PRAISE FOR
JAMES GRIPPANDO
AND
CASH LANDING

"Action-packed . . . Buoyed by Grippando's strong characters . . . *Cash Landing* is one of Grippando's most hard-edged novels and shows how the best-formed plans quickly spiral out of control when greed and stupidity enter the equation."
South Florida Sun Sentinel

"Grippando makes the best use of reality as he spins fictional gold with *Cash Landing*."
Mystery Scene

"Fast-paced . . . recalls the caper novels of Donald E. Westlake."
Booklist

"Spellbinding."
Huffington Post

"Grippando supplies a satisfyingly wild ride through *Presumed Innocent* territory."
Kirkus Reviews

"Gripping . . . Grippando keeps the tension high."
Publishers Weekly

By James Grippando

Cash Landing†
Cane and Abe
Black Horizon*†
Blood Money*†
Need You Now†
Afraid of the Dark*†
Money to Burn†
Intent to Kill
Born to Run*†
Last Call*†
Lying With Strangers
When Darkness Falls*†
Got the Look*†
Hear No Evil*
Last to Die*
Beyond Suspicion*
A King's Ransom
Under Cover of Darkness†
Found Money
The Abduction
The Informant
The Pardon*

And for Young Adults
Leapholes

* A Jack Swyteck Novel
† Also featuring FBI agent Andie Henning

JAMES GRIPPANDO

CASH LANDING

HARPER

An Imprint of HarperCollins*Publishers*

HARPER

An Imprint of HarperCollins*Publishers*
195 Broadway
New York, New York 10007

Copyright © 2015 by James Grippando
Author photo © Monica Hopkins Photography
ISBN 978-0-06-229546-0

First Harper premium printing: March 2016
First Harper hardcover printing: June 2015

HarperCollins® and Harper® are registered trademarks of HarperCollins Publishers.

Printed in the United States of America

Visit Harper paperbacks on the World Wide Web at
www.harpercollins.com

10 9 8 7 6 5 4 3 2 1

For Tiffany

CASH
LANDING

November 2009

G etting rich in Miami was easy. Or so Ruban Betancourt was told.

Miami had *boomtown* written all over it—again. The Great Recession was over. The perils of reckless borrowing and NINA loans—"no income, no assets, no problem"—were yesterday's news. Cash was king. A new Bentley Continental GT like Paris Hilton's? Cash. Hitting Miami Beach to clean out Chanel at Bal Harbour Shops? More cash. A penthouse in Sunny Isles? All cash, no mortgage required. Brazilians, Argentinians, Mexicans— anyone with a Latin fortune was flush with cash and buying up Miami.

Ruban saw the expensive cars and jewelry all around him, but he wasn't plugged into the "new economy," and he didn't understand it. One year the banks loved him, couldn't give him enough credit, and talked him and his wife into a house and NINA loan that they couldn't possibly afford. "All you need is a pulse and credit score," their mortgage broker had assured them. As it turned out, that pulse thing was optional. Fraudulent loans to dead people were soaring, right along with bank profits. Two years into their subprime mortgage, the Betancourts were in foreclosure and out on the street, their dream house scooped up for a song on the courthouse steps by investors who paid—what else?—cash. Front end and back end, the banks won. But not this time. Ruban got smart and looked to the skies. Not at the new high-rise condos and office towers that had reshaped Miami's skyline. His eye was on "money flights"—commercial jets pregnant with bags of U.S. currency in their cargo bellies.

"Touchdown!" shouted Ruban.

He was in the passenger seat of a borrowed pickup truck, listening to the Miami Dolphins football game on the radio. The color commentator added his patented "*All RIGHT, Miami!*" over the airwaves. Ruban slapped a high five with his brother-in-law, Jeffrey Beauchamp, who was behind the wheel. The truck was parked alongside Perimeter Road near Miami International Airport. Jeffrey's uncle, Craig "Pinky" Perez, was in the backseat, a fully loaded Makarov 9-millimeter semi-automatic pistol tucked under his belt.

"They're still gonna lose," said Pinky.

The pessimism was warranted. The team was "rebuilding," and just eight weeks into the new season they already had five losses.

"Maybe I should buy the team," said Jeffrey.

"Maybe you should shut up," said Pinky.

"Maybe *you* should—"

"*Everybody*, shut it!" said Ruban. "Just shut up and watch the fucking planes."

The family dynamics were wearing thin on Ruban. He'd approached a couple of buddies to pull off the heist with him, two pros with balls as big as globes but who had passed because it sounded too risky. He was stuck with family. Pinky would probably be okay, with an impressive criminal record to prove it. Jeffrey, on the other hand, was five foot six inches tall and weighed three hundred pounds, and the number-one woman in his life was still his mother. Always smiling, he loved to laugh, even at himself. But he was as gullible as a ten-year-old. It was like asking the actual loser on *The Biggest Loser* to knock off a bank, with the added dimension of drug addiction, which meant that he spent half his life coked-up and bingeing, the other half sleeping it off. Jeffrey would be the driver. *Just* the driver.

"Hey, is that it?" asked Jeffrey as he peered out the windshield.

Their truck was south of the airport on the other side of a twelve-foot fence of chain link topped with barbed wire. They had a clear view of the runway and control tower.

"Looks like a jumbo jet to me," said Pinky.

The plane descended from the west, flying over the uninhabited Florida Everglades. Ruban had counted almost four dozen landings since 1:00 p.m., a typical afternoon at MIA, the second-busiest airport in the country for international traffic. But Ruban was getting antsy. The scheduled arrival time for Lufthansa flight 462 from Frankfurt was 1:50 p.m. It was now two o'clock. He smiled as he spotted the telltale bump on the forward double-deck section of the fuselage of the Boeing 747.

"That's it, bro!"

"Yeah, baby!"

The landing gear deployed, the nose lifted, and the plane touched down at the west end of the runway. The engines whined as the plane rolled past them. The airline's logo—a circle of gold on the deep-blue tail—seemed to smile on them like the Florida sun.

"Payday," said Ruban.

"All RIGHT, Miami!" said Jeffrey. "Touchdown!"

The idea of a heist had been planted in Ruban's brain over the summer. He was nearly floored by what his old friend was telling him. "Money flights happen every day, bro. Eighty million dollars. A hundred million dollars. Every fucking day." The Miami branch of the Federal Reserve Bank of Atlanta is just northwest of the Miami International Airport, a distance of about four miles "as the crow flies," a fifteen-minute ride by armored truck. When a foreign bank has more U.S. currency on hand than needed, it physically ships the bills to the United States for deposit at one of the twelve Federal Reserve Banks. South Florida's cash-hungry Latin community made Miami a prime destination.

Ruban had been planning and preparing for months. He'd studied enough maps of the area to know that the Lufthansa flight flew right past the Miami Fed upon approach to the south runway. The shipment's ultimate destination, however, was as irrelevant as the world economic events that impacted the value of the U.S. dollar and fueled these money flights. To Ruban and his partners in crime, the 747 was nothing more than bags of cash, low-hanging fruit, theirs for the taking.

Ruban's phone rang and he answered immediately. It was his source—the old friend who had tipped him off about the "money flights." This was the call he had been waiting for: time to move.

"Understood," he said into his cell. "Ten minutes."

He hung up. Clearing customs was normally a two-hour process, but the armored-car guards were moving faster than usual. The Lufthansa container had been transported from the aircraft to the warehouse. All bags had been inspected for tampering and tearing, the cash accounted for, and the bags resealed. The process of loading the armored truck was soon to begin. In another half hour the money would be heading north on the Palmetto Expressway at fifty-five miles per hour—unless Ruban made his move.

"Drive," Ruban told his brother-in-law.

"How much we talking about?"

"Forty-some bags. Two million per bag, give or take, depending on the mix of bills."

The math was beyond Jeffrey. "Sweet," he said as he steered onto the Perimeter Road.

It was a short drive to the airport warehouse on Northwest Eighteenth Street. Ruban and Pinky put on latex gloves to make sure there would be no fingerprints when they pulled themselves up on the loading dock. Jeffrey parked outside the open cargo door. He kept the motor running. The time was 3:08 p.m.

Ruban could hardly believe that the enormous bay door was wide open, though he knew it would be. It was one of the many lapses in security that would make this job so easy. Each of those vulnerabilities had been spelled out to him in advance. Bricks of bills lay exposed on the concrete floor. Federal law prohibited any private citizen—including armored-truck guards—from carrying a weapon into the customs clearance site, so the guards were required to remove all weapons before entering the warehouse and performing any clearance tasks. The CCTV cameras were monitored by the security staff at the main terminal, well away from the warehouse, and the crooks would be long gone before the weekend security guard noticed anything awry on one of his many screens and contacted police. The kicker in this incredible equation was that the gaping bay doors led directly to a public-access road running parallel to the building. A fast-moving getaway vehicle could bypass the airport perimeter fence and the gatehouse and be on the expressway in less than sixty seconds.

Ruban had gotten all this information from a trusted old friend, a childhood buddy he'd grown up with in Cuba.

Ruban's given name was "Karl," which is not a Hispanic name, but decades of Soviet influence in Cuba had many faces, including that of Ruban's father, a Russian soldier who never married Ruban's mother and who was shipped off to Afghanistan, where he was killed, when Ruban was three. Karl and his older sister were half-Cubans—"Rubans"—who lived on a single mother's salary of twenty dollars per month, paid in *moneda nacional* and supplemented by rice-and-beans rations and other "necessities" provided by the Cuban government. They owned no car. Their television worked intermittently, but in any case they watched only what the government allowed them to watch. The Castro regime's ban on international travel by Cuban citizens meant that no one in the Betancourt family had left the island since 1959. Ruban was among the next generation of refugees, part of President Clinton's Cuban crisis, having left only when he'd decided to leave for good, at the age of seventeen. If ever he returned, it would be as a rich man. He would stay at the Hotel Nacional, along with the European tourists. He'd drink mojitos all day and lounge on the white-sand beaches at Veradero. But first there was work to do.

His real job as a restaurant manager kept him too busy to indulge in hobbies, yet Ruban did have one: his gun collection. Mostly Russian-made pistols. They would come in handy in this new job.

"Ready, Ruban?" asked Pinky. The "Ruban" nickname had stuck. Not even his wife called him Karl.

"Let's do this," said Ruban.

Ruban and Pinky put on sunglasses to hide their eyes and pulled ski masks over their heads. They got out of the truck, and hauled themselves up onto the loading dock. Pinky pulled a Makarov 9-millimeter semi-automatic pistol as they ran into the warehouse. Ruban gave the order, first in English and then in Spanish.

"Down on the floor! Everybody down!"

The scene was exactly as Ruban had been told

it would be. A cavernous warehouse littered with crates and plastic packing wrap. Canvas bags lay right by the doors, protected by only a handful of unarmed guards and warehouse workers. They complied immediately and dropped to the floor.

The thieves moved quickly. Ruban grabbed four bags, two in each hand, nearly his own body weight in fifty- and hundred-dollar bills. Pinky brandished the Makarov, never letting his guard down, but grabbed two more bags with his free hand.

"Like bags of cement," Ruban said, groaning. Easy money didn't mean easy to carry. One bag was dropped in their race back to the truck.

"Shit!"

"Leave it! Go, go, go!"

They left it on the floor, threw the five bags into the bed of the truck as they hopped down from the loading dock, and jumped into the cab.

"*Vaya!*"

Jeffrey hit the gas. The truck sped away. The men pulled off their ski masks, slapped high fives, and showered themselves with hoots and hollers of congratulations. Jeffrey felt the excitement. Maybe too much.

"Hey, Ruban?" He was driving so fast that the steering wheel was vibrating in his hands. "Tell me where we're going again?"

Ruban slugged him in the arm. They'd gone over the escape countless times. "Shit, Jeffrey! Turn here!"

A hard right, and the tires squealed as they ran the stop sign. They were deep into the warehouse district.

"Left!" shouted Ruban.

Jeffrey steered toward the Miami Tile & Marble Depot. It was closed on Sundays, but the garage door opened as they approached. The black pickup entered and continued through the warehouse without stopping, passing pallets of tile and marble stacked floor to ceiling on either side. As the garage door closed behind them, a cargo door opened before them. It was the rear loading platform, where a delivery truck was backed up against the elevated dock. Its roll-up door was wide open. Jeffrey drove the pickup straight into the empty box of the delivery truck, stopped, then switched on the running lights so they could see. Ruban and Pinky jumped out of the pickup, secured the axles to the bed of the delivery truck with chains, and chocked the wheels with wooden blocks.

"Done!" shouted Ruban.

Pinky pulled down the roll-up door. Ruban banged on the metal wall between him and the cab. The driver was Marco, a forklift operator who was the lone security guard on Sundays, a friend of Pinky's.

"Go!"

They jumped into the bed of the pickup. Canvas bags of money lay between them as the delivery truck pulled away from the loading dock.

"Home free," said Pinky. "So easy!"

Ruban leaned back against one of the bags, a lumpy mattress of money. "Too easy."

That's what worries me.

2

The search for a black pickup truck with an extended cab was in high gear.

It was led by the FBI but involved an alphabet soup of state and local agencies, from the FHP (Florida Highway Patrol) and FDLE (Florida Department of Law Enforcement) to the MDPD (Miami-Dade County Police Department) and its airport substation. Countless squad cars were on alert in the tri-county area, north to Palm Beach and south to the Florida Keys. FBI and MDPD helicopters were airborne, crisscrossing the skies. The black pickup was their Holy Grail, but they were also searching for discarded money bags, weapons, latex gloves, or ski masks along the road. Mindful that profiling was a legal no-no, law enforcement had an eye out for any vehicle with three men inside, possibly Hispanic, especially if it was fast moving and seemingly in getaway mode. The access road by which the thieves had fled was completely shut down, and the entire warehouse and surrounding area was a secured crime scene.

Special Agent Andie Henning was the first FBI agent to reach the warehouse.

Andie was entering her fifth year with the Bureau, all but the last six weeks of which had been in the Seattle field office, where she'd spent eighteen months in the bank robbery unit. She'd made a name for herself in a lengthy undercover assignment in the Yakima Valley, and she was promised more of that work if she transferred to Miami. So far, the promise had been unfulfilled. She was assigned to "Tom Cat," a multi-jurisdictional task force that focused on the growing number of organized-crime syndicates involved in cargo heists. On the upside, the transfer did at least put two thousand miles between Andie and her ex-fiancé. But that was another story.

"I see the Bureau sends the newbie on Sunday afternoons," said MDPD lieutenant Elgin Watts. He was one of the cofounders of Tom Cat.

Andie wasn't exactly a "newbie," but she knew what he meant. "Littleford is on his way."

Supervisory Special Agent Michael Littleford was the head of the FBI's bank robbery unit, a twenty-five-year veteran.

A dozen officers from MDPD were already on the scene, most of them with Tom Cat. It wasn't Andie's place to tell them—at least not yet—but Tom Cat would be playing a supporting role in this case. The typical cargo heist involved truckloads of everything from designer clothes to pharmaceuticals, and law enforcement's key to success was finding the warehouses the syndicates used to store the stolen goods. Here, the stolen currency had been on its way to the Federal Reserve Bank, and the warehouse was just the starting point. The FBI would assert its bank robbery jurisdiction as soon as Littleford arrived.

"How much did they get?" asked Andie. They were standing in front of the thirty-six bags of cash that the thieves had left untouched. The empty armored truck hadn't moved, its doors wide open.

"Not sure yet," said Watts. "But if you're a trivia nut, I'd say at least a few million more than the JFK Lufthansa heist. We may be looking at a new record."

Anyone in law enforcement who'd worked a bank robbery or armored-truck heist knew about JFK, but this wasn't the time to debate the dollar value in 1978 versus the twenty-first century. "Who was first on the scene?"

"Officer Foreman. He works out of the MDPD airport substation."

"How many witnesses?" asked Andie.

"Four guards and four warehouse employees. They're sitting over there, with Foreman," he said, indicating with a jerk of his head.

Andie wondered which one would be trading in his uniform for prison garb. "A job like this doesn't happen without inside help."

"Yup," said Watts.

"What about camera surveillance?"

"Two outside cameras, four inside. They're all monitored by airport security from the main terminal. Crooks were outta here before security noticed anything and dispatched police."

"You think the guy watching the screens was in on it? Maybe looking the other way?"

"Honestly, I don't. I talked with the director of airport security. The weekend staff is shorthanded. Just three guys watching dozens of screens that cover the entire airport."

"Wouldn't they be more focused on this particular warehouse when a hundred million dollars in cash is clearing customs?"

"The policy is not to give advance notice of a cash delivery to the guards who watch the CCTV screens, or to anyone else who isn't part of a very small need-to-know circle. It makes sense: the more fifteen-dollar-an-hour employees who know exactly when a hundred million bucks'll be spread across the floor in the warehouse, the more people you tempt into planning an inside job."

Andie couldn't disagree with his logic, but she still suspected an insider. Her gaze drifted back to the eight men who were in the warehouse at the time of the heist—the armored-truck guards, in particular.

"Which one you got your eye on?" asked Andie.

"One of the guards. Octavio Alvarez. Cuban-American guy."

Watts was showing his bias from Tom Cat experience, where the "Cuban connection" was always part of any investigation into a cargo heist. Cuban-American crime syndicates in Miami preyed on Cuban nationals in Havana and other cities. The price of a trip to Florida was an indefinite stint as a "lumper" offloading truckloads of stolen cargo, followed by a string of heists around the country. For some young men, the risk of incarceration in the United States outweighed the risk of a leaky boat across the shark-infested Florida Straits.

"Why Alvarez?" asked Andie.

He shrugged. "Just a hunch."

It was possible that his hunch was correct, but Andie was trying to clear her head of the stereotypes that might apply in a Tom Cat case. Cargo theft, at the FBI, was part of "Major Thefts," grouped together with stolen jewelry, art, vehicles, and the like. Bank robbery was part of "Violent Crimes," grouped together with gangs, kidnapping, murder for hire, and serial killings. It wasn't about turf wars. It involved different training, made investigators think differently, and changed the way they looked at things. As far as criminal enterprises went, cargo heists were comparatively low risk, while thieves who targeted money flights had historically shown an uncanny knack for ending up dead or in prison. The "hunches" an investigator followed early on were critical, which in Andie's mind underscored the need for the FBI to take control of the crime scene.

Where the heck are you, Littleford?

"I'll want to talk to all of the guards," said Andie.

"Better move fast. Braxton Security will have its lawyers here any minute. That's rarely a good thing for the flow of information."

Andie checked her watch. Littleford was hands-on, and she knew he would want to be part of the witness interrogations. She'd give him two more minutes, tops.

"Tell me more about the CCTV cameras. What'd we get?"

"Not much more than the eyewitnesses gave us. Outside cameras confirmed the getaway vehicle was a black Ford F-150. Also picked up a plate number, but it turned out to be stolen from some old lady's Cadillac in Doral, so that leads us nowhere. Inside cameras show both perps, but at the end of the day, we're left with two males of average height and build wearing ski masks and sunglasses."

"I'll get my tech people to see about enhancing it."

Andie sent a quick message to her tech agent, then walked toward the cargo lift. Watts showed her where the black pickup had parked and pointed out the bag that never made it to the truck. It was still on the floor where the thieves had dropped it.

"Expensive case of the dropsies. Check for prints," said Andie.

"I'm sure we'll get some, but not any from the perps. Witnesses say they wore gloves."

An FBI van pulled up outside the open cargo doors. Several agents jumped out and entered the warehouse. Another van was right behind. Special Agent Littleford hopped up on the loading dock and entered the warehouse.

"Fill me in," he said to Watts. "And FBI takes jurisdiction from here."

The direct approach. Andie listened as Watts gave Littleford the same quick recap, and then Littleford followed up with some questions of his own.

"No shots fired? You confirmed that?" he asked.

"Correct. None."

"How well armed were the perps?"

"At least one handgun, for sure. Witnesses agree that it looked like a semiautomatic."

"I've already told tech to work on the security video," said Andie. "Hopefully we'll get a make and model on the gun."

"Which they've dumped by now, if they're smart," said Littleford.

Watts agreed. "Seems to me they came here knowing that none of the guards would be armed and wanted to have as many hands free as possible to carry out the money bags. But it would be safe to assume more firepower in the truck to ward off any pursuit. The BOLO says 'armed and dangerous,'" he added, referring to the "be on the lookout" alert.

Littleford started across the warehouse, taking Andie with him. "Let's talk to the witnesses," he said, but then he stopped short at the bag of cash that the thieves had dropped.

"This is our best friend right here," he said. "Even if they wore gloves and we don't lift a single print."

"How so?" asked Andie.

"We have no shots fired, no blood, and no one hurt. Well, that's all about to change. I don't have to be the fly on the wall to hear them arguing already: 'Dude, *you're* the one who dropped the bag. That comes out of your split.' Oh, yeah. It's gonna get ugly. Real ugly."

Andie returned the thin law enforcement smile. This wasn't the undercover work she'd transferred across the country to do, but she liked the way Littleford operated.

"Come on," he said. "Let's go find their insider."

3

Five sealed canvas bags lay in a heap, a virtual mountain of concealed cash lying on the cracked and oil-stained garage floor.

The transfer of the money bags from the getaway truck to the trunk of Ruban's car had gone off without a hitch. Marco from the tile depot had supplied the "borrowed" black pickup, and it was his job to ditch it. Jeffrey and his uncle left in separate cars and in opposite directions. Ruban drove off with the money, but only after assuring his coconspirators that all five bags would remain sealed until it was time to make the split. They agreed it would be that night in the garage at the Betancourts' rental house.

"Open it, bro," said Jeffrey.

Ruban was standing over the bags with a kitchen knife in his hand. Pinky was beside him. It was just the three of them. The others would get their money later.

"Hold on," said Pinky. "What if there's one of those blue dye packs inside? You know, the ones that explode in your face when you open the sack of money."

"Alvarez says there's no dye packs," said Ruban.

"What if some kind of tracking chip starts beaming out a signal to the cops when you open the bag?"

"Alvarez says no. Nothing but money inside."

Jeffrey chuckled. "Dumb fucks need to watch more cop shows. Open the bag, bro."

He tried to puncture it with a kitchen knife and nearly broke the blade. The bag was impenetrable. "I need a power tool."

Jeffrey got an electric drill and a steel bit from the tool board. Ruban used it like a jigsaw to cut a fist-sized hole in the bottom of the bag. He reached inside eagerly, grabbing and pulling brick after brick through the hole. The bag hemorrhaged fifty- and hundred-dollar bills until it was empty.

"Ho-leee shit," said Jeffrey, staring at the pile of money on the concrete floor.

"Pretty, huh?" said Ruban. "Four more just like it."

"Who's going to do the counting?" asked Pinky.

"I'll do it," said Jeffrey.

"You can't count that fucking high."

"Then let Savannah count it," said Jeffrey. "She'll get it right."

Savannah was Ruban's wife, and Jeffrey's younger sister. The joke in the family was that "Savannah got the looks, but Savannah got the brains"—which, strangely, always made brother Jeffrey laugh. She was a Latina beauty with none of her brother's weight issues. "Wow," "gorgeous," "sexy," and "*linda, como su madre*" were typical of the ways people described her. Ruban was handsome, not in the classic sense but more in the bad-boy Marc Anthony mold, so it was plain to see why he'd fallen for the neighborhood version of J-Lo. Some said there was nothing he wouldn't do to keep her.

"Savannah's not home," said Ruban. "I made sure of that."

"How much does she know?" asked Pinky.

Ruban looked right at his accomplice, making sure he understood. "*Nada*. Savannah knows nothing."

"But she has to find out some time," said Jeffrey.

"She finds out when I'm ready to tell her. Got it?"

"Yeah, sure. Whatever you say."

"I'll count the money," said Ruban.

It took hours to cut open the bags, count each bill, and divide each player's take into separate piles. Three times Jeffrey had gone out to "use the bathroom." Each time he'd come back all wired up and sniffling, unable to stop pacing a circle around the money. Clearly he'd been blowing coke. That was one drug Ruban had no use for. Some guys claimed it was an aphrodisiac, but as far as he could see, doing coke only made you want to do one thing: more coke.

By midnight, there were seven stacks on the floor. Ruban announced the final tally. One million for Alvarez, the armored-car insider. Another million for Marco.

"The rest is ours," said Ruban. "Three-way split."

"How much? *How much?*" asked Jeffrey.

"Two-point-five million and change."

"Woo-hoo! Wait. Is that before or after taxes?"

It was late, Ruban was exhausted, and he was

in no mood for his brother-in-law's jokes. "Listen up," he said. "I'll make sure Alvarez gets his money. Pinky, did you and Marco work out a time and place to get his share to him?"

Pinky had brought Marco into the heist. They'd met in prison. "I'll take care of it."

"Please tell me you have a plan in place," said Ruban.

"I said I'll take care of it."

"Damn it, Pinky. I don't want phone calls flying back and forth about splitting up the money. I gave Alvarez clear instructions: third Tuesday, eight a.m., corner of U.S. 1 and Bird. Boom. Octavio knows to be there, no phone calls needed. You and Marco were supposed to do the same."

"Alvarez is different. The FBI will be watching the guards like a hawk. Nobody knows to keep an eye on Marco."

"We can't get sloppy anywhere."

"Here's a plan," said Jeffrey. "I'll take my money now. I am going to *par-tee* tonight."

"No, you're not," said Ruban. "We are going to lay low."

"Low, uh-huh, *real low*," Jeffrey said in the deep, rhythmic voice of a rapper. He arched his back and mimicked a limbo dance, his shirt rising up to expose his big belly above the beltline. "How low . . . can you go . . . bro?"

Ruban smacked him across the head, knocking Jeffrey onto his ass. "I'm serious. Stop goofing off."

Jeffrey picked himself up. "It's my money, bro."

"We're in this together. If one of us gets caught, we all get caught."

"They catch me, I don't give up nobody," said Jeffrey.

"Just listen to me," said Ruban. "This is how it's going to be. We don't go out drinking and partying. We don't flash money. We all get up and do what we do on a regular Monday morning."

"Cool. I sleep till noon," said Jeffrey.

"The perfect cover for you would be to go out and start looking for work," said Ruban.

"Fuck that," said Jeffrey. "I don't ever have to go back to work now."

"It's about perception," said Ruban. "You ever see the movie *Goodfellas*, Jeffrey?"

"No. What's that, gay porn?"

"It's about the guys who pulled off the biggest heist ever from JFK airport. It went perfect."

"Just like us."

"Yeah. Except we don't want to end up like them. They were snorting coke before they even counted up the money. It was fucking Mafia wars before it was all over. Like a dozen guys ended up dead."

"Yeah? So? That was them."

"It could be *us*. This is no bullshit, bro. We gotta lay low."

"What do we do with the money while we're laying low?" asked Jeffrey.

"We stash it," said Ruban. "Ninety days, minimum. We act like this never happened."

"No, no," said Pinky. "We gotta launder it. I saw

this in a Ben Affleck movie. You buy shit, you go to the casino, you—"

"Forget it," said Ruban. "Laundering the money is what the cops expect us to do. If we do what they expect, we get caught."

"So when you say stash it, you mean what?" asked Pinky.

"Simple. First, we put the money in vacuum-sealed bags."

"Vacuum-cleaner bags?" asked Jeffrey.

"No, moron. It's a machine. I bought it already. It seals things in plastic so no air and no water can get inside. You can use it on anything. Food, clothes—"

"Money."

"You got it. So we seal the bricks into packets that hold anywhere from ten to twenty-five grand, and we stuff the packs inside PVC pipe. I bought the pipe already, too."

"Okay, then what?"

Ruban walked toward the rack of tools on the other side of the garage and grabbed a shovel. "We bury it."

"You want to stick seven and a half million bucks in the ground?" asked Pinky.

"Yup."

"Where?"

Ruban smiled a little. "Where no one will find it."

Jeffrey grimaced, clearly not in love with the idea. Pinky was more vocal. "This is stupid. Marco and Octavio get their money, but we gotta bury ours?"

"I'm not related to those guys," said Ruban. "We're family. We need to act as one unit. And this unit is flying under the radar."

"Fine," said Pinky. "Seal up the money, and each of us buries his own share."

"I don't trust you guys to bury it," said Ruban.

"I don't trust you to keep my money," said Pinky.

"This is not negotiable," said Ruban. "I'm keeping control."

"Not of my money, you're not."

"Mine neither," said Jeffrey.

"Stay out of this, Jeffrey," said Ruban.

Pinky stepped closer. "Give me my money, bro, before this gets ugly."

Jeffrey backed away from them nervously. "Guys, come on. Let's not fight."

Pinky pulled his cell from his pocket, his gaze fixed on Ruban. "No one's going to fight. Either I walk out of here with my money, or I call my sweet little niece and tell her what her husband's been up to today."

"I'm going to tell her myself," said Ruban.

"Bullshit," said Pinky. "You want to sit on the money until you figure out some explanation that doesn't involve you stealing it."

Their eyes locked, and the glares intensified. Neither man blinked, and Ruban could feel the power shift in the air. The honeymoon had barely started.

Already it was over.

4
.

It was five a.m. when Ruban returned home. He tried not to wake Savannah as he climbed into bed, but his head hit the pillow so hard that she stirred. She snuggled up next to him.

"How did it go?" she asked.

He'd told her only that Jeffrey was doing coke again, which was true, and that the "intervention" would probably keep him out late, which was a lie. His muscles still ached from burying the money: his share, along with Octavio's and some of Jeffrey's. Pinky had gotten his way.

"I'm really worried about Jeffrey," he told her.

"I love you so much for that. I don't know what my poor mother would do without you. Did Jeffrey give you a hard time?"

"Oh, yeah. He gave me a hard time, all right."

Pinky's insistence that each man hide his own money had emboldened Jeffrey, and it had been World War III to get Jeffrey to leave behind a "with-hold" of five hundred thousand dollars for Ruban to bury. "You can take the rest and stash it yourself," Ruban had told him, "but if I see you flashing money, you forfeit half a mil." It had seemed like a workable solution at the time, but Ruban was having second thoughts.

"I'm afraid he's going to take us all down," said Ruban.

"That won't happen," she said.

"Don't be so sure," he said. They were speaking about two entirely different things, but Ruban wasn't ready to tell her about the money. Net yet.

"Jeffrey can't hurt us," she said.

"Sure he can. He's a cokehead."

She ran her finger lightly across his chest. "That's him, not us. You are strong. You are smart. You have a beautiful, sexy wife." She kissed the side of his mouth, but he didn't react.

"One slip and all that's gone," he said. He propped himself up on his elbow, looking at her in the darkness. There was just enough moonlight streaming through the blinds for him to see. "The slightest slip, that's all it takes. Poof, you can lose everything."

"Ruban, you're kind of scaring me."

He hesitated, wondering if it was the right time. He eased into it. "Tonight wasn't about an intervention."

"What?"

"It was about money."

"You mean our money?"

He didn't answer. She looked at him with concern. "Ruban, are we in money trouble again?"

The fear in her voice was eerily reminiscent of the bad old days of lying awake at night and wondering how much longer they'd be able to make their mortgage payments, wondering if the bank would work with them, if they could avoid foreclosure, if tomorrow would be the day that the MDPD officers would show up with a court-issued writ to haul them and their possessions out into the front yard. It was a journey they'd taken together, and he'd been honest with her every grim step of the way. This was different. Savannah wasn't part of this.

"Jeffrey messed up royally this time," he said.

"Does he need to borrow money? Don't give him money to buy drugs."

"No. It's not that."

Ruban reached for his smartphone on the nightstand, brought up the front page of the *Miami Herald*, and handed it to her. She read it to herself, her confused face aglow from the LCD screen.

"Are you saying Jeffrey is involved in this?"

"Yes," said Ruban. "Jeffrey and your uncle."

"Oh, no. I swear, I wish my scumbag uncle had never gotten out of prison. There is not a member of my family that he hasn't shamed or hurt. This has always been my biggest fear—that Jeffrey would get mixed up with him."

"He's mixed up big-time."

She glanced at the display, her eyes widening. "It says here the heist could be in the millions of dollars. They stole all that?"

"With some other guys."

"Who?"

"One of Pinky's friends," he said, a half-truth. "They made off with nine-point-six million dollars."

"Where does it say that?" she asked, checking the article again.

"It doesn't say it."

"Then how do you know?"

If he was going to tell her, this was his opportunity. But it was hard to come clean when part of him still couldn't believe that he'd even attempted such a thing, let alone gotten away with it. Even after he'd held the money in his own hands, Ruban Betancourt as mastermind of Miami's biggest heist in history didn't feel at all like the truth.

"That's where I was all night," he said. "I helped them hide their share of the money."

She sat up, practically jackknifing in the bed. "Ruban—no!"

Her reaction made him jump, and it pushed him even farther toward the new truth. "What was I supposed to do, Savannah? The two of them showed up at our house with big bags of money, the cops were looking for them, and neither one of them had any idea what to do."

"They should turn it back in."

"You can't just give back the money and make this go away. This is no different than robbing a bank, and your uncle had a gun. Using a firearm to steal this much money could land both of them in prison for the rest of their lives."

"Oh, my poor mother."

"We don't have to tell your mother. We don't have to tell anyone."

She fell back into the pillow. "What are we going to do?"

"It's under control for now. They promised not to spend the money and to keep it hidden until we figure out what to do."

"You can't trust them to keep that promise!"

They were on the same page, but he needed to allay her concerns. "It's fine. The money is buried in sealed bags."

"All of it?"

One more lie wouldn't hurt. "Yes. All of it."

"But if you helped them hide the money, that makes us part of it."

He took her hand. "No. It makes *me* part of it. Not you."

Even in the darkness, he could see that he'd touched her heart. She sat right back up and held him tight.

"Oh, honey. My family is so screwed up, and you spend so much of your life picking up the pieces. But this is way more than I can ask."

"No, we're all family. I'll make this right. Just don't tell Jeffrey or your uncle that you know anything. They trust me on this. If they find out I told you, they will dig up that money and all hell will break loose."

"I won't say a word. But please don't let this drag on. We have to decide something quick."

She embraced him tightly. Ruban lay back into the pillow. Savannah nuzzled up against him and laid her head on his chest.

"Do you really think you can fix this?"

"Yes. We'll be fine. Just remember: keep this between us. I'll handle it."

"Okay. I promise." She pulled away.

One more thing to add to the list on an unbelievable day: she'd bought it.

Ruban was dead tired, but he couldn't close his

eyes. As he lay staring at the ceiling, the truth started to replay in his mind. He and Pinky rushing into the warehouse. The money grab. The getaway. He shook off those unforgettable images and glanced over at his wife. The curve of Savannah's body beneath the bedsheet. She was right beside him, as close as ever—as close as the bag of money, the two million dollars that he'd dropped and left lying on the warehouse floor.

Don't think about that.

He reached over and rested his hand gently on her hip. "Are you okay now?" he asked.

"I'm much better."

Ruban took a deep breath and let it out. The air conditioning cycled off. The bedroom fell quiet.

"Me, too," he said into the darkness.

5

On Monday morning Andie and Agent Littleford paid a visit to Braxton Security. A fleet
of armored trucks was stationed less than two miles
from the Miami Fed, the vaults of which were officially short 9.6 million dollars. Andie wondered
if the crooks might be right across the street at
Doral Country Club, smoking cigars and thumb-
ing their noses at law enforcement from the mani-
cured greens of the "Blue Monster," one of the most
famous golf courses in the world.

"You golf, Andie?" asked Littleford.

Andie glanced out the passenger-side window as
they cruised past the groomed fairways. "Nope."

"If you ever want to drop four hundred bucks for
five hours of aggravation and eighteen reasons to
swear your head off, this is the place."

"I'll keep that in mind."

Littleford looked ready for a round of golf, his
khaki pants and short-sleeved Hawaiian shirt not
just for weekends. Sunday afternoon's interviews
at the airport warehouse had gone as expected.

No one had broken down, confessed, and pleaded for mercy. Two of the guards were targeted for a follow-up. Alvarez in particular. Andie and her supervisory agent met with him in a conference room at the office suite. The assistant general counsel for Braxton was also in the room, along with a junior member of the in-house legal staff. Andie did the interviews. Each took about an hour. They called Alvarez back for a short but to-the-point follow-up. The Braxton lawyers gave the FBI the green light to turn up the heat. Andie ran with it.

"Mr. Alvarez, let me spell this out for you: We think you're holding back."

"Me? No. Nothing to hold back."

Andie allowed the blanket of silence to settle over them. It was amazing what a nervous target might say when left to stew, no question pending.

Alvarez had lived in Miami for almost fifteen years, having come to Florida just six months after graduation from high school in Havana. It was impossible to land a job at Braxton with a criminal record, and his was clean, at least since coming to this country. Andie wondered about the inaccessible juvenile record he may have left behind in a country that shared nothing with the United States.

She leaned closer, resting her crossed forearms on the table. "One of the warehouse workers says he saw you using a cell phone before the heist."

It was a bluff, but the FBI was convinced that someone from inside the warehouse had signaled the robbers. The guy remained cool.

"That's a lie," said Alvarez. "I never use my cell on duty."

Andie didn't miss a beat. "Let me be clear, Mr. Alvarez. We are going to turn that warehouse upside down and inside out. Maybe you cloned somebody's cell so it couldn't be traced to you. Maybe you used your sister's cell. Maybe it's a disposable. Whatever phone you used, you had to ditch it somewhere in that warehouse. We are going to find it. I'm giving you a chance to tell me now, before all bets are off."

"Maybe you didn't hear me the first time," he said, not the slightest quake in his voice. "I never use a cell on the job."

"Suit yourself," said Andie. "But remember what I tell you today. Count One: Octavio Alvarez did conspire to obstruct commerce by robbery by taking approximately nine-point-six million dollars in United States currency by actual and threatened force and violence. Count Two: Octavio Alvarez and his coconspirators did knowingly commit such crime of violence through the use of a firearm. I'm guessing fifteen years in federal prison on count one. Another ten to fifteen on count two. Those are just the obvious charges. I'm sure the U.S. attorney will tack on two or three more, including an order of restitution in the full amount of the heist that will follow you around for the rest of your life. My guess is that you'll be a sixty-year-old man wishing he could afford his prescription for Viagra by the time you get out of prison and make love to a woman again. Have a nice day, Mr. Alvarez."

Alvarez addressed the company lawyers. "Is that all?"

"Yes, Mr. Alvarez. You're excused."

He rose, the junior lawyer escorted him to the door, and Alvarez left the room.

"You think he's our man?" asked the general counsel.

"Hard to say," said Littleford. "If he is, we know he didn't use a cell phone registered under his own name."

"How do you know that?"

Andie explained. "We don't need a warrant to get the transactional details from a person's cell. That includes time and date of phone calls, the GPS coordinates of the caller's location, and the numbers dialed. Alvarez's cell is clean all yesterday afternoon. No calls. Same with all the Braxton guards."

"As they should be," said the lawyer. "Guards can't talk on their cell while on duty."

"Which is why we think our insider used a phone that's not registered in his name and ditched it somewhere in that warehouse," said Littleford.

"Or it could be in a thousand tiny pieces and flushed down the toilet," said Andie.

"So what's next?" the lawyer asked. "Will you wiretap his phone? Follow him?"

"We'll let you know," said Littleford.

"There's one other thing we should discuss," said Andie. "The reward."

"We're on that," the lawyer said. "Braxton will offer two hundred fifty thousand dollars for information leading to the arrest and conviction of those responsible and the return of the money."

"I got a problem with that," said Littleford.

"That's a big reward. What's the problem?"

"Don't make the reward conditional on return of the money."

The lawyer smiled a little, but it wasn't a friendly smile. "No offense, but it's the FBI's job to catch the crooks. Braxton's primary interest here is the return of the money."

"You're asking someone to risk his life by coming forward and fingering the guys who did this. Arrest and conviction is enough. Don't be a prick who says, 'Sorry, we only recovered nine million of the nine-point-six million, so no reward.' That makes you no better than those car ads that offer a top-of-the-line luxury sedan for ninety-nine dollars a month, but the fine print requires you put twenty-nine thousand down on signing."

"I disagree. Thankfully, no one was injured here. All we're talking about is money, so the reward is conditioned on its return."

"You're not seeing the big picture," said Littleford.

"I assure you, a lot of careful thought and consideration goes into the formulation of our rewards."

Littleford nodded, as if to acknowledge the party line. "Let me give you and your company a little different perspective. Everyone remembers the big Lufthansa heist at JFK in December 1978 because Martin Scorsese made a movie out of it."

"*Goodfellas*. I know. It's practically required viewing in our line of work."

"See, that's the problem. People forget all the other heists, all the other robberies in New York. But I remember because my old man was with NYPD when I was a kid. A big hit puts ideas in crooks' heads. A few months after JFK, New York had eighteen bank robberies—*eighteen in three days*. Five on Monday, ten on Tuesday, and three more on Wednesday. Two of them were big hits over a million dollars, like JFK. Mayor Koch went nuts, warning these guys in the newspapers and on TV to remember what happened to Dillinger."

"That's a nice history lesson, but we have an excellent safety record."

"History repeats itself. You have a lot of armored trucks out on the streets of Miami every day. Hundreds of gangbangers and small-time crooks with big ideas saw the news reports of this multimillion-dollar job at the airport. A quick tip is the fastest way to solve this case. It's your best shot at recovering your money. And catching these crooks is the best way to make sure we don't see eighteen armored truck heists in the next week."

The lawyer thought about it for a moment. "I see your point. I'll recommend to headquarters that we go with arrest and conviction in the reward. No condition that the money be returned."

"Good call," said Littleford. "Follow up with Andie on this. She'll be taking a major role in this investigation."

"Will do."

"I'll be in touch," said Andie.

The agents left the building and walked to their car. "Nice work in there," said Andie.

"Thanks."

They got inside and closed the doors. The sun was blazing, and the temperature had climbed at least ten degrees since their arrival, well into the

eighties. It was legitimately beach weather, Littleford cranked the A/C. "Ah, November in Miami,"
he said. "Not like Seattle, is it?"

"No. It sure isn't."

He put the car in gear, but kept his foot on the
brake. "Hey, I know you didn't transfer here to be
assigned to my unit, but we do good work here."

"I see that."

"A lot of young agents think they want the undercover assignments, the stuff movies are made of. I'm
just saying: I like what I see in you. Keep an open
mind."

She smiled a little. Strokes were hard to come by
in the Bureau. Especially for the Andie-come-lately.
"Thanks. I will."

Littleford pulled out of the parking lot and onto
the street. They passed a long line of armored trucks
that were parked on the other side of the chain-link
fence. Dozens of trucks. Maybe a hundred. As they
passed, Andie was thinking of Littleford's history
lesson on the spate of robberies in New York, and
she found herself counting the trucks lined up in
the nearest row.

She stopped at eighteen.

6

Ruban stuck to the plan and went to work, just another week on the job.

Monday through Wednesday brought no surprises. Thursday was his monthly meeting with a Nicaraguan seafood supplier who, as usual, wanted to jack up the price on the shrimp that went into Ruban's signature dish: Russian borscht with grilled *camarones* in a Cuban marinade. They met at eight a.m. and haggled, over steaming cups of coffee, in the empty dining room at Café Ruban.

Café Ruban was Ruban's brainchild, a combination of Russian and Cuban cuisine that made for unique dishes, from the appetizer of caramelized yucca with caviar, to Russian pastries that made for a divine dessert when soaked in Cuban coffee. The café had originally opened in Miami's Little Havana, where it was a complete disaster. Hard-line expats vehemently opposed the notion that anything positive, much less edible, could come out of a Soviet-dominated Cuba. Ultimately, that mind-set worked to Ruban's advantage. As far as he could tell, his nearest competition was O! Cuba in St. Petersburg—Russia, not Florida. He moved his restaurant north to "Little Moscow" in Sunny Isles, where it was just starting to flourish when his and Savannah's financial world blew up.

"Come on, Ruban," his supplier pleaded. "Another nickel a pound. You can afford it."

Little does he know. "No," said Ruban. *"Nyet."*

Not that Ruban cared about a few pennies here or there. It was all about keeping his boss happy, who insisted on a hard line with suppliers.

Café Ruban bore his name, but Ruban didn't own it. Not anymore. It was a great concept, and one wealthy Russian customer had loved it so much that he offered to buy it. Ruban wasn't selling. Then he and Savannah fell behind on their home mortgage. Seriously behind. Their banker promised that if they brought the payments current, the bank would rework their loan to something they could afford. Ruban went to his Russian friend and borrowed $20,000, secured by the restaurant. He paid the bank, which then flatly refused to renegotiate the loan. The promised "work-out" was a lie, of course, the same lie that thousands of distressed homeowners heard at the height of the mortgage crisis. Their adjustable-rate mortgage skyrocketed, putting them even deeper into default. The bank foreclosed on the house. Café Ruban had a new Russian owner, who was smart enough, and lucky enough, to keep Ruban as a salaried manager.

Ruban couldn't wait to buy the place back.

His supplier agreed to another month of shrimp

at the current price. Ruban got a high five from his chef.

"Boss man will be very happy," she said.

"Hope so," said Ruban. "He seems pissed that I'm not doing Savannah's birthday party here."

"I think he understands."

Chef Claudia had known Savannah since high school, and Savannah had been the one to suggest that she and Ruban pair up to open a restaurant. The foreclosure, however, had killed the restaurant's positive vibe, at least from Savannah's standpoint.

"You're coming Saturday, right? Club Media Noche."

"I don't get off till midnight."

"It's Savannah's twenty-ninth birthday, not her forty-ninth. We'll still be going at midnight."

She laughed. "Then I'll be there."

"Great."

Claudia started toward the kitchen, but Ruban stopped her. "Hey, let me pick your brain a little bit. I'm having some paralysis by analysis with the gift. What do you think Savannah would really want?"

Claudia smiled a little, but it was half sad. "You know what she *really* wants."

He knew. Better than anyone. "Okay, short of that, what would work?"

"Go with something that sparkles."

"Jewelry?"

"I don't mean fireworks."

They had hocked her nicest jewelry trying to

save the restaurant—another reason not to have her party there. He hadn't bought her a piece since the foreclosure. "I'm going to make that happen," he said.

"She'll be happy."

Claudia went to the kitchen. Ruban crossed the dining area, toward the liquor stockroom. He needed to check the inventory and make sure his new bartender wasn't robbing him blind, but a knock on the front window got his attention. It was Pinky, the other new millionaire in Ruban's family by marriage. He was right outside the restaurant, standing on the sidewalk.

Ruban went to the front door and unlocked it, but he didn't let Pinky in.

"Let's walk," he said, and he took Pinky around the side of the building. They talked as they walked down the alley.

"What are you doing here?" he asked.

"You said no cell phones. All I have is a cell."

Pinky was old school, the opposite of his drug-addicted nephew. With Pinky, if you receive an order, you follow it; you disobey it, you die.

"This better be important," said Ruban.

"I can't get in touch with Marco. Have you talked to him?"

They stopped at the alley's dead end in front of the Dumpster. Funny, a restaurant could serve the most unique cuisine in south Florida, but all garbage smelled alike.

"No," said Ruban. "You're the one who's supposed to give him his cut."

"I've been to his apartment twice. No sign of him."

"Does he have a wife, a girlfriend?"

"Nah. Marco's a loner. The only thing I could think of was to check where he works."

"Shit, Pinky! You went back to the tile depot?"

"What was I supposed to do? I need to track him down. I don't want him to think we're stiffing him."

"What'd they tell you at the tile place?"

"Nobody's seen him all week."

Ruban started to pace. He did that whenever stress kicked in. "You think the cops got to him?"

"I don't know. That's why I came here. I was hoping you knew something."

"You and Marco should have worked out a time and place to meet before we did the job. That's what I did with Alvarez. He knows exactly where and when—"

"I know, I know. Third Tuesday after blah blah blah. Marco and me didn't do that. So it doesn't help for you to tell me what we should've done."

Ruban stopped pacing and drew a breath. "You're right. No more 'shouldas.'"

"So what do we do?"

"First off, don't *ever* go back to the tile warehouse again. Don't go to his apartment, either."

"Then how am I supposed to find him?"

"You do what I told everyone to do Sunday night: keep your normal routine, go to work, and go home every day just like before. You let Marco find *you*."

"What if he doesn't come?"

"We owe him a million dollars. He'll come."

"What if he doesn't?"

Ruban looked him right in the eye. "If we don't hear from him, we got much bigger problems than finding Marco."

On Saturday morning Ruban picked up his brother-in-law in South Miami. It was time to spend some money.

Week one was in the bank, so to speak. Still no word on Marco, but otherwise it had gone without a hitch. Ruban had followed the news coverage on television, and he'd overheard a couple of customers at the restaurant talking over Cuban mojitos made with Russian brandy—*Hey, did you hear about that airport heist?*—but that was it. The FBI had no leads, at least none reported in the media. Ruban still dressed the same, still acted the same, and still drove a ten-year-old Chevy Malibu with a driver's-side quarter panel that didn't quite match the rest of the car. He pulled up in front of a neighborhood ice cream parlor called Whip 'n Dip. Jeffrey climbed into the passenger seat with his breakfast in hand.

"You're eating a banana split at ten o'clock in the morning?"

"It's got milk, bananas, and nuts. It's practically health food."

Ruban drove east along the tree-lined and "historic" Sunset Drive. Jeffrey navigated while eating. A long string of weekend cyclists crossed the road ahead of them. They were in High Pines, a quiet neighborhood of sixties-vintage ranch-style houses, most of which had been updated by upper-middle-class families with young children. It was where Jeffrey's friend lived, "Sully the Jeweler," a wholesaler who normally sold only to dealers, though he did some business on the side for customers who met his minimum purchase requirement and paid in cash. Today was Savannah's birthday. Ruban had dug up a single pack of vacuum-sealed fifty-dollar bills to cover it.

"What are you going to get her?" asked Jeffrey.

"Something nice. We'll see what your friend is selling."

"Is this a total surprise? Or did you tell her about the money?"

"It's a surprise. But, yeah, I told her." He left out the biggest part of the lie, that he'd led her to believe that Jeffrey and his uncle had pulled off the heist alone.

"She's okay with it?"

"She will be."

"Savannah hasn't said a word to me about it."

"I told her not to. I don't want anyone talking about it, so it's best you not say anything to her, either."

Especially anything about me.

They were driving past an old, abandoned cemetery, four acres of pine trees and greenery that made this quiet neighborhood even quieter. Jeffrey scooped a mouthful of gooey chocolate sauce from the plastic dish. "You should get her a wristwatch. Sully is the go-to guy for Rolex."

"That could work."

"He gives good prices. I bought one."

Ruban cut a sharp glance from the driver's side. "You bought a Rolex? Shit, Jeffrey. I told you not to spend any money."

"Bro, *you're* spending money."

"It's Savannah's birthday."

"I bought one Rolex. That makes us even."

Ruban breathed out his anger. "Fine. One watch. But that's it. Don't spread the money around yet. It's too soon."

"No worries, bro. No worries."

They parked in the gravel driveway beneath the shade of an enormous royal poinciana tree and walked to the front door. Jeffrey tossed his empty dish into the bushes, wiped his hands on his shirt, and knocked firmly. No answer. He dialed Sully on his cell, got no answer, and dialed again. Still no luck. A minute later, a six-foot-six mulatto shuffled to the door, half-asleep, wearing only boxer shorts. He had an athletic build, and the way he scratched himself made Ruban guess baseball.

"Did I wake you up?" asked Jeffrey.

"No," he said, scratching yet again. "Some asshole kept ringing my cell."

"What a coincidence," said Jeffrey, choosing not to fess up. Instead, he made quick introductions, and they entered the living room. "Ruban wants to buy a Rolex for his wife. My sister."

Sully looked at Ruban, who was enough of a Latin heartthrob to have one pretty wife, and then his gaze drifted to Jeffrey, who didn't exactly convey the impression that good looks ran in the family. The expression on Sully's face was typical, and Jeffrey handled it as usual.

"Savannah got all the looks," said Jeffrey.

"I would have never guessed," he said dryly. Sully went to the closet in the hallway. He returned with a metal strong box, which he opened with a key. Inside was an assortment of high-end watches, mostly Cartier and Rolex. He removed a man's Rolex.

"This one here you might like for yourself," said Sully.

"That's the one I bought," said Jeffrey.

"Diamond-encrusted Rolex Daytona," said Sully. "Forty-five thousand."

Ruban's jaw dropped. *"Forty-five thousand?"*

"Too steep? Maybe this one," he said as he pointed to a Cartier. "I practically gave that one to Jeffrey for thirty thousand. You can have the same deal."

Ruban shot another harsh look at his brother-in-law. "You said you only bought one watch."

"I said one *Rolex*," said Jeffrey.

"Look, I'm a wholesaler," said Sully. "I don't sell to people who buy one watch. I'm making an exception for you because Jeffrey tells me he's thinking of getting into the business."

"Is that so?" asked Ruban.

"We'll talk about that later," said Jeffrey.

"Yeah, you bet we will," said Ruban.   .

"Okay, fine," said Sully. "One woman's watch is what you want?"

"Twenty grand is my top price," said Ruban.

Sully shook his head, not pleased. "Twenty grand? I don't know. I have a two-tone gold that goes for no less than twenty-five even in the discount shops. And at that price, it's probably a knock-off or stolen. I sell the real deal. I guess I could go twenty, seeing how Jeffrey bought four of them."

"Four!" said Ruban, the numbers quickly adding up in his head. "A hundred grand on ladies' watches? Seventy-five more on men's? Are you out of your damn—"

Ruban stopped himself, his gaze locked onto his brother-in-law's face.

Jeffrey froze. "What are you looking at?"

Ruban hadn't noticed his brother-in-law's teeth earlier. "What is that in your mouth?"

"Nothing."

He nearly lunged at him, prying his lips apart. The gold crowns on the bottom sparkled back at him. "Are you getting your teeth capped?"

"Guys, guys," said Sully. "Do you want to buy a watch or don't you?"

"No, forget it," said Ruban. "Jeffrey, let's go."

Ruban grabbed his brother-in-law by his shirt and pulled all three hundred pounds from the couch. Jeffrey made an awkward apology to Sully, stumbling as Ruban dragged him out the front door. Ruban waited until they were back in the car before dressing him down fully.

"Who are you buying four ladies' Rolexes for?"

"None of your business."

"Jeffrey, if you are giving twenty-five-thousand-dollar watches to strippers, I am going to kick your ass from here to Yemen."

"I'm not giving them to anyone. They're an investment."

"Oh, bullshit. Jeffrey, if you start flashing money, we are dead meat. Either law enforcement is going to take notice, or you'll be targeted by some of the scariest motherfuckers you've ever met in your life. There are entire gangs out there who do nothing but steal from other criminals. Do you understand what I'm saying? For the last time: Lay low."

Jeffrey didn't answer.

"And don't forget that I'm still holding a half million dollars of your share. If you flash money, you lose it. Final warning." Ruban backed the car out of the driveway and headed toward the highway.

"Sorry, bro," Jeffrey said softly.

"I'm telling you this for your own good," said Ruban.

"What should I do with the watches?"

Ruban grumbled, searching his mind for a solution. There was none. "Keep the damn things, I guess. But no more gold caps. Stop with the bottom teeth."

"Okay."

They rode in silence for a couple of blocks. Then Jeffrey spoke in his most contrite voice. "You want to give one of the ladies' Rolexes to Savannah? No charge. You can have it."

Ruban glanced over. His brother-in-law looked like a scolded schoolboy, his multiple chins resting on his chest.

"Shit, you're pathetic, you know that?"

Jeffrey dabbed at the chocolate and strawberry stain on his T-shirt. "Yeah. I do know. People tell me all the time."

Ruban sighed. Puppy-dog eyes. Jeffrey bore little resemblance to his younger sister, but both were masters of those sad puppy-dog eyes.

"Oh, all right, Jeffrey. One for Savannah. But no freebies. I'll buy it from you."

"Thanks, bro."

"You're welcome." *Dumb fuck.*

Savannah wanted to go dancing at midnight. What Savannah wanted, Savannah got. That was Ruban's rule. And for the first time in his life, he had the money to back it up.

Dinner had been at their favorite restaurant—which didn't bear Ruban's name—their go-to place in Kendall, not far from the house they'd once owned. Her dress wasn't new, but it was the red one that advertised to the world that Ruban Betancourt had the sexiest wife in Miami. They were sitting in the car, parked outside Club Media Noche, when he decided to give her the birthday present like none he had ever given her before.

"Go ahead, open it," he said, smiling so big that he was about to burst.

She returned the smile from the passenger seat. "What did you do?"

"Just open it."

She untied the ribbon and tore off the wrapping paper. The insignia on the box gave away the surprise.

"Are you kidding me? A Rolex?"

He reached over and opened the box for her. They were parked just outside the club entrance, and the diamonds sparkled in the multicolored glow of the neon sign.

"Is this a *real* Rolex?"

"The real deal."

She seemed concerned. "How much did you pay for this?"

"It's beautiful, right?"

She breathed deep, obviously aware that he'd dodged her question. "Did you use some of that money?"

He smiled. She didn't.

"Ruban, are you crazy? You said *all* the money stayed buried until you figured out what to do."

"And you said you were okay with it."

"*Okay* with it?" she said, her anger kicking in. "I said I was okay with not calling the police and turning Jeffrey and my uncle in. We still may have to do that eventually."

"No!"

She withdrew, his tone too sharp.

"I need a little more time to figure it out," he said in a more reasoned voice.

"Fine. You figure it out. But you can't touch this money. That's just stupid."

"Is it?"

"Yes. And, oh, by the way, it's stealing."

"Yeah, like the banks don't steal?"

She didn't respond right away. They'd had this talk on many sleepless nights before. "You can't make this about what happened to us."

"I've looked into it," he said. "The five bags that Jeffrey and your uncle stole add up to less than a drop in the bucket. That plane was carrying eighty-eight million dollars. This bank in Germany ships that much every week. Sometimes even more."

"That's not true."

"It *is* true. Losing nine or ten million is *nothing* to this bank. It's all insured, anyway, so the bank doesn't really lose anything."

"That doesn't make it okay to take it."

"Was it okay to take our house? My restaurant?"

"Honey, I know all that hurts. I still feel it. But Jeffrey and my sleazeball uncle really screwed up this time. If you start digging up the money and spending it, we're as bad as they are. Really, what were you thinking?"

"I was thinking that I haven't bought you a piece of jewelry in forever. I was thinking it's your birthday and that you would like it."

"I *do* like it. But, shit, Ruban. This is the stupidest thing you have ever done."

He sank into the driver's seat, his head rolling back as he gazed at the ceiling. Savannah was going to be an even harder sell than he'd thought. "All right, I'm sorry. I'll take the watch back."

"Promise?"

"Yes," he said. "But . . ."

"But what?"

"Why don't you wear it tonight?"

"Forget it."

"Come on. Once in her life, every woman should know what it feels like to have a Rolex on her wrist. Try it on."

"No."

"Please," he said, pushing it toward her. "Just for grins."

She resisted at first, then let him slide it up over her hand.

"There you go," he said with a smile.

She hesitated, but it was impossible not to say *something* nice. "It *is* gorgeous," she said.

He kissed her neck. "Like you."

She held it up to the light, admiring the sparkle. "Wow. Honestly, it's the most beautiful thing I've ever seen."

"Wear it to the party."

"Ruban, no. How could our friends look at this watch and *not* think you robbed a bank?"

"I'll tell them the restaurant is doing really well, which it is. The place is packed every night."

"But that doesn't make *us* rich."

"Nobody needs to know that. This is your night. How many twenty-ninth birthdays are you going to have in your lifetime? Wear it. It's just a few hours."

She leaned closer to him, torn for another moment, but then she nodded. "Okay. I'll wear it tonight. But then it goes back to wherever it came from."

"Deal," he said. "Come on, my beautiful wife. Let's go knock 'em dead."

8

·

Marco Aroyo was blinded by the light. His head throbbed with pain. A stream of blood and sweat stung his eyes, one of which was almost completely swollen shut. His wrists and ankles burned from the taut metal chains that shackled him to the wall.

The man asking the questions was a silhouette, his enormous frame hidden in the shadows behind the white-hot spotlight.

"One last time," the man said, his voice hissing. "Where is the money?"

Running. Aroyo wasn't good at it, but that was all he'd been doing since the heist. Running and hiding, afraid to go home or to work. Afraid to contact Pinky or Ruban about his share of the money, afraid even to make a phone call that might divulge his whereabouts. Aroyo was running for his life.

"I don't have it. I swear, I don't!"

It had been Aroyo's responsibility to get rid of the pickup truck. No one had told him how dangerous that job would be. When they'd loaded the pickup into the delivery truck and he'd pulled away from the tile warehouse, Aroyo had thought that his million-dollar cut would be the easiest money he ever earned. Before the pickup was even backed into the chop shop for disassembly, however, the breaking news was flashing on every television screen in Miami: "Black Ford F-150 pickup truck involved in multimillion-dollar heist at Miami International Airport." Locked up in a chop shop and surrounded by sharp tools is no place to be when a garage full of goons suddenly puts two-plus-two together and realizes that the guy with the black pickup has a treasure map in his head.

"You are a *liar*!" the man shouted, as he kicked Aroyo in the groin again. "Where's the money?"

Aroyo doubled over in pain, the chains rattling as he dropped to his knees and fell to the floor. He could barely breathe, let alone speak.

"It's . . . the truth," he somehow managed to say.

The man kicked him harder, this time in the kidney. It was as if someone had switched off the light. Aroyo struggled to remain conscious. The man stepped closer and grabbed Aroyo by the hair, forcing him to look up.

"This is not going to end well for you, Marco."

"Please, I'm begging."

"Tell me now, and it ends quickly. Keep up this game, and we do it my way."

Aroyo looked up, barely able to see. "Nothing to tell," he said, breathless.

He slammed Aroyo's head to the floor. "Now you've done it," he said. "Now I have to get my tools."

Aroyo closed his eyes, his face still pressed against the floor. He felt the vibration of firm footfalls as the man stepped away. He heard the sudden hiss of a propane tank, and the roar of focused flame suddenly pierced the darkness. It floated toward him like a blue comet, landing not quite near enough to burn the skin. Slowly, steadily, the heat intensified, singeing the hair on his bare chest. It was painless, so far, but he could smell it burning.

"Okay, okay! I'll tell you!"

"Too late," the man said, as he turned up the flame. "You chose *my way*."

Aroyo would have told him anything, wanted to tell him everything. But the scream he heard next was his own.

Ruban and Savannah were still dancing at two a.m. The club was packed, and a dozen friends from the birthday celebration were partying with them.

Media Noche was *the* nightclub in midtown, and every Saturday night it pulsated with live Latin music. Ruban was nearing his limit on the Cuba libres, and Savannah wasn't far behind with her vodka and cranberry. They told the bartenders, cocktail waitresses, their friends on the dance floor, and everyone else they ran into that they were celebrating. All wished Savannah a happy birthday, but for Ruban it was a double celebration. Bragging about the restaurant again made him feel like the old Ruban, and he told a few of his closest friends that he was even thinking about buying it back. The Rolex on Savannah's wrist was enough to convince them that it wasn't just a pipe dream.

At first, Savannah had seemed embarrassed by the compliments on her gift. She'd even told a few that it wasn't real. Sometime after midnight, however, Ruban caught her smiling and letting a girl-friend try it on.

"Come with me, beautiful," he said as he took her hand and led her onto the dance floor. It was a slow ballad, and he wrapped Savannah in his arms.

"I love my party," she whispered into his ear.

"Do you love your present?" he asked.

"I love *you*." She ran her nails along the back of his neck. "Hey, wanna get down and dirty?"

"Really?"

"Grab a shovel. Let's dig up some money."

He stopped dancing, surprised, and took a step back.

"Just kidding," she said, smiling as she pulled him close again.

He held her tight, and they swayed to the music. All was good. Savannah was beautiful. They were in love the way they used to be. It might take some time, but she would come around to loving the money.

Ruban could feel it.

9
.

"We may have our first break," Andie said into her phone.

She gave Littleford the quick rundown. Tom Cat had stepped up patrol along the Miami River since the heist, figuring that the crooks might make the pickup truck disappear by putting it on a freighter along with the usual haul of stolen vehicles. They had a hit.

"We found the pickup?" asked Littleford.

"A stolen delivery truck," said Andie. "Watts searched the cab and thinks the pickup might be, or might have been, in the box. Just to be safe, I told him to get a warrant."

"Good. Where's the truck?"

"Seabird Terminal B, just down the street from the Miami River Rapids Mini Park."

"I'll meet you there."

It had been a week of dead ends for the FBI. They had footprints and tire tracks from the warehouse, but not a single fingerprint, and no DNA to work with. The eyewitness descriptions of the thieves were sketchy and conflicting. FBI tech agents were able to enhance the security camera video, but only up to a point. Not even techies could see through ski masks. At bottom, they were looking for two men of average height and weight. About the only thing the witnesses agreed upon was that they spoke Spanish with an American accent. Even less helpful were the hundreds of calls that had flooded the tip line. A six-figure reward was serious motivation, and it didn't have to be a case of Hatfields versus McCoys for folks to report a "suspicious neighbor" down the street. Law enforcement wheels had been spinning all week, no traction at all. Until Sunday morning.

The shipping area near Miami River Rapids Mini Park is upriver, closer to the airport and well away from the upscale riverfront development in downtown Miami. Many old, sketchy cargo terminals had been shut down by Homeland Security after 9/11, but commerce continued to flow, some of it as polluted as the river itself. Huge cranes worked around the clock, hoisting mountains of metal containers onto Caribbean-bound freighters. Some carried electronics and other dry goods. Others carried vehicles with the VINs scratched off. Trucks and four-wheel-drive vehicles were particularly in demand, as any Miamian who *used to* own a Range Rover would attest. Andie wondered about a certain black pickup.

Andie parked her car along the chain-link fence. Coils of razor wire stretched across the top like a man-eating Slinky. If that weren't enough to protect the three-story stack of containers on the other side of the fence, the Dobermans might make thieves think twice. Littleford pulled up right beside her. Together they walked toward a white box truck that had been pulled aside and separated from the cargo that was being loaded onto a freighter bound for Jamaica. Lieutenant Watts from MDPD was waiting for them.

"Do you have your search warrant yet?" asked Andie.

"Any minute," said Watts. "We got the VIN through the windshield and ran a vehicle check. Belongs to an appliance store in West Kendall. It was reported stolen the Monday morning after the MIA heist, when the driver showed up for work and saw that it was gone. My guess is that it was stolen the Saturday night before the heist."

"So were a lot of other vehicles. What makes you think this one might have a pickup truck inside it?"

Watts showed them a sealed evidence bag with a piece of paper inside. "We found a handwritten note tucked under the visor on the driver's side."

"You searched the cab without a warrant?"

"It's a stolen vehicle. We can take an inventory."

He was technically correct, but when there was time to get a warrant, Andie didn't like to take chances. "What's on the note?"

"Time entries. The first one is 1:55 p.m."

"That was the scheduled arrival time for flight 462," said Andie.

"Notice that it's crossed out," said Watts. "Someone wrote in 2:08. That's the actual arrival time. Then you have two more time entries below those. Three forty-five is crossed out and somebody wrote in 3:58. Thirteen minutes later."

"Which is exactly how many minutes late the flight was," said Andie.

"You got it. My theory is that this second entry— 3:45 changed to 3:58—was an estimated time for some kind of rendezvous involving this truck. This box is plenty big to hold an F-150."

Andie's gaze turned toward the truck. The suspension was even between front and rear, no sign of any load in the box. "That pickup probably weighs six thousand pounds. It's not inside there now, that's for sure."

Littleford had made the same observation. "They could have brought the pickup here in the delivery truck and shipped it on another freighter. One that's long gone."

"Exactly," said Watts. "And if I'm right about this, they would have made some modifications to the box to keep the truck from rolling out the back door."

Another car pulled up, and a young assistant state attorney got out.

"Here's our warrant," said Watts.

The prosecutor had a pissed-off expression on her face, clearly not very happy about coming out on a Sunday. "You know, you don't need a warrant to inventory a stolen vehicle," she said.

Andie immediately pegged her as one of those prosecutors who would talk out of the other side of her mouth and blame the cop just as soon as a key piece of evidence was excluded at trial for failure to get a warrant. "Belt and suspenders," said Andie. "That's me."

They walked toward the back of the truck where one of the MDPD officers was standing. Watts told him to open it. The rollup door wasn't locked, and one good shove was enough. The box was empty.

Andie shone her flashlight inside, which criss-crossed with the more powerful beam from the officer's heavy-duty flashlight. The chains and timbers used to secure the truck were readily visible, as were tire tracks on the bed of the truck.

"I'll be damned," said Littleford.

"We'll want to get a comparison to the tracks at the airport warehouse," said Andie.

Watts was about to climb inside, but Littleford stopped him. "Keep it clean for forensics," he said.

Andie aimed her flashlight toward the forward end of the box, where four lengths of steel chain lay in separate piles. "Could that be dried blood on that chain?"

"Hard to tell," said Littleford.

Andie's flashlight picked up a string of brown dots across the metal bed of the box. "Definitely could be blood," she said as her beam came to rest on something in the far corner.

"What's that?" asked Littleford.

"Candy bar, maybe. We could get lucky and find saliva."

She wanted to climb inside and look, but she

knew better than to contaminate the crime scene, especially if blood was involved. The MDPD officer brought binoculars from his squad car. Andie focused on the object in the corner. The zoom was powerful enough for her to see ants at work.

"It's not a candy bar," she said as she lowered the binoculars. "That's a human finger."

Littleford borrowed the binoculars. "Whipped him bloody with chains and cut off his finger. If he's alive, he's in bad shape. If he's dead, he didn't die a pleasant death."

"Check that out," said Watts, pointing toward another section of the floor.

Andie aimed her flashlight at the black smudges. "Looks like burn marks," said Andie.

"I'm leaning toward unpleasant death," said Watts.

"Most unpleasant," said Andie.

"I'll put MDPD homicide on alert."

He started toward his squad car. Andie and Littleford stayed behind the open delivery truck.

"What do you think?" asked Andie.

"I predicted it in the warehouse when I saw that bag on the floor. I think it's the guy who dropped two million dollars on his way to the truck."

"Forensics will be interesting. I can stay and wait for them. No need for you to hang around all Sunday afternoon."

"Thanks. Call me when you know anything." He started toward his car, then stopped. "Hey, Henning."

"Yeah?"

"How do you like the bank robbery unit so far?"

Andie was still learning his sense of humor, and she was not yet sure that he could handle hers. She resisted the urge to fire back a smartass response.

"I'll get back to you on that, Chief."

10

·

Ruban woke up feeling lousy, and it wasn't just the rum-soaked night at Club Media Noche. Savannah held him to his promise. Her joke on the dance floor about getting "down and dirty" and digging up some money had been just that—a joke. It must have been the alcohol. She'd put the Rolex back in the box before going to bed, and first thing in the morning she gave Ruban the order: "Take it back. Today."

What Savannah wants, Savannah gets.

He drove to South Miami and talked to Sully, who actually seemed glad to see him. He invited Ruban inside and directed him to a seat on the couch, apparently smelling another sale.

"Did you decide to buy the watch after all?" he asked.

Ruban removed the box from his coat pocket and laid it on the table. "No. I ended up buying one that you sold to Jeffrey. My wife didn't like it, so we have to return it."

Sully smiled with amusement. "This isn't Nordstrom. I don't do returns."

"I know this is a hassle, so keep a thousand for your trouble, give me twenty-four, and we'll call it even."

"Are you not hearing me? I don't do returns."

"I'm giving you a thousand dollars for nothing. Jeffrey paid you twenty-five grand."

"All sales are final."

Ruban checked his anger, but his glare made the point. "You're being unreasonable. That's not smart."

Sully blinked, and the point seemed to have been made. He reached for the Rolex box and opened it. "I can't take this back. It's been worn."

"One time. How can you even tell?"

Sully sniffed the band. "I can smell the perfume on it."

"So wipe it off."

"You let your wife wear the watch, and then I'm supposed to take it back? Fuck no."

"All right, I'll take twenty grand."

"Take a hike."

"You're starting to piss me off," said Ruban.

Their eyes locked, but Ruban didn't flinch, and he could feel Sully backing down.

"Fine," said Sully. "Twenty. I'll get the cash."

He went to the closet. It wasn't the best deal Ruban had ever negotiated, but he'd told Savannah so many lies lately that he was having trouble keeping them straight. It was important to tell her the truth about *something*, and his return of the Rolex was a good place to start.

"Get out," said Sully. He was pointing a gun at Ruban from across the room. He hadn't gone to the closet to retrieve cash.

"Whoa. Relax, pal."

"Don't tell me to relax. Your brother-in-law is cool. You're not. Take the watch, and don't let me see your face around here again."

"You're gonna shoot me over this? Really?"

"Only if you make me."

Ruban studied him. Sully didn't look at all comfortable holding that pistol. Ruban wondered if he'd ever fired the thing.

"What you got there?" asked Ruban. "Taurus nine-mil?"

"What's it to you?"

Ruban rose from the couch. "Yeah, looks like a Taurus."

"Take the watch and walk straight to the door," said Sully.

Ruban left the watch on the table and started slowly away from the couch. "I used to own a Taurus," he said.

"Walk toward the door." He pointed in that direction with the gun—only for a second, but it was long enough for Ruban to get a side view of the pistol.

"Taurus makes a nice sidearm," said Ruban. He was walking slowly, straight at Sully.

"Toward *the door*," said Sully.

Ruban kept coming, his gaze locked on Sully like a laser. "I'm going to give you one last chance to take twenty thousand on the return."

The gun was beginning to shake, and Sully was

starting to look like a man who wished he hadn't injected it into the discussion. "No deal," said Sully.

Ruban took two more steps, not much farther to go.

"Stop right there!" said Sully.

Ruban took another step, then the last.

"Stop, or—"

Ruban grabbed the barrel of the gun and pointed it toward the floor. Sully froze.

"First of all," Ruban said in a firm, even tone, "I knew you don't have the balls to shoot me. Second, I know the Taurus. I saw the white dot on the frame when you pointed toward the door. A red dot means it's ready to fire. You left the safety on, dumbass."

Sully swallowed the lump in his throat. In one quick motion, Ruban snatched the gun away, removed the safety, and shoved the barrel up under Sully's chin.

"I'll take my twenty-five grand now," he said, speaking right into his face.

Sully raised his arms slowly. "No problem."

In another quick motion, Ruban pressed the slide against Sully's ear and racked it, taking a nick out of Sully's earlobe as the first round entered the chamber.

"Ow!" Sully was bleeding.

Ruban pressed the gun to the back of Sully's head. "Shut up and lead the way."

Sully did as he was told. A safe was built into the wall in the back of the closet, and Sully's hand shook as he dialed the combination and opened it. He reached inside and removed a vacuum-sealed pack. Ruban recognized it as one of the packs he'd given to Jeffrey on the night of the heist, and he knew it contained precisely twenty-five thousand. He stuffed the pack under his shirt. Then he shoved Sully into the closet and closed the door.

"You stay in there till Tuesday," he said loud enough for Sully to hear. "You got that?"

"Uh-huh."

Ruban left through the front door, tossed Sully's pistol into the shrubbery on his way out, and stashed the money in the trunk of his car before driving away. He was halfway home when he realized that he'd walked out with at least two thousand dollars more than he'd expected to get from Sully on the return, which would buy a nice birthday present for Savannah. But no more dealing with scumbags who did business out of a closet. It was time to shop like real people, people with class, people with money. He hopped onto the expressway and headed to downtown Miami.

The Seybold Building is a ten-story retail center filled with nothing but jewelry stores and dealers. People came from all over the world to shop there, and Ruban had heard many a customer at Café Ruban gushing about their new bauble from Seybold. He breezed past the first few shops in the arcade, which sold mostly antique rings and other vintage jewelry. Midway down the mall he found a shop that sold "contemporary designs," more Savannah's style. He spotted a pair of earrings for two grand. Sold. He went inside and told the clerk.

"Would you like those gift-wrapped?"

"Yeah, I would."

Ruban browsed the glass display cabinets while

the clerk wrapped the earrings. He wandered toward the selection of fine watches, where a Rolex caught his eye. It looked identical to the watch he had just "returned" to Sully.

"Are you interested in a watch as well?" the sales associate asked.

"Maybe. How much is that ladies' Rolex?"

The clerk unlocked the cabinet and laid the watch on a velvet pad. "This is a nice one. Twelve-karat gold with diamond and ruby bezel. It goes for twenty-five hundred dollars."

Ruban did a double take. "You mean twenty-five *thousand*, right?"

He chuckled. "No. You can have *ten* of them for twenty-five thousand. Honestly, it's a discontinued style. Twenty-five hundred is what we're asking. I might be able to go a little lower, if you pay cash."

Ruban was too angry to speak.

"Sir?"

"Sorry," said Ruban. "Just the earrings today."

He took the shopping bag, the clerk thanked him, and Ruban left the store. He tried to focus on how happy the earrings would make Savannah, but he couldn't let go of the fact that Sully had charged his stupid brother-in-law ten times the full retail price on four ladies' watches. His markup on the men's watches was probably just as outrageous.

No wonder he'd pulled a gun.

Ruban's cell rang. He took the call while walking back to his car. It was Savannah's uncle—Pinky.

"We got a problem with Marco."

Ruban stopped on the sidewalk. "What now?"

"I was just watching the noontime news. The cops found the delivery truck by the river."

"Damn it, Pinky! Marco's only job was to supply the pickup and then ditch it. You hired him. You said he could handle it."

"Don't put this on me. It was *your* idea to put the pickup inside the delivery truck and put everything on the freighter. Marco was just in charge of execution."

"How hard is that to execute?" Ruban said, his voice rising. "Now it's all fucked up!"

"Relax, all right?" said Pinky. "They didn't say anything on the news about finding the pickup. That's gone. Maybe there wasn't room on that freighter for the delivery truck. But if the TV news got it right, there's a bigger problem. They found bloody chains inside the delivery truck. And somebody's finger."

Ruban froze. "Shit. Is it Marco?"

"They didn't say."

"Did you ever get hold of him after we talked Thursday?"

"No."

"So you still got his money?"

"Yeah. Still got it."

Ruban started toward his car again, as if walking might help him think. "Where is it?"

There was silence on the line. Then Pinky laughed and said, "Where it'll be safe. We settled this the night of the split. You hide your money, I hide mine."

"This isn't yours. It's Marco's. I'll hold it."

"What, you don't trust me, bro?"

Ruban unlocked his car, and before he could answer, a homeless man approached from behind.

"Hey, my man. Don't I know you?" He was holding a sign that said "Dog Bless You," which was either his attempt at humor or "Exhibit A" in his trial for public intoxication.

Ruban waved him off, climbed behind the wheel, and locked the door. "Pinky, if Marco's toast, we need to split up his money."

"We don't even know he's dead yet."

"Don't be stupid. Can't you see what happened here? Marco shot his mouth off to the wrong person. They beat him with chains and cut off his finger to find out where he hid his money, and they didn't believe him when he said he didn't get paid yet. He's dead."

"Probably."

Another thought came to Ruban's mind, one more important than money. "Do you think Marco gave us up?"

"How the fuck do I know, bro?"

"He was your friend."

"He's a two-bit car thief I met in prison. Look, all I can tell you is I'm outta here. No way am I going to work tomorrow like everything's normal. I'm cracking open my vacuum-sealed packs and getting the hell out of Miami."

"Pinky, don't. We have to hold it together here."

"Bullshit. Your brother-in-law is stuffing coke up his nose and dropping money at strip clubs like there's holes in his pockets. He's wearing a target on his chest. Either you get him to tone it down, or I might take some target practice myself."

"That's not cool. Jeffrey is your nephew."

"He's a fuckup. This is the big leagues. There's a chance Marco didn't give us up. But if somebody even twists Jeffrey's fat finger, there's *no chance* he won't give us up. You gotta take control of the situation. If you don't, I will."

"Don't threaten me."

"No threat. Here's the deal. Get fatso under control, and we split Marco's share. Otherwise, I keep it. That's all I have to say."

Pinky hung up. Ruban tossed the cell onto the passenger seat. Week one had been a dream. Week two was shaping up to be a nightmare. Pinky's question had hit the nail on the head: *"What, you don't trust me, bro?"*

Ruban didn't trust anybody. *Gotta take control.*

He started the engine and nearly ran over the homeless guy as he backed out of the parking spot. The driver's-side window squeaked as he lowered it.

"Dog bless you," he said as he drove away.

11

·

Andie stopped by Littleford's townhouse after dinner. It had been a busy afternoon, and his place was on her way home from the crime lab.

"Tire tracks match," said Andie. "The pickup used in the heist was definitely inside the delivery truck at some point in time."

They were seated in matching Adirondack chairs on the backyard patio. The sun had set, and a half-moon was rising over the tall ficus hedge. It was the peak of autumn in south Florida, that one night each November when Miamians step out of their air-conditioned boxes and ask, *Hey, where did the humidity go?*

"That gives us something," said Littleford. "Stay on Tom Cat this week to keep looking for the pickup, but my bet is that it's probably cruising down the streets of Nassau or Santo Domingo as we speak."

"Or chopped into pieces that will soon be sprinkled across South America."

"What about the finger?"

"More bad news: no fingerprint."

"Ants?"

"Not just ants. Dermestids. Flesh-eating beetles. Every trace of epidermis is gone. I swear, you find the most bizarre insects at these cargo terminals on the river."

"What did you find out about the blood on the chains?"

"B-positive. It matches the DNA from the finger. Male victim. Unfortunately, we have nothing from the MIA warehouse to compare it to, so no way to know if it was one of the perps in the heist."

"Any other prints to work with?"

"MDPD pulled some from the handwritten note that was found under the visor, and from the cab of the delivery truck. But no hits in the databases."

Littleford's wife came out and handed him a slice of cheesecake on a plate. "You sure you wouldn't like some, Andie?" she asked.

"I'm fine, thank you."

"You know, dessert is actually a required activity in my unit," said Littleford.

"You do make it tempting. But my plan is still a steady diet of undercover work after this case is cracked."

He shaved off a slice with his fork and savored it. "Great cake, Barbara."

"Thanks, honey," she said. "Do you bake, Andie?"

"Only when I lie in the sun."

"Excuse me?"

"Sorry, bad joke. No, I'm not much of a cook."

"But she can shoot the cap off a Coke bottle at fifty yards," said Littleford.

It was a slight exaggeration, but Barbara didn't

seem impressed anyway. "Michael says you moved here from Seattle."

"That's right," said Andie.

"Are you seeing anyone?"

"Hey, a new world record!" said Littleford. "Fifteen seconds until Barbara puts out the feelers for her poor, lonely divorced cousin."

"Stop, Michael. John is not poor."

"I didn't mean he's—"

"I know what you both mean," said Andie. "No, I'm not dating anyone. But I'm not looking to date right now. Thank you, though."

"Great answer," said Littleford.

Barbara rose. "Well, if you change your mind . . ."

"I'll let you know," said Andie.

Barbara smiled and left them alone.

Littleford set his plate on the armrest. "Well, wasn't that just dandy? I spend all week trying to convince you to stay in the bank robbery unit, and in two minutes my wife has you running for undercover work."

Andie laughed. "Don't worry about it."

"Okay. Let's talk about this week. I want you to coordinate with MDPD to find out who lost a finger."

"No problem."

"Any reason to go back to the MIA warehouse?"

Andie considered it. "I still think one of the guards—probably Alvarez—called the perps from the warehouse and told them when to come. But we've practically turned that warehouse inside out looking for a phone. Nothing."

"Your initial reaction is probably spot-on," said

Littleford. "He went into the bathroom, made the call, smashed the phone into a thousand tiny pieces, and flushed it down the toilet."

"We should keep our eye on Alvarez. At some point he needs to meet up with someone and get his cut of the stolen money."

"Unless someone else is putting the money through the laundry and it ends up in his Cayman Islands account. Maybe we go back to Braxton and talk to Alvarez again."

Littleford's wife was back with two demitasses. "Espresso?" she asked.

"Is it decaf?" asked Andie.

Littleford made a face. "Real dessert, real coffee. Get with the program, Henning."

Andie smiled and took the cup.

"I forgot to ask," said Barbara. "How do feel about lawyers?"

"Barbara, give it a rest," said Littleford.

"Sorry." She went back inside.

"My wife has a great heart, but she's one of those married people who will never rest until the rest of the world is married, too."

Andie felt the need to shift gears. She opted for the perfect diversion with any man and made the conversation about him. "Not to change the subject, but ever since those interviews at Braxton, I've been meaning to say that I loved the way you worked in those eighteen robberies in three days after the Lufthansa heist at JFK. I thought you were bluffing, but I Googled it. That was no bull."

"Nope. August 1979."

"So, your dad was with NYPD?"

"No. That part of the story I made up."

"Are you kidding me?"

"No. He was never even a cop."

"Oh, man," she said, smiling. "You had me totally buying it. What did he do? Wait, don't tell me. Aromatherapist, right?"

He smiled, then turned serious. "He drove an armored truck in the Bronx."

"For real? Why didn't you tell the folks at Braxton?"

He shook his head. "I don't really tell anyone."

Andie paused, confused, not sure why he'd be embarrassed by it. "Why not?"

"You really want to know?"

She wasn't sure. "Yeah. If you want to tell me."

He put down his demitasse and looked out across the yard as he spoke. "It happened on a Tuesday," he said. "I was in my last week of the third grade and couldn't wait to start summer vacation. My dad was in the parking lot outside a shopping center. Four men stormed the truck. Two of them had guns. They got away with two hundred and ninety-two thousand dollars. No one really knows why, but they shot both guards before they ran off with the money. One lived. Dad was dead before I got home from school."

Andie didn't know what to say. "I'm so sorry. I had no idea."

"It's okay. I don't really talk about it, especially with the armored-transport companies. Can you imagine what they would say? 'Oh, there goes Littleford again, bumping up the reward money, still trying to make us pay for never finding out who killed his daddy.' "

Andie studied his profile, which was more like a silhouette in the dim afterglow of the sunset. "Did they offer a reward?"

"Sure did."

"I'm going to take a guess here," she said. "Was it good only for information leading to an arrest, conviction, *and* return of the money?"

Finally, he looked at her. "Smart girl."

Andie sat forward in her chair and spoke without so much as a blink of her eyes. "We're going to catch these guys."

He looked off again toward the long shadows on the lawn. "Yeah," he said quietly. "I know we will."

12

Jeffrey Beauchamp was in celebration mode. It was the one-week anniversary of his becoming a millionaire. His pockets were stuffed with money, his nostrils were numb from coke, and the perfect ass of one of his favorite porn stars was grinding down on him in a four-minute lap dance.

"Easy, baby," he said.

"Oooh, Jeffy, you naughty boy. I knew there was a dick somewhere under that big belly."

The men at the next table laughed. So did Jeffrey.

The lap dance was a well-honed art form at the Gold Rush in downtown Miami. Completely naked women worked on very drunk men, and the old song about a fool and his money was perpetually at the top of the charts. Many a hungover patron had awakened the morning after to find that the same five-dollar cocktails he bought for himself were fifty dollars when purchased for a dancer, and that the love of his life who couldn't say enough about the enormous bulge in his pants had "mistakenly"

charged him $1,200 for a hundred-dollar dance—
Oops, sorry, sweety. Dancers were from all over the
world: Thailand to India, London to São Paulo, and
Caribbean goddesses galore. The biggest draw was
the weekly "HEAD-liner," usually a porn star of
some note. Most customers were from out of town,
save for a handful of regulars that included a former
congressman and an ex–state attorney who'd lost his
job after flashing his badge to get in without a cover
charge—and Jeffrey.

"Don't you ever go home, Beauchamp?"

He smiled. Lap dances 24/7, legs and eggs for
breakfast, grilled chicken and a side of friction for
lunch. "This *is* my home."

The music got louder. Bambi worked her ass to
a more strategic position, slow and steady. "Jeffy?"

His head rolled back, and the mirror on the ceiling offered a bird's-eye view of Bambi at her bouncy
best. "What?"

"Can I get a Rolex?"

"Uhmm. Okay."

"One with diamonds?"

"Uh-huh."

"I want it right now."

"Ohhh. Ohhh. Oh-kay."

Bambi slid off his lap. Jeffrey knocked back another shot of tequila and pushed himself up from his
chair. Half of his ass was hanging out of the back of
his pants, and he could feel the cold air on his skin,
but he didn't care. He wiped away the coke residue
from under his nose, and Bambi followed him past
the line of pole dancers and across the bar to a dark

booth in the back. Sully was with a pair of Venezuelan strippers. Jeffrey recognized one, but the other girl was new. He liked the snake tattoo coiling up her arm. Very hot.

"Whah . . ." Jeffrey started to say, but the words wouldn't come. That last shot of tequila had hit him like a mule kick. He tried again. "Whah . . . hoppin . . . to ya' ear, bro?"

Sully tugged at the bandage. "It's my Vincent van Gogh look."

"Huh?"

"Nothin'. You need another Rolex?"

Bambi nodded. "Jeffy said I could have one."

Sully snapped his fingers at the new girl with the snake tattoo. The Rolex was the only thing she was wearing, and it made her pout to hand it over.

"You like this one?" Sully asked as he handed it to Bambi.

She stepped up on the table and pressed the watch against her pubic hair. "You like it, Jeffy?"

She was so close, so in his face, that he had her scent. "Yeah, yeah. I lub it."

"Twenty-five grand," said Sully.

"Puddut in my ah-count," said Jeffrey.

"No," said Sully. "No more account."

"Why?"

"That's my new rule. Cash on delivery."

Bambi turned around, bent over, and grabbed her ankles to give Jeffrey his favorite view. "*Please*, Jeffy?"

"Okay, cash," said Jeffrey. "My car."

"Let's go," said Sully. "Excuse us, ladies."

Sully slid out of the booth. Jeffrey staggered past

the pole dancers and toward the door. The girl with the snake tattoo followed.

"Hey, Jeffy," she said. "I like watches, too."

Ruban was sinking deep into the couch, a wink away from sleep, when Savannah shoved him. The ten-o'clock news was on the television.

"They think they found the truck that was used in the heist," she said, her voice filled with urgency.

He sat up and got his bearings. The report was nearly over, but a final image of a delivery truck flashed on the screen. He was relieved not to see the pickup, but that was not something to share with Savannah.

"That could be."

The reporter reminded viewers to call Crime Stoppers tip line if they have "any information about the possible victim," and the newscast moved to the night's next story.

"They found a human finger in it!" said Savannah.

Ruban wasn't sure what to make of that, but he was concerned enough to prod Savannah for more details. "Did they say anything about a black pickup?"

"No. What do you know about a black pickup?"

"Jeffrey told me," he said.

Savannah moved closer, her nails digging into his forearm. "Do you think that finger could be my uncle's?"

"No," he said, thinking up another lie on the fly. "Pinky said they hired someone to get rid of the truck. I suppose it could be that guy."

"Oh, my God, Ruban! This is the kind of thing I was afraid of! We need to go to the police."

"Just calm down."

His phone rang, and it made them both jump.

"Keep an eye on the news and see if there's any update," he told Savannah. Then he stepped away to take the call where she couldn't overhear. The voice on the line was Jamaican.

"Ruban, you got big trouble, mon."

It was the bartender at the Gold Rush. He used to work with Ruban at the restaurant. Ruban should never have backed down on burying Jeffrey's entire share in his yard, but a hundred bucks a night for Ramsey to keep an eye on Jeffrey was Ruban's finger on the pulse of a bad situation.

"What now?" he asked.

"Your brother-in-law is out of control, mon. *Toe-tuh-lee* out of control."

Ruban cut one last glance toward Savannah before ducking into the kitchen. She was glued to the television, waiting for any follow-up on the heist. "Tell me," he said into the phone.

"He's crazy, mon. Money, coke, girls. Tonight he buying Rolex watches for duh strippers."

"*What?*"

"Ruban, I don't know where Jeffrey gets dis money. Not my business. But if the cash don't run out soon, he goin' to end up dead in the parkin' lot."

Ruban started to pace, back and forth, from the stove to the refrigerator. "That's what I've been telling him. I been telling him, and telling him, and telling!"

"You tellin' him, mon, but he ain't listenin'. You

got to *do* somethin'. Or it goin' to be one revoltin' situation."

Ruban stopped at the sink, ran his hand through his hair, and let out a mirthless chuckle. The Jamaicans had such a way with words. "You got that right, bro. One revoltin' situation."

Ruban woke before five a.m., but not on purpose. He thought he heard Savannah on the phone. He buried his head in the pillow and hoped he was dreaming.

They'd gone to bed at midnight, and not on good terms. Whatever good he'd done by returning the Rolex was lost with the replacement gift. The earrings were on sale at the mall, he'd sworn to her, no funny money involved. Savannah wasn't fooled.

"Ruban, wake up!"

He opened his eyes. The room was dark, and Savannah was practically on top of him. Her cell was pressed to her ear.

"Jeffrey's in trouble!"

He groaned and rolled onto his side. Savannah tugged his shoulder and forced him to look at her. "He needs to talk to you!"

He checked the clock on the nightstand. "I need sleep."

She shoved the phone at him. "He sounds scared to death. Talk to him!"

"Fine," he said as he took the phone. "Jeffrey, I have no coke. Time to go to bed. Good night."

He hung up and tossed the phone aside.

"Ruban, what are you *doing*?" she screamed.

The phone rang immediately. Savannah answered,

and Ruban could hear the urgency in her voice as she spoke into the phone. "Jeffrey, are you okay? Where are you?"

Ruban stayed in the bed, but his wife was up and began to pace at the foot of the bed. Ruban wasn't trying to listen, but she was talking in a loud, excited voice. Her end of the conversation was the same line, over and over again: Oh, my God. Oh, my God. Oh, my God. Finally, she lowered the phone and spoke to Ruban.

"Somebody has Jeffrey."

Ruban got up on one elbow. "What do you mean, *has* him?"

"Abducted. Kidnapped. Whatever you want to call it. They took him from the parking lot at Gold Rush."

"When?"

"Thirty minutes ago."

He fell back into the pillow. "Oh, shit."

Savannah was back on the phone. "Jeffrey, listen to what I'm saying. I want you to do whatever they . . . Jeffrey? Are you there?"

Even in the darkness, Ruban could see the panic in her expression.

"He's gone!" she said. She dialed back frantically, then put the phone down. "No answer. Ruban, what are we going to do?"

He sat up on the edge of the bed. "First, we calm down. Freaking out will just make things worse."

"I need to call the police!"

Ruban snatched away the phone before she could dial. "We are *not* going to call the police."

"My brother has been kidnapped!"

"You don't know that he's been kidnapped. Nobody has asked for a ransom. For all you know, he left the Gold Rush with some prostitute who is threatening to kick his ass because he ran out of money."

"No, that's not what this is. I could hear it in his voice. This is bad."

"This is exactly the thing I warned him and your uncle about when I told them to stash the money. A guy with no job, no money, and no life is asking for trouble if he suddenly starts acting like he's a high roller. The strippers aren't the only ones who take notice."

"What money? You made sure it was buried. All of it. That's what you told me."

He had told her that, the night of the split. Or had he? He wasn't sure. Time to tap-dance. "They must have held out on me and stashed some on their own. My point is—"

"*My* point is that we're talking about my brother. We have to help him!"

"Yes, and I'm looking out for him. If we call the cops, this whole heist that he and Pinky pulled off will unravel. Jeffrey will spend the rest of his life in jail," he said, no mention of his own skin. "We have to work this out ourselves."

"How?"

"We wait for him to call back."

"*Wait?* What if Jeffrey ends up like that guy in the back of the delivery truck? The only thing left of *him* is a finger!"

"That's not going to happen to Jeffrey."

"How do you know that?"

Ruban had to dig deep for the answer to that one. "Because Jeffrey has a family who cares about him. And I'm not going to let it happen."

Savannah sat beside him on the edge of the bed. She was staring blankly into the darkness, but her head was resting on his shoulder. He seemed to have chosen the right words.

"What are we going to do?"

He took her hand. "We go to work, like we do every Monday morning. And we wait."

13

Savannah had to be at the dry cleaners by seven a.m. Ruban drove her.

"My brother's missing and I'm going to work," she said, staring out the passenger-side window. "This is crazy."

It was their normal Monday routine: Savannah on her feet, behind the counter, hour after hour, smiling and assuring yet another rich wife of Coral Gables that her Hermès gown would no longer smell of Dom Perignon, caviar, and Chanel No. 5. The restaurant was closed on Mondays, but Ruban still had to show up and tally the weekend receipts.

"There's nothing else to do until we hear from Jeffrey."

Or his kidnappers. He didn't say it, and neither did Savannah. But she was thinking it. Constantly.

Savannah climbed out of the passenger seat slowly. She hated her job at the cleaners. Marathon shifts behind the counter on Mondays, Fridays, and Saturdays, however, made up for the paltry wages she earned Tuesday through Thursday as a part-

time assistant at a daycare center. Nurturing pre-
schoolers was its own reward. Customers at the dry
cleaners only made her feel unworthy, even when
they were trying to be nice in their own way—
women like Mrs. Willis, third wife to a rich investment banker, who had come in to drop off a killer
cocktail dress with a small red-wine stain at the
hem. She and Savannah were just about the same
height and weight, not to mention age.

"I don't think it will come out," Savannah had
told her.

"You sure?"

"Not without discoloring the fabric, which would
be a shame. Such a gorgeous dress. I mean, *I* would
wear it with a little stain like this on it. But that's
just me."

Mrs. Trophy-Wife had reached for her dress,
paused, and then pushed it across the counter
toward Savannah. "Why don't you keep it, sweetie?
I think you'd dress up nicely in it."

The stain had actually come out, no discolor-
ation, good as new. But Savannah never told the
customer. It was the closest she'd ever come to stealing, but she'd managed to rationalize it.

*Sweetie? Dress up nicely? Up your liposuctioned butt,
lady.*

She was afraid Ruban was starting to engage in
the same mental gymnastics, convincing himself
that it was okay to buy a Rolex and earrings for his
wife with Jeffrey's stolen money.

Like the banks don't steal, Savannah.

She'd heard him say that many times. Too often,
especially of late. It was a slippery slope.

"Everything is going to be okay," Ruban said from behind the wheel.

She hesitated before closing the car door. "Are you sure?"

"Definitely. It's better to wait at work than to sit at home."

"You promise to call me as soon as you know anything?"

"I promise."

She closed the door, and Ruban drove out of the parking lot.

Ruban didn't go to work but to a coffee shop in West Miami, where he had some business with a certain Jamaican bartender.

Ramsey Kincaid was waiting for him at an outside table. Ruban joined him, laid an envelope on the table, and pushed it toward Ramsey.

"Here's half," he said.

Ramsey tucked the envelope into his fanny pack without bothering to count the money. His dreadlocks were tucked up under a knit cap. A Bob Marley tattoo bulged on his right bicep. He'd come straight from work at the Gold Rush, having pulled the eleven-to-seven shift.

"How's our boy this morning?" asked Ruban.

"I dunno."

"Huh?"

Ramsey tore open a pack of sugar. His hand was shaking so badly that more of it ended up on the table than in his coffee. "We got a problem, mon. A big problem."

Ruban stared at him. They had agreed on the

telephone that the best way to get Jeffrey to stop flashing money was to scare the living crap out of him. Ramsey had agreed to do it, for three thousand dollars.

"Ramsey, I swear, if my brother-in-law OD'd and died on you, I will—"

"No, no, no. Jeffrey not dead, mon."

"Where is he?"

"I dunno."

Ruban tightened his glare. "Stop saying you don't know and start explaining."

"It all went fine at first. Jeffrey partied all night, like he do every night. Finally, he leaves at four o'clock in the morning. I walk him to his car. He's so wasted that he practically falls into the trunk. My friends, they took him—"

"Wait a minute," said Ruban. "You didn't go with them?"

"No, mon. I work till seven o'clock in the mornin'."

"I paid you three grand. You said *you* would do it."

"No, mon. I said I would *get it done.* Kidnapping is not my thing. I got you professionals."

Ruban was ready to grab him by the throat. "You idiot! I didn't tell you to bring in more people."

"Hold your horses, mon. You didn't tell me *not* to."

Ruban breathed out his anger. "Who are your friends?"

"Not really friends. More like friends of friends."

"You don't even know these guys, do you?"

"Friends of friends, mon."

Ruban leaned into the table, pointing his finger

as he spoke. "Listen to me, Ramsey. You need to get Jeffrey back right now."

"Okay, mon."

"I mean *right now*."

"No problem. Well, maybe there be one problem. The ransom."

"What the hell are you talking about? There's no ransom."

"Your brother-in-law, he got one big mouth, mon. Before we even shove him inside the trunk of the car, he sayin' shit like 'Oh, please, please, Mr. Kidnapper, don't hurt me. I got lots of money. I pay you a million dollars.'"

Ruban's head was about to explode. "I hope your friends didn't believe him."

"Not my friends, mon. Friends of friends."

"Whoever. Do they think Jeffrey actually has a million dollars?"

"They called me one hour ago. They want a handsome ransom. Hey, dat rhyme."

"How big?"

"I jis told you. One million."

"No way."

"Come on, Ruban. Dis is your brother-in-law."

"I'm not paying a million-dollar ransom. I'm not paying anything."

"These are bad dudes, mon. They will kill him."

Ruban looked off toward the rush-hour traffic, thinking. Then his gaze shifted back to Ramsey. "Here's my counteroffer: Tell your friends to let Jeffrey go."

"Not my friends, mon. Friends of friends."

"I don't care who the fuck they are, Ramsey."

"You don't understand, mon. Bad dudes. Very bad."

He leaned forward, his forearms resting on the table, his eyes cutting through the Jamaican like lasers. "Do you know who Jeffrey's uncle is?"

"Nuh-uh."

"Craig Perez. He goes by Pinky. Ask around about him."

"What you telling me, mon?"

Ruban had no intention of involving Pinky, but it was the best bluff he could come up with. "Tell these bad dudes to let Jeffrey go. Or Pinky comes looking for *you*."

14

.

Ruban left his assistant manager in charge at the restaurant and picked up Savannah at the dry cleaners. It wasn't even lunchtime, and the early pickup made Savannah think the worst. The tension was written all over her face as she slid into the passenger seat, shut the door, and braced for the unspeakable.

"Please tell me Jeffrey is okay," she said.

The motor was running, but they were still in the strip-mall parking lot. People were coming and going from the cleaners and the drug store, oblivious to the worried-looking woman talking to her husband in the car.

"I'm sure Jeffrey is just fine," said Ruban.

"It sounds like you don't know."

"I only heard from the kidnappers. I didn't talk to Jeffrey."

Her concern heightened. "They wouldn't let you speak to him?"

"It wasn't like that. They passed a message to me

through one of the bartenders at the Gold Rush. A Jamaican guy."

"Is he working with them?"

He couldn't tell Savannah that he'd hired Ramsey and that his plan to scare Jeffrey had backfired. He kept it vague. "No. I don't think so."

"What's the message?"

"If we want Jeffrey back, the ransom is a million dollars."

She sank a little deeper into the passenger seat, her gaze fixed blankly on the dashboard. "How easy is it for you to dig up a million of what they stole?"

Very easy, if they counted Ruban's share and the million he was holding for Octavio. "That's putting the cart before the horse. We don't pay a million. We negotiate."

She glanced over. "How do you know it's negotiable?"

"Everything's negotiable."

"Ruban, this is a kidnapping, not an eBay auction."

"We can't get emotional about this."

"Not get emotional? This is my brother!"

"Take a breath, okay? Only a fool would hand over a million dollars just because some thug says so. Have you ever met the Mendoza family two doors down from us?"

"Who—what do they have to do with this?"

"I'm making a point. A couple of months ago I got to talking with the *abuelo* when he was out walking the dog. Five different members of his family were kidnapped before they finally left Medellín.

The old man didn't give me specifics, but they never paid the first ransom demand. It was always negotiated down."

"Ruban, this isn't Medellín."

"It's also not Kabul. We're not up against the Taliban or some other lunatics trying to make a religious or political statement. This is all about money. We negotiate."

She considered it, but not for very long. She looked at him from across the console and spoke in a firm voice: "No."

"*No*, what?"

"No negotiation. If they hurt Jeffrey, I swear I will never forgive you, Ruban. Pay the million dollars."

He chuckled, but not because it was funny. "Whoa, whoa, whoa."

"Whoa what?"

Only a half million of Jeffrey's share was buried in their yard. "Let's think this through," he said.

"What's there to think about?"

Ruban stared at the steering wheel, searching for something to say other than the truth of the matter: paying a million dollars meant dipping into *their* share. Then it came to him.

"Your first instinct was right, Savannah. When I bought you that Rolex, you said we can't touch the money."

"But this is different."

"No, it's not. If we ever have to explain this to the police, they won't care what we spent it on. All they'll know is that we hid the money, and a million dollars is missing."

Her expression tightened. It was her nervous look, which meant he was getting through to her.

"Okay. Then what do we do?" she asked.

"The way Jeffrey has been burning through money, he clearly has some serious cash stashed away somewhere. We find it, and we use it to pay the ransom."

"How is that better?"

"At least we can honestly say that we never touched any of the money that was under our control."

"I guess that makes sense. But how do we even know where to look?"

"If you were Jeffrey, where would you stash your money?"

"I have no idea."

"Savannah, come on. Your brother is a thirty-two-year-old cokehead who lives with his mother. Apart from the bedroom he's had since middle school, the only world he knows is the Gold Rush. We can only hope that he didn't stash his money at the strip club. Really, where do you think it is?"

She sat up and turned, her left shoulder leaning into the seat back. "No, absolutely not. If we start tearing my mother's house apart looking for Jeffrey's money, I'm going to have to tell her that Jeffrey got kidnapped, and she's going to have a heart attack. Literally, she will run for her rosary and drop dead on the floor."

"She is not going to die."

"We cannot drag my mother into this. She knows nothing about the heist."

"Would you rather she hear about it from the kidnappers?"

"There's no reason for them to call her."

"You're right. They won't call. When Jeffrey cracks under pressure and tells them where his money is, they'll just smash down her front door and put a gun to her head. Is that what you want?"

"God, no!"

"We need to find that money, hide it someplace else, and send your mother on a monthlong vacation to Fiji."

She leaned back and considered it. "All right," she said, breathing out a heavy sigh. "But let me be the one to break it to her."

"Now you're making sense," he said as he backed out of the parking space.

She shook her head, staring out the window. "None of this makes any sense," she said under her breath.

"*Ay, Dios mío!*"

Ruban rolled his eyes as he walked into the kitchen to refresh the cold compress. His mother-in-law had not taken the news well. For ten minutes she'd been moaning, wailing, and calling for divine intervention. Savannah was beside her on the couch, trying in vain to console her.

"*Mi niño, mi niño precioso!*"

Right. The "precious boy" whose idea of "laying low" was to spend ten times retail on discontinued Rolexes and give them to strippers. *Idiot.*

"Ruban, hurry!" Savannah called from the living room.

He went to the freezer, wrapped fresh ice in the washcloth, and returned to the critical care unit—er, living room. His mother-in-law was on her back with her feet up on the couch and her head in Savannah's lap. Savannah took the compress and placed it on her mother's forehead.

Beatriz Beauchamp was filled with more melodrama than the human body could possibly contain. Anything from the death of her husband to her parakeet's loss of appetite was enough to land her on the couch, praying to Saint Lazarus. Savannah had inherited her beautiful face, but nothing more. The rest of her—the carrying on, the five-foot frame, the extra poundage—she'd passed on to her son.

Ruban sat in the armchair facing them. "We need a plan to help Jeffrey," he said.

"*Sí, sí. El plan de Dios.*"

"No, not God's plan. *We* need a plan."

Savannah shot him an angry look. "Not *now*, Ruban."

"This can't wait," he said, and then he spoke directly to his mother-in-law. "Savannah and I have decided to pay the ransom."

"Why no call the police?"

Good question, but he was ready for it. "The kidnappers said they will kill him if we call the police."

"*Ay, no!*"

"Totally agree. Ay, yai, yai; yada, yada, yada. But we need to come up with some money."

Savannah patted her mother's forehead with the cloth.

"How much?" asked Beatriz.

"A *lot*," said Ruban. "We think Jeffrey might have some cash around the house."

"*Sí, sí.* He won it in the lottery. Pick Six."

"The lottery, huh? What a lucky boy," said Ruban. "Do you know where he keeps it?"

"*Sí.* I found it when I cleaned his room. Under his mattress."

Under the mattress. The thought of Jeffrey as his coconspirator was suddenly enough to make Ruban want to shoot himself. "I'll be right back."

Ruban went down the hall. The door was closed but unlocked. He went inside, not sure what disaster to expect, but the room was neat and tidy—just the way a doting Cuban mother would keep it. No coke mirrors on the dresser. No pornography on the walls. Not so much as a hint of dust on the windowsill or nightstand. The bed was made with military precision. Ruban went straight to it and flipped the mattress. Benjamin Franklin was staring back at him through the vacuum-sealed packs. Ruban had marked each pack with a dollar value on the night of the divvy. Ruban did the quick math on Jeffrey's stash, gathered it up, and went back to the living room.

"Four hundred thousand," he said as he laid the packs on the coffee table. "Your brother burned through a million-plus in one week."

"That's not possible," said Savannah.

"Add it up."

She didn't bother. "Maybe he stashed more somewhere else."

"What about it, Beatriz?" asked Ruban. "Any more excellent hiding places besides the mattress?"

"Maybe ask El Padrino," she said. "I think Jeffrey gave some for him to hold."

"Who's El Padrino?" asked Ruban.

"His godfather," said Savannah.

"I know what *el padrino* means. Who *is he*?"

"Carlos Vazquez," said Savannah.

"Where does he live?"

"*No sé*," said Beatriz. "Jeffrey is the only one in the family who stays in touch with him. The rest of us . . . no."

"Should I even ask why?"

"He became a priest," said Beatriz.

"You cut him off because he became a priest?"

Savannah squeezed the excess water from the washcloth into the bucket at her feet, careful not to drop what remained of the ice cubes. "A Santería priest."

Ruban had seen Santería in Cuba, and it was still practiced in certain parts of the Afro-Cuban immigrant community in Miami. A Hialeah group had successfully defended the right to conduct animal sacrifices, all the way to the U.S. Supreme Court. To Ruban, the killing of chickens, doves, and turtles to provide spirits the nourishment needed to possess priests during rituals was more voodoo than religion.

"Jeffrey gave his money to a Santería priest?" he asked, incredulous.

"For safekeeping," said Beatriz.

Ruban stared at the vacuum-sealed packs on the table. Four hundred thousand dollars. If they added it to the half million of Jeffrey's money that was buried in the yard, they were close to the ransom demand. But paying the full amount made about as much sense to Ruban as giving it to a Santería priest.

"Brilliant," said Ruban. "Just brilliant."

15

.

Savannah wanted lunch, but with $400,000 in the trunk of the car, Ruban refused to stop. He dropped her at the dry cleaners and drove straight home. Jeffrey's stash fit inside the leftover PVC pipe. He sealed it up, gave the liquid cement a minute to dry, and buried it in a foot of sand beneath the patio tiles in the backyard.

Under the mattress? He gathered up his tools and shook the sand from his shoes. *You gotta be kidding me, Jeffrey.*

Ruban put away the tools in the garage and went to the locked cabinet in the TV room. His gun collection was short one Makarov semi-automatic revolver, the Soviet Union's standard military and police sidearm for forty years, which Pinky had brandished at the airport warehouse, and which now lay at the bottom of the Miami River, never to be seen again. Ruban had other Russian weapons, but if he was going to "lay low," it was best never to leave the house again with anything Russian made: it seemed likely that at least one of those security guards had managed a good enough look at Pinky's Makarov to peg its origins. Plenty of non-Russian choices remained. He grabbed a Glock and one clip of standard 9-millimeter ammunition and another clip of military-issue tracer ammo. It was overkill, but he was suddenly feeling the need to be prepared for anything.

It was time to visit *El Padrino*.

Finding an address for Carlos Vazquez proved much easier than expected. Facebook apparently had no problem with Santería priests, at least not the ones who had 18,000 "likes" and posted no photographs of animal sacrifice. Vazquez had no physical church. Services were held at his personal residence in Hialeah, and the Facebook comments and photos pointed Ruban to the exact house. It was less than fifteen minutes away.

Ruban left the crappy old car in his driveway and instead pulled the dusty tarp off of his motorcycle in the garage. The Kawasaki Ninja ZX-14R was a precision machine that, in the eyes of most drivers, was nothing but a blur shooting by on the expressway. Long rides to nowhere had been a therapy of sorts. Until the accident.

He hadn't ridden since.

The ignition fired, but the engine didn't respond. Disuse and neglect beneath a dusty tarp had taken a toll. He tried again, and this time it answered with a roar. He rolled out of the garage and onto the street with a measure of caution, like a cowboy back on the horse that had thrown him. He observed the speed limit on the shady neighborhood streets, but as he approached the expressway, he felt the tug of the past, the need for speed. Halfway up the entrance ramp, he gunned it.

Traffic was always heavy on the Palmetto Expressway, but he threaded his way between cars and around trucks as if they were mere cones on a test track, cutting the fifteen-minute ride in half. The power was addictive, and part of him wanted to keep going. But he forced himself to focus. He took the second Hialeah exit, worked the side streets east toward his destination, and parked in front of the ranch-style house. His heart was pounding as he climbed off the Kawasaki.

The Vazquez residence was like thousands of other sixties-vintage houses in Hialeah—a concrete shoebox with four cars parked in the front yard for the three families who shared 1,800 square feet of living space: three bedrooms, and two baths. Ruban removed his helmet and started up the sidewalk. His escorts to the front door were a couple of chickens, clucking and blissfully unaware of their starring role in an upcoming Santería ritual.

Ruban rang the bell. An old man opened the door just far enough for the chain to catch. Ruban wasn't sure how to address a Santería priest. "Father Carlos Vazquez?"

"*Babalawo* Vazquez," he replied.

"I'm Jeffrey Beauchamp's brother-in-law."

The door slammed in his face. Ruban knocked again but got no answer. He walked toward the driveway and stopped. Parked alongside the house was a brand-new Cadillac Eldorado. The temporary tag was still in the window. Ruban felt his anger rising. He went back to the front door and pounded hard enough to conjure up a host of Santería spirits. Finally, Vazquez answered.

"Did you take Jeffrey's money?" It was a demand, not a question.

"No, *señor*. It was a gift to the church."

"Yeah, I see the church needed a new Cadillac."

"I pray every day for Jeffrey."

"He needs his money back. He's in trouble."

"Money doesn't solve trouble. Money makes trouble."

"Then you'll be very happy to give it back."

He chuckled and wagged his finger as he spoke. "Not *to*-day, *señor*."

Ruban leaned into the door before Vazquez could shut it, and he wedged his knee into the crack to make sure it stayed open. "Jeffrey needs his money."

The two men locked eyes through the opening, the taut chain between them. The old man made a strange guttural sound that welled up from his belly and shook in his throat. Slowly, it grew louder, but it had a rhythm to it, like some kind of chant.

"Go-o-o-o," he said.

"I'm not leaving until I get Jeffrey's money."

"G-o-o-o. Or feel the wrath of the Orisha."

"I'm not—oww!" Ruban shouted, pulling his leg from between the door and frame.

"Orisha very angry now."

"Bull-*shit*, Orisha. You just jabbed me with a fucking pen!"

"Go-o-o-o-o. Or I call the police. I'm dialing," Vazquez said as he showed Ruban his cell phone. Then the door slammed. Ruban pounded on it.

"Open the damn door!"

"Police are coming!" Vazquez shouted from inside the house.

Lay low. It was getting harder and harder to follow his own rule, but hanging around for the police to arrive would have made him even stupider than Jeffrey. He gave the door one good kick, letting Vazquez know that this wasn't over. Then he went to his motorcycle, put on his helmet, and rode away.

Vazquez was a piece of shit, but he wasn't the problem. Jeffrey was the problem, and the four hundred thousand dollars that Ruban had found under his mattress was well short of the solution. Ruban needed answers that didn't involve a Santería priest who had the police on speed dial.

He stopped for gas before getting back on the expressway. Half a tank would do it. He stepped away from the pumps to make a phone call before getting back on the bike. The last time he'd spoken to Savannah's uncle, Pinky had said he was getting out of town. Ruban took a shot and dialed his number. Pinky answered, and Ruban got right to the point.

"Jeffrey's been kidnapped."

"I know."

"You know?"

"Yeah. He called me at four o'clock this morning to ask for money. He begged me to help him out. I told him, 'I'm your uncle, not your bank. Call your sister.'"

"Pinky, the kidnappers want a ransom. This is serious."

"Not my problem. Jeffrey got into this trouble. He can get out. If you and Savannah want to help him, be my guests."

"I need Marco's share to pay the ransom."

Pinky laughed.

"What's so funny?" asked Ruban.

"Now I get it. You think I'm stupid? This has scam written all over it."

"Scam? Pinky, you're making no sense."

"Jeffrey gets kidnapped, and the first person he calls to pay a million-dollar ransom is his Uncle Pinky? Give me a break. He ain't kidnapped. This is *you* trying to scam me out of Marco's cut."

"That's not true. He called you first because he knew I'd kill him for getting into this mess."

"Bullshit, Ruban. A million dollars was exactly Marco's share. Like that's a coincidence. I'm outta here. You got that? I'm keeping Marco's money, and I'm gone. Fuck all of you."

He hung up before Ruban could say another word.

Ruban should have headed south, but he wasn't going home. He rode north toward I-75, a toll road that cut across the Everglades. He'd taken it all the way to Tampa before, one of many long rides on his motorcycle. This time, he wasn't going nearly that far.

The day had started out badly and was only getting worse. Vazquez was scum. Pinky was no better. Ramsey was an idiot. Jeffrey was a problem with no solution. A million-dollar ransom would be a Band-Aid, at best. Times like these were all about self-preservation.

Midday traffic on I-75 was nothing compared to south Florida's busiest thruways. Ruban was sharing five lanes with just a handful of cars, and he was feeling the tug of the past again, the need for speed. Not because he wanted to go back. He wanted to put it behind him—for good. The accident that had landed his motorcycle under a tarp in the garage had left him, and his Kawasaki, without a scratch. Savannah was another story.

Ruban had buried the needle on his Kawasaki many times, but always while riding alone. Savannah was okay riding with him around town, but never on the expressway. He bought her a bodysuit of leather and Kevlar, protective boots and gloves, and a state-of-the-art helmet, but still she refused to hop on the seat behind him and flirt with death on the virtually deserted I-75 after midnight. Until it was time to leave their house. The night the bank came.

"Ruban, they're taking the car!"

The house was empty, and they'd been ordered out by midnight. The front door was wide open, and Savannah was watching the men in the driveway. The repo team moved quickly.

Ruban went to the gym bag on the floor. In it was his pistol collection, and he would go down shooting before turning *that* over to the bank. He zipped it open and grabbed a Glock. "They're not taking another fucking thing."

"Stop!" she shouted.

"They can't have it!"

"It's a stupid car!"

Ruban gripped his pistol. He'd been pushed too far, but there was a reasoning part of him that understood she was right.

"It's not worth going to jail over this," she said.

No. She was definitely right. If he was going to risk jail, it would be for something big—big enough to make the bank regret the day they'd messed with Ruban Betancourt.

He stood in the doorway and watched the repo men back their car out the driveway, then the orange taillights disappearing into the night.

"Let's go," he said.

The car was gone, but they still had wheels. Ruban had already lost ownership of his restaurant, and Savannah had offered up her jewelry before letting him cash out his beloved motorcycle in their losing battle to stay afloat. The Kawasaki was next door in the garage. Their neighbors had been foreclosed on the month before, the thirteenth in the neighborhood, and the house was empty.

They waited in the garage until one a.m. to make sure the repo men were out of the neighborhood, no one watching. Savannah's girlfriend in Broward had said they could stay with her for a few nights. Ruban strapped their bags to the motorcycle. Helmets on, they were off.

The expressway was theirs for the taking, but Ruban watched his speed. This was Savannah's first time on the interstate. He hadn't invested in microphones for the helmets, so they'd worked out a system: a tug at his right elbow if she needed him to slow down. Twenty minutes of smooth riding, just below the speed limit. No signal from Savannah. He bumped it up to seventy. Still good.

Then something took over him. Ruban couldn't get the repo men out of his mind, the feeling of powerlessness as he'd watched them drive away in his car. He needed to grab back the power.

Steadily, he increased velocity. The g-forces mounted. So did his anger. Savannah tightened her hold around his waist, but he felt no tug at his elbow. He checked the speedometer. Ninety-five and rising. At this speed, with each upward tick, the increase in vibration, wind, and engine roar was on an order of magnitude. He was beginning to feel like a man again, not that poor, impotent bastard whose financial carcass could be picked clean by some vulture in a pinstripe suit. At ninety-eight, he felt it: Savannah tugged his elbow. They were so close. He had to break a hundred. She tugged harder. Just another second was all he needed. She jerked his arm so hard that she nearly sent them into a spin.

Her doctor would later explain the phenomenon to Ruban. It was the same sensation some people get when they walk too close to the edge of a balcony and feel like they're going to jump. Savannah had felt that terrifying sensation and couldn't control it.

She'd tugged and pulled at his arm and had to get off that bike. Ruban cut the speed from ninety, to seventy, to sixty, but she tugged even harder. They were down to fifty or so when she just couldn't stand it anymore. She let go.

Savannah!

Ruban felt the vibration of the engine, felt in control of the beast, as the motorcycle sped down the expressway in the afternoon sun.

The leather-and-Kevlar suit had saved Savannah's skin, literally, and the full-face helmet had prevented catastrophe. Had she managed to stay in a smooth slide, like the professional racers, she might have been unhurt. But she'd extended her arm, trying to stop herself, which only sent her body into a tumble—over and over again. She spent weeks in the hospital. Left arm broken in three places. A fractured pelvis that lacerated her appendix. The appendix turned out to be the real disaster. The resulting infection had spread to places it should never have spread. The pain lasted for months, but the real loss was something Ruban could never make up to her, though he would try.

Whatever Savannah wants, Savannah gets. Except for the one thing she could never have: a child.

Ruban exited the expressway and drove toward one of the huge landscape nurseries that sprouted from the fertile soil along the Everglades border. The pavement gave way to a gravel road, and dust kicked up behind him. Fifty acres of mature palm trees lay before him. He was less than a mile from I-75, but it was legitimately the middle of nowhere. Here, even the most inept insurance fraudsters avoided detection, flocking to irrigation canals in broad daylight, dumping an overpriced vehicle in eight feet of opaque water, and then reporting it stolen. Ruban parked his motorcycle in the grass at the edge of the canal, opened the storage compartment, and removed his Glock.

For two years he'd been promising Savannah that he'd get rid of the motorcycle. Selling it would have gained him nothing, since the bank that had foreclosed on their house held a judgment lien on his bike. More to the point, a sale would have done nothing to slay his demons.

He reached below the frame and scratched out the motorcycle's vehicle identification number with his key. Then he walked to the middle of the road. Neat rows of countless trees, palms of every variety, stood between him and the interstate. Even though he couldn't see beyond the nursery, he was roughly dead even with the spot where Savannah had jumped. He turned to face his Kawasaki, raised the pistol, and took careful aim at the gas tank. He squeezed off one shot. A direct hit, but there was no fire, no explosion. The puncture hole did its job, however, spilling gasoline all over. Ruban changed out the standard 9-millimeter clip for military-issue tracer ammunition—the other clip he'd packed just for this purpose. Some marksmen liked to follow the trajectory of a bullet in target practice, and tracers had just enough powder outside the casing to emit a visible white light—and just enough spark to ignite gasoline.

Ruban squeezed off a second shot, and the Kawasaki burst into flames.

He watched from a distance. It had taken him three years to save up for that machine, but he'd been planning this moment since the accident. His old biker friends might have seen it as wasteful, but Ruban had enough money now to buy hundreds of motorcycles. If he wanted them. But he didn't. He wanted only one thing, the thing that the bank and this motorcycle had taken away.

The fire burned hot for several minutes, and when it was down to almost nothing, Ruban walked back toward his bike. A quick kick to the frame toppled the charred remains. What was left of his Kawasaki tumbled down the steep embankment and into the black canal. The hot metal sizzled, and it sank to the bottom, gone, forever.

Civilization was a mile up the road. Ruban dialed a cab on his cell, told the driver to meet him in twenty minutes at the only gas station around, and started walking.

What Savannah wants, Savannah gets.

Ruban just needed to figure out how money could buy it back.

16

·

The severed finger came through for the FBI.

"We got a DNA match," Andie said. She was with Littleford in his office on the second floor.

"CODIS does it again?" he asked. The Combined DNA Index System (CODIS) is an FBI-funded computer system that stores DNA in searchable profiles for identification purposes. Convicted felons are in the database.

"Yup," she said as she laid the report in front of him. "Marco Aroyo," she said. "Forty-one years old. Lengthy criminal record. Six years in prison for grand theft auto."

"Does he steal delivery trucks used in getaways?"

"I'd like to find out."

"Where does he live?"

"Sand Dunes apartments in West Miami. Also happens to work at a ceramic tile warehouse less than a mile from the airport."

Littleford smiled. "Now we're on to something. I'll take the apartment. You check out the warehouse."

Andie coordinated with Lieutenant Watts at MDPD while driving to Miami Tile & Marble in the warehouse district near the airport. On the off chance that Marco was still alive and had actually shown up for work minus a finger, she wanted backup. It was just before two p.m. when she pulled into the parking lot. The roar of jet engines in the air made her feel even closer to the airport than she was. A 747 passed almost directly overhead on approach to the runway. Andie glanced up and wondered how many millions were in the cargo belly.

Watts met her outside the warehouse, and together they went inside to the manager's office. The manager was on the phone. Andie was able to catch his eye through the little window in the door, mostly because a good-looking woman was an unexpected sight in this mostly male environment. A flash of her badge got his full attention. He ended the call and stepped out to meet her in the busy warehouse area. Andie and Lieutenant Watts introduced themselves.

"Mahoney," he said, reciprocating. "Todd Mahoney."

They shook hands, and the calluses confirmed Andie's first impression that he'd worked his way up from the warehouse to the front office. Mahoney looked out of place in a necktie, and he wore the short-sleeve dress shirt of a blue-collar man only half-committed to management. He was middle-aged and overweight, but he had the tough, stocky look of a guy who could move a full pallet of ceramic tile without a forklift.

"We're here about Marco Aroyo," said Andie.

A forklift beeped behind them. It was backing up with a two-ton pallet of marble tiles in its load. Mahoney pulled Andie out of the way.

"Good luck," said Mahoney. "Haven't seen Marco in over a week. Hired a replacement for him this morning. He didn't even pick up his last paycheck."

"Have you checked with his family?"

"Marco's a piece of shit. He's got no family."

That explained the absence of a missing person's report. "What kind of guy was he?" asked Andie.

"Rhodes scholar. Sang in the Vienna Boys' Choir. Just like all the knuckleheads here."

The forklift was beeping and coming at them even faster than before. Mahoney pulled Andie out of the way again. "Hey, moron!" he shouted at the driver. "Can you do your job someplace where no one will get killed?"

The driver shrugged, as if to say *My bad*, and moved to a different stack of tiles. Mahoney looked at Andie and said, "*That's* what Marco was like."

"Did you know he was a convicted felon?" asked Andie.

"He mentioned it, yeah. I take what I can get."

"I'm sure you've heard about the Lufthansa heist from MIA eight days ago."

He smiled a little, almost wistfully, which Andie was finding to be a common reaction. To the average Joe, there was an odd Bonnie and Clyde–like romanticism about making off with millions in the back of a pickup truck.

"Yeah," said Mahoney. "That's not far from here."

"Marco is a person of interest in the heist."

"Marco? You shittin' me?"

"Why does that surprise you?"

Mahoney looked across the warehouse, stared down a couple of goofballs who were slacking off, then answered. "From what I heard on the news, that was close to ten million bucks. Hard for me to think of Marco the millionaire. Kind of funny, actually."

"I don't think Marco's laughing," said Andie. "We have reason to believe he's severely injured. Could even be dead. We need to find him."

His expression changed, as if he suddenly recalled that things hadn't ended so well for Faye Dunaway and Warren Beatty on the silver screen. "Like I said, haven't seen him."

"Was your warehouse open on the Sunday of the heist?"

"No. We're never open on Sundays," he said, but then a light seemed to go on. "But Marco was here."

"How do you know?"

"Two months ago, right around Labor Day, he said he needed extra hours. He asked if he could be the security guard on Sundays. We've had some problems with theft on weekends, so I said okay."

"He was here by himself?"

"As far as I know."

"Do you have any security cameras that might have caught any activity on that afternoon?"

"Seriously? Here? The last warehouse in this

area to install security cameras had them stolen."

"Did you notice anything unusual here when you came to work Monday morning?"

Mahoney shook his head. "Nope."

"Two vehicles are of special interest." She described the pickup and showed him a photograph of the delivery truck. Again he shook his head. Detective Watts jumped in. "Do you mind if I look around a little?"

"Be my guest," said Mahoney. "I really gotta get back to work."

"One second," said Andie. "Do you know anything about Marco's friends? People he hung out with?"

"Marco didn't have any friends here. He kept to himself. But there was this one guy who used to drive him to work every now and then. They'd meet for lunch sometimes, too. In fact, he stopped by here earlier this week looking for Marco."

Andie reached for her notepad. "You know his name?"

Mahoney scratched his head, thinking. "Marco used to call him Pinky."

"Does he wear pinky rings?"

"I asked Marco the same thing. He got the name in prison. Communal showers, no privacy. Supposedly he's got a dick down to his knees, so they started calling him 'Pinky,' as a joke. Like calling a tall guy 'Shorty.'"

Andie didn't write that in her notes. "Anything else you remember about him?"

"Hmm. No. I really couldn't even tell you what

he looks like. Just the pinky thing sticks out. No pun intended."

"Not much to go on," said Andie. "Unless he's hiding out in a nudist colony."

"Wish I could be more help," said Mahoney.

Andie put away her notepad, empty. "So do I."

17

.

Jeffrey's eyes blinked open, but only for an instant. It hurt too much to open his right eye, so he used only his left. The light was annoying, but slowly the strange room came into focus.

He was on his back, lying on a floor of cool, unfinished concrete. A bare bulb hung by a wire from the ceiling. He pushed himself up and wanted to stand, but he could rise only to a seated position. His wrists and ankles were chained to an exposed metal stud in the wall. There was enough slack to move no more than a couple of feet in any direction—left, right, or upright. The chains rattled as he lowered himself back to the floor.

Whoa, head rush.

That simple up-and-down motion stirred the fog in his brain, reminding him why his right eye hurt so much. He could feel the swelling. He could almost feel that boot again, the steel-toed battering ram that had rearranged his face. His pleas for mercy— *Stop, stop, I'm begging you!*—had been useless.

The night was coming back to him now. Staggering out of the Gold Rush and into the parking lot. Someone grabbing him from behind. The sharp blow to the back of his head, and some guy cursing the "fat son of a bitch" as they shoved him into the trunk of his own car. Jeffrey had offered them money on the spot, but the lid slammed shut, and off they went. Not far. A few minutes later the car stopped, but he wasn't sure where they were when the trunk opened. The men didn't let him out. They handed him a phone and said, "Call someone who thinks you're worth your weight in gold, you fat fuck." He didn't want to get Savannah involved, so he tried his uncle. Pinky was absolutely no help: "You got yourself into this, get yourself out." Only then did he phone his sister.

He had no memory of what he'd said to her. He remembered someone snatching the phone away and slamming the trunk shut. The next ride was much longer. He was pressed against the spare tire, and it was hard to breathe. His belly was so big he couldn't even roll onto his side. He must have passed out at that point. The next thing he remembered, he was on the floor with his face pressed against the concrete. A garage? *Yeah, must be.* His kidnappers must have pulled him out of the trunk, dropped him on the floor, and chained him to one of the wall studs.

He opened his left eye as wide as he could, and his gaze swept the garage in monovision. He spotted the tool bench along the wall, and his right thumb began to throb. The pain was rushing back to him. His memory was becoming clearer. He remembered the needle-nose pliers, the angry voice of one sadistic bastard, and the laughter from his buddies who were looking on.

Where's the money, Jeffrey? Where's your fucking money?

It made him cringe just to think about it, and the sound of his own screams replayed in his mind. He tried to sit up again, then stopped. He heard footsteps outside. Someone was coming. He listened carefully. Just one set of footsteps was all he could discern.

Please, God, not the maniac with the pliers.

The door opened—not the big garage door, but the side door. Jeffrey caught his breath, sat up, and then did a double take. He recognized that beautiful face. He knew that perfect body, even with clothes on. It was Bambi from the Gold Rush. She came to him and knelt at his side.

"Oh, my God, Jeffy. Are you okay?"

"No. Look at my thumb. They ripped out the nail."

"Oh, you poor, poor thing."

He tried not to get emotional, but his lower lip began to quiver, and he couldn't help himself. The sweet sound of her voice was too much. He started crying—a little at first, then uncontrollably.

"Oh, honey," she said as she cradled his head against her bosom. "Don't cry."

He pulled himself together. "Can you get me out of here? Please?"

She changed her tone—not harsh, but firm. "I can't do that, Jeffy."

He sniffled. "Why?"

"Only you can get you out of here."

He looked around, puzzled. "I'm chained up. I can't do anything."

"These are really bad guys you're up against, Jeffy. But they're not unreasonable. They know you have money."

"I don't. I really don't! I burned through all of it. Every cent is gone."

"They don't believe you."

"It's true!"

"They think there's more stashed somewhere."

He didn't answer.

She stroked his chin, forcing him to look her in the eye. "Does your brother-in-law have more?" she asked.

He was silent.

"I want to help you," she said. "But you have to be honest with these men. You have to tell them how much money you have."

"I told you—I'm broke!"

"I don't mean just you. I mean the whole family, Jeffy. Did your family come into some money?"

He looked down at the floor, but she gently tugged his chin again, forcing him to look at her through his one good eye. *Such a sweet face.* "Uh-huh."

"A lot of money?" she asked.

"Yeah."

"Can you tell me about that?"

He hesitated, and for an instant he was tempted to answer. But finally he shook his head. "I can't. I can't tell anyone."

She moved a little closer, pressing more of her hard body against his flabby torso. "You can tell me. It will be our secret."

"If I tell you, everyone will be mad at me."

"No, they won't, Jeffy. They're your *family*. Look at you," she said as she cupped his face gently with her hands. "So cute. The only way they will be mad at you is if you don't do *everything* in your power to make these mean, mean men stop beating on your precious head. You want them to stop, don't you?"

"Yeah. I do. I really do."

"How much can you pay, Jeffy? Whisper it in my ear."

She nuzzled against him, letting a wisp of hair brush his face. The smell pushed him over the edge. It was Bambi's trick to finger herself and then wear her own scent on her neck the way other women wore perfume.

"Four hundred thousand," he whispered. "That's all of it."

She kissed him on the forehead. "That's my boy. So smart. So, so smart. You'll be back where you belong in no time. Now, tell me where all that money is."

He struggled. No way did he want to drag his mother into this. "I can't tell you."

"Jeffy, you can tell me anything."

"No."

"Please, Je—"

"I said *no*."

It had startled both of them. Jeffrey had never said no to her, much less with an edge. She pulled away from him and shot an icy glare. "You disappoint me."

"I just can't tell you that."

"Fine. Be that way."

"I'm sorry."

She rose and stood over him, looking down as if he were a pile of something she'd just stepped in. "It's too late to apologize, *Jeff*," she said, emphasizing that he was no longer "Jeffy."

"No, I really am sor—"

"Save it. You had your chance. You don't have to tell me where it is. You can tell *them*."

A shiver went down his spine. He wanted to fix things, but his mind was a blank, and he couldn't find words. He watched in silence as she walked away, and the door slammed on her way out.

18

Ruban picked up Savannah from work at seven. He didn't take the usual route home, but Savannah was either too tired or too distracted to notice until they were on the turnpike.

"Where we going?" she asked.

"It's a surprise," he said.

"I've had enough surprises for one day, thank you."

"This is a good thing. You'll like it."

She looked out the passenger window. A sea of Miami suburbia twinkled beneath the purple-black night. "Whatever."

Definitely tired.

The speed ripples in the road sent a vibration through the car. They were approaching the pre-paid toll lanes. Ruban steered with one hand while holding the transponder against the windshield so that the electronic eye could read it. Ruban was one of the last remaining drivers in Miami who still owned one of those clunky old transponders that attached to the window with suction cups, and the cups were shot.

"I know I told you not to spend any money," she said. "But I really think we can afford a new gizmo."

"Not if we have to keep digging your brother out of trouble."

"You shouldn't have helped him hide the money. We should have just gone to the police and begged for mercy."

"We can't go back now."

She breathed in and out, looking out the window again. "I'm just so worried about him."

Ruban reached across the console and squeezed her hand. "Everything is going to work out. Ramsey will get him back. He promised me he would."

"You talk like this Ramsey is Spider-Man or something. What if these are the same guys who cut off that man's finger in the delivery truck?"

"These aren't the same guys. These are small-time punks."

"How do you know?"

He glanced over. She was a bundle of nerves. He had to put her at ease, and this time, nothing short of the truth would do it. "The guys who kidnapped your brother are friends of Ramsey."

"You told me he wasn't in on it."

"He's not." He hesitated, not sure how it was going to sound, but he said it anyway. "I hired Ramsey to scare Jeffrey."

"Excuse me?" she said. It was that accusatory tone, not at all a question.

"Jeffrey was out of control. He wouldn't listen to

anyone. I asked Ramsey to put a scare into him so that he'd stop flashing money."

"So he's not really kidnapped?"

"Well, he is, actually. It backfired. Ramsey asked his friends to meet up with Jeffrey in the parking lot outside the Gold Rush to scare him. But your brother is such a marshmallow that he started offering them money before they even laid a hand on him—before they even asked for a dime. So they grabbed him, and now they want some serious money. It's just a mess. But it's not the same guys who kidnapped Marco. It can't be."

"Ruban, what on earth were you thinking?"

"It'll be fixed."

"Yeah, and *we* have to fix it. Jeffrey got kidnapped because your plan backfired."

"Don't worry. I've got another plan."

Another sigh from Savannah. She wasn't happy. "This changes everything. I mean, yes, Jeffrey stole some money. *A lot* of money. But he didn't hurt anybody. Now he could be killed, and it's *our* fault."

Ruban changed lanes and steered toward the turnpike exit. He fumbled again for the clunky transponder as they passed the electronic tollbooth.

"Where are we going?" she asked. The perfect change of subject.

"Close your eyes."

"Ruban, I am not in the mood for surprises."

"I'm trying to help you. If you want to feel better, play along for two minutes."

"Oh, all right," she said, groaning.

They were passing Miami-Dade County's other airport, Kendall-Tamiami Executive, a smaller general-aviation facility that served mostly light single-engine propeller planes. It was right across the street from several residential communities. Ruban made sure Savannah kept her eyes closed as he steered onto Country Walk. He drove past several one- and two-story houses, then stopped at the end of the cul-de-sac.

"Okay," he said. "You can open your eyes."

It was dark, but there were enough streetlamps and porch lights for Savannah to recognize the neighborhood. It looked pretty much the way it had before the banks had foreclosed and taken over eight of the ten houses on the street.

"It's our old house," she said.

"Wrong. It's our new house."

"What?"

"I bought it back."

Her mouth fell open, and it took her a moment to form words. "Why would you do that?"

"I want you to be happy."

"This doesn't make me happy."

"You cried when we lost this house."

"I'm over it."

"Come on," he said. "Get out for one second and check out the curb appeal."

"Curb appeal? Who have you been hanging out with, those sharks on that real estate reality show?"

"Just take a look. You'll fall in love again."

"Ruban, no! You just bought a house? With stolen money?"

"No, it's not what you think."

"Do not lie to me. Where else would you come up with the money for a house?"

"It's not a done deal, okay? But I just want you to see how easy this could be."

"How easy *what* could be?"

"All this money."

"Stop!"

"No, listen to me. This goes on every day in south Florida. The only person who knows I'm involved is my real estate agent. We put down a nonrefundable cash deposit, no names involved. We don't close for another hundred and twenty days, after it's safe for us to start spending money. Until then, the seller doesn't even know who the buyer is."

"This is insane. Ruban, it's not *our* money."

"Fuck the banks, Savannah. They ruined us!"

"You need to get control of yourself right now. We agreed not to touch any of the money that you buried—not to get me a birthday present, not even to pay Jeffrey's ransom. And now you want to buy a house?"

"Not a house. *Our home.*"

"No, it's not ours. We can't go back to where we were."

"Yes. Yes, we can."

"No. This ginormous house was when we were talking about four kids, two dogs, and—"

"We can have all that."

"No, we *can't.* Ruban, you can't buy back what's lost."

His cell rang. He checked the number. It was from the Gold Rush. "This could be Ramsey," he told Savannah. He took the call. It was.

"Mon, you got to come up with the money. Fast!" He was talking very quickly, almost breathless.

"Slow down," said Ruban. "Start at the beginning. What's the deal?"

"The *deal* is they gonna kill your brother-in-law if you don't pay up."

"I told you I'm not paying a million dollars."

"They don't want a million no more. They want four hundred thousand."

Ruban froze. It was the exact amount he'd found under Jeffrey's mattress. "They're bluffing," he said.

"No, no. They ain't bluffing. They know Jeffrey got four hundred thousand, and they know it's in your mother-in-law's house. They gonna break into the house and take it, mon, if you don't give it to dem."

Ruban's head was starting to spin. He covered the phone, looked at Savannah and said, "Jeffrey talked. He told them the money is in your mother's house."

"Oh, no!" she said.

He spoke into the phone. "I'll give them fifty thousand."

Savannah grabbed him, her eyes wide with anger and fright. Ruban waved her off, but Ramsey was equally shocked.

"You *crazy*, mon. Fifty thousand?"

"Just see if they'll take it."

"They ain't gonna negotiate, mon. Lemme send you the video."

"What video?"

"You'll see what I'm talking about. You check

your text message in one minute and you call me back at this number." Ramsey hung up.

Ruban waited with his cell in hand.

"What did he say?" asked Savannah.

"Hold on." His phone chimed with an incoming text. There was no written message. Just a video. He tapped to open it, and Jeffrey's face filled the screen. Ruban caught his breath.

"What is it?" asked Savannah.

The video streamed without audio for several seconds, starting with an overview of Jeffrey's swollen and bruised face. It looked as if someone had used him as a punching bag. Then it zoomed in, a close-up of complete terror. One more zoom, this time to his mouth, which was forced open with a tool of some sort. Needle-nose pliers. The audio kicked in, and Jeffrey's scream cut through the silence in their dark car.

"Oh, my God!" Savannah shouted as she covered her ears.

Ruban shut it off and tried to tuck his phone away. Savannah grabbed his hand and began prying it from his fingers.

"What is it?"

"Leave it!" he said. "You don't want to see."

Tears filled her eyes, but she kept tugging at his hand, trying to get his phone. "What did they do to Jeffrey?"

"Savannah, just calm down."

"I can't calm down! Did they kill him?"

"No, he's not dead."

"What did they do?"

Ruban squeezed the phone in his fist even more tightly, no answer for her. Savannah slugged him in the shoulder.

"Tell me what they did to my brother!"

There was no way to sugarcoat it. "They took his gold caps," he said, then added the worst of it. "And some teeth with 'em."

She screamed almost as loud as Jeffrey had, then buried her face in her hands, crying. Ruban reached over and laid his hand on the small of her back, but there was no time to console her. His phone rang. It was Ramsay.

"You see dat, Ruban? You see?"

"Yes. I saw."

"You got to pay up. You got to give 'em what they ask for."

He glanced at Savannah, who was glaring right back at him. "Okay," he said. He was speaking into the phone, but it was for Savannah's benefit as well. "We'll pay them what they asked for."

Ramsey was so relieved that the line crackled with his sigh. "Very smart, mon. You give 'em what they ask for, this ends better for everyone."

"You call them right now and tell them the exchange is tonight," said Ruban. "I'll meet you at the Gold Rush in one hour."

Ramsey agreed and hung up. Ruban looked at his wife. "It's taken care of," he said in his most reassuring tone.

"Pay the ransom," she said, her voice shaking.

"I will."

"Pay the ransom," she said, her fear turning to

anger. "And put this stupid house out of your head. This is going too far. Listen to me, Ruban, or I swear I will leave you."

Their eyes met for a few seconds, but it seemed much longer. Never, not in all they had been through, had Savannah threatened to leave him.

He looked past her, toward the five-bedroom house and the front yard that was just the right size for a pair of soccer goals. Then he turned the key and started the car.

"All right," he said. "It's done."

19

·

Ruban drove home faster than he should have. Any run-in with the law was to be avoided, even a speeding ticket, but he got away with it this time. He parked in the driveway and tried not to draw comparisons between the dream house in Kendall and the shitty shoebox of a rental that he and Savannah had called home since the foreclosure. He grabbed a shovel from the garage, walked around to the patio behind the house, and started digging. Savannah checked on him as he was putting the pavers back into place. The sealed eight-inch PVC pipe lay beside the shovel.

"You buried Jeffrey's money at our own house?" she asked.

Ruban didn't answer. He was nowhere near ready to confess that he was the one calling the shots when they'd divvied up the stolen money, that the cash under Jeffrey's mattress was only part of Jeffrey's take, and that Ruban had held back a half million bucks to keep Jeffrey under his thumb. He just gathered up the PVC pipe and carried it to the garage. The only way to remove the cap from the end of the pipe was to cut it off. Nearly a dozen vacuum-sealed packs of cash spilled out of the tube when he finished sawing. Savannah brought a gym bag from the closet, and he stuffed the money into it. Then he went inside the house and unlocked his gun cabinet.

"Do you really need that?" asked Savannah.

He chose the MRI "Baby" Desert Eagle and two clips of 9-mil parabellum ammunition, ten rounds apiece. His collection included handguns with even more firepower, but he loved the grip on the Baby, and the Israelis knew how to make a reliable combat weapon. He tucked it into his belt. "No way am I going unarmed."

She didn't press it. He kissed her good-bye, told her to make sure to lock the door, and went to his car. She waved from the front window, as if to say "good luck." He waved back, as if to say he'd need it, and drove away. He was on the Dolphin Expressway, halfway to the strip club, when Ramsey called on his cell.

"No need to come to the Gold Rush," said Ramsey. "Meet me at Dadeland Mall. In the parking lot on the west end. The one closest to the expressway. My friends say we do the exchange there."

"I thought you said they weren't your friends."

"Friends of friends, mon. That's all."

Ruban harbored enough doubts to be glad he'd packed the Baby Eagle. "Okay. I'll meet you there." Ruban exited the Dolphin, got on the Palmetto, and drove south.

Dadeland Mall was one of the busiest shopping centers in Florida. A lot of locals avoided it, but everyone knew where it was, and South American tourists visited by the busload as part of organized vacation packages. Parking was never easy, but on a Monday night, an hour before closing, the western lot near the Saks Fifth Avenue anchor was a good choice for the exchange. It wouldn't be overly crowded, so business of any description could be done without witnesses, but there would be just enough innocent bystanders to prevent Ruban from pulling a gun. Ruban entered the parking lot from Kendall Drive and drove slowly past Saks. He wasn't sure where to go, exactly. A text message from Ramsey filled in the blank: "Park at the end of row eleven."

The lot was about half full, with most vehicles parked closer to the building. He drove past them to the end of row 11 and stopped. He turned off the engine. Dadeland was in a safe suburban area, most people having no memory of the mall's bloody cocaine-cowboy shootout of July 1979 that had reinforced Miami's brand as the most violent city in America. Still, Ruban wanted to be able to hear the footfalls of anyone who might approach, so he lowered the windows, which also eliminated the glare on the glass, giving him a clear view of the lighted parking lot. He took the gun from his belt and laid it between his legs on the seat, where he could grab it quickly. Then he waited.

A minute later, he heard a knuckle-rap on the

passenger-side panel. It was Ramsey's way of letting him know it was him, unnecessary as it was: there weren't many men with dreadlocks in the lot outside Saks. Ramsey opened the door and slid into the passenger seat.

"You got the money, mon?"

Ruban handed him the gym bag. Ramsey opened it and peered inside at the vacuum-sealed plastic packs. "You bring me money or you bring me bacon, mon?"

"There's exactly four hundred thousand. The five packs of hundreds make two-fifty. Six packs of fifties are one-fifty. Count it, if you want."

"I trust you, mon." Ramsey dialed on his cell and reported to the kidnappers. "He brought it. It's all here."

Ramsey kept the phone to his ear, listening, but Ruban couldn't hear the other end of the conversation. Then he hung up and put his cell away.

"Where's Jeffrey?" asked Ruban.

"He's comin' right now," Ramsey said, pointing.

Ruban peered through the windshield toward the dark access road that ran along the other side of the chain-link fence. The road wasn't lit up like the parking lot, but even at a distance of fifty yards, there was no mistaking the three-hundred-pound bowling ball staggering toward the entrance gate. Someone was at his side, and it appeared to be a woman.

"Who's with him?" asked Ruban.

"She's one of the strippers from Gold Rush."

"Is she in on this?"

"No, mon. Not her. Not me, neither. We just tryin' to help Jeffrey through dis revoltin' situation."

Ramsey's favorite phrase, but this time it made Ruban want to reach for his pistol. *I'll give you a revoltin' situation.* "What if I don't believe you?"

Ramsey smiled. "What you gonna do, mon? Call the cops?"

It was the age-old conundrum, the reason criminals loved to prey on other criminals. Ruban held his stare a moment longer, then returned his attention to Jeffrey and his escort. They were just reaching the gate, fifty feet away, still too deep in the darkness for Ruban to get a good look at the woman.

Jeffrey suddenly seemed to recognize Ruban's car, which energized him. He broke free, no longer needing the help of his escort. She let him go, seeming to have no intention of getting any closer, where the lights of the parking lot might expose her. Adrenaline carried Jeffrey across the remaining ground. He yanked open the rear door, fell into the car, and slammed the door shut.

"Oh, thank you, bro! Thank you, thank you!"

Jeffrey lay sprawled across the backseat. The dome light remained on, and Ruban looked over the seat to check out Jeffrey's condition. It wasn't as bad as the video, but his face was still a purple mess. Dried blood dotted his shirt.

"Jeffrey, smile for me."

He forced the stupidest grin Ruban had ever seen. He still had his top teeth, enough to form words, but the bottom was a row of bloody nubs.

"They laughed at me when they took my caps," he said.

Ruban felt a surge of anger. He grabbed a fistful of Ramsey's shirt collar. "Your friends didn't have to do this to him," he said, his voice hissing.

"Easy, mon!"

"You could have sneezed on him and Jeffrey would've given you whatever you wanted."

"It's not me, mon. It's them. They bad dudes, mon. They like doin' dis shit."

The dome light blinked off. Jeffrey groaned in the darkness, his words barely audible. "I want to go home, Ruban. Take me home, please."

Ruban locked eyes with Ramsey, still gripping him by the collar.

"Take him home," said Ramsey.

It was the first thing Ruban had heard all night that made any sense. He released his grip and started the engine. The Jamaican opened the passenger-side door, and Ruban nearly pushed him out onto the pavement. The car pulled away so quickly that the door slammed shut purely on the force of his acceleration.

Jeffrey's groaning turned to deep, pathetic moans. "I want to go home."

Ruban speed-dialed Savannah as he drove toward the parking lot exit. "I got him," he said into his cell.

"Oh, thank God! Is he okay?"

Another deep moan from the backseat only fed his anger. "He'll be fine," he told her.

"Are you okay?"

"I'm fine."

"So you didn't need the gun after all?"

Ruban chose his words carefully, thinking of Ramsey, his sadistic friends who "like doin' dis shit," and this revoltin' situation. "No," he said. "I didn't need the gun."

Not tonight.

20
.

Ruban drove straight home. Before heading to his mother-in-law's place and letting Beatriz see her son in this condition, he wanted Savannah to clean him up. But first he laid down some ground rules.

"Jeffrey, wake up."

Jeffrey was curled up in the backseat. Ruban shook him gently, trying to wake him. "Listen to me," said Ruban.

He grunted but seemed to be reasonably alert.

"Savannah has no idea I was part of the heist. She thinks it was just you, your uncle, and one of his friends. You got that?"

"Uh-huh."

"If you say anything to make her think I was part of this, you are going to wish the kidnappers had never let you go. Understand?"

"Yeah, whatever you say, bro."

"Good. Come on," Ruban said, pulling him from the seat. Jeffrey was a complete load, absolutely no help in getting out of the car. His arms hung limply over Ruban's shoulders, and Ruban managed to pull him from the backseat piggyback style. Jeffrey would have fallen flat on his face in the driveway if he hadn't draped his body over Ruban's back. Ruban struggled to put one foot in front of the other, Jeffrey's feet dragging behind him like disc plows. Savannah hurried out to meet them in the driveway.

"Oh, you poor boy. What did they do to your face?"

Jeffrey grumbled something unintelligible, drooling on the back of Ruban's neck as he tried to speak.

"We should take him to the emergency room," said Savannah.

Ruban could barely stand beneath the weight. "*I* need the emergency room."

The front steps were a challenge, but they finally got Jeffrey inside and laid him on the couch. His battered face looked even worse in the light. Savannah raided the medicine cabinet and brought out everything from painkillers to cotton balls. Ruban acted as his own chiropractor, arching and twisting his spine until it popped back into place. He watched from the armchair as Savannah tended to her brother's face.

"Open your mouth, Jeffrey." She dabbed his gums with a wet washcloth, but even a gentle touch made him scream. "Thank God it's just the bottom teeth," she said.

"They only took the gold," said Ruban.

"He needs a dentist."

"They have really good ones in Thailand. Cheap."

"Please be serious."

"I'm totally serious," said Ruban. "That's where I'm sending him. Your mother, too. Jeffrey told his kidnappers that his cash was in your mother's house. They both need to get out of Miami. Out of the country is even better."

"We'll talk about that later." She put two Tylenol in Jeffrey's mouth and told him to swallow.

"Let's talk now," said Ruban. "We got a major problem. Don't forget that these guys started out asking for a million dollars. They settled for four hundred thousand, but now they know Jeffrey's an easy mark. If we don't get him the hell out of Miami, they'll come back."

Savannah looked at her husband with concern. "What about you and me? Are we easy marks? What if they kidnap one of us?"

Ruban caught his brother-in-law's eye, reminding him about the ground rules they'd established in the car. "What about it, Jeffrey? What'd you tell them about Savannah and me?"

"Nothing, bro. I told them the money was mine, nobody else's. They wanted to know who could find it, and I said my uncle or my sister. That's it."

Good dog. Ruban sat forward in his chair, his interrogation mode. "Did you tell them how you got your money?"

"I said I cashed in a lottery ticket."

That jibed with what El Padrino had told him at the Holy Santería Church of Our Lady of the New Cadillac.

"Did they believe you?" asked Savannah.

"They didn't say they didn't," said Jeffrey.

"It was a good try," said Ruban. "But I'm pretty sure they know it didn't come from a lottery ticket. Ramsey basically dared me to call the cops and report the kidnapping. He knows I can't, which means he knows that Jeffrey's money isn't legit."

"That doesn't mean they know it's from the heist," Savannah said. "What'd you tell Ramsey when you hired him to watch Jeffrey?"

Jeffrey tried to sit up, but he was in too much pain. "What?" he asked, grimacing. "Hired?"

Ruban shot his wife a look that said "*Shut it.*" Savannah shoved two more Tylenol in Jeffrey's mouth. "Here, baby. Take your medicine."

He spat out the pills. "What did you say about hiring Ramsey to watch me?"

"I misspoke," said Savannah.

"No, I heard you."

The cat was out of the bag. "I did it for your own good," said Ruban.

"So you hired Ramsey, and Ramsey got me kidnapped?"

That was Ruban's take, but he saw no upside in agreeing with Jeffrey. "We don't know what happened."

"Bull*shit*," said Jeffrey. "That's exactly what happened. I'm not going to Thailand. I'm not going nowhere."

"Oh, you're going, all right," said Ruban.

"No, I'm not. You just tell your friend Ramsey to leave me alone."

"What for? So you can shove more coke up your nose and throw money at the Gold Rush whores?"

"Fuck you, Ruban."

"Fuck *me*?" Ruban said, rising. "Who's going to protect you next time?"

"Nobody asked you to protect me."

"Your *sister* did."

"Yeah, like you protected her when you knocked her off your motorcycle?"

Ruban went at him, but Savannah jumped between them before he could take a swing. "Stop it!"

Ruban froze. Jeffrey peered up through his fingers, instinctively having brought his hands up to cover his face.

"I can't have you fighting each other," she said.

"You're lucky I don't knock the rest of your teeth out," said Ruban.

"You're lucky I don't tell—"

"That's enough," said Savannah, stopping Jeffrey in mid-sentence. And it was a good thing she had. Ruban was pretty sure he was on the verge of outing his role in the heist.

"Both of you—listen to me," said Savannah.

Ruban stepped back. Jeffrey was breathless from the excitement, his belly heaving.

"We are going to work through this," she said. "It doesn't matter who kidnapped Jeffrey. If they think he had only four hundred thousand dollars, this should be the end of it."

"That's exactly what they think," said Jeffrey. "I told Bambi that's all I had left, and she believed me."

"Who's *Bambi*?" asked Ruban.

"She's the woman who brought me to the parking lot. She's my friend."

Ruban groaned. "Bro, she made you walk alone

to my car so I couldn't see her face. She ain't your *friend*."

"Yes, she—"

"It doesn't matter!" Savannah shouted. It was loud enough to startle both men into silence. She caught her breath and kept talking. "Listen to me. Thanks to Ruban, we paid less than half the ransom they asked for. So even if you had a right to this money—which you don't—you have no right to hold a grudge against us."

"Fine. Just so long as I can spend what's left."

"You have more money here in Mom's house?"

"No. I gave some to El Padrino to hold for me."

"How much?" asked Ruban.

"None of your business."

Ruban shook his head. "You're never gonna see that money again, Jeffrey. I already talked to him. He won't give it up."

"Not to you. But to me he will."

"Quiet," said Savannah. "No more blowing through money. Jeffrey, if and when you get back anything from your godfather, you give it to Ruban, and we straighten this out. Maybe we hire a lawyer."

"*NO!*" they shouted in unison.

"Okay, maybe not a lawyer. But no more spending sprees."

"It's my money."

"You can't touch it, and the only way to make sure you don't is for Ruban to take control."

"But I need my money, Savannah."

"No. You told this Bambi that the ransom was every last cent you had. As long as we all keep acting like we don't have any money, then they have no reason to kidnap any of us. Once upon a time, you had four hundred thousand dollars. It doesn't matter if you cashed in a lottery ticket or stole it from a drug dealer. Now it's gone, and there's no more. End of story. Am I right, Ruban?"

Ruban was still reeling from her "hire a lawyer" comment, but otherwise Savannah was making sense. "I can act broke for as long as it takes," he said. "I'm not sure Jeffrey can."

"He can if he doesn't know where his money is."

"This sucks," said Jeffrey.

"Jeffrey, do you want me to tell Mom you've been practically living at the Gold Rush?"

She was playing on Jeffrey's worst fear: daughter forces Mom to see the truth; Mom goes into instant cardiac arrest—or, worse, kicks her deadbeat son out of the house.

"Shit," he said softly.

"Do you promise to play by the rules this time?" she asked.

He made a face, but it was more tooth pain than an expression of disagreement. "I guess so," he said, wincing.

"Good," said Savannah. "It's settled. Next problem. I'm going to see if I can get a dentist on the phone. You boys behave yourselves."

She left the room to get her phone. Ruban fell into the armchair. Jeffrey tried to find a more comfortable position on the couch, but he was like a beached whale, and his butt sank even deeper into the crack between the cushions. Both men avoided eye contact, and the silence was getting awkward.

"Ruban?"

He didn't answer. His anger was still smoldering, and starting a conversation without Savannah in the room to referee was a risky proposition.

"I'm sorry I brought up the motorcycle," said Jeffrey. "And I know you didn't knock Savannah off it."

Ruban sighed. He hadn't expected an apology, and it was decent of Jeffrey to try and remove the sting from words spoken in anger. But it didn't really matter that he hadn't knocked Savannah off of his motorcycle. He might as well have.

"Thanks, bro," he said without heart. "I appreciate that."

"Even when those guys ripped out my caps, I never said nothin' about you having any of the money or being part of the heist. I stuck to my guns and told them I had only four hundred thousand. That's why they asked for that much ransom."

It rang true, and Ruban had figured as much.

"And I won't tell Savannah you were part of the you-know-what. So, are we cool?"

Ruban glanced over. Jeffrey's face was a swollen mess, and the loss of his gold caps had left his lower mouth misshapen. He was such a pain in the ass, but he was clearly reaching out for Ruban's approval, which made it hard to stay angry. All he seemed to want was someone to say "You done good, Jeffrey."

"Yeah, we're cool," said Ruban, but he didn't feel it. "For now."

21
.

Savannah stayed behind and watched television, alone, while Ruban drove Jeffrey home.

She'd cleaned him up as best she could, but she didn't want to be there for the wailing when her mother laid eyes on his battered face. The dentist would see him first thing in the morning. It was up to Ruban to decide how much cash to give Jeffrey to fix his teeth.

"Yuck," Savannah said. Jeffrey had left a spot of blood on the arm of their couch. She got a rag to clean it up, which took only a few minutes, but that was long enough for her to lose the storyline on the TV drama she was watching. She channel-surfed for more mindless entertainment, but nothing captured her interest. It wasn't the networks' fault: there was more than enough "so bad, it's good" programming to distract the average viewer. It was Savannah's lack of focus. Her mind was elsewhere.

The trip to their old house in Kendall had been an unexpected setback. Jeffrey's mention of the motorcycle accident had completed the emotional double whammy. It had taken the doctors a while to assess the full extent of the injuries to her fallopian tubes, and after six long months of depression, she'd made it a point not to dwell on "the situation." But tonight was like a punch in the gut, going back to the place where they'd planned to raise children coupled with the blunt reminder that she couldn't have them.

Ruban, you can't buy back what's lost.

The only person ever to say it was fixable was Jeffrey's godfather—El Padrino—who'd told her that she would remain barren only so long as she lived a sinful life. She'd told him and his Santería beliefs to get lost, not even bothering to point out that she was no more of a sinner than millions of women who seemed to have no trouble at all popping out babies. But now she wondered. In hindsight, maybe it was punishment for the multimillion-dollar sin she had not yet committed, the biggest sin of her life: letting her brother and uncle hide all that money, telling the police nothing. Until this, she'd never really stolen anything. Never concealed anything so big. Well, maybe *one thing*.

It had to do with her dream job. The one that had slipped through her fingers.

Miami had its share of distinguished private schools, but for anyone who wanted the one-stop option of "pre-K through 12," Grove Academy was of singular distinction. The wooded five-acre campus was in Coconut Grove, right on Biscayne Bay, and students who didn't come to school each morning in a Lexus or BMW might arrive by boat. No class had more than twelve students. Mandarin Chinese was mandatory beginning at age three. Classrooms had the latest SMART Board technology, and any student who didn't have a brand-new laptop every September was living in the Dark Ages. About once every decade, someone made it through the fifth grade without being named a "Duke TIP kid," but the best of the best weren't aiming for Duke, or any other college south of Cambridge, with the possible exception of the one in New Haven.

Savannah would never forget the day she'd landed the job in the art department.

Or the day she'd lost it.

"Headmaster Burns wishes to see you in her office, Savannah."

She looked up from the desk in her tiny office. Savannah was one of two apprentices who worked under the Grove's perennial art teacher, who was standing in the open doorway. The school day had not yet begun, but in forty-five minutes a dozen seventh-graders would flood into the art room, expecting to work with acrylics.

"Now?"

"Yes. Right away."

Savannah glanced nervously at the clock on the wall, concerned that she wouldn't be ready for class. But when the headmaster called, the newest teacher's assistant at the Academy didn't say "Later." She laid her work aside and hurried downstairs to the administrative offices.

"Please have a seat," said the headmaster.

Headmaster Burns wasn't smiling, which Savannah took as a very bad sign. Burns was the consummate administrator who had the ability to smile through the most difficult of circumstances, whether she was telling you that your house was on fire or, far worse, that your child wasn't going to be in the honors Singapore Math program. No smile meant something serious indeed, which was only confirmed by the fact that the assistant headmaster was also in the office.

"Is something wrong?"

"Let me get straight to the point," said the headmaster. "We are here to educate our students, but nothing at Grove Academy is more important than the safety of our children."

"Of course."

"That's why our hiring process is so selective."

"I'm honored to work here."

That was an understatement. For five years, Savannah had been an art instructor at West Miami Middle School, where 80 percent of the students spoke English as a second language. The principal had put in a word for her at Grove Academy, and Savannah had impressed them enough to land an apprenticeship. It was actually a pay cut, but the point was that the position had become available only because the Academy had sent Savannah's predecessor to earn his M.F.A. from the School of the Art Institute of Chicago—on full salary, all tuition paid. This was Savannah's chance to earn the same distinction, to be somebody, to beat down the joke that she'd heard since high school: you can take *la niña* out of Hialeah, but you can't take Hialeah out of *la niña*.

"Your employment here is exactly what this meeting is about," said the headmaster.

It was suddenly difficult to breathe. "What do you mean?"

"We don't require teachers' assistants to complete job applications under oath, but we take any misrepresentations or omissions on the application very seriously."

"As you should."

"We have zero tolerance for misrepresentations and omissions when it comes to criminal history."

Savannah's throat tightened, but she knew exactly what the headmaster was talking about. "I can explain—"

"Please, don't make it worse by lying to my face. We've dug all the way back to the arrest record on this."

"But—"

"Ms. Betancourt, your services are no longer required here. Return to your office immediately, pack up your personal belongings, and be gone before first period."

A pair of headlights flashed through the venetian blinds. Savannah went to the front window and checked the driveway. Ruban was back.

Other than her, Ruban was the only person who knew the story behind her firing—*both sides* of the story. He knew how devastating it had been for her. He knew the timing couldn't have been worse. She'd lost her job five days before they'd lost their house. Five days before the repo men had come for the car and they'd ridden off on Ruban's motorcycle. They'd had each other in those times, only each other, and she'd told him everything she was thinking and feeling. But there was one thing she would never tell him.

The car lights went out. She heard the car door close.

It was hard for her to describe what had been going through her mind on that night, when she'd climbed onto the back of that motorcycle, the last thing of value they owned, even though they didn't actually own it anymore; they possessed it only as long as they could hide it from the bank. She'd wrapped her arms around Ruban's waist, and they'd sped down the interstate, the engine roaring, the vibration rattling her bones. She remembered that urge to jump, but what came later was fuzzy. Later, the doctor in the hospital would call it a phobia, an uncontrollable sensation that had taken over and made it impossible for Savannah to spend another moment on that speeding machine. Ruban had accepted the diagnosis. Savannah had, too, for a while, but only because she'd wanted to believe that the experts were right. Deep down, she knew differently. What had made her jump from that motorcycle was no phobia. It wasn't a panic attack. It had been a split-second decision, but in the blurry moment it had seemed like an answer. Her broken heart was beyond repair. Behind the tinted shield of her helmet, tears were pouring down her face.

She'd just jumped.

The front door opened and Ruban came inside.

She went to him, wrapping her arms around him as tightly as she should have on the night that had changed their lives.

"What's that for?" he asked.

She couldn't let go of him. "Nothing," she whispered, holding back tears. "It's just . . . nothing."

22

·

It was Andie's first sunrise on South Beach. A sliver of orange emerged from the Atlantic as she approached the Third Street lifeguard tower on Miami Beach. The tide was out, leaving the shoreline in the middle distance, but the gentle rhythm of breaking waves could be heard in the shrinking darkness. A handful of joggers passed on the boardwalk, but the beach was deserted, save for Andie and a dozen other early risers who had gathered for the seven a.m. yoga class. Andie had transferred to Miami knowing no one, and she wasn't having an easy time making friends outside of law enforcement. Her new friend Rachel taught the class.

"You actually came," Rachel said with surprise.

Andie was a regular at the studio three nights a week. Rachel had been bugging her to try the beach class, though she would have denied that yoga instructors ever "bugged" anybody.

"This is spectacular," said Andie.

"Even better, it's free. But I do take tips, and hopefully today's group will understand that telling me to 'go to bed early' or 'choose my sticky mat carefully' aren't the kind of tips that pay my grocery bill."

"Not very Zen of you," Andie said with a smile.

"Hey, I'm not running a yoga cult here."

Andie didn't bring it up, but she'd actually discovered yoga after busting a Seattle instructor who'd convinced his female students that signing over their worldly possessions and having sex with the instructor were necessary to awaken Kundalini.

Class lasted one hour. Andie didn't make it to the first downward-facing dog pose. In a perfect world, she would have turned off her cell and started the day right. Her unit chief had other plans. Andie stepped away from the class, walked to the other side of the lifeguard stand, and took his call.

"We got a lead through the tip line," he said.

"Great. How many does that make now? Nine thousand, or nine thousand and one?"

"This seems real. Auto mechanic. He works at a body shop near the river. Says he knows what happened to the black pickup."

Since the heist, agents from the FBI's auto-theft unit had been combing the auto-repair districts between the airport and the ports along the Miami River. The suspicion was that the black pickup had been reduced to parts at a chop shop.

"So the reward actually worked?" asked Andie.

"We'll see. Go talk to him. Lieutenant Watts is bringing him in now."

"I'll be right there."

Andie never went anywhere without a clean set of work clothes in the trunk of her car, so she drove straight to the office, made a quick change in the restroom, and met Watts in the interrogation room. Leonard Timmes, a nervous-looking man in his mid-thirties, was seated on the other side of the Formica-top table. The Miami field office was a smoke-free building, but exceptions were made for informants on the verge of running out the door if they didn't get a nicotine fix. The bright fluorescent light seemed to bother Timmes' eyes, and Andie suspected that he hadn't slept much the night before. It wasn't unusual for a tipster to change his mind and decide not to get involved after all, and Watts had done well to bring Timmes in pronto.

Andie introduced herself and thanked him for coming. Timmes lit up another cigarette, his third. Andie spent the first few minutes trying to put him at ease, but nothing short of Valium would have done the job. She moved straight to the heart of the matter before Timmes could shut down.

"Ever seen this man?" she asked as she laid her iPad on the table. She had photographs and everything else she needed on her gizmo.

"That's the guy," said Timmes. "Marco is his name."

Bull's-eye. "When's the first time you saw Marco?"

"It was a Monday. Before the heist at MIA."

"Did you talk to him?"

"No. I just listened. I was getting ready to put a clear coat on a Toyota pickup. My boss brought him over to have a look. He wanted to borrow a truck."

"Borrow?"

Timmes took a drag on his cigarette, then glanced at Watts. "The lieutenant said there weren't gonna be any questions about that."

Watts confirmed it with a nod, from which Andie inferred that this was a typical deal: Timmes would help with the investigation into the heist, but he wasn't there to bring down the chop shop and put his boss and coworkers in jail for auto theft.

"How long did Marco want to borrow it?" asked Andie.

"He said he'd have it back Sunday night."

"The Sunday of the heist?"

"Right. But he didn't like the Toyota. He said he needed a cab with a rear seat."

Two gunmen, a driver, probably some weapons. It made sense. "Did your boss show him another truck?"

"No. We didn't have anything like that. But my boss told him I could probably get what he was looking for."

"Did you get him one?"

Another long drag on the cigarette, followed by another exchange of eye contact between Timmes and Watts. The detective answered for him: "Let's just say one came in."

"Right," said Timmes. "One came in on Friday. A black Ford F-150."

"Did Marco pick it up?"

"I assume he did. He was supposed to get it Saturday, but I didn't work Saturday because I agreed to come in the next day for the drop-off. We don't usually open on Sundays."

"So you were at the shop when the truck came back?"

"Right. Me and two other guys."

"Who?" Andie didn't expect an answer, and she didn't get one.

"Mr. Timmes doesn't remember that information," said Watts.

"Right. I don't remember. Not important anyway. What you need to know is that when the pickup came back on Sunday, it was inside the box of a delivery truck."

Andie retrieved another photograph for him. "Like this one?"

"Bingo," said Timmes.

"Who was driving the delivery truck?"

"Marco was."

"Anybody with him?"

"No. Just him."

"What happened next?"

"We took the pickup apart."

"You chopped it?"

"That's a very loaded term," said Timmes. "We salvaged the parts and loaded the pieces back into the delivery truck. Then Marco drove away. The whole job probably took us three hours, I'd say."

"What time did you start?"

"Around three-thirty."

The timing fit. Timmes was proving to be quite credible. "Did anybody leave with Marco in the delivery truck?"

"No. He came alone, left alone."

"Where did he go?"

"I got no idea. Never saw him again, never heard from him."

"Did he pay you?"

"No. My boss paid me, and I went home. Later, I was watching the news on TV. That's when I heard about the heist at the airport. Some guys in a black pickup truck got away with millions. So I called my boss."

"What did you tell him?"

"I was kind of joking, but I was serious, too. I told him we didn't get paid enough."

"Did your boss confirm that it was the pickup used in the heist?"

"He didn't have to. We all knew Marco was suddenly a very rich man."

"Did anybody talk about tracking him down?"

"Not to me."

Andie leaned into the table, giving her question a little extra oomph. "Do you know anybody who might cut off Marco's finger and beat him bloody to find out where he was hiding his cut from the money flight?"

Timmes crushed out his cigarette and dug into his pack for another. "I don't know any people like that."

Andie glanced at his hands. They were shaking. "Then why are you so nervous about coming here?"

"I'm not nervous." He struck a match, and it took several tries, but he finally steadied the flame long enough to light another cigarette.

"This is very helpful, Mr. Timmes. Thank you."

"Do I get the reward?"

"Too early to say. You will, if this information leads to an arrest and a conviction of the criminals responsible for the heist."

"Well, that's not exactly what I wanted to hear," he said. "From what I've seen on the news, this Marco is probably fish food in the Miami River. You can't arrest a dead man. I should still get the reward."

"It doesn't work that way."

His nervousness gave way to anger. "This is bullshit. I gave you everything I promised Lieutenant Watts I would."

"And the FBI is very grateful," said Andie.

"Then give me my damn money!"

There was a knock on the door. Andie excused herself and left the room. Watts followed. It was one of the other agents on the case.

"I lost track of Alvarez," he said.

Andie's interview at Braxton Security had focused on Alvarez, and he continued to be the FBI's primary suspect among potential insiders at the armored-car company. Agent Benson had been assigned to tail him.

"You *lost* him?" said Andie.

"I watched him enter his apartment last night around ten o'clock. He was supposed to be at work by six a.m. to start the daily merchant drops, but he never came out. I called Braxton and had them check on him and see why he didn't show up for work. They got the landlord to open the apartment. He's gone."

"He can't just vanish," said Andie.

"He's not in his apartment, and I never saw him leave."

Andie looked at Watts. "Make another sweep along the river."

"You thinking what I'm thinking?"

"Just a hunch," she said. "We may have more fish food."

23

—
•

Ruban's morning was full. First stop was the daycare center. He dropped Savannah off at 6:30 a.m.

Sometimes it was a pain having to drive Savannah everywhere, but Ruban didn't complain. She'd stopped driving after the accident. There seems to be a clinically recognized phobia for just about every disabling fear—phobophobia: fear of phobias—but not for fear of driving. "Post-traumatic Stress Disorder" was what the emergency-room physician had labeled Savannah's condition. A major panic attack had landed her in Jackson Memorial Hospital. She'd stopped cold in the middle lane of I-95, unable to move, backing up rush-hour traffic out of downtown Miami for two miles behind her. It wasn't car trouble. Savannah suddenly couldn't deal with cars changing lanes around her, cutting her off, stopping short, speeding past her, blinking lights, horns blasting, dump trucks roaring—*can't breathe!*

"What time should I pick you up?" he asked as the car pulled up to the curb.

"Six."

She reached for the door handle, then stopped to tap out a message on her cell phone. "I'm forwarding you the text I sent to Jeffrey with the bus info he needs to get to the dentist. He has to be there by eight sharp. Can you call him and make sure he gets there?"

"I guess so. Can't you call him?"

"I'm not supposed to use my phone at work."

Drop-off at the daycare center started at 6:45. Savannah only got to work there three days each week, and he knew how important this job was to her. "Okay. I'll make sure."

He kissed her good-bye and drove back to the expressway; next stop, downtown Miami. He was in a hurry and making good time. Ruban took the baseball stadium exit, drove around the block, pulled up under the bridge, and stepped out of his car. The interstate rumbled overhead as commuters poured into the city for another workday. The homeless didn't seem bothered by the noise. A half dozen or so were sleeping soundly on cardboard mattresses. A woman was loading her possessions into a shopping cart, another pointless day. An old man was urinating in plain view. A familiar face approached, and Ruban reacted too slowly to avoid him.

"Hey, you again," the man said. "I told you I knew you!"

It was the guy on the street outside the Seybold Building with the "Dog Bless You" sign.

Ruban went in the opposite direction and scouted out three more-reliable candidates. Jorge, the one-armed Iraq War veteran with the sad eyes. Marvin, the retiree who had lost everything to Bernie Madoff. Alicia, the ponytailed, twenty-year-old runaway who could have been your niece or cousin. Ruban had used them before, and they knew the drill. They climbed into the backseat of his car and rode to Coral Gables.

The intersection of U.S. 1 and Bird Road was prime panhandling territory. Thousands of commuters sat in their cars every morning waiting for the traffic light to change. Some were too busy talking on a cell phone or putting on makeup to notice the sad faces outside their car windows. Others noticed but looked away uncomfortably. A few generous souls rolled down the window and offered spare change, a dollar, sometimes more. These were the folks that Ruban and his team counted on.

"Everybody out," said Ruban.

The homeless trio stirred in the backseat. A twenty-minute car ride was their most comfortable sleep of the night. Ruban hurried them along and handed each of them a sign for the day. *Family Man, Lost My Job. Army Vet—Don't Do Drugs. Pregnant, Please Help.*

Ruban didn't "own" the Bird Road intersection. He just rented it every Tuesday from a former gangbanger who owned all the major intersections on U.S. 1 between Coconut Grove and Pinecrest, two of Miami's most wealthy suburbs. It was Ruban's job to staff the intersection once a week, collect the money at the end of the day, and drive his team back to sleep under the bridge. The owner of the Bird Road intersection got the first

$200. Ruban got the next $100. The homeless kept the rest. Anyone who didn't pull down the $300 daily minimum to cover the overhead was black-listed and out of the rotation.

"I'll be back after the evening rush hour," Ruban told them. He returned to his car, opened the door, and nearly fell over from the odor.

"Shit!" he said, which was exactly what he smelled. He suspected the old guy. This gig was hardly worth the effort. It was typical of the small-time dealing that had made him jump at the chance to "think big." He couldn't wait to stop laying low and enjoy the spoils of the heist.

"Ruban!"

He turned and saw his friend, but if Octavio Alvarez hadn't spoken, Ruban would never have recognized him. Alvarez was wearing old clothes, a big hat, sunglasses, and a phony beard. Before the heist, they'd agreed that Ruban should have no contact with an armored-car guard. The plan was for Octavio to show up as a homeless person at the Bird Road intersection and collect his share from Ruban in a backpack. But that meeting wasn't until the following week.

"What the hell are you doing here today?" asked Ruban, "It's *next* Tuesday."

"I know. We gotta talk. Get in the car."

"Dude, get out of here!"

"Get in the car!" Alvarez said as he opened the door and jumped into the passenger seat.

Ruban didn't like it one bit, but he complied. His heart was pounding so hard that he thought he was having a Savannah-style panic attack. He slammed the door shut and glared at his friend.

"What is the matter with you? I don't have your money today."

"I know, I—" Alvarez stopped himself, making a face. "What is that smell?"

"Never mind that. Your money is hidden. You'll get it in a week."

"I need it right away."

"No! That's not what we agreed."

"I'm being followed."

"That's what makes it even stupider for you to come here. Now they know *me*!"

"Don't worry, I shook the tail. I snuck out the window last night, and nobody followed me. You're acting like I showed up in my Braxton uniform. No one is going to recognize me dressed like this."

Ruban breathed a little easier—but the odor hit him again. Alvarez, too.

"Damn," said Alvarez. "I gotta roll down a window."

"No, I don't want anyone to see us!"

Tinted windows did more than keep out the sun. Ruban started the car and blasted the air. Alvarez stuck his nose right up to the vents and drew it in.

"Who's following you?" asked Ruban.

"I'm not sure. But I'm worried. I heard about Marco."

"What did you hear?"

"Just what's on the news, but I'm not stupid, bro. Somebody at the chop shop must have figured out Marco was part of the heist. They followed him to the river and did a chop number on him until he told them where his money was."

"Pinky doesn't think he told them anything. That's why they killed him."

"Pinky doesn't know shit. What if Marco gave up my name?"

"Not possible. Marco never knew your name."

"You swear?"

"Yes."

That seemed to make Alvarez feel better, but it left an obvious question. "Then who is following me?" asked Alvarez.

"Have the cops been questioning you?"

"Of course," he said. He told him about the FBI interview. "Two agents. An older guy named Littleford. A woman named Henning. She's kind of hot, actually."

"I'm sure she thinks you're cute, too. What the fuck does it matter that she's hot?"

"I'm just saying. But you make a good point. It doesn't matter. Just like it doesn't matter who's following me. I'm being followed. Period. I need my money, and I need to get out of Miami."

"Bad idea. I'm not going to let you do that, bro."

"Not gonna *let* me?"

"Your money is hidden. It stays hidden, and we are all staying put until the cops decide that the MIA Lufthansa heist is headed for the cold-case files."

"That was a good plan before Marco got whacked."

"It's still a good plan."

Alvarez leaned forward, took in another blast of fresh air from the A/C vent, then shook his head.

"This started out as us grabbing a few bags of cash from a big-ass German bank that ships a hundred million dollars *every week*. A little payback for their banker buddies in Miami who took your house and are still driving around in their Porsches and BMWs."

"Those fuckers back in Frankfurt don't even care if the plane lands," said Ruban. "They still get rich. It's all insured."

"All true," said Alvarez. "But everything has changed now. Marco got chopped to pieces in the back of a truck, and somebody's following me. Time for a new plan."

Ruban didn't tell him that Pinky was ready to make a run for it, too. And he didn't dare tell him about Jeffrey. "We're going to be okay. We have to hang together."

Alvarez paused, as if he sensed that his words wouldn't be received well. "I'm thinking about going back to Cuba."

Ruban could hardly believe his ears. "You're *what*?"

"The FBI can't touch me there. My sister still lives in the middle of nowhere, twenty miles west of Guantánamo. I can stash the money and hide out with her for six months. A year if I have to. When the FBI stops looking for me, I dig up my money, and I'm set for life."

"Great plan," said Ruban, scoffing. "But what do you do when you set foot on Cuban soil and they throw you in jail for defecting when you were seventeen years old?"

"That's not gonna happen, bro. That's the kind

of shit people talk when they run for mayor of Miami."

Ruban shook his head, laughing without heart.

"What's so funny?" asked Alvarez.

"Think back fifteen years," said Ruban. "I still remember that look on your face when we got on that *balsa*. A wood crate sitting on top of inner tubes, plastic bottles, and anything else that would float. Powered by a lawnmower motor. A jar of fireflies so we can see the compass at night. You know you're in trouble when there's no room to bring anything with you except for a coffee can to bail out the water."

"That was one balls-out trip. Good thing we had that virgin with us—somebody to pray to God we make it across the Florida Straits."

They shared a smile, but it was tinged with a measure of sadness. "We were the lucky ones," said Ruban, and he could see the memories clouding Octavio's eyes. They'd been part of the Cuban raft exodus of summer 1994. Some made it all the way to U.S. shores. The Coast Guard plucked another 31,000 from the sea and shipped them to overcrowded refugee camps at the U.S. naval base in Guantánamo. An unknown number succumbed to twelve-foot waves, storms, dehydration, exposure, rafts that had no business being anywhere near the water, or just plain bad luck, their fates sealed at the bottom of the ocean, or in the bellies of sharks.

"What if I had told you then that you were going to be a millionaire before you were thirty-five?" asked Ruban.

"I'd have called you crazy."

"And what if I'd also told you that, nine days after all that money was yours to keep, you would look me in the eye and say you're going back to Cuba?"

That got a real laugh. "I would've called you *fucking crazy*."

Ruban's expression turned very serious. "That's exactly my point, bro."

Alvarez took a minute to consider it, staring down at the air vent. Then he looked across the console and said, "All right. I get it. I'll hang tight."

"Good man," said Ruban.

Alvarez reached for the door handle. "But next Tuesday's meeting stands. I get my money."

"A deal's a deal," said Ruban.

Alvarez nodded, opened the door, and climbed out on the passenger side. "Ruban?" he said before closing the door.

"Yeah?"

"Take some of my money," he said, sniffing, "and buy yourself an air freshener."

Ruban smiled as the door closed and Alvarez stepped away from the car. Then he pulled out into traffic, ignoring the sad and hungry faces of the homeless as he merged into the morning rush hour.

24
.

Savannah was on edge.

Morning drop-off at the daycare center had gone fine, nothing unusual. At nine o'clock, however, the director called Savannah into her office. Two lawyers had arrived unexpectedly, and the younger one closed the door after Savannah entered.

"What's up?" asked Savannah. She was trying to sound cheery, but the men in business suits made her voice crack.

"We have a very serious matter on our hands," said the director.

Savannah took a seat and listened.

"We have a court order," said the lawyer.

The last time Savannah had seen one of those, she'd lost her house. This time, her thoughts raced to an even scarier place: the heist. Maybe the lawyers represented the airline, the bank, the airport, or the Federal Reserve. Maybe they were prosecutors from the U.S. attorney's office.

"How does this involve me?" she asked.

The director opened her desk drawer and handed her a paintbrush. Savannah was the center's art instructor, but teaching lawyers to paint happy faces seemed beyond her expertise.

"Did you make that sign out in front of the daycare center?" the lawyer asked.

"Yes. Why?"

"We have to change it," said the director.

The lawyers were intellectual-property specialists. The illegal "Mickey & Minnie Daycare Center" needed a new name and new mascots, or it would be shut down immediately. Savannah tried not to look too relieved as this "very serious matter" was explained to her.

"I'll get right on it," said Savannah.

It took her about an hour. The ears were a challenge, but Mickey and Minnie were transformed into "Mikey and Millie," Miami's friendliest raccoons.

Savannah cleaned her brushes and could breathe again, but it wasn't the alleged trademark infringement that had her so upset. When she'd walked into the main office and seen the suits, she'd seriously thought that the Justice Department was on the premises and that she'd be leaving in handcuffs. It was so unnerving that she violated the no–cell phone rule to check on Jeffrey. She called him from the bathroom.

"Did you make it to the dentist?" she asked.

"No. I'm in bed."

It was after ten o'clock. "Jeffrey, you were supposed to be there two hours ago."

"I'll get there when I get there."

"Aren't you in pain?"

"I rubbed coke on my gums. I'm all numb. It's fine."

Savannah didn't bother with the "just say no" lecture. Drugs had been an on-and-off problem for Jeffrey since high school. He'd turned things around for a while, but losing his job had sent him into a downward spiral, which was now going on two years. Moving back home wasn't just about a place to live. Savannah suspected that, unbeknownst to Mommy, at least half her monthly Social Security check was going up Jeffrey's nose.

"Get your butt out of bed and go to the dentist," she said. "Or I'm telling Mom about the strippers."

Jeffrey groaned. Their mother could look the other way about drug addiction, a treatable illness, but strippers were for perverts, and perverts couldn't live in Mommy's house. Savannah hung up, knowing that she had him, and went back to work.

She stayed busy the rest of the morning helping three-year-olds paint self-portraits. Her favorite little girl was vomiting and had to be picked up early, one more reason to put today in the "not as fun as usual" category. But the real source of her stomachache—Savannah's, not the little girl's—was the afternoon appointment with the social worker from the Florida Department of Children and Family Services.

DCF was the Florida agency in charge of placing neglected or abandoned children. It was Savannah's best shot at adoption, though it wasn't where her journey had begun. She and Ruban had been trying for months. They'd started with a private adoption agency. Naturally, she'd been nervous about it. Even though all criminal charges against her had been dropped, no conviction, her prior arrest had cost her a job at Grove Academy. She'd gone into the meeting with the private adoption counselor fully prepared to explain that her brother Jeffrey had borrowed her car, that she was stopped for speeding the next day, and that the neatly rolled joint the police had spotted on the backseat "in plain view" had belonged to Jeffrey, not her. She never got to give the explanation. Her arrest wasn't the problem.

"I'm afraid I have bad news for you." The counselor's words had caught Savannah off guard. Their first meeting with the private adoption agency had gone well, she'd thought.

"How bad?" asked Savannah.

"Your application has been rejected."

Ruban was seated beside her, but Savannah did the talking. "We've barely even gotten started. You said there would be a series of meetings. You were going to come to our house, talk to our references, all that stuff."

"How should I put this?" asked the counselor. "Sometimes there's a red flag that halts the adoption process cold."

"I think I know what you're talking about," said Savannah. "But there is a perfectly innocent explanation for this 'red flag.'"

"Look, I'll be honest with you. You *might* find an agency that will approve you, but I doubt it. Certainly *this* agency will not approve you, no matter what the explanation."

"That's not fair. The charges were dropped."

Ruban took her hand. "Let's go, Savannah."

"No," she said firmly. "This is crazy. We both have jobs. We own a house. We're good people. Okay, there was an arrest. We can explain that. But an arrest is not a conviction."

The counselor closed her file. "First of all, it doesn't help matters for you to misrepresent the criminal history."

"I'm not misrepresenting anything."

"Look," said the counselor. "At the end of the day, a private adoption agency is a business. We can't *stay* in business if a birth mother has any doubt in her mind about the placement of her child in a safe environment."

Ruban nudged her. "Savannah, really. Let's just go."

"No. I was arrested, but I was never even prosecuted. The case was thrown out."

The counselor appeared momentarily confused. She glanced at Ruban, who wouldn't look her in the eye, and she seemed to sense the marital disconnect. "Mr. Betancourt, is there something you haven't told your wife?"

Ruban said nothing, so the counselor answered for him.

"Mrs. Betancourt, your husband is a convicted felon."

Savannah's mouth opened, but words didn't come. From the day she'd met Ruban, she'd known he was a risk taker, which she was not, and which had drawn her to him. This was not the kind of boldness she'd bargained for.

She pushed away from the table, smothering the urge to scream.

"Thank you for your time," she told the counselor. "Ruban, we should go now. You and I need to talk."

It was a bitter memory, and Savannah put it out of her mind as she led the DCF social worker to the play area behind the daycare center. The two women sat alone at one of the picnic tables. A sea of eucalyptus mulch stretched from their table to the monkey bars. Sprawling oaks shaded the entire playground.

Savannah had given up trying to find a private adoption agency that would place a child in the home of a convicted felon. The international door had closed just as quickly; under federal law, a felony conviction was an absolute bar to international adoption. Savannah's hope was that a state agency would be more flexible about her husband's situation. She also hoped that working at a daycare center would help her chances, since the center didn't seem to have any problem with her husband. This was the day that DCF was to observe Savannah on the job and speak to her coworkers.

"Sorry if I seem nervous," said Savannah.

"You don't have to apologize."

The DCF social worker went by "Betty," but her name was Beatriz, which Savannah took as good luck, since that was her mother's name. "This is just really important to me," said Savannah.

Betty nodded, seeming to understand. "As I told you before, you have a complicated application."

"I know. I'm so grateful that you've been able to carry us through this far. If I can just have a shot at giving DCF the total picture, I know I'll be approved."

"Well, let's be clear. There are circumstances where DCF can work around a . . ." Betty paused to find a suitable euphemism for "felony conviction," acutely aware that they were on a children's playground. "Where DCF can work around a *situation* such as your husband's. Especially if it was a long time ago and there are mitigating circumstances."

"That's exactly the case here."

"Then there's hope," Betty said. "But this is far from a sure thing. I want to caution you not to get your hopes up too high."

Savannah took a breath, reeling in her excitement. "I won't," she said, but that was her biggest lie yet.

An even bigger lie than her application.

25

·

Friday was Andie's date night.

Andie had dodged plenty of matchmaking efforts since moving to Miami. At her unit chief's house on Sunday evening, she'd been polite but clear about her lack of interest in meeting Barbara Littleford's cousin—the poor, recently divorced attorney who "isn't poor." Undeterred, Mrs. Littleford followed up midweek with a voice-mail message straight from Cupid's quiver. "Just meet him for a glass of wine after work on Friday. He could be your type."

A lawyer? My type?

Ironically, Andie's ironclad excuse would come from Barbara's husband. He and the assistant special agent in charge of the Miami field office arranged her "date" with Special Agent Benny Sosa. It was Andie's first undercover assignment in Miami.

"Did I put on too much cologne?" Sosa asked from the driver's seat.

Sosa was a handsome ex-jock with hair a little too styled, muscles a little too big, and shirt a little too tight. It only seemed fitting that he'd overdo the love potion. Andie's allergic sniffles began just two minutes into the car ride.

"It's pretty powerful," she said, as she lowered the window.

"Sorry. I thought it would be in role."

They were headed to Night Moves, a private club for couples who liked to swap partners. The club's owner, Jorge Calderón, also owned a paint and body shop near the airport—the chop shop that Marco Aroyo had used for the black pickup after the heist. According to the FBI's source, Leonard Timmes, Calderón spent every Friday night at the club. It was their best lead of the week. There was no further information on Marco Aroyo. Octavio Alvarez had returned to work at Braxton Security on Tuesday; no more suspicious activity. The plan at Night Moves was for the hot new couple to prowl their way over to Mr. Calderón and see if anything came up, so to speak.

They pulled into the parking lot just before midnight, and Sosa found the last open space. Night Moves claimed to be south Florida's largest "adult lifestyle" nightclub, the "premier playground for sexy couples and select singles." Theme nights were popular. Andie was relieved to see that they'd missed Thursday's "Sushi in the Raw Night." Eating raw fish off the hairy chest of some man she'd never met wasn't her cup of Japanese tea.

"No cover charge tonight if you wear pink pasties," said Sosa, pointing to the sign outside the entrance.

"Not gonna happen," said Andie.

The club was BYOB, no liquor license, so Andie brought a faux bottle of vodka to share. Dance music greeted them as they stepped into the entrance lobby. The sign on the wall said "*DO NOT ENTER* if you are offended by any form of nudity or sexual activity," but the disrobing came later. "Smart and sexy" attire was required of anyone who didn't dress in line with the night's theme of pink pasties, "schoolgirl," or whatever. The bouncer gave Andie the thumbs-up on her backless black cocktail dress. The attendant at the front desk checked their photo IDs, which were convincing fakes; then she ran their names through the club's database. Andie was Celia Sellers.

"First-timers, I see," said the attendant. "I'll ask a couple of our club mentors to show you around."

"That's not necessary," said Andie.

"It's mandatory. I'll be right back."

Mentors and a tour weren't mentioned in the FBI field dossier that Andie had studied. The bouncer explained after the attendant stepped away:

"It's not really mandatory. It's for newbies they want to impress."

Flattered, I'm sure.

The attendant returned with the mentors and made the quick introductions. The tour protocol was to separate the men from the women. Agent Sosa went off with a good-looking Latino who could have been his fraternity brother. The men disappeared into the noisy dance studio. Priscilla took Andie down the hall to a quiet lounge where they could talk.

"You two married?" asked Priscilla.

"No. Just dating."

"When's the last time you had sex with someone else?"

"Too long." She wasn't lying.

"Good attitude," said Priscilla.

A handful of couples were at the bar, all fully clothed and in keeping with the "smart and sexy" dress code. Andie wasn't in South Beach, but so far the look and feel of the club was no different. Night Moves was not your grandmother's swing club, no *Charlie's Angels* wannabes inviting men with long sideburns to have sex on skanky shag carpeting. Priscilla led her to a seat on the couch, crossed her legs, and smiled. The tattoo script on her calf jumped out at Andie: *Not all who wander are lost.*

"Let me tell you what's happening right now," said Priscilla. "Your boyfriend is getting the full tour. First, he'll see the dance floor, which can be pretty erotic. Some people will be dressed, others will be undressing. Some will be touching, a few might be doing more. Then the tour will head over to the Red Room. This is where you can actually do the things you were fantasizing about on the dance floor. If you feel like it, you can bring along some new friends you've only just met. The Red Room can suit any member's comfort level. Some people like to do it in the open, where anyone can watch. The *luv-nasium*, we call it. Others like a private cabana. Some of our members will walk around completely naked. Others want a robe. It's up to you."

Andie considered her response, mindful that she

needed to work within the restrictions on acceptable agent conduct in the FBI undercover operations manual. "I'll be honest: I'm not going to make it to the Red Room on my first visit."

"Don't worry. It's not even part of tonight's tour for you," said Priscilla. "But your boyfriend will come back from there all pumped up for an orgy and ready to sign on the dotted line for a lifetime club membership. My advice to you on the first visit is to have fun and keep your clothes on. Then go home and have the best sex you and your boyfriend have ever had."

"That sounds like good advice," said Andie.

"It is. You're the kind of people we want. You have class. You're beautiful. And as much as the club's marketing materials say that the membership is mostly people in their twenties and thirties, an awful lot of folks only *wish* they were that young again. The club needs more people like us."

Andie tried not to smile too cynically. Priscilla was clearly in the wishful category.

"So," Priscilla said, rising. "Let me show you the dance floor."

Priscilla led the way, and Andie followed her through the set of chrome-clad double doors at the end of the hallway. Inside, it was the typical loud music and flashing lights. The dance floor was spacious but packed, maybe fifty couples. Andie saw more bare skin than Priscilla had led her to believe she would. The "pink pasties" theme had apparently drawn out the exhibitionists in spades. Low-slung couches and tables surrounded the dance floor. Many of the tables had a brass pole. Housewives in

G-strings honed their amateur stripping skills. Men in tight briefs played underwear model. A few even had the six-packs to pull it off. On the enormous wall behind the DJ were at least a dozen flat screens. Technologically, it was a match for even the greatest of sports bars, except that the only thing to watch was porn.

"See that guy over there?" asked Priscilla, pointing with a subtle nod.

Andie shot a discreet glance across the dance floor. The man's partner was in the process of removing his shirt.

"Good-looking, right?" asked Priscilla.

"I'd say so."

"Fair warning: He's only got one testicle. I know, you think I'm shallow, and your politically correct reaction is probably, '*Oh, one nut, so what?*' Funny thing about balls, though. You don't really pay much attention to them, but you kind of miss them when they're not there."

Andie wasn't sure how to respond. "Like grandparents, I guess."

Priscilla laughed. "I like you. Yeah. Grandparents."

Andie looked away, but Priscilla tugged at her arm. "Over there," she said, "at the end of the bar. That's definitely someone you should know about."

She meant another man who was definitely in the "wishful" age category. The brunette on his right arm and the blonde on his left were little more than half his age and, in Andie's quick estimation, well out of his league.

"He's really not much to look at," said Andie.

"Craig has the biggest unit in the club."

"Oh."

"I'm not kidding. I measured it. That thing goes from my elbow to the tip of my little finger, no exaggeration. It must take ninety percent of the blood in his entire body to get it . . ."

Priscilla went on and on, but Andie had tuned out after "little finger." She was thinking back to her conversation at the tile depot earlier in the week. At the time, the warehouse manager's quip about the prison nickname for Marco's friend had seemed superfluous. Not anymore.

"Excuse me," said Andie, "but did you say from your elbow to your pinky?"

"Yeah. All the way to the tip of it. Can you believe that?"

"By any chance, do people call him Pinky?"

"As a matter of fact, they do. It's a joke. They call him Pinky because—

"He's enormous," said Andie, finishing for her.

"Exactly. How did you know that?"

Andie glanced across the bar. It had to be the same Pinky, Marco's friend, which was satisfying on many levels. She'd hit pay dirt without having to eat hairy sushi, wear pink pasties, or take a weeklong shower.

"Let's just say his reputation precedes him," said Andie.

26

.

On Saturday morning, Ruban dug up more money.

Friday had been another gangbuster night at the restaurant, and it was after two a.m. when he'd finally gone home. He woke before sunrise so neighbors would not see him digging in the yard. He took only what he needed, left the rest in the PVC pipe, and covered up the hole. A flick of a knife removed the vacuum-sealed packaging. The bills went into a backpack. Savannah was still in bed when he stepped out of the shower, and it wasn't his intention to wake her before leaving. He almost made it.

"Where you going, honey?"

He was at the front door, reaching for the knob. She was standing across the room, wrapped in her peach terry-cloth robe, her hair up in a chip clip.

"Oh, you're up."

"I am now," she said. "Where are you going?"

"Back to the restaurant," he said, lying. "A pipe broke in the kitchen last night. I need to see if I can fix it. Got my tools right here," he said, patting his backpack of money.

"Can't you call a plumber?"

"Ha," he said, smiling. "Do you have any idea what a plumber charges on a weekend? I'd have to get Jeffrey to knock off another money flight to cover his bill."

She folded her arms, clearly not amused. "Please don't joke about that. Jeffrey's lucky to be alive. I'm still very worried about him."

"We both are." He laid his backpack on the floor, keeping a safe distance between Savannah and what was really inside it. Then he crossed the room and put his arms around her. "I told both him and your mother that they should pack their bags and get out of Miami. I can't put a gun to their heads and force them to go."

Savannah laid her head against his chest, but she kept her eyes wide open, thinking. "I think we should turn in the money."

Ruban froze, then took a step back. "You what?"

"We don't have to tell the police that Jeffrey stole it. We can say that we were walking along a bike trail and saw a hundred-dollar bill on the ground. We looked around and saw another one, and then another one. Then we found a whole bag of money that the crooks had buried, and some animals must have dug it up."

Animals? Dug up? It was actually possible. He took another step back, suddenly feeling the need to sit, and leaned against the back of the couch. "That's just a bad idea."

"Why?"

"We find millions of dollars in a bag, and we just turn it in? That's our story?"

"Yeah. We did the right thing. Why is that a bad idea?"

"It's not believable."

"Why not?"

"First of all, where do you think we live, Mayberry? Nobody in Miami finds that much money and just turns it in."

"That's not true. I remember a story on the news just a few years ago. An armored car got in an accident and overturned on I-95. Two kids turned in the money."

"No. I remember that story, too. It was almost a half million dollars that spilled out of the truck. Two kids found fifty-five bucks and returned it. The rest of the folks, they just kept the money. The city practically threw a parade in honor of the kids who stepped up, because no one could believe they did it. *That's* Miami."

Savannah walked around the couch and sat on the armrest. She was right beside Ruban, leaning against him. "I'm afraid that the longer we keep this money hidden, the harder it is to figure out what to do about it."

Ruban reached for her hand and held it. "It's going to be okay."

"What about Pinky?"

He felt a chill. "What about him?"

"You still have his share of the money, right?"

He didn't, but he'd told her otherwise, and he was sticking to it. "Yeah, his and Jeffrey's share. Or at least I thought I did. Jeffrey had some cash I didn't know about. Enough to come up with a four-hundred-thousand-dollar ransom. I suppose Pinky does, too."

"We can turn in whatever we have. How much is it?"

He'd never told her, and putting an exact number on it would make it even harder to maintain equilibrium in the ebb and flow of lies mixed with truth. "Savannah, put this idea out of your head. If we don't have all the money, turning in part of it doesn't solve anything."

She sighed deeply. "Pinky is such a scumbag. Even if we could convince Jeffrey to turn in the money, he'll never make this right."

"You never know what will happen."

"Have you been in touch with him?"

"Last time we talked, he said he was leaving Miami."

"Just as well. He scares me. He was always nice to me when I was a little girl. Used to bring me presents whenever he came over to the house. But even before he went to prison, he scared me."

"I'll take care of Pinky."

She looked at him with concern. "What does that mean?"

"Don't worry. I'm not going to do anything stupid."

"You promise?"

"You have to trust me on this, Savannah."

Their eyes met and held. Then she smiled a little, but it was a sad one. "Okay. I trust you."

Ruban drove south and didn't stop until he was almost to the Florida Keys. It was his first visit to Eden Park.

The Eden Park mobile home community was twenty-seven acres of manufactured housing, a flat and treeless tract of agricultural land that the county had rezoned "residential" to accommodate thousands of migrant workers who worked the surrounding fields of beans and tomatoes each winter. Like many who'd lost a house in foreclosure, Ruban and Savannah had considered the manufactured-housing option before deciding to rent. Some mobile home parks were beautiful, having made it from one hurricane season to the next with nary a sign of damage from wind or rain. Eden Park was not one of them. When it came to tropical storms, Eden Park was like that unknowing kid in middle school who walks around all day with the "Kick Me" sign pasted to his back. It bore the scars of every major storm to make landfall in the last decade. Empty lots aplenty, the demolished houses long since hauled away. Some homeowners bought storm-damaged units on the cheap and fixed them up, good as new. Some bought as-is, unable to afford the necessary repairs. Windows remained boarded with plywood year round, the roof perpetually covered with blue plastic tarps, the "temporary" fixes that never went away.

The bluest of all was at the end of Eden Lane.

Ruban stopped and parked alongside the gravel road that bisected the park. He rolled down the window and sat behind the wheel for a minute. Just ahead, a little farther down the street, boys and girls were kicking a soccer ball. They looked to be around kindergarten age. In a place like Eden Park, video games were a luxury. Kids learned to kick a soccer ball almost before they could walk. All of these youngsters were good. One boy, in particular, was skilled for his age. Good ball control, dribbled with both feet, excellent speed. Ruban watched him with passing interest, focusing more on the feisty little girl who kept stealing the ball from him.

Ruban, you can't buy back what's lost.

Savannah was so wrong. She could not have been more wrong.

Ruban climbed out of the car, grabbed one more glimpse of the Eden Park World Cup, and walked to the front door of the trailer with the blue roof. He had his backpack with him. He knocked firmly. No one answered. He knocked again, and the main door opened, but the storm door remained closed. The old woman on the other side of the screen wasn't smiling. Her expression soured even more when she recognized Ruban.

"What the heck do you want?" she asked.

"Can we talk?"

"We got nothing to talk about."

"Please. I want to make things right."

She scoffed and shook her head.

"It could mean some money for you," he said.

Money. The magic word with Edith Baird. She had once been a pro at working the system. When her daughter and Ruban had dated, Edith was living comfortably in a four-bedroom house with a swimming pool. A felony conviction for welfare fraud put an end to the scam. Unfortunately, the pendulum swung too far in the opposite direction, and now the monthly assistance check wasn't even close to what she needed.

"You got two minutes," she said, as she opened the screen door.

Ruban thanked her and went inside. The living room was a cluttered mess. In fact, it wasn't used as a living room. An ironing board stood in the middle of it. Several damp loads from the morning wash hung on the drying racks. Mostly children's clothes. Lots of pink.

"How are you doing, Edith?"

Edith was a large woman with enormous flabby triceps that sagged over her elbows, and ankles so swollen that Ruban would have sworn she didn't have any. Her old sundress was at least two sizes too small, which didn't make it any easier to bend at the waist. Just lowering herself into a chair seemed to leave her breathless.

"How's it look like I'm doin'?"

"Mindy okay?" He meant his ex-girlfriend, Edith's only child.

"Locked up. Another parole violation. At least if she's in jail, I know she's not selling her body and doing drugs. I guess that's something to be thankful for. That can't be what you're here about—to talk about Mindy."

"No." Ruban moved to the edge of the couch, leveling his gaze at Edith. "I'm here about my daughter."

"Kyla ain't your daughter, Ruban. You never married her mother, and you gave up any possible paternal rights you had when I adopted her."

"I understand. And I regret that."

"Well, that's a damn shame. It's too late now."

"Is it?"

" 'Course it is. Kyla's lived with me her whole life. She'll be five years old next month."

Ruban paused, making sure he struck the right tone. "Edith, I was watching the children play soccer out on the street before I came up to your door. How many kids are you raising in this trailer?"

Edith glanced at the drying racks in the middle of the living room. "Three. Kyla, Alex, and Dylan. They share the other bedroom."

"How much longer can a girl share a room with two boys?"

"As long as she has to."

"Do the fathers help with the boys?"

"Mindy don't even know who the fathers are," she said. "You're the only boyfriend she ever had. And what a piece of shit you turned out to be."

Ruban averted his gaze, then looked her in the eye. "I'm sorry about that. I've changed."

"Yeah, so has Mindy. For the worse."

"I want to help."

She scoffed again, dubious. "Really? How?"

The backpack was at his feet. He picked it up and handed it to her. "Open it."

"What's this?"

"Have a look for yourself."

She unzipped it, peeked inside, and froze. "Money," she said, gasping. "My God, how much is this?"

"A hundred thousand dollars."

"Where did *you* get that kind of money?"

"I'm doing all right these days."

"Baloney."

"It doesn't matter where I got it," he said. "The question is: Do you want it?"

"What kind of question is that?"

Ruban replied in the most level, matter-of-fact tone he could muster. "Do you want it, Edith?"

"Well, of course I want it. Who wouldn't want a hundred thousand dollars? But I've been around the block. I know there ain't no such thing as somethin' for nothin'."

He spoke in the same even tone. "I want to adopt Kyla."

"Ha!" she said, half laughing, half scoffing. "You want Kyla?"

Ruban was deadpan, no change in his expression.

"Well, that's just beautiful," said Edith. "You want Kyla. *Kyla*. Do you think you can just walk in here and buy a little girl like she's for sale?"

His tone didn't change. "Yes. I do."

Silence. Ruban took it as a good sign. If it weren't in the cards, she would have thrown him out immediately.

"I love that child," said Edith.

"A hundred thousand dollars is my opening offer, Edith. It's negotiable."

"And she loves me."

"You make a strong case. You will be treated fairly. I'm sure we can agree on a number."

Edith blinked. Another good sign. Ruban saw a flicker of hope, a sparkle in her eye that bespoke the old Edith—the one who'd pretended to be deathly ill and then split ten thousand dollars with the doctor who'd billed Medicare for treatment never rendered.

"How can I be sure this money isn't counterfeit? For all I know, you went into some fancy copy center and printed it yourself."

"Take one. Pick any bill you like."

Ruban removed a stack from the backpack and laid the bills on the table, fanning them like playing cards. "Take a closer look," he said. "Some bills are crisp. Others are worn around the edges. These aren't freshly printed fakes with consecutive serial numbers. *These* have been circulated."

She seemed to take his point, but he could still see suspicion in her eyes.

"Take one," he said.

Edith pulled one from the middle of the stack.

"Keep it," said Ruban. "Take it to any department store in Miami. They'll check the watermark, test the paper with that colored marker pen they use. They'll tell you it's real. Then you call me."

Ruban rose. He reached for the backpack, but she held on to it for a second or two, and he could feel the pull as he retrieved it. A look of angst came over her as she finally let go of the money.

Ruban smiled thinly, then turned serious. "Don't worry. This offer is not going away. You think about it, and let me know. Good to see you again, Edith."

He swung the backpack over one shoulder and let himself out.

27

Pinky woke in the Red Room. Alone.

Closing time at Night Moves was five a.m., but it wasn't unusual for Pinky to find an empty bed in one of the private cabanas and sleep till noon on Saturday. It was a perk of being one of the club's "Select Gentlemen," a handful of members with "special talents" who weren't required to have a woman in their company to enter the club. They serviced the women of other members.

He fumbled in the darkness and found the dimmer switch on the wall. Even at full power it was mood lighting at best, which was fine. His eyes couldn't have handled an all-out assault.

His head pounded as he stepped out of the cabana. He wasn't sure what he'd been drinking all night, but it made everything a blur. Almost everything. He remembered leaving the bar with two women. It was a typical scenario. Their husbands had been dancing with other women most of the night, and the wives were curious to find out if the anatomical rumors about Pinky were true. As always, he was more than happy to deliver. Mornings after, how-ever, were getting more and more difficult.

Damn, my back hurts.

He straightened out the kink in his spine, pulled on his pants, and walked to the locker room. Mem-bers paid extra for a locker and shower access, but for the Select Gentlemen that was another freebie. Pinky had a prime locker directly across from the viewing window that looked out onto the "luv-nasium," where some of the hottest action in the club took place, usually around two a.m. He found his key and opened the locker. His shaving kit was on the top shelf, where he'd left it. His cash was not.

"Fucking bitches!"

Another five thousand dollars, picked clean. It was the second time since the heist that prostitutes claiming to be another man's wife had lured him into a cabana, plied him with a special BYOB con-coction until he passed out, and then cleaned out the cash from his locker. He could never prove it, of course. There were no cameras in the locker rooms, security or otherwise. He was starting to feel as stupid as his nephew at the Gold Rush.

At least I'm actually getting laid.

He showered, got dressed, and headed down the dimly lit hall to the exit. His friend stopped him in the lobby before he reached the door. It was the club owner, Jorge Calderón.

"I need to talk to you," said Calderón.

"What about?"

"In my office. It's important."

Pinky followed him. "Important" could mean a lot of things, especially between two old friends who'd known each other since their sophomore year at Miami Senior High School. They'd drifted apart after graduation but reconnected a decade later, when Calderón owned the body shop. Pinky couldn't count the number of stolen vehicles he'd pushed through Calderón's chop shop. Business was so good that Calderón had branched out with Night Moves. Pinky held no financial stake in either business, but the club benefits were definitely tangible.

"Have a seat," said Calderón.

Pinky settled into the chair. Calderón sat behind his desk.

"Bro, why so serious?" asked Pinky.

"I'm sorry, Pinky. I can't have you hanging here no more."

"What?"

"Every other Select Gentleman in my club is under thirty. You're forty-five. You had a good run. But it's time."

"But I don't look forty-five."

"Now you sound like Priscilla. Have you stood in front of a mirror lately?"

"So you're kicking me out of the club?"

"No. You're welcome to come if you bring a woman with you. But no more Select Gentleman status."

"This is really harsh, bro."

"It's nothing personal," said Calderón. "This is business."

"Business?"

"I'm grooming the club to sell it. I have investors coming in from Brazil, Singapore, all over. These people have a keen eye for what a club like this is worth. It has to be top notch. I can't have my Select Gentlemen asking for the AARP discount on their club dues."

"I'm not that old."

"You're closer than you think. The point is, if I'm going to get top dollar for this club, I have to get rid of the dinosaurs."

"Speaking of dinosaurs, size does matter."

"Not to these buyers. They're looking for a first-rate operation, with some style and flash, not a red-light-district freak show."

"Ouch. Now you're really getting harsh, bro."

"I'm sorry, but I'm not just testing the waters here to see what I can get. I need to sell this place."

Pinky's gaze drifted toward the montage of photographs on the wall. "Nurses Night." Pinky had been on fire at that event. *Hard to believe it was twelve years ago.*

"What if *I* buy the club?"

Calderón smiled and shook his head. "You can't raise that kind of dough."

Pinky had told his old friend nothing about his involvement in the heist, not a word about chopping the pickup truck at Calderón's shop, and even less about the job his bodywork mechanic had done with a blowtorch on Marco Aroyo.

"What if I could raise the money?"

"Get real, Pinky. I'm asking five million."

Pinky did the quick calculations. His share was $2.5 million. He still had Marco's share of one million. He'd blown through at least a hundred grand, but it wasn't beyond reach.

"Would you take four?"

"No way. Five is practically land value. My broker would lock me up in an insane asylum if I went a penny lower. And let's stop pretending like you even have four."

"Give me two weeks. I can get five."

"Are you serious?"

Pinky glanced at the photos on the wall again. Nurses galore, and his equipment had been just what the doctor ordered. "Never been more serious in my life, bro."

"His real name is Craig Perez," said Andie.

She'd stopped by the Littlefords' townhouse to update her supervisor, and she was on his patio again. Littleford had the Saturday edition of the *Miami Herald* in his lap. He was one of those tactile nostalgic types who clung to a real weekend newspaper, especially when relaxing in his Adirondack chair on a perfect south Florida afternoon in November. His gaze was fixed on a pair of blue jays in the poinciana tree as Andie filled him in about Pinky.

"I'd like to get a wiretap."

He turned his attention from the blue jays to Andie, thoroughly unimpressed. "You have a guy with a big schmeckle and one prior for auto theft who stopped by the tile depot looking for Marco Aroyo after the heist. Is that it?"

"And who also quit his job two days after the heist. I tracked that down this morning."

"Still not enough," said Littleford.

"I went back and watched the video from the

security cameras. Pinky has the same build as the perp with the gun. Similar walk, too."

"You're getting warm."

"No offense, Michael, but that would have been enough for my supervisor in Seattle."

"You're not in Seattle."

"I have a hunch about this one."

"A hunch isn't probable cause for a wiretap."

She had another angle, but just then Littleford's wife stepped out to say hello.

"Andie, hi there. So sorry you weren't able to meet up with my cousin John last night."

"Talk about a schmeckle," Littleford muttered.

"What was that, honey?" asked Barbara.

"Nothing," he said.

Barbara smiled at Andie. "Perhaps we can set something up for next weekend."

"I'll have to check my calendar."

"Please do," said Barbara. "And let me know. I'll leave you two alone now." She stepped back into the kitchen and closed the sliding glass door. Littleford apologized.

"No worries," said Andie. "Back to our man. Forget the wiretap for now. Let's put a tail on him. We don't need probable cause to do that."

"No, but we do need money. Between the tail on Al-varez and your undercover gig at Night Moves, we've already blown through half our surveillance budget."

"Can't you request an increase?"

"Not based on what you've told me. Look, Andie. Miami-Dade has the Marco Aroyo homicide investigation. From the FBI standpoint, this is basically a property crime that doesn't involve terrorism, cyber threats, public corruption, civil rights, or major crime syndicates. Unless this Pinky has a direct link to al-Qaeda, there's no chance in hell that I can get a budget increase to tail him."

The blue jays were fighting, drawing Andie's gaze toward the tree.

"Sorry," he said. "I didn't mean to sound condescending. But in the world we live in, my unit does more with less. It's expected. Frankly, I find it to be part of the challenge that gets me up every morning. Working a case means *working* a case, not putting in a budget request for the latest gadget that makes teenage boys in movie theaters say, '*Ooo, awesome.*'"

"Okay. I get it."

"I'm probably not helping my efforts to recruit you into the bank robbery unit, am I?"

"On the contrary. I really do get it."

They sat in silence for a moment. But a supervisor who believed in what he was doing and didn't try to oversell it—that only made Andie want to work harder.

"You have any objection if I tail him on my own time?" she asked.

"No, but understand that it truly will be in your free time. It doesn't count toward availability pay, you won't get credit for unscheduled duty, and you won't get reimbursed for any of your expenses."

She shrugged. "What else am I gonna do with my weekend? Have a blind date with Barbara's cousin?"

He smiled. "Keep me posted on what turns up. And, who knows? Maybe you'll get that wiretap after all."

"Count on it," she said.

28

•

On Tuesday morning, Ruban had a million-
dollar delivery to make. Rush hour was just
getting under way, and he was right on time.

Three lanes of northbound traffic crept along
U.S. 1 toward downtown Miami. The western
suburbs drained into the northerly flow from Bird
Road. In peak traffic, commuters could easily wait
at the intersection through four or five light cycles,
a good twenty minutes, just to make that dreaded
left turn. Shaded by the elevated Metrorail tracks
overhead, it was a prime panhandling opportunity
for anyone with the street credentials to work it. On
this Tuesday, like every Tuesday, it was up to Ruban
to decide who had what it takes and who didn't.
The usual homeless suspects rode in the backseat of
his car, with the notable exception of the previous
week's disaster, the guy who'd deposited the chief
symptom of irritable bowel syndrome on Ruban's
upholstery. The others had lost or forgotten their
"Please Help" signs—of course. Ruban gave them

new ones and sent them off with the standing order about the three-hundred-dollar minimum.

Chicken scratch, compared to what was in the backpack on the seat beside him.

Ruban pulled onto the shoulder and watched his team get into position. They knew the drill. No one walked straight toward the shade beneath the tracks and curled up for a nap, which was surprising. Usually, at least one joker sat down on the job from the get-go. Ruban did notice an old man going from car to car in the far lane, collecting a buck or two for the puppet figures he'd fashioned by hand from palm fronds. Grasshoppers and butterflies were his big sellers. He was an artist. He was also a squatter, operating without authority, and, technically, Ruban should have flexed his muscles and told him to beat it. This morning, however, he was in no mood for small-time Miami.

I can't wait to be done with this crap.

He put the car in gear and pulled back onto Bird Road. Westbound traffic was nonexistent, so he zipped right across the street to the parking lot in front of the convenience store, the designated meeting spot for the delivery.

Ruban felt good about this split. Pinky was a dirtbag. Jeffrey was a loser. Marco—who the hell knew how far out into the bay the river currents and tides had carried his body? But Octavio Alvarez had been his buddy since boyhood. They'd started boxing together at the gym as seven-year-olds, knocking each other around the ring, equally determined to be Cuba's next gold medalist. They used to watch the Cuban national *béisbol* team practice through a hole in the right-field fence, then scrape together their *moneda nacional* to buy a scoop of chocolate ice cream at the world-famous Coppelia. Test scores and other academic indicators landed them in separate high schools, and most of Ruban's friends at the Vocational Pre-University Institute of Exact Sciences stopped talking to him after he got kicked off the college track for violating the government's ban on access to the Internet. It didn't seem to matter that he hadn't been planning to overthrow the regime, that he'd been searching for information about his dead Russian father. Alvarez was the old friend who had stuck by him. More than stuck by him. "Let's get a raft to Florida," he'd told Ruban. So they did.

And, of course, if it hadn't been for Alvarez and his work at the armored-car company, there would have been no heist.

Ruban checked his rearview mirror. A homeless man was approaching from Bird Road. He was wearing blue jeans, an army jacket, a beanie, and sneakers. The gnarly beard and cheap sunglasses were the finishing touches on a convincing disguise. If Ruban hadn't known Alvarez was coming, he would never have known it was him. Ruban lowered the window.

Alvarez stepped up to the driver's side and held out his hand. "Got any spare change, Mr. Trump?"

Ruban handed him the backpack. He'd brought all hundreds for Octavio, to lighten the load, but a cubic foot of tightly packed currency was still a good twenty pounds. "Don't spend it all in one place."

"Thanks, bro."

"Good luck."

Alvarez slung the backpack over one shoulder, smiled, and walked away from the car. Ruban continued to watch in the rearview mirror. The westbound lanes on Bird Road were still clear, the rush-hour traffic headed in the opposite direction. Alvarez didn't even bother to look before crossing, or perhaps he'd looked but just didn't see. Ruban saw and heard it all—the flash of blue metal on wheels, the moment of panic as his friend froze in the middle of the street, the sickening thud of a human body on the losing end of a hip-to-hood collision with a speeding blue automobile.

"Octavio!"

The impact sent Alvarez flying at least thirty feet before he landed on the pavement. The car screeched to a halt, but Alvarez was motionless, his body a grotesque heap on the road. Ruban rushed from his car. His gaze locked on to Alvarez, but out of the corner of his eye he saw the man with the puppets made from palm fronds—the homeless artist—running toward Alvarez.

The artist grabbed the backpack, flung open the passenger-side door, and jumped in. The car sped off in reverse. With no plate on the front bumper Ruban couldn't get the license number. Only when the driver reached the end of the block did he back into a driveway, turn the car around, and squeal away. By then the car was too far away to see the plate on the rear bumper.

"Shit!"

Ruban started toward his friend, then stopped. Several other commuters had jumped out of their vehicles and were already tending to him. One was on a cell phone, presumably talking to 911. A pool of blood stained the pavement. Alvarez wasn't moving.

Ruban took another half-step forward, then stopped. His conscience was nudging him toward his friend and telling him to do all he could to help. Another voice told him that there was nothing he *could* do, at least not anything that other Good Samaritans weren't already doing. The most compelling message was also the most frightening: staying at the scene would mean talking to the police, which would link him directly to the armored-car insider who'd organized the heist.

Sorry, old friend.

Ruban gathered one last glimpse of the lifeless body in the road, then turned away and got into his car. He headed west out of the parking lot, against rush hour, no traffic to contend with. He checked his rearview mirror and saw the flashing lights. An ambulance and two squad cars were arriving. It was a good thing he'd left, and not just because the victim was Alvarez. As he drove away, one thought burned in his mind.

The guy driving the car, speeding away in reverse: he looked a lot like Pinky.

29
.

Savannah had a knot in her stomach.

It had nothing to do with her usual tasks at the daycare center. Drop-off went smoothly. Flagpole proceeded as usual: *I pledge a lesion, to the flag* . . . Only two kids wet their pants during the early-morning recess. The cause of her indigestion was the scheduled follow-up meeting with the Department of Children and Family Services. It was supposed to happen at nine a.m. while her three-year-olds were in "movement" class with the dance instructor. Betty could have really good news for her. Or really, really bad.

At five minutes before nine, Betty phoned from her car. She was in the daycare parking lot and wanted Savannah to step outside to meet her.

The knot tightened.

Savannah quickly herded her children into the playroom. The kids were supposed to sit cross-legged in a big circle for movement class, but Savannah's class was more like an amoeba. A colleague helped her out, and Savannah tried not to appear too distressed as she excused herself, exited the building, and found Betty standing beside her hatchback.

"Savannah, I'm sorry to call you out to the parking lot, but I was afraid there might be tears in front of the children."

It was a dagger to the heart. "I'm not going to be approved?"

She shook her head. "No. You're not approved."

Savannah took a breath. When Betty had said "there might be tears," Savannah had reached inside herself and vowed there wouldn't be. Yet she found herself wiping one away.

"Is it because of . . ." She stopped and glanced over her shoulder to make sure no one was within earshot. "Because of Ruban?"

"Yes."

"But you told me that his criminal record was not a definite bar."

"That was true," Betty said. "There are circumstances where DCF can work around it, depending on what the conviction was for. Especially if it was a long time ago."

"Ruban was eighteen. A teenager. Did you tell the review committee that?"

"I did."

"I don't get it. If ever there was a case with—what did you call it? Circumstances?"

"Mitigating circumstances."

"Right. This is one of those cases. It's a proven fact that organized criminals in Miami would go down to Havana and tell teenage boys they could have a free ride to Florida. Ruban took the bait, and then when he got here, they told him he had to hijack a truckload of designer jeans or something, or they would send him back to Cuba. He got caught, and he did his time. He wasn't deported. He straightened himself out and is a U.S. citizen. There's no reason he shouldn't be a father."

Betty didn't answer.

"So . . . don't you agree with me?" asked Savannah.

The social worker looked away, then back. "Let me say this: I don't think you're lying to me."

"No, I'm not lying. It's the truth."

Betty hesitated, as if searching for the right words. "When I say I don't think you're lying, I mean that in my judgment you absolutely believe it to be true."

"Of course I believe it. I confronted my husband about this when the private agency told me he had a felony conviction. He told me the whole story."

"Yes. That's what he told you: a story."

Savannah's defensive instincts kicked in, and she had to check herself to keep from speaking too loudly. "Are you accusing him of making this up?"

"I'm very sorry to be the one to tell you this, Savannah. We did a thorough background check on your husband. He was convicted of a felony, but it wasn't when he was a teenager, and it wasn't for hijacking a truck."

Savannah glanced toward the older children on the other side of the fence. An argument was brewing on the monkey bars. Another assistant handled it. Savannah refocused. "When was it?"

"You really don't know?"

"Apparently not."

"His first conviction was five years ago."

"That was before we met. But wait: *first* conviction? There's more than one?"

"I'm afraid so.

"What for?"

"Domestic violence."

That knot in her stomach was only getting worse. "That's not possible. I'm his first wife."

"I understand your confusion. Florida is one of the few states with old laws on the books making it a crime to cohabitate, but fortunately the legislature saw fit to extend domestic-violence protection where a man and a woman are unmarried but in the same household. Your husband was living with his accuser."

"Well, domestic violence can mean a lot of things."

"Yes, it can. And all too often it's a pattern of conduct. That's why I came here today. I didn't want to just make a phone call and cancel the appointment." She reached out and gently touched Savannah's hand. "I'm worried for you."

A warm breeze rustled the palm trees behind them, but Savannah suddenly felt chills. "What did he do?"

Betty reached into her satchel and pulled out the DCF file. "Is there someplace we can go to discuss this?"

"No. I don't want to go anywhere. Tell me now. Tell me exactly what Ruban did."

Betty cracked open the file and put on her reading glasses. "Let's start at the beginning," she said.

30

A white tarp lay atop the pavement in the ghostly form of a life cut short. Yellow tape cordoned off a block-long stretch of Bird Road, from busy U.S. 1 to the corner convenience store.

"Special Agent Henning," Andie said with a flash of her badge to the perimeter control officers.

Police beacons swirled atop a half dozen squad cars, and sparks belched from a line of roadside flares, as Florida Highway Patrol directed traffic toward a slow-moving detour. The reroute affected only westbound traffic, but rubberneckers in the eastbound rush hour were doing their best to make everyone late for work. A crowd watched from a parking lot. Several snapped photographs, seizing the opportunity to update their Facebook page with something more exciting than the usual captivating close-up of what they were eating for breakfast. Two ambulances were on the scene, but paramedics were in standby mode, nothing to be done. A plain white van from the medical examiner's office was parked in the outer lane, its rear doors agape, a gurney at the ready. The black T-shirts worn by the MDPD investigators were standard-issue, but they seemed to underscore the fact that this was indeed a fatality, a cause for mourning.

"Lieutenant Watts is right over there," the officer said as Andie ducked beneath the police tape. "Next to the body."

The 911 callers had described the victim as a homeless Hispanic man, but the first officer on the scene quickly noted the fake beard. It was equally strange that a homeless man would carry a wallet with a valid driver's license and a current employee identification card from Braxton Security. Andie was on the scene before official confirmation that it was the same Octavio Alvarez who was a person of interest in the MIA heist.

"That's definitely him," Andie said as she peeled back the tarp.

Watts was at her side, along with Sergeant Collins from the MDPD Traffic Homicide Unit. A media helicopter whirred overhead, drawing their attention from the bloodied asphalt to the crisp blue sky.

"What do we know about the vehicle?" asked Andie.

"Blue two-door sedan," said Collins. "Witnesses don't agree on the make or model. That may not sound like much to go on, but this is my ninety-first hit-and-run this year. 'Blue two-door sedan' is more than we started with in better than half of them."

"Did anyone get the tag?" asked Andie.

"Yeah. Ran it. No connection to any blue sedan.

It's from a jeep that was reported stolen eight weeks ago."

It was premature to point out every possible connection between the heist and the hit-and-run, but Andie made a mental note that the body shop that chopped a certain black Ford pickup would also be a ready source of stolen license plates.

A detective from the traffic homicide unit approached. "Got something," he told the lieutenant. Andie listened as they talked. It was about a homeless man selling origami grasshoppers made out of palm fronds. Three witnesses had seen him grab the victim's backpack, jump in the car, and flee with the hit-and-run driver.

"Get those witnesses down to the station for an artist composite," said Watts.

"Will do, sir."

He left quickly, so Andie put her question to Watts. "Are there cameras at this intersection?"

"None," said Watts.

"How soon can you get the manpower to check the business establishments along the street? Their security cameras could have picked up the car, or Mr. Homeless Origami, maybe even the driver."

"We'll get to it," said Collins. "But keep in mind that this is a hit-and-run accident, not a terrorist threat to blow up the Port of Miami."

The FBI wasn't the only law enforcement agency to feel the pinch of budgetary priorities. "I'll see if I can get assistance from my tech agents," said Andie.

The MDPD officers thanked her, and Andie excused herself. Octavio Alvarez was a major point of overlap between the heist and the hit-and-run, but Andie didn't want the MDPD traffic unit to become the proverbial tail wagging the dog. She found a quiet place in the parking lot, dialed Littleford, and quickly filled him in.

"Can't think of a single good reason for an armored-truck driver to be out on the street pretending to be homeless," said Littleford.

"Neither can I," said Andie. "I see this as a prearranged meeting to deliver to Alvarez his cut from the heist. He knew he'd be under FBI scrutiny, so he came disguised as homeless."

"Why would he choose such a busy intersection at the height of rush hour?"

"The same reason a drug dealer chooses to make a drop on Lincoln Road Mall at lunchtime. If you don't totally trust the other side of the transaction, do it in a public place where you're less likely to end up staring down the barrel of a gun."

"So, no guns here—but they ran him over."

"That's how I see it. This hit-and-run was no accident."

"Is that what MDPD is saying?"

"Not yet, but look at the facts. No skid marks; I could see that with my own eyes. The driver put stolen tags on his vehicle to keep us from tracking him down. An accomplice on the street not only grabbed the backpack but probably alerted the driver when Alvarez arrived. They knew Alvarez was going to be here today, ran him down, and took off with a backpack full of money."

"We don't know that money was inside."

"But it's a fair assumption, given what happened

to Marco Aroyo. You predicted it: the crooks are turning against each other. Now we have two dead, and somewhere in this band of thieves is a pig collecting all the acorns."

"Definitely plausible," said Littleford. "Where do you want to go with this?"

"Surveillance."

"On who?"

"Pinky. I spent all day Sunday tailing him on my own time. I e-mailed you some photographs. Did you look at them?"

"I did," said Littleford.

"I see a resemblance to the armed suspect in the video from the MIA security cameras. Don't you?"

"I see two men wearing ski masks and dark sunglasses."

"I'm talking about body type."

"Yeah, I suppose there's *some* resemblance," said Littleford.

"Enough to put a line in our budget for surveillance on him?"

"Enough to put a written commendation in your file for tailing him on your day off and on your own dime."

"Gee, thanks."

"Drawing conclusions from facial comparisons in photographs is difficult enough. I've used body comparisons to corroborate facial comparison, but a body comparison alone is pretty flimsy stuff."

A noisy bus passed on the street, spewing diesel fumes. Andie plugged one ear. "We're talking about one investigative tool, not the key piece of evidence in a criminal trial."

"Does Pinky own a blue sedan like the one in the hit-and-run?"

"No. But he's done time for auto theft. He could have easily gotten his hands on one before coming here."

"Let's wait and see. You did the right thing telling MDPD to check for video from private security cameras. If we get a good enough shot of the driver for our experts to do facial mapping and confirm some similarities to Pinky, I'll green-light the surveillance."

"By the time we get that video, Pinky could be long gone."

"Do you have evidence that he's about to flee?"

"He's been living out of a hotel, never goes home. If Priscilla over at Night Moves wasn't trying to be my new best friend, I would've never known where to find him. Come on, boss. This is time sensitive. Are you really going to make me beg?"

"Don't beg," he said. "And don't take this the wrong way, either, but . . ."

"But what?"

He sighed so heavily that, even on the phone, Andie could feel the sage about to impart his wisdom.

"It goes back to the unit assignment you requested when you transferred to Miami," he said. "I'm still hoping you stay in bank robbery. But in the subconscious world of showing the FBI where you really belong, maybe a part of you wants the big break in this case to come from a lead you developed in an undercover role."

"Are you psychoanalyzing me, boss?"

"It's called mentoring."

Andie knew better than to disrespect a well-meaning supervisor, but it bugged her that he thought she was "subconsciously" angling for a way out of his bank robbery unit. "Is that what you really think? Pinky's resemblance to the suspect in the warehouse video is me seeing what I want to see?"

"A tattoo, a guy with one arm, or some other distinctive physical attribute would be one thing. But in this case we can't even compare the guy's hands, because the crooks were wearing gloves. If we could take grainy CCTV video and identify suspects based on subjective comparisons of body types, we'd have a hundred-percent arrest and conviction rate in every case involving cameras."

"Pinky isn't someone I plucked from the general population. He was Marco Aroyo's friend."

"I understand."

"You're leaving me no choice but to bring him in for questioning. As soon as I do, Pinky will book a one-way trip to Timbuktu, and he'll probably take Aroyo's and Alvarez's share of the heist with him."

He paused, which Andie took as a sign that she was getting through to him. She pushed a little harder. "Look, I totally get your message about the budget. I understand that everything we do in this unit needs to yield results. But I wouldn't have spent my day off following Pinky if I thought this was just a shot in the dark."

There was silence on the line, which was better than a knee-jerk no. Another bus passed on the street, this one noisier than the last.

"I tell you what," said Littleford. "I'll send it to

the Digital Evidence Laboratory for a quick look and have a forensic expert compare your photographs to the security-camera video. Maybe they'll latch onto something distinctive."

"And if the expert sees what I see? Then what?"

"I'll push through the funding for surveillance on Pinky."

Yes. "Thank you."

"Don't thank me. Just catch me a crook before these dumb sons of bitches kill each other off and the money's gone for good."

"You got it," said Andie.

31

.

Ruban drove to his mother-in-law's house and waited until 11:30 a.m., which seemed long enough for the "accident" scene to clear. It was time to go back.

The hit-and-run driver was Pinky. Ruban was almost sure of it. Who else knew about the prearranged meeting with Alvarez? Ruban had said too much, way too much, when he'd chewed Pinky out for dropping the ball on Marco's cut—for not making a plan like the one Ruban had made with Alvarez: *"Third Tuesday, eight a.m., corner of U.S. 1 and Bird. Boom. Octavio knows to be there."* Thanks to Ruban, Pinky knew to be there, too. Pinky and his "homeless" friend, whoever he was. Ruban had to find out.

"Beatriz, I need to borrow your car."

Ruban's car was in her garage, where it would stay. He had to assume that police would interview his homeless crew about the accident. Each was under a standing order *never* to tell the police who they worked for or how they got to the intersection, but these were not Navy SEALs, impervious to interrogation. They didn't know Ruban's name, but they could describe his vehicle. Never again would his wheels see the light of day.

"Jeffrey needs my car to get his cereal when he wakes up," said Beatriz.

"Cereal?"

"*Sí.* He wake up every day at noon. I ask, 'Jeffrey, where you going?' He say, 'To buy cornflakes.'"

Poor Beatriz, born long before the advent of the breakfast-buffet code for drugs. Cornflakes was cocaine, butter was crack, cocoa puffs were cocaine with marijuana, and so on.

"Fry him an egg," said Ruban, a vague allusion to the old public service announcement. He grabbed the keys and was out the door.

Rush hour had ended, but each November marked the return of snowbirds to Miami, so it took Ruban nearly an hour to drive through the gauntlet of New York, New Jersey, and Ontario license plates back to the intersection. Traffic had resumed a normal flow, no police tape or squad cars on the scene. The only sign of what had happened were the remains of expired road flares, a scorched chain of burn marks on the pavement. Ruban stopped at the red light, lowered the window, and waited for the homeless Iraq War vet to approach.

"Round up the crew," said Ruban.

"Huh?" he said, not recognizing Ruban at first. Then it kicked in. "Oh, hey. Whaddaya mean round everyone up? We're not even close to earning out." He meant the daily three-hundred dollar minimum.

Ruban slipped him a fifty. "I'm covering you

today. Get the group together and meet me at the entrance to the Metrorail station."

The traffic light changed, and Ruban drove around the block to the station. He parked the car, purchased four one-way rail passes from the machine, and waited outside the turnstiles. Five minutes later, his crew walked up. It was turning into a hot day, and four hours of standing in the sun had his team sweating out some head-spinning odors. Ruban sat them down on a bench in the shade by the parking garage. The pregnant young woman who wasn't actually pregnant started to complain about cutting the day short, but Ruban made good on his promise to pay, which shut her up. Then he started his interrogation.

"There was a homeless guy selling grasshoppers made out of palm fronds this morning," said Ruban. "I need to find him. Anybody seen him before?"

The vet shook his head. So did the others.

"Did any of you see the accident this morning?"

"Saw it after it happened," said the vet.

"Did anyone actually see it happen?"

More shaking of heads.

"Did any of you talk to the police?"

Silence. Ruban had made it clear never to talk to the police, and he was sensing a breach of the rules. "I'm not going to get mad at anyone for telling me what happened," he said as he opened his wallet. "There's another fifty here for anyone who cuts through the bullshit."

The vet spoke up. "Cops interviewed all of us. Asked us the same questions you're asking now."

"What'd you tell them?"

"Nothing."

Ruban went right down the line—*you, you, you?* They all said the same. Nothing about the accident, nothing about the guy selling grasshoppers, nothing about their arrangement with Ruban.

Ruban could have stopped there, but if Pinky had turned against him and Octavio, it was a declaration of war. He had to be absolutely sure. He searched the Internet on his phone and found Pinky's mug shot from the Florida Department of Corrections website. He didn't want to plant his idea in their minds that Pinky had been the hit and-run driver, so he kept his question general.

"Any of you seen this guy before?" he asked, showing the photo.

Three heads were shaking. The vet took a closer look. "Never seen him in person. But I saw his picture."

"When?"

"One of the cops showed me. Wanted to know if I ever seen him. Looks just like that guy there," he said, pointing at Ruban's phone.

"Which cop asked you that?"

"A woman. Don't know her name. She wasn't dressed like a cop."

Ruban recalled Octavio's description of the FBI agent who had interviewed him at Braxton. "Was she good-looking?"

"I'd do her."

"You'd do a fruit bat with rabies."

"She was *very* pretty," said the unpregnant woman.

Ruban elicited a few more details, then gave each

of them another fifty and a one-way Metro pass. "I want all of you to go back downtown and keep your mouths shut. You got that?"

They nodded.

"Good," said Ruban. "Now get lost."

He watched them push through the turnstiles and made sure they got on the escalator leading to the elevated platform. Then he walked to his car. A bad day was only getting worse. A dead friend. A back-stabbing relative with an unknown accomplice. And now an FBI agent was on a trail that could lead her right through Pinky and all the way to Ruban. He got in the car and closed the door. His phone rang before he could start the engine. It was Jeffrey.

Just what I need.

"Bro, why'd you take the car?" asked Jeffrey. "I gotta be somewhere."

"I heard. Cornflakes run, huh?"

Jeffrey laughed the way druggies laughed when they thought they were so clever. "Yeah. Corn-flakes. You got a problem with that?"

"I got more problems than you can imagine, but this one I can solve right now. I'm putting you on a diet. You understand what I'm saying?"

"Sure, bro. But that just makes more problems. If I don't get my cornflakes, my memory comes back. I start remembering shit like who was at the ware-house that night. Pretty sure it wasn't just me and my uncle. I seem to recall this third guy. It's still kind of fuzzy. I can see his face, but can't quite re-member his name. Maybe Savannah would know it."

Ruban was seething. The contrite, boyish Jeffrey who had wanted Ruban's approval was gone. *Drugs.*

"You piece of shit. Are you threatening me?"

"No. You're doing this to yourself. I turn into a total asshole when I don't get my cornflakes. Pick some up on the way home."

He hung up. The screen on Ruban's phone went dark, but as he laid it on the console, an image re-appeared. It was the mug shot of Pinky that he'd retrieved earlier.

What a fucked-up family, he said to himself, which triggered another thought entirely. He knew what drugs could do to someone's personality, but he wondered if Jeffrey's new attitude was more than just an addict in need of a fix. Ruban wondered if Uncle Douchebag had been talking to his nephew.

Don't get paranoid.

He started the engine, pulled away from the station, and drove toward Café Ruban, avoiding the intersection that had changed everything.

32

·

A text message told Ruban to meet Savannah at the bus stop at six p.m. Normally he picked her up right at the daycare center, but she didn't answer when he texted back to ask about the change. He spotted her at the bus shelter on the corner, seated on a bench, waiting. He pulled up to the curb and reached over to unlock the door. Savannah climbed into the passenger seat.

"Why are you driving Mom's car?" she asked.

Ruban steered into the flow of evening rush hour. Their car was still in his mother-in-law's garage, but the truth was way too complicated.

"Our car is shot," he said. "The mechanic wants two grand to fix it. Time for a new one."

"With what money?"

"We'll figure it out."

"Just don't touch any of Jeffrey's."

Jeffrey's money. Ruban was relieved to hear her put it that way. It meant that Jeffrey had not yet regained his memory about Ruban's involvement, even though Ruban hadn't brought him cornflakes.

"Wouldn't touch it," he said.

Dusk was turning to darkness. The streetlamps flickered on. Ruban glanced over, but Savannah was looking straight ahead into the fuzzy glow of oncoming headlights.

"So. What's up with picking you up at the bus stop?"

"I spoke with the Department of Children and Family Services today," she said.

Ruban bristled. "Savannah, I told you I didn't want to go that route."

"I thought it was worth a shot. I was wrong. Not only did they say no way on adoption but the social worker also said it was best for you not to come on the campus anymore."

"That's bullshit. So from now on I have to drop you off and pick you up at the bus stop?"

"Yes."

"They're treating me like a child molester because of a dumbass conviction when I was a teenager?"

"No," said Savannah. "Because of a conviction for domestic violence that you didn't tell me about."

Oh, shit.

"Ruban? I want the truth."

She was looking right at him, her laser-like gaze intense enough to burn through metal. Ruban pulled into a gas station and parked. He gathered his thoughts before speaking.

"Her name was Mindy," he said. "We lived together for eight months."

"Did you hurt her?"

"No."

"What did you do to her?"

"Nothing."

"Men don't get convicted of domestic violence for doing nothing."

"They do when women lie."

"So this Mindy is a liar? Is that your answer?"

Ruban looked away, toward the motorists vying for a spot at the gas pumps, then back. "Mindy was a mess. Not as bad as your brother, but bad enough for me to tell her I was moving out if she didn't stop the drugs. A week later, I came home from work and found her totally strung out on meth. That was it."

"You left?"

"Tried to leave. She went berserk."

"Meaning what?"

"The whole scene was sick. She was crying, hanging on to me, promising never to do it again. It went beyond begging me to stay. I was shoving my things into a suitcase, and she kept pulling them out and stuffing them back into the drawer. Finally, I just decided to leave everything and go. She grabbed onto me, and I shook her loose. That's when her temper took over. She started hitting me."

"Did you hit her back?"

"No. Never. I just kept walking."

"What did she do?"

He hesitated, his gaze again shifting toward the gas pumps. "You really want to know?"

"Yes. I want to know."

He looked her in the eye, her face aglow from the dashboard light. "She ripped off her blouse, called me a user, and said I should fuck her one more time because that's all I ever wanted anyway. Then she ran into the bedroom and got my gun."

Savannah caught her breath. "She was going to shoot you?"

"I didn't wait to find out. I went for the gun and managed to take it away from her. That's when the cops showed up. The neighbors heard us arguing and dialed 911."

"Did you tell them what happened?"

"Didn't get the chance. They rushed in with weapons drawn. First thing they saw was Mindy on the floor with her blouse ripped off and me standing over her with a pistol in my hand. In ten seconds they had me facedown with my hands cuffed behind my back. They took Mindy into the bedroom to talk to her away from me. The story she told them was that she was kicking me out of the apartment and I refused to leave—that I pulled a gun and started ripping off her clothes."

Savannah blinked twice, as if it were too much to process. "That's unbelievable."

"Yeah, that's a good word for it," said Ruban. "Because nobody believed me. They believed Mindy."

"Did the police give her a lie-detector test?"

"If they did, they didn't tell me about it."

"Is there any way you can prove she was lying?"

"You want me to *prove* it to you?"

"Not to me," she said, suddenly energized, as if a bright idea had come to her. "To the adoption agencies that turned us down. Maybe they'd change their mind if we could prove that your conviction was based on a lie."

"How could I possibly prove that? Mindy and I were the only people in the room."

"If you could find some way—"

"Savannah, *forget* the adoption agencies," he said, a little too firmly.

The sparkle in her eye faded, gone as quickly as it had appeared. "Forget them? I've explored everything. DCF was our last option, and now *they've* said no."

"We don't need DCF. We don't need the adoption agencies."

"We do if we want to adopt a child!"

He heard the distress in her voice—had heard it many times before. He reached across the console and took her hand. "Actually, we don't. We really don't."

"What are you getting at?"

"There's one more thing you should know about me and Mindy."

His tone was apologetic, but Savannah seemed to sense the excitement in his voice, too. He was eager to move beyond saying how sorry he was for what had happened after the motorcycle accident; he was finally able to fix it.

"What is it, Ruban?"

He swallowed hard and took a breath. And then he told her.

33

The sun was setting in her rearview mirror as Andie drove across the causeway to Miami Beach. Special Agent Benny Sosa was with her, but this time it was no undercover date at Night Moves. Andie had the much more delicate assignment of interviewing Octavio Alvarez's girlfriend less than twelve hours after his death. They were about ten minutes from Westwind Apartments when Andie phoned Lieutenant Watts for the latest on the hit-and-run.

"The only development is more of a nondevelopment," said Watts.

"Meaning what? Nobody called in and confessed?"

"That happens," said Watts. "But let me give you a more common 'for instance.' Driver runs over a pedestrian. Driver panics and flees the scene. Driver talks to a smart lawyer. Driver parks his car in the Grove ghetto with the door wide open and the motor running, then calls MDPD and reports that it was stolen an hour or two before the accident."

Andie kept her cynicism in check, but she was suddenly thinking about Barbara Littleford and her poor, available cousin: *How do you feel about lawyers, Andie?* "If I hear you correctly, no one called in today to report that his blue sedan was stolen a few hours before this morning's hit-and-run."

"That would be correct," said Watts.

"So, what does that tell you?"

"The driver could be afraid to come forward. Maybe he thinks a witness got a look at him. Could be a warrant out for his arrest. Maybe he's an illegal alien."

Maybe he's afraid the police will recognize him as the gunman in the heist. "Keep me posted," she said.

Andie thanked him and hung up as the causeway fed her into the North Miami Beach version of Main Street. Palm trees lined the sidewalks. Locals strolled past mom-and-pop restaurants and shops where customers were known by name. Delis and corner markets that were strictly kosher. A gas station that was full service. Westwind Apartments was well away from the older, traditional neighborhood. The two-story white building was just a short walk from the ocean, popular with beach lovers, catering to a mixture of overnight hotel guests, seasonal renters, and year-round tenants. Andie found a parking spot on the street, right behind a long row of Vespas, the Italian-made motor scooters that were *the* method of transportation in Miami Beach for anyone who fancied himself immortal and zipped around, oblivious to the fact that to the average driver in south Florida scooters were the equivalent of bugs on a windshield.

Andie and Sosa checked in with the attendant at the front desk, who directed them down the hall to apartment 103. A young woman answered, and Andie identified herself with a flash of her badge. "I'm sorry for your loss," said Andie, "but we'd like to talk to you about Octavio Alvarez."

"I already talked to Miami-Dade police. What's this about?"

Andie made a strategic decision not to mention the heist. If Jasmine knew about it, she'd say nothing; and whether she knew about it or not, pointed questions from the FBI would only put her on the defensive and shut down the conversation. "Just a follow-up. Gathering as many facts as we can about the hit-and-run."

It was enough to get invited inside.

Jasmine Valore was a pretty brunette with the toned body of someone who had no cause for embarrassment at the beach. She wore jeans shorts, flip-flops, and a tank top, just like every other young woman Andie had seen on her way into the building. A background check had told Andie that she was a graduate of Miami Beach Senior High and a part-time student at Miami Dade College with no criminal record. She lived alone in a small one-bedroom apartment. The smell of cooked oatmeal wafted from the tiny kitchen, a reasonably healthy dinner for a young woman on a budget. The living room was tidy, but space was severely limited; Jasmine had to move her bicycle to make room for guests to sit on the couch.

"This doesn't even seem real to me," said Jasmine, her voice hollow. "I can't believe Octavio is gone."

"How long did you know him?"

"A few months. I met him at a party and we got to be friends at first. We started going out over the summer."

"Sorry to be personal, but how well did you know him?"

She shrugged. "He was my boyfriend. He would stay here sometimes. I stayed at his place. We weren't talking about moving in together or getting engaged, if that's what you're asking."

"Are you involved in the funeral arrangements?"

"Yeah. He has no one else. His entire family still lives in Cuba. Braxton is paying for everything. It was part of his benefits. They don't pay squat to their armored-car drivers, but at least they have insurance to cover burial costs if something happens."

"When you say they don't pay squat, is that something Octavio told you?"

"Every once in a while."

"Did he ever talk about ways to fix that?"

"Like what? Winning the lottery?"

"No. Just anything."

Jasmine glanced out the window, her expression turning more serious as her gaze drifted back to Andie. "There was one thing. We had a pretty big argument when I found out about it. I didn't like it."

Andie reeled in her anticipation. "Tell me."

"The detective from MDPD told me that Octavio was dressed like a homeless guy. I didn't mention this to him, but maybe I should have. All the panhandling at that intersection is controlled. Octavio had a piece of the action. He drove downtown once a week to round up a group of homeless people and took them to Bird Road. They split the money."

That was news to Andie, but it wasn't what she was hoping to hear. "That's it?"

"Yeah. Octavio told me it wasn't illegal, but I thought it was scummy."

"Do you think that's what he was doing at the intersection this morning?"

"It's the only thing that makes sense to me. Maybe he dressed up like a homeless guy and was sort of working undercover, you know? Checking up on his team, making sure they weren't goofing off or stealing from him. I just wish he would've listened to me and dropped that stupid gig." She sniffled back the first sign of tears. "Maybe this wouldn't have happened."

Andie studied her expression. Either Jasmine knew nothing about the heist, or she deserved an Academy Award. Andie backed off.

"If I may ask, what are you doing for the funeral arrangements?"

Jasmine sighed. "The funeral home pretty much takes care of it. They work with the insurance company to pick out the casket and such. Mostly I've been making phone calls, sending e-mails and text messages, letting Octavio's friends know what happened."

"Can I ask you a favor? I'd really like to have a list of the people you've called."

"Well . . ." Jasmine hesitated, but Andie didn't read it as anything more than the normal pushback to any invasion of privacy. "Why do you want that?"

Andie continued to steer clear of the heist. "We

think the driver in the hit-and-run may be someone who knows Octavio."

"You mean a friend of his? That's terrible. Why would you think that?"

"If you were Octavio's wife, I would share that level of detail. But as it is, I hope you'll work with us and understand that your list could be very useful to our investigation."

"I don't really have a list. I've just been calling people as I think of it."

"Could you give me the names of his closest friends?"

Jasmine got her phone from the coffee table and rattled off a few names and numbers. Andie jotted them down. None was familiar, and Pinky was not among them.

"Any others?" asked Andie.

"I'm sure I forgot someone," said Jasmine. "It's a work in progress, especially with Octavio's older friends. I could make a final list and give it to you."

"Perfect," said Andie. "There's one other thing I'd like you to do. When is the funeral?"

"Thursday or Friday. It depends on when the medical examiner releases the body."

"Is there an online registry where people can post memories of Octavio or express condolences?"

"Yeah, that's part of the package deal with the funeral home. It should be up tonight."

"Good. Here's what I want you to do. Before the funeral, make a list of everyone you think should be there. After the funeral, circle the name of anyone on that list who doesn't show up. Then go through the list again. If someone whose name is circled didn't call you, didn't respond to your text or e-mail, or didn't go to the online registry to post something, I want you to put a star next to that person's name. Can you do that?"

"Yes. Of course. But can I ask you a question?"

"Sure."

"Is there someone in particular you're looking for?"

"The answer to that is yes," said Andie.

"You're not going to tell me his name, are you?"

Andie shook her head. "No, Jasmine. You are."

34
.

Ruban was waiting for a response, any response, but Savannah appeared numb. They were still parked in her mother's car at the gas station, Savannah staring through the windshield at nothing.

"You have a child?" she said finally. It wasn't really a question. More of an expression of disbelief. "And you never told me?"

"I didn't even know Mindy was pregnant when I moved out. It was one of the reasons my lawyer advised me to plead guilty and avoid jail time. I told him the abuse charges were all a lie, but he said I would have to be crazy to stand trial with a pregnant ex-girlfriend accusing me."

Finally, she looked at him. Half of her face was in darkness, the other half aglow from the lights around the gas station. "I don't know what to say, Ruban."

"You're acting like this is totally a bad thing."

"How is it a good thing?"

"Don't you see what I'm getting at, Savannah? Kyla could be our child. We could adopt her."

Her mouth fell open. "No, we can't."

"I'm serious. We can make this happen."

"*Make* it happen? You can't just throw something like this at me, before you even know if I *want* it to happen."

"But this is what you've always wanted."

"Yes, but not like this. 'Hey, honey, I had a child with another woman. Hey, let's adopt her. Hey, isn't that a great idea?' Shit, Ruban."

"So you'd adopt a stranger's child, but not *my* child?"

"I didn't say that. Don't make me the bad guy here."

Ruban reached for his phone. "I took a picture of her. Let me show—"

"No! Don't do that to me."

Ruban paused for a moment, just long enough for the tension to break. "Sorry. You're right. That's not fair."

"No, not fair at all," said Savannah. "Because even if I wanted this to happen, it *can't*. You're talking in circles. A felony conviction for domestic violence is a deal killer for adoption. Period. End of story."

"No," he said. "There is one clear exception."

"There's no exception," said Savannah. "I talked to DCF."

"Not about this, you didn't: I'm allowed to adopt my own biological child, if I can get the consent of everyone who has parental rights."

Savannah blinked hard, as if trying to make sense of it. "Honestly, I don't know if that's true or not.

But put that aside. You were convicted of domestic violence. Why would your ex-girlfriend consent to the adoption?"

"Kyla's mother is irrelevant. She's in jail. Kyla's grandmother—Edith—is the only person with parental rights. She adopted Kyla."

"Fine. Why would Kyla's grandmother consent after you were convicted of abusing her daughter? This is a hopeless situation."

"I've talked to Edith. She's willing to let the adoption go through."

Savannah did a double take. "I don't understand. How could she do that?"

"Think about it, Savannah: Would Edith consent to the adoption if the domestic violence charges against me were valid?"

He could almost see her mind at work, but he didn't wait for her response. "The answer is clearly *no*," he said. "Mindy's own mother knows that those accusations and my conviction were bogus. That's the only reason she would consent."

Savannah still seemed troubled. "I just don't understand. Even if it was all a lie, why would anyone give up a child she adopted and raised for almost five years?"

Ruban hesitated. It was the moment of truth: the cash.

"She's not just giving Kyla up to anyone. I *am* the father. She's also raising two other kids that Mindy had with other men, so Edith has more than she can handle. I think she feels guilty about the way the whole conviction went down, and how it's keeping us from adopting our own child now. And . . ."

"And what?"

Back to that moment of truth. Money, money, money. Ruban couldn't go there. "I told her about you. What a great mother you would be."

"Really?"

"Yeah. The way this played out, it was *all* about you. That was the tipping point."

Savannah's expression started to change, as did her posture. She seemed to be opening up. "I'm going to think about this."

"You should."

"I'm not promising that I'm going to say this is a good idea."

"I understand."

"But if we do move forward, when can I meet her?"

"Kyla?"

Savannah shook her head. "No, no. We're nowhere near that point. Edith. I would want to talk to Kyla's grandmother first."

"Oh."

She was waiting for more. Ruban was searching for words.

"'Oh'?" said Savannah. "That's all you can say?"

"I hadn't really thought about you meeting Edith."

"You didn't think we would adopt Kyla without me meeting the grandmother, did you?"

"Is that really necessary?"

Savannah shot him an expression of curiosity. "Is there some reason you don't *want* me to meet her?"

"No. Not at all."

"Is there some reason she wouldn't want to meet me?"

"Not than I can think of."

"Okay, then, there you have it. Why don't you see if you can make that happen?"

"A meeting? Between you and Edith?"

"Or the three of us, if that's more comfortable for her."

Ruban drew a breath. It wasn't the plan he'd envisioned, but he saw no conceivable way to convince Savannah that the meeting shouldn't happen. Unless, of course, Edith refused to meet with her.

"All right," said Ruban. "I'll take care of it."

35

·

The tilapia in the refrigerator still smelled fresh, so Savannah cooked it up with steamed kale and wild rice for dinner. Ruban had a full night at the restaurant and couldn't stay, so she ate alone at the kitchen counter.

The house was too quiet, and the fifth mental replay of her talk with Ruban about Kyla was the point of overload. She grabbed the TV remote and switched on the local news. The lead story was a hit-and-run traffic fatality during the morning rush hour, but it didn't really capture Savannah's attention until the "exclusive live report" shifted to the street outside Braxton Security headquarters.

"The victim has been identified as twenty-eight-year-old Octavio Alvarez," the reporter said into the camera, microphone in hand. "In a breaking development, Eyewitness News has confirmed that Mr. Alvarez was one of the Braxton Security guards on duty when, little more than two weeks ago, thieves made off with nearly ten million dollars in cash from a warehouse at Miami International Airport."

Savannah almost dropped her fork.

The reporter continued, fighting off a long wisp of hair that was caught in the gentle evening breeze. "While the heist remains unsolved, sources tell Eyewitness News that law enforcement has been actively investigating the possibility of an inside job. Miami-Dade police have declined to comment on any suspected connection to this morning's fatal hit-and-run accident involving the Braxton guard, but we will keep viewers apprised of any further developments. Reporting live from Doral, this is Cynthia—"

Savannah hit the mute button, grabbed her phone, and speed-dialed Ruban. The clatter of a busy restaurant was in the background, and she nearly had to shout for Ruban to hear her.

"Slow down," said Ruban. "What's the matter?"

She told him, her voice racing.

"Octavio who?" he asked.

"Diaz—no, Alvarez. I don't know. The important thing is that the news made it sound like he could have been part of the heist."

"Did you talk to Jeffrey?"

It seemed like an odd first question. "No. Jeffrey still doesn't know I know anything."

"Okay, good. Don't talk to him."

"Don't talk to him? Ruban, this is serious. First it was my uncle's friend. Now it's the guard from Braxton. Two of the people involved are dead. And you say don't talk to Jeffrey? What if he's next?"

"He's not."

"How do you know that?"

"Because—"

He stopped short and asked her to hold on. The restaurant noises in the background faded, as he'd apparently moved to someplace more private. "We don't have to worry about Jeffrey," he said. "It's Pinky who concerns me."

"Forget him. My uncle can take care of himself. Jeffrey can't."

"That's not my point. I don't see Pinky as next on the hit list. I think he's behind what happened to these two guys."

Savannah felt chills. "Then we need to go to the police," she said. "I don't care if he is my uncle."

"We can't go to the police. Your uncle has me in a box."

"What are you talking about?"

Savannah waited for a response, and she could almost sense him struggling over the line. Then he answered.

"There's something I need to tell you."

"Then tell me."

"Do you promise you won't get mad?" he asked. "No matter how bad it is?"

"Ruban, just tell me what is going on!"

"Okay. Here's the deal. Do you remember that Sunday night when I came home late and told you that it wasn't an intervention? That Jeffrey and your uncle pulled off the heist?"

"How could I forget that?"

"I told you that I made them hide the money until we figured out what to do. You and I agreed that we should do what we could to keep Jeffrey out of jail."

"Yes, I remember all that."

"And you were so grateful to me for helping out your family."

"Yes, Ruban! What are you getting at?"

He breathed so heavily that it crackled over the line. "Your uncle is using that against me."

"I don't understand."

"He's *blackmailing* me, Savannah. If we go to the police, he is going to tell them that I was part of the heist."

She couldn't speak for a moment, and then it came all at once. "Oh, my God! What—*how?*"

"He's going to tell the cops I was his accomplice. I'll go to jail."

"No! He can't get away with that. Jeffrey will stand up for you. He knows you weren't involved."

"The police will think Jeffrey is lying to protect his brother-in-law. Your uncle is holding all the cards right now. He can put me away for the next thirty years."

Savannah's hand was shaking, and she gripped the phone a little tighter to steady her nerves. "Ruban, I . . . I am so sorry."

"Don't apologize. It's not your fault."

"But you were just trying to help Jeffrey, and now you're caught in the middle."

"I can handle this," he said. "But you have to stick with me. We cannot go to the police. Not yet."

"When?"

"As soon as I figure out how to deal with your uncle."

"Do you really think he killed these two men?"

"I really do. I've called his phone, and the number

doesn't work anymore. He quit showing up for work. He never goes to his apartment. Plus, I just think he's capable of doing something like this."

It wasn't the most far-fetched thing she'd ever heard, but a thief in the family was one thing. A murderer was quite another. "I'm scared for Jeffrey."

"You don't need to be."

"He's already been kidnapped once."

"That was my fault for trying to scare him. It had nothing to do with what your uncle did to his friend Marco and Octavio Alvarez."

"I'm still scared, Ruban."

"There's no reason to be, Savannah. As bad as your uncle is, he's not going to hurt his sister's kids. You and Jeffrey have nothing to worry about."

"What about you? You hid the money. What if he goes after you?"

"I'll be okay."

She stopped pacing and stood at the counter. From there, she could see down the hallway all the way to the locked cabinet in the other room. "Ruban, are you carrying a gun?"

"It's not anything to worry about."

"Did you take one of your pistols from the cabinet?"

"I'm taking precautions," he said.

"I don't like this. People are dying. You're packing a gun. Jeffrey is—" She stopped herself, sensing that he wasn't listening. She overheard him speaking to someone in the background. Then he was back on the line.

"Savannah, I have to go now. We can talk more about this when I get home."

"I'm not staying here by myself."

"If I thought you were in danger, I would be the first one to tell you to get out of the house. But you're not."

"I'm going to my mother's place. Pick me up there."

"How are you going to get there? You don't have a car."

She breathed out, exasperated. "I'll take the bus."

"Okay. Go to your mom's. That's a good plan. But this is all going to be okay, Savannah. I promise. And I love you."

He said good-bye and hung up before her reply. "Love you, too," she said to no one.

She immediately dialed her mother. Jeffrey answered.

"Is Mom home?" she asked. "I want to come over for a while."

"Yeah, she's here. What time are you coming?"

"It could be an hour. I have to take the bus."

"No, I'll pick you up."

"With what car?"

"Yours. It's in our garage."

"Ruban said the engine is shot."

"That's bullshit. He told me the same thing so I wouldn't drive it. There's nothing wrong with the engine. I've been driving it all day."

Savannah hesitated, not sure what to say. "Why would he swap cars?"

"I don't know. Ask him."

Another lie. *Best to keep Jeffrey out of this.* "I will."

"You want me to pick you up or not?"

"Can you come get me now?"

"Sure. Be there in ten minutes."

The call ended, and Savannah laid the phone on the counter, her mind awhirl. The lies and half-truths were starting to pile up, and the best spin she could put on it was that Ruban was trying to protect her and keep her from worrying. The spin was getting harder to swallow.

She walked to the end of the kitchen counter, where her daycare satchel lay. Tomorrow's lesson plan was inside: group time, story time, small-group activities. Tucked beside it was another folder, which contained copies of the court records that the DCF social worker had given her. Savannah glanced over the papers once more, then dialed Betty's home number.

"I'm so sorry to·call you at home."

"Not at all," said Betty. "I said you could call me whenever, and I meant it."

"I have a favor to ask," said Savannah. "I was looking over the records you gave me. I notice that the victim's name is blocked out."

"Yes. Her identity was sealed by court order. That's not the typical situation in domestic-violence cases, but it's not unheard of."

"Ruban told me her first name·is Mindy. Is there any way to find out her last name?"

"Why don't you just ask your husband?"

"I could do that," she said, drawing a breath. "But I don't want him to know that I'm looking into this."

"Ah, I see. Savannah, are you having some difficulties?"

"No. Nothing to worry about."

"It's like I told you earlier, I'm concerned about you."

"You don't have to be."

"Okay. I won't pry. But why do you want to know her name?"

Savannah swallowed hard. Perhaps Ruban would have a perfectly good explanation for the little lie about the car engine, and she could probably forgive him for that. But if there were still more lies, bigger lies, she wasn't so sure. "I want to talk to Mindy," said Savannah. "I want to know the truth about her and Ruban."

There was silence on the line. Then Betty answered. "I'll see what I can do."

Savannah took one more look at the docket sheet in the case of *State of Florida v. Karl Betancourt*, her finger running over the printed black bars that obscured the victim's name.

"Thank you," said Savannah. "Thank you very much."

36
.

The call from Savannah left Ruban's brain throbbing. A stabbing pain behind his right eye forced him to dim the lights and sit quietly at his desk for a minute. It was his classic stress headache.

He was alone in the cramped office at Café Ruban, which wasn't much of an office at all. There was no window. The constant clatter of the kitchen came right through the walls. The only way to open the closet door was to pick up and move the printer and the fax machine. The filing cabinets were somewhere behind thirty-pound bags of rice, canned chicken stock, and the overflow of other dry goods from the stockroom.

Ruban tucked his cell into his pocket, leaned back in his squeaky desk chair, and closed his eyes, willing the headache away. It was only getting worse.

Lies. More lies. There were almost too many to keep track of.

He'd come so close to telling Savannah the truth about the heist, even closer than on the night he'd climbed into their bed with the smell of money on his hands and lied for the first time. He wasn't sure when he'd conjured up the story that Pinky was threatening to blackmail him if they went to the police—that Pinky had the power to put Ruban away for thirty years, and that Savannah just needed to stand by her man and all would work out. Such a great lie. It almost felt like the truth. If it was in fact Pinky who'd killed Marco and Octavio, it wouldn't be long before Ruban was in his crosshairs. The lie he'd told Savannah wasn't all that far from the truth.

So why is my head pounding?

There was a knock at the door, and his assistant manager stuck her head into the room. "Our sous-chef is threatening to walk out again. I've had it with him. You need to deal with this."

Ruban's head chef had the night off, leaving the sous-chef in charge. "I'll be there in two minutes," he said.

"Okay, but it's getting pretty intense. And there are lots of knives in that kitchen."

She was only half kidding, but Ruban seemed to recall that an argument at a fine restaurant in Coral Gables had been settled in that very fashion. The thought triggered a moment of panic. Ruban unlocked the desk drawer and opened it. To his relief, the gun was still there—no armed lunatic in the kitchen.

Ruban had always kept a gun at the restaurant, just in case, but Savannah's instincts had been correct. After the hit-and-run, he'd gone to his cabinet at home and swapped out the revolver for a pistol with more firepower. Ruban wasn't eager to use it. In fact, he was determined to avoid a confrontation with Pinky, at least until the immediate shock and anger over the hit-and-run subsided. He couldn't say what he would do if he met up with Pinky in his current frame of mind. Would he feel the impulse to avenge his friend's death? Did he even have the capacity to act on it? He didn't want to find out. If he didn't hunt Pinky down, he couldn't self-destruct. But if Pinky came looking for him . . .

Can't let it come to that.

No one—not Pinky or Jeffrey, and definitely not Savannah—knew of the friendship. He and Octavio had lost touch years earlier. In early summer, Octavio had reached out to him, a blast from the past. He'd heard on the street that Ruban had a criminal record and thought he might be up for something big. They'd met at a bar after work to talk it over. "It's why we got on that shitty raft and came here," he'd told Ruban with that wry smile. "To be millionaires, right, bro?" The plan was finalized by the Fourth of July weekend, which was the last time Ruban and Octavio had spoken or met in person. Their strategy to prevent law enforcement from connecting the dots between two boyhood friends from Cuba was ironclad: No contact the four months before the heist, and none for six months after it. There were only two exceptions. The phone call on the disposable cell from the MIA warehouse, after which Octavio would crush the phone to bits and flush it down the toilet. And the face-to-homeless-face exchange at Bird Road.

There was no contingency plan for the death of one of them.

It killed Ruban that he couldn't even go to the memorial service. A message from Octavio's new girlfriend had come to him through the restaurant's Facebook page that afternoon. Ruban didn't know Jasmine. She and Octavio had met during the pre-heist blackout. Ruban couldn't even drop a note to express his condolences. He couldn't do *anything* that linked him to Octavio, especially with Eyewitness News pegging him as the possible insider in the airport heist.

The door opened. It was his assistant manager again. Ruban shut the desk drawer before she could catch a glimpse of the gun.

"Ruban, I'm serious. I *need* you."

He locked the drawer. Only he had the key. "Coming."

They went straight to the kitchen, where one angry sous-chef was shouting obscenities at his "incompetent and disrespectful" line cooks. Ruban pulled him aside, but the rant continued. They stepped out into the alley for some fresh air. A cigarette seemed to calm him. Ruban pretended to listen as the sous-chef got everything off his chest. As in most kitchens, the problem was egos. At Café Ruban, things seemed to come to a head whenever Chef Claudia took a night off and the sous-chef took over.

"I'll fix it, I'll fix it," Ruban said a dozen times.

The chef crushed out his cigarette and, after a little more stroking from Ruban, returned to the kitchen. Ruban went back inside to check on the dining room. It was packed, which made him smile. So was the bar, which made his smile even wider. Profits surged when customers tipped back cocktails while waiting for a table. Ruban went down the line and thanked each customer for waiting. It was the time of year for more tourists than locals. Tonight, there were no familiar faces, save one: the woman sitting alone at the end of the bar, who managed to wipe the smile from Ruban's face.

"Hello, Ruban." It was Edith Baird. She'd put on lipstick and brushed her hair, but Ruban recognized the same sundress from their talk in her trailer.

He moved closer so none of the guests at the bar would overhear. "What are you doing here?" he asked through clenched teeth.

"That peek inside your backpack led me to believe you must be doing well. I wanted to stop by and see *how* well."

"Let's go outside," he said.

"I haven't paid for my martini."

"I got it," he said.

"That's what I like to hear."

She followed him out of the bar, and he led her to the rear exit. He was in the alley again, and they were standing exactly where the sous-chef had crushed out his cigarette a few minutes earlier.

"Don't ever come here again," said Ruban.

"Not very hospitable of you. This was a long drive for me."

"I don't want you contacting me. I'll get in touch with you. That's the rule."

"All these things are negotiable."

"No," he said. "That's not negotiable. Got it?"

"Sure," she said. "I got it."

"Good. Did you test out the hundred-dollar bill I gave you?"

"Yup. Went to Macy's this afternoon. No problems. It's the real deal."

"There's more where that came from."

"I'm glad to hear that," she said. "Because it's going to take a lot more."

Ruban hesitated. He recognized that sly expression on her face, the old Edith. "You mean more than a hundred thou?"

She sighed heavily, then turned on the phony southern accent that she liked to use. It had always annoyed Ruban. "You know, I'm very, very fond of Kyla. Now, I could see my way clear to let her stay with her daddy. But it's just going to break my heart to say good-bye to her."

"How much do you want?"

Another sigh. "Oh, my. How does a person put a price on such things? Not seeing her sweet face every morning. No more kisses good night."

"Edith," he said flatly. "How much do you fucking want?"

"Not a penny less than two-fifty," she said, the accent suddenly gone. The old Edith was in her negotiating mode.

"I'll give you one twenty-five."

"That's an insult."

"I'm off at midnight," he said. "Let's talk."

"I'm in bed by then, sweetheart. Come by the trailer on Thursday. Bring your wallet."

He wanted to tell her exactly how he felt, but he held his tongue. His trail of lies to Savannah was like bile in his throat, and he had a sickening sense that she was beginning to see through it. No explanations could remove all of Savannah's doubts. But Kyla might just make them go away.

"All right," he said. "I'll see you Thursday."

37

Andie was hunting for a parking space, which was a form of extreme sport on Miami Beach, something that could quickly turn as violent as your average African safari. The trick was to target an unsuspecting gazelle walking along the sidewalk with her car keys in hand, stalk her at a steady and patient three m.p.h. all the way to her parked car, and then pounce on the opening as she pulls away. Andie found her mark and staked her claim in front of Dylan's Candy Bar.

Dylan's is at the geographic heart of Lincoln Road Mall, a pedestrian-only, eight-block stretch of open-air shopping and dining. The mall was loaded with places like Dylan's, celebrity-owned shops that sightseeing guides on double-decker buses liked to point out to tourists. *"The store on your left with the giant lollipops in the window is owned by Ralph Lauren's daughter . . ."* Andie crossed Meridian Avenue and found an open café table beneath the palm trees outside the coffee shop.

The report from the FBI's body-mapping expert

had actually been good, although the phone conference had taken much longer than necessary. Scientists loved to explain their methodologies, and Dr. Vincent was no exception. "Contrary to that old saying about a picture being worth a thousand words," he'd told them, "images do not speak for themselves: they require interpretation. I applied several accepted methods of photo-anthropometry, morphological analysis to your images, including the overlaying of two similar-size images, known as photographic superimposition; the rapid transition between two images, or the 'blink technique'; and the gradual transformation of one image into another, known as 'swipes.'" Five minutes later, they were at the bottom line: "I can say to a reasonable degree of scientific certainty that the man in Agent Henning's photographs is the same man in the CCTV video from the warehouse."

It was a small victory for Andie, and her unit chief was true to his word: surveillance on Craig Perez, a/k/a Pinky, was an approved line item in the operational budget. There was just one problem: Pinky had vanished. He'd checked out of the motel where Andie had found him over the weekend. According to the postman, he hadn't picked up the mail at his apartment in almost three weeks. He had no cell-phone account and was presumably using a disposable. Andie had one lead to follow. It didn't involve another trip to Night Moves, but it did require a meeting between "Celia," Andie's undercover persona, and Priscilla.

"Good to see you again, sweetie," Priscilla said as she pulled up a chair at Andie's table.

She looked surprisingly suburban-like to Andie,

nothing particularly sexy about her cotton blouse and khaki shorts, her makeup not overdone. Apparently she saved her "gotta have it right now" message for the club. Andie was second-guessing her own choice of red lipstick and a tight skirt for Celia. They ordered a couple of decafs from the waitress, and Priscilla lit a cigarette.

"I was hoping you'd follow up," she said with a puff of smoke.

"Are you surprised?"

"No," she said, then smiled. "Maybe a little. The club really is in a state of flux."

"How do you mean?"

"Jorge's trying to sell it."

Jorge Calderón, the owner of the chop shop. He was on Andie's list, but Celia had to be very discreet if she was going to make this about him as well as Pinky. "Why would he want to sell it?"

"I don't know. Why? You want to buy it?"

Andie could have joked about the toxic site and EPA issues, the things that must have spilled on those floors. She let it go. "I don't think I could afford it."

The waitress brought their decafs and left. Priscilla tasted hers and said, "You'll never guess who wants to buy it."

"Who?"

"Pinky."

Andie almost dropped her cup. She'd worked out a strategy in advance to turn the conversation in this direction, but she was more than happy to run with a *gimme*. "Is Pinky rich?"

"I didn't think so. Apparently I was wrong."

Two men took the table next to them. Their dogs

immediately drew interest from passersby, and Andie couldn't help overhearing that the two-hundred-pound mastiff was "Laurel," and the skinny Thai Ridgeback was "Hardy." She didn't spoil the magic by telling them that they had it backward.

"So, you want to join Night Moves?" asked Priscilla.

"Uhm . . ."

It was the classic undercover challenge: how to appear interested in sex without ever actually having it. "Here's the problem," said Andie. "My boyfriend is a definite no-go on the club."

"Really? I heard he was totally into the place."

Sounds like Sosa. "He was all for *him* having sex with other women. He's not at all into *me* having sex with other men."

"Yeah, very common problem," said Priscilla. "You think you could change his mind?"

"Never."

"Too bad. Maybe you should find a new boyfriend."

Andie suddenly imagined herself walking into Night Moves with Barbara Littleford's poor cousin, the attorney. It was a bizarre thought, and she shook it off. "I had another plan in mind."

"Tell me."

"I was hoping we could work out something a little less formal than a club membership."

"You looking for something specific, sweetie?"

"Yeah," she said. "Something in an extra large."

"You naughty girl," Priscilla said, smiling. "You mean Pinky?"

"I do," said Andie. "I really want to meet this Pinky."

38
.

Ten a.m. Ruban awoke alone in their bed.

It felt good to sleep late, no need to get up and take Savannah to work, but the way it had come about bothered him. Savannah had called the restaurant around eleven p.m. to ask how late he was planning to work.

"Definitely after midnight," he'd told her.

"I'm tired, and I have to be at the daycare center at seven. I'll just sleep here at Mom's house tonight."

"Okay. I'll pick you up around six-thirty and take you to work."

"Don't worry. Jeffrey will drive me. He can use our car. Which is sitting in my mother's garage and running fine, no engine trouble."

A lie. A trap. A quick and light explanation, no need to panic. "Ah, busted."

"Why did you lie, Ruban?"

"I'm sorry. I shouldn't have tried to trick you into buying a new car. I'm just tired of driving that old piece of junk. But I promise I wasn't going to use any of Jeffrey's money to buy a new one. I swear.

We'll talk about it tomorrow, okay? Sweet dreams, honey."

Lies to cover lies. Damage control was becoming a way of life. This lie was the littlest of all, about their stupid car, but it was the most worrisome. For the first time, Savannah had set him up. She was trying to catch him off guard. An ambush.

Piss me off.

Ruban rolled out of bed and pulled on his jogging shorts, T-shirt, and running shoes. Over the summer he'd started a fitness routine to get in shape for the heist, but he hadn't gone running since. He hated it. His sole motivation had been the fear that something would go wrong at the warehouse and that they would have to flee on foot. Day after day, even in the unbearable heat and humidity of August and September, he'd hit the jogging trail. Without fail, a side-stitch would kick in around the one-mile mark. To push through the pain, he'd tell himself that he needed to outrun the cops; but an even louder voice in his head would tell him to quit, that in any getaway he only needed to outrun Jeffrey.

He followed his usual route from his driveway, down the street and into the park. He'd never reached the point where running was effortless, not even when he was running every day. This morning was like starting over. He continued onto the "heart trail." The wood-chip path was easier on his knees, and there were fitness stations along the way where the ambitious could stop and do chin-ups and other challenges. He passed several stations, no time to stop even if he'd wanted to. At 10:30 sharp he had a meeting at the sit-up station.

He arrived a minute early and waited. An old man jogged past him. Ruban waited another minute, walking with hands on hips as he caught his breath. Sweat was soaking through his shirt. The breeze felt good. Then he heard footsteps on the trail. Another jogger was approaching. One look and he knew it was her. She was exactly Octavio's type.

She stopped at the station, climbed onto the inclined sit-up board, and started crunching her abs. She spoke without breaking her rhythm.

"I know you can't come to the funeral," she said. "And I know why."

Ruban didn't react. Jasmine had said the same thing at midnight, when she'd called him at the restaurant—right before she'd told him that they needed "to meet and talk business." Ruban had chosen the time and place.

"I wish I could be there," he said.

No break in the sit-ups. Jasmine was a machine. "Octavio told me a lot about you."

"Like what?"

"All the things you would expect. And maybe a few more." She stopped in the up position, her eyes locking with Ruban's. "About nine or ten million more."

If there had been a reason to wonder what kind of "business" she'd been talking about on the phone the night before, all doubt had been removed. "What do you want?" he asked.

"Octavio's share."

He scoffed, almost chuckling. "You expect me to hand it over, just like that? A half million dollars?"

"Nice try," she said. "I know it was a million. I want all of it."

"And what if I tell you that I don't have any idea what you're talking about?"

Jasmine started another set—down, up; down, up—speaking without effort. "The FBI came to see me yesterday."

"Who was it?"

"The same woman who interviewed Octavio at Braxton. Special Agent Andrea Henning."

Ruban made a mental note; he'd heard plenty about a female agent, but this was the first time he'd heard a name. "What did you tell her?"

"Nothing," she said, getting in a few more reps before adding the qualifier: "Yet."

"What did Henning want to know?"

Jasmine counted off the last few—"forty-nine, fifty"—then stopped and caught her breath. "She was pretending it was all about the hit-and-run accident. But you and I both know what it's really about."

Ruban didn't answer.

"Anyway," said Jasmine. "Henning asked me to pass along the name of any of Octavio's friends who should be at the funeral but don't show up."

Ruban considered the logic; Henning wasn't stupid. "Are you planning to give her my name?"

"I haven't told her a thing about you," said Jasmine.

"That wasn't my question. I asked, are you planning to."

Jasmine shrugged. "Are you planning to give me my share?"

Her share. He wasn't even buried and it was no longer *Octavio's* share. "What does it get me?"

"Everything you had with Octavio."

"Why should I trust you?"

"What choice do you have?"

She made a compelling argument. "All right," he said. "But we do have a slight problem. Octavio had his share with him in a backpack when he was hit. It was stolen."

"That's not my problem," said Jasmine. "That's yours."

"I'm saying that I don't have his money."

"I'm telling you to get it."

"You're quite the ball buster."

"Yes, I am." She resumed her sit-ups. "Let's meet again next week. Same time, same place. Now get lost."

Ruban watched her rip off another twenty reps, fast and furious. She looked capable of sustaining that pace well into the hundreds. There was nothing more to say anyway. He started down the woodchip trail and headed home.

He wasn't sure how she expected him to come up with Octavio's million dollars in a week. She seemed to think she had him backed up against the wall, and she'd asked a legitimate question: *What choice do you have?*

Ruban didn't know Jasmine. What was even clearer was that she didn't know him.

Ruban always had choices.

39

.

It was Party Animal Night at the Gold Rush. Jeffrey arrived at ten p.m., a cross between a drunken hyena and a coked-up teddy bear.

"Party, party, party," said Jeffrey as he entered. "Here come the party."

His pockets bulged with cash again. Ruban had been dead wrong about El Padrino refusing to give back Jeffrey's money. All it had taken was one visit to the "church" and two hours of whining and blubbering. His godfather had coughed up two vacuum-sealed packs just to make him go away.

Jeffrey slipped the hostess a couple hundred bucks for a good table. She led him through the crowd, right up to the edge of the runway. Dance music blasted. Jeffrey had not only replaced the bottom row of caps, but he'd finished out the top, and his gold smile glistened beneath the flashing colored lights. He'd promised Ruban that he would never return, but that was bullshit. The Gold Rush wasn't dangerous. The danger was Ruban, who'd hired that Jamaican bartender to scare him. The bartender's friends, not the folks at the Gold Rush, were the problem. The club was like home.

"How's this?" asked the hostess.

He settled into a bench seat that was designed to fit three across. In Jeffrey's case, it was just barely big enough for him and the dancer of his choice. "Perfect," he said as he handed her another fifty bucks of gratitude.

"Party Animal" was Jeffrey's favorite theme night, the T-and-A version of a big-cats circus act. Pole dancers wore tiger-ear headbands and spiked collars, hissing and pawing at the crack of a dominatrix's whip. The guest "trainer" for the night worked the runway from end to end, dressed only in a black tuxedo tailcoat, top hat, and five-inch heels. The lounge was packed, and the crowd was overwhelmingly male, but there was a smattering of women who'd avoided the cover charge by agreeing to wear the fox tails or bunny ears supplied at the door.

A dancer wearing a zebra-striped bow tie and nothing else stepped down from the stage and sat right beside him, letting Jeffrey feel the warmth of her bare arm against his. Her accent sounded Russian, but she could have been one of the women from Romania or Slovakia who seemed to flood into the Gold Rush every November.

"How about a bottle of Cristal, cutie pie?"

That would set him back about ten Benjamins. *No problem.* "Make it two," Jeffrey said.

Zebra Girl signaled to the bartender, an exaggerated gesture that made her breasts rise before his eyes. Jeffrey would have liked to pull her even closer, but club rules forbade any physical contact that wasn't dancer-initiated. It was strictly enforced—which Jeffrey had learned the hard way.

"I'm Sylvia," she said.

Jeffrey mumbled his name, and Zebra Girl told him what a "big, strong" name it was, how cute his eyes were, how much she loved his gold caps and tattoos—all the things men heard from naked women who worked for tips. Jeffrey wanted to enjoy it, but his head was buzzing. Too much cocaine. He'd never actually overdosed, but he frequently overdid it, which made him sweat, which made him stink, which turned off the dancers. He could feel the dampness building in his armpits. The odor couldn't be far behind. The polite thing would have been to excuse himself and slather on the overpriced cologne sold by the attendant in the men's room, but he didn't budge. He wasn't trying to impress Zebra Girl. She was hot, no doubt about it, but he was looking for someone else.

"Is Bambi here tonight?" he asked.

"She's your girl, isn't she?"

He almost blushed. "I just wondered if she was here tonight."

"Sorry to break your heart, cutie pie, but Bambi doesn't work here anymore."

"Where did she go?"

"She decided to join the convent. But here's the good news. She told me to take care of you while she's gone."

The bachelor party at the next table was getting louder. Two drunks staggered over to Jeffrey's table. The short one had something to say, but his tongue was almost too thick to get the words out. "Hey, beautiful. I'm getting married tomorrow."

"Congrats," she said.

He leaned forward, palms flat on the table, barely able to stand. "Lemme ask you this," he said with a goofball grin. "I seem to be lost. Can you tell me how to get to Pussy Lane?"

Zebra Girl was deadpan. "Yeah. Stick your tongue down the best man's throat and make an immediate U-Turn."

The groom grabbed his wounded heart, as if punched in the chest, and fell back into his chair. The entire bachelor party erupted in laughter. They had their story. Jeffrey had a new crush.

"That was fucking awesome," he told her.

She reached under the table and laid her hand on the wad of cash in his pants pocket. "Stick with Sylvia, cutie pie," she said as her fingers slid between his thighs. "Who needs Bambi?"

The bottles of Cristal arrived. The bartender delivered them himself. It was Ramsey.

"Are you crazy, mon? What you doin' bok at dis place?"

Sylvia removed her headband and put the zebra ears on Jeffrey. "He's a party animal. Can't you see that, Ramsey?"

He placed the bottles on the table. "Yah, mon. I see very clearly."

Ruban smelled garlic. It penetrated the kitchen walls, wafted through the duct work, and filled the restaurant's business office.

The Wednesday-night special at Café Ruban was

"Garlic Shrimp under a Fur Coat," a signature salad in which Cuban *camarones* replaced herring in a traditional Russian dish of layered seafood, potatoes, egg, and mayonnaise, topped with shredded beets. The culinary marriage worked, except when one of the line cooks lost the ability to discern between a garlic head and a garlic clove.

I smell like a Brooklyn pizza parlor.

His attention returned to the computer screen. All evening he'd been trying to find fifteen minutes of alone time, and finally he'd managed to get away to the office. He just wished the government website would load a little faster.

Come on, come on . . .

One of the last things Octavio had told him was that a good-looking female FBI agent had interviewed him at Braxton. He knew from his homeless crew that a "hot" FBI agent had visited the accident scene and shown them a photograph of Pinky. Jasmine, too, had spoken to a female FBI agent. She'd even given him a name, but he needed more specifics on what this Agent Henning looked like.

He was scrolling through the FBI's official website, which had a separate menu button for "Women in the FBI." In its apparent eagerness to shake the image of a boys' club, the FBI liked to showcase some of its two thousand female agents. There was a mother-daughter profile, a testimonial from the first female member of the Underwater Search and Evidence Recovery Team, and more. It seemed crazy to put the faces of FBI agents out on the Internet, but the search engine had taken him directly to this site: "Henning" had to be there. He scrolled down and, sure enough, he found her name: *Special Agent Andrea Henning.* She might as well have had her own Facebook page.

The FBI is stupider than Jeffrey.

There was just one sentence written about her, but it was enough to confirm that she hadn't been selected at random. She was "the most recent female agent to make the 'Possible Club,' an informal honorary fraternity for agents who shoot perfect scores on one of the toughest firearms courses in law enforcement." The woman could shoot, which earned Ruban's immediate respect. The bio didn't mention what type of pistol she used, but he pegged her for high performance with interchangeable grip sizes and trigger lengths to suit her needs and hand size. Probably a Sig Sauer. Maybe the P250?

He clicked on the thumbnail, and her image filled his computer screen.

Damn. A shooter and a babe.

He clicked the PRINT button. The old machine squeaked and rumbled as it spat out the image. Ruban retrieved it from the bin.

Agent Henning, he said to himself, burning it into his memory. *I will never forget your pretty face.*

40

•

Jasmine sat alone in the funeral parlor. The viewing had officially ended at ten p.m., but she stayed longer.

An open casket sometimes invites drama, especially with a young and handsome corpse, but Octavio's had been a quiet viewing. No wailing. No finger-pointing. No prayers or eulogies. Twenty-two guests had signed the registry. A half dozen of Jasmine's girlfriends had come by to show their support. Octavio's coworkers and fishing buddies had made an appearance but didn't stay long. Octavio was without family in the United States, but he'd kept in touch with a sister who lived in Oriente Province in eastern Cuba. A family friend from Hialeah had brought a camera and snapped a photograph for Octavio's sister. Jasmine thought it was weird, but Octavio didn't seem to mind.

The viewing was optional under the funeral package, and Jasmine's initial instinct had been against having one. A graveside service seemed sufficient. Agent Henning's unexpected visit to her apartment had changed her mind. It was clear enough that Henning's interest was in the heist when she'd asked Jasmine to make a list of everyone who should attend the funeral but failed to do so. The logic, however, applied with equal force to the hit-and-run. Maybe the driver *was* someone Octavio had known. Jasmine had no intention of helping the FBI solve the heist, but it still seemed like a good idea to create such a list for her own use. Maybe it would reveal Octavio's killer.

"We need to close up for the night," the manager told her in a gentle voice.

Jasmine was seated in the front row of white folding chairs, ten feet away from the casket. "Just a moment longer, please?"

He nodded, seeming to understand, and walked away quietly.

Jasmine rose and slowly stepped forward. She stopped at the kneeler but remained standing, resting her hand on the coffin's edge. Octavio was handsome in blue, and Jasmine had selected his favorite shirt. To look at him now, no one would ever have guessed that he'd been killed in a car accident. She'd chosen not to see the body until after the work had been done, but she'd been told that the deadly blow had been to the back of his head.

"I lied," she whispered.

To Agent Henning, she meant. She and Octavio had talked about so much more than she'd led the FBI to believe. The heist, of course, was one omission. Octavio's promise to marry her was another.

Jasmine reached toward his body. Stillness was by definition a part of death, but the only Octavio she'd ever known was full of life, and it was disturbing to see him exhibit absolutely no sign of it. Her hand trembled as she laid it atop his. His skin was cold, so cold. Much warmer memories brought a tear to her eye. She wiped it away and collected herself.

"It was a good plan," she said softly. "A really good plan. I'm not sure what went wrong, but I promise you, I'll figure it out. I'll make this work. You'd like that, wouldn't you?"

She leaned over and kissed his forehead. "We were a *great* team."

She sensed the manager standing in the rear of the parlor, and a quick glance over her shoulder confirmed that her time was up. She knew that the casket would be closed and sealed when she left, and she would never see Octavio again.

"Good-bye, my love."

She turned away and headed toward the door. The manager expressed his sympathies again, which she said she appreciated. He offered to escort her to her car, but she declined, preferring to be alone. The moon peeked through the clouds to help her find her car key. She climbed into the driver's seat and closed the door.

Octavio is gone.

It seemed unbelievable, but Jasmine could do nothing to bring him back. The best she could do was to carry out their plan and make sure the risks Octavio had taken and the work he had done were not in vain. Jasmine's meeting with Ruban had been a good start. But what if he really couldn't recover Octavio's share? What if that money was gone for good?

She and Octavio had spent many nights together thinking through the "what ifs." *What if Ruban screws you over? He's your friend, but what if his wife gets greedy? What if they pay you less than they owe you?* They'd understood the risks from the very beginning, but what really bothered him and Jasmine was the split: How did two shitheads like Jeffrey and his uncle end up with more than two million each, more than double Octavio's take? It was an injustice that Jasmine had been working hard to correct, even before Octavio's death. It was time to redouble her efforts.

Jasmine dug her cell from her purse. She knew the number by heart and dialed. He answered on the third ring, and Jasmine turned on her "club" voice.

"Hi, Jeffy," she said sweetly. "It's me. Bambi."

41

.

Ruban took the turnpike south to Eden Park Mobile Home Community. His meeting with Edith Baines was set for ten a.m. Kyla was in the balance.

Savannah had slept in their bed Wednesday night, but the kiss good night had been cool, and the ride to the daycare center in the morning had been downright chilly. She'd accepted his explanation for lying about the car, but she refused to believe that he hadn't planned on using "Jeffrey's money" to buy a new one. She'd get over it in a day or so, and he could live with her anger. What he couldn't risk— and what he couldn't tell Savannah about—was the possibility that a witness had seen Octavio, moments before he was run down in the street, talking to a man in a white Chevy with a nonmatching gray quarter panel. Getting rid of the old piece of junk was the preferred solution, but a paint job would do the trick. Ruban dropped it off that morning. Metallic blue. It would be ready late Friday afternoon.

Until then, he was stuck in an economy-class rental that should have come with pedals.

He parked on the road outside Edith's mobile home and went to the door. Edith was still wearing her pajamas, which wasn't a pretty sight. It also told him that Kyla and her half brothers had probably walked without an adult to the bus stop on the other side of the busy highway outside Eden Park. He suddenly felt better about the deal he was cutting for Kyla.

He followed Edith into the kitchen and took a seat at the table.

"Coffee?" she asked.

"No, thanks."

She grabbed her pink bathrobe from a hook beside the refrigerator and slipped it on. Fabric pills stretched from the frayed collar to the ragged hem, and the elbows were threadbare. Ruban's guess was that she'd been wearing that robe since Mindy was in kindergarten.

Edith pulled up a chair on the opposite side of the table. "I see you brought your backpack."

It was on the floor at Ruban's feet. "We'll get to that."

"Yes, sir. You bet we will."

He leaned forward to make a point, but his hands stuck in maple syrup.

Edith reached behind her and grabbed a wet dishrag from the sink. "Damn kids," she groused as she wiped down the Formica. "I'm always tellin' 'em to clean up after themselves."

Another wild guess, but Ruban figured the syrup

had probably been there about two weeks. "Not a problem," he said.

"You sure you don't want any coffee?"

"No. This is going to be short and sweet."

"Fine by me. I ain't budging: Two-fifty, that's my number."

Ruban grabbed his backpack and laid it on the table. "That's too bad. There's only one-fifty on the table."

Edith reached for it, but he pulled it back. "Whoa, girl."

"I need to count it," she said.

"You can count it after we cut a deal."

"It's not complicated. Pay me two hundred fifty thousand dollars, you adopt Kyla. You hire the lawyer and I'll sign whatever is needed."

"I said one-fifty."

"That won't get the deal done."

"Yes it will. Our *new* deal."

"Adopting Kyla is all we talked about."

"I came up from one hundred to one-fifty. You raise the price, I raise the demand."

She shifted uneasily, as if sensing what he was about to ask.

"I need my name cleared," he said.

Edith shook her head. "I can't do that."

"Mindy can," he said.

"Then talk to Mindy."

"You know that's impossible. There's an injunction. I can't call, write, or get within a hundred yards of her."

"What do you want me to do?"

"Tell your daughter to recant her testimony."

"Say what?"

"I want Mindy to state under oath that the charges she brought against me were lies."

"You're asking too much."

"Everything she said was a lie."

"Maybe it was, maybe it wasn't."

"You *know* it was. You wouldn't let me adopt Kyla if any of that was true."

"I don't know anything, Ruban. I wasn't there. That's all between you and Mindy."

He opened the backpack and removed the money, one brick of bills at a time. Fifteen in all. "One hundred fifty thousand dollars," he said.

Edith's eyes were like saucers.

Ruban took five bricks and pushed them toward her. "Fifty thousand now."

Edith stared at the stack of bills, but she didn't move.

Ruban separated the rest of the money into two stacks of five bricks. "Fifty thousand when Mindy recants her charges against me under oath. Another fifty thousand when the adoption is final. And no one, not even Mindy—*especially* not Mindy—can ever know that I paid you. Those are the terms."

Edith looked at him suspiciously, her eyes narrowing. "Where on God's green earth did you get all this money, Ruban?"

"Do we have *a deal*?"

"Seriously—where did this money come from?"

"Deal? Or no deal?"

Edith considered it, here gaze darting back and forth from the stack of money to Ruban's steely expression, her elbows resting on the table. Not for a nanosecond did Ruban believe that she actually cared where the money had come from. She just needed another minute for all that cash to speak to her.

"Deal," she said as she wrapped her arms around the bricks of bills, raking them toward her.

Ruban grabbed her wrist, stopping her cold. "If you take the money, there's no going back. You understand what I'm saying?"

Their eyes locked, and then Edith blinked. "Understood."

Ruban released his grip. Edith drew the cash into her bosom and smiled. Ruban tucked the rest of the money into his backpack and pushed away from the table. "When should I follow up about Mindy?" he asked, rising.

"I'll speak to her this weekend."

"Good enough," he said as he slung the backpack over his shoulder.

Edith followed him to the front door. "Pleasure doing business with you, sir."

"You won't regret it," he said, and then his voice took on a more chilling tone. "Unless you screw me. Then you will regret the day we ever met."

"We're cool. Nothing to worry about."

He let himself out and walked to his rental car, the backpack on his shoulder a wee bit lighter.

42

A ndie was alone in her car, three blocks from her friend's yoga studio and hardly able to believe that she was going to make it to class.

Rachel had switched from teaching beach yoga at sunrise to a sweaty Bikram class indoors. "A ninety-nine-degree hothouse is right up your alley," Rachel had said in several invitations, but Andie was always full of excuses. Around four-thirty that afternoon, she'd noticed a lull in her workday. It had lasted just long enough to delude her into thinking she could squeeze in an early-evening class.

Her cell rang as she turned onto Collins Avenue. It was Lieutenant Watts at MDPD headquarters. The offer of a reward from Braxton had reeled in another credible informant.

"Shit."

"Excuse me?"

"I mean good," said Andie. "I'm on my way."

For the second time in as many weeks, Watts had snatched her away from yoga. It seemed as though every time she grabbed her sticky mat, someone made a grab for the reward. The first informant, Leonard Timmes, had been helpful but not a home run. Timmes worked at the body shop that had chopped the getaway truck, and his tip had linked Marco Aroyo to the acquisition and disposal of the black pickup. Aroyo was dead, however, and Andie's bet was that no one would ever find the body that had been separated from his finger, which meant that the FBI was a long way from an arrest and conviction in the heist. Hopes were higher for informant number two.

Andie reached MDPD headquarters in Doral around six-thirty. Watts met her outside the interrogation room. Andie peered through the one-way glass and saw a middle-aged, overweight woman seated alone at the table.

"Her name's Edith Baird," said Watts. "Walked into the station alone about fifteen minutes before I called you."

"Out of the blue?"

"Yeah. Funny thing. We were all pissed off when Eyewitness News leaked that Octavio Alvarez was a suspected insider in the heist. That leak may turn out to be a blessing. Ms. Baird saw it on TV and has been mulling it over since Tuesday night. She says that if Alvarez was working on the inside, she has the name of his buddy on the outside."

"No doubt in my mind that Alvarez was involved," said Andie.

"Same here. One caveat," Watts said as he handed her the dossier. "She has a criminal record."

Andie read it. It was like so many she'd seen in her

short tenure in south Florida, which was the undis-
puted king of Medicare fraud. "Basically we have a
scam artist angling for a hefty reward."

"It's a criminal investigation, not a beauty con-
test," said Watts. "We don't get to pick our players."

"Okay. Let's hear her story."

Watts opened the door, and Andie followed him
inside. Edith kept her seat through the introductions. Andie thanked her for coming in and got her
permission to call her "Edith." Chitchat followed,
just enough for the law enforcement officers to size
her up and develop a rapport. Andie steered clear of
the criminal conviction, at least at the start.

"Tell me how you know Octavio Alvarez," said
Andie.

"I know him."

"How well?"

Her expression tightened. "Well enough."

"How long has it been since you last saw him?"

"It's been a while."

"How long?"

"A while."

"Okay," said Andie, "let's back up a bit. What
brought you into the station?"

Edith breathed a heavy sigh, glancing at Watts.
"I already told the detective. I heard on the news
that you think Alvarez did an inside job at the airport. I know who helped him."

"We'd love to hear his name."

"I'm sure you would," said Edith. "And for two
hundred and fifty thousand dollars I'll give it to you."

"Let me explain how the reward works," said

Andie. "You give us the information. If that tip leads to an arrest and conviction, Braxton pays you the reward. Fair enough?"

"Bullshit. I don't operate that way," said Edith.

"We're not being cute. That's the way rewards work."

"You're not listening. *I* don't operate that way."

"Okay. Tell me what you want."

"I'm sure you've checked me out. You know I got a record. So let's cut the crap. You don't trust me, and I don't trust you."

"If you have helpful information, we can build trust."

"Yeah, sure we can. I know what's going to happen. I'll give you the name. You'll check it out. You'll get your arrest and conviction. Then you'll come back to me and say, 'Oh, we were already following that lead when you came down to the station. Too bad, Mrs. Baird. No reward for you.'"

"I have never seen that happen," said Andie. "The whole crime-tip system would crumble if police started playing that game."

"I don't give a rat's ass about the system. I care about my reward. So here's how we're going to do it. You give me a list of all the names you have so far. I'll add my guy's name to the list. If it's a new one, and he's your man, I get the money."

"That's nice in theory, Edith. But our investigative files are confidential. We aren't going to give you a list of names."

"Then you don't get a name from me. It's as simple as that."

The terms were unacceptable, but Andie could

play along well enough to keep the conversation from shutting down. "I'm not going to say no," said Andie. "But I can't say yes."

"Yes is the only word I want to hear."

"I can't just go back to my unit chief and tell him we need to hand over our list of suspects to a convicted felon."

Edith smiled. "Then don't tell him."

"You've been around the block," said Andie. "You know how these negotiations work."

"Yes, I do."

"Good. Then let's be honest. If we're going to play by your rules, I need more than your promise to give me a name. I'll be laughed out of the FBI if I tell my boss that I have an informant who is willing to identify a suspect only on the condition that we reveal every name in our file first. If you expect me to even consider making a pitch like that, you have to give me *something* to show that you're a highly credible informant."

Edith said nothing, but her body language told Andie that her words were resonating.

"You know I'm not being unreasonable," said Andie.

"*Shhh!* I'm thinking," said Edith.

Andie gave her a minute.

"All right," Edith said.

"All right, what?"

Edith laid her hands atop the table and laced her fingers together, as if ready to talk. "Get me a coffee," she said, "and I'll give you a little something."

43

.

Ruban heard his ringtone in the darkness. He sat up in the bed. Silence, except for the gentle sound of Savannah's breathing.

Was I dreaming?

He looked around. The curtains were drawn and the room was dark, save for the greenish glow from his cell phone, which was charging on the night-stand. His gaze came to rest on Savannah's face, half-buried beneath twists of long brown hair. She was sound asleep.

Ruban had told her nothing about his latest talk with Edith. He was still trying to figure out how to avoid the meeting that Savannah wanted with her. Edith would surely demand more money to face Savannah's questioning, and there was no way a face-to-face encounter with Edith would give Savannah any sort of reassurance. Expunging his criminal record was the answer. Ruban needed to *prove* to Savannah that the domestic violence con-viction was built on lies. It wasn't enough to point out that Edith would never consent to Kyla's adop-

tion if Ruban were truly an abuser. He needed un-
equivocal refutation of the charges by his accuser.

He lay back and let his head sink into the pillow.
It took a while for his eyes to close. As soon as they
did, his cell rang again. He grabbed it before it could
wake Savannah.

"Hello?" he whispered.

"It's me, mon. Ramsey."

"Hold on." Ruban slid out of bed, careful not to
wake Savannah, and went into the bathroom. He
took a seat on the cold tile floor, his back against the
closed door, and kept the light off. "What are you
calling me for?"

"It's your brother-in-law, mon. He been kidnapped again."

Ruban could have crushed the phone with his
bare hand. "You son of a bitch. Are you playing me
for another ransom?"

"No, no, mon. I never played you the last time.
We both got double-crossed."

"Go to hell, Ramsey."

"No, listen to me, mon. Jeffrey just rang me."

"Why would he call you?"

"He's afraid to ring you, mon. He thinks you be
pissed at him for going back to the Gold Rush."

Ruban could barely comprehend it. "He went
back?"

"This is what I'm sayin', mon. Jeffrey came by
the club tonight. It was like old times. All coked up,
he blowin' through his money. Buyin' the expensive
bottles of champagne. His friend Sully selling him
the Rolexes."

"Sully was there?"

"Of course Sully was there. These dancers are smart business ladies. They see Jeffrey walk into the club, they get on their cell phone and ring Mr. Sully the Jeweler. They make a thousand dollars every time he sells a nice watch."

"Was Jeffrey with that dancer who walked him to my car? Bambi?"

"No, mon. Bambi is gone. Jeffrey was with Sylvia."

"Who's Sylvia?"

"Ah, she's a sharp one. Romanian."

Ruban's anger was rising. He could almost smell the con. "Are you working with *her* this time, Ramsey?"

"No, you got it all wrong, mon. There was no 'last time,' and there's no '*this*' time.' I been tryin' my best to help you and your brother-in-law. Tonight I go to his table and I say, 'Jeffrey, are you crazy, mon? What you comin' back here for? Dis place not safe for you.' I tell him I can be his Guardian Angel."

"His what?"

"I says I can keep an eye out for him. I promise to tell him if anyone comes into the club that he should be worried about."

"Sounds like you did a pretty shitty job."

"I did my best, mon. I be workin' the bar. I can't help after Jeffrey left."

"Did he leave alone?"

"No. With Sylvia. Then three hours later, five o'clock in the morning, Jeffrey rings me on my cell. He's crying. He's scared. His voice is shaking. He says he's been kidnapped again and needs his Guardian Angel to help him."

"This sounds like such bullshit."

"It's no bullshit! This is real, mon!"

"What kind of idiot do you think I am? You stung me last time. We're not going down this road again."

"Ruban, you be making a big mistake, mon. This is no trick!"

"Jeffrey's broke, isn't he?"

"What?"

"I thought he was broke already, but obviously he had more bills stashed somewhere. Now he's burned through his reserve, too. So you, Jeffrey, and this Romanian bitch cooked up a second kidnapping to con me out of another ransom. Well, fuck you, Ramsey! It's not happening."

"You're wrong, mon. This is no scam. Jeffrey's in real trouble. He needs help, big time."

"Jeffrey needs help? Fine. Tell him to call his mother. And don't call me again."

He disconnected, his cell screen went dark, and the bathroom got blacker. Ruban took a deep breath. There was a light rap on the bathroom door.

"Ruban?" Savannah asked. "Is everything okay in there?"

He pushed himself up from the floor, put his cell in the vanity drawer, and opened the door. "It's fine," he said in a calm voice.

"Who were you talking to?"

"No one."

Savannah scratched her head, more sleepy than confused. "I heard you talking to someone."

He kissed her on the forehead and started toward the bed. "It was nobody," he said. "Nobody important."

44
.

Andie spent Friday morning at the Histori-cal Museum of Southern Florida, getting bumped from one curator to the next. A series of seeming dead ends eventually linked together into a chain that led to an old Cuban exile named Valentín Cruz.

"Happy to help," said Cruz. He gave Andie his home address and agreed to meet there at lunch-time.

Thursday's interrogation of Edith Baird had yielded little of substance. Andie had left MDPD headquarters with little more than hints, generali-ties, and Edith's promise to deliver a name for the tidy sum of $250,000. The best "freebie" was Edith's remark that Octavio Alvarez and his accomplice had been boyhood friends in Cuba. Andie knew from the FBI dossier that Alvarez had come to the United States in the 1994 exodus, the third-largest wave of Cuban refugees in American history. It stood to reason that two childhood friends—men who had remained close enough to pull off a daring heist years later—might also have made that dangerous journey from Cuba together. Immigration records provided the names of all 38,000 refugees processed in the summer of 1994. To Andie's surprise, however, it was virtually impossible to identify "raft mates," unless the refugees were related. Valentín Cruz held the missing link—she hoped.

The Cruz residence was in Cutler Ridge, a vintage 1970s suburb midway between Miami and the Florida Keys. His boxy, one-story house was a relic of a lost architectural era, neither its jalousie windows nor its flat roof meeting the hurricane building codes of the twenty-first century. Cruz greeted Andie with a smile and took her to his garage.

"*El Museo*," he called it. The Museum.

Cruz was a wounded veteran of the ill-fated Bay of Pigs invasion who believed that God had spared his life on that bloody Cuban beach in April 1961 for a reason. He'd devoted his life in exile to the successful resettlement of Cuban refugees. His crowning accomplishment was in the summer of 1994, three years after the collapse of the Soviet Union, when the end of Eastern Bloc subsidies pushed Cuba to the breaking point and thousands fled in desperation. Cruz served as director of the Key West Transit House on Stock Island, a nongovernmental way station of sorts for the *balseros* who survived the ninety-mile journey from Cuba. The Transit House received refugees from the Coast Guard and funneled them to the Catholic charities in Miami, which conducted orientation and resettlement efforts for as many as three hundred new arrivals a day.

"My plan was to turn the Stock Island house into a museum," said Cruz, "but we couldn't afford the rent. We tried moving to Coconut Grove, right next to City Hall, but that fizzled. Our last shot was an old firehouse in Little Havana that the city was willing to lease for one dollar a month, but the building was falling down and we couldn't raise the money to fix it up. So all the things I collected and saved for El Museo del Hogar de Tránsito—the rafts, the photographs, the papers—it's all here."

Andie was drawn toward the hunk of Styrofoam hanging from the ceiling. "Is that one of the rafts?"

"*Sí*. It washed up around Marathon. I had to get rid of many, many like it. No room to store all of them. This one I keep. It landed on the beach upside down. There was no one on it. We hope the rafters were picked up at sea. But we will never know."

It was a chilling piece of history. Cruz was eager to share more of it—enough to fill the museum that was never built—but Andie's needs were pressing and quite specific. "I want to know about the records you kept."

Cruz moved another raft out of the way and led her to the stacks of boxes at the back end of the garage. They covered the entire wall, each column three-deep and twelve boxes high. "This is everything," he said.

"I was hoping for a searchable CD or, at worst, a floppy disk. It's all on paper?"

"Yes. We worked the old-fashioned way. My hope was to scan these records into a computer, but that never happened."

"How is this organized?"

"Chronologically, more or less. The peak was in August, but around May we could see the first signs of a coming flood. Dozens of Cubans occupied the Belgian ambassador's residence and asked for asylum. Another group entered the German embassy. Things just kept escalating. By late June we were getting hundreds of letters from people in Miami telling us that their father, their aunt, their cousins—whoever—left Cuba on a raft a week ago, ten days ago. The family had no information. Did their loved ones make it to shore? Did the Coast Guard pick them up? Did they drown? Did the Gulf Stream carry them out to sea?"

"So that's what you have in these boxes? Those letters?"

"That's part of it. Like I said, we heard from so many worried families. We wanted to help, but imagine the task. Thousands of people left Cuba without documents, or they lost their papers at sea. So we started doing our own interviews and getting detailed information about the rafters who came through the Transit House."

"More than what the Coast Guard collected, you mean."

"Way more. The main concern of the government in those stage-one interviews was to verify that the refugees were actually from Cuba. You have to remember that rafts were also coming over from Haiti, which was a whole different process. Only Cubans got automatic asylum. Our job was to unite families."

"That's what I'm asking. You collected more than name, date of birth, what town they were from in Cuba?"

"We got all the information we could. The day they left Cuba, where they pushed out to sea, where they landed. Everything."

"What about the names of other refugees on the raft? Did you get that information?"

"Of course. It was important to know who they traveled with, especially if any passengers were lost at sea. If the raft had a name, we wrote that down, too. *La Esperanza. Tío B.* Anything that could help link a rafter to family or friends."

Andie smelled pay dirt. "Let me be more specific. If the Coast Guard told me that a man named Octavio Alvarez landed in Key West on August twenty-third, could you tell me who else was on his raft?"

"*Sí, sí.* He would have come through the Transit House. That's where the Coast Guard sent the rafters who made it to Key West."

"Can you show me which box that information would be in?"

"Well, this isn't exactly the National Archives. Even with a specific date, I can only give you a general idea where to look."

Andie sized up the wall of boxes. It was no small task, but buried somewhere beneath tons of yellowed paper was the name of Octavio Alvarez's accomplice—she could feel it.

"Good enough," she said. "Let the fun begin."

45

·

Not again. Jeffrey couldn't shake the thought. It reminded him of that old Bill Murray flick, *Groundhog Day*, except there was nothing funny about getting kidnapped over and over. He recalled staggering out of the Gold Rush, crossing the dark parking lot, freezing up at the press of a gun into his lower spine. The first kidnapping had left him wary of strangers, and he would never have left the Gold Rush with Sylvia, but it turned out that Bambi hadn't run off to join the convent after all. In fact, Bambi called to invite him *and* Sylvia to come party at her place. "Sylvia's one of my best friends," Bambi had told him over the phone, a girl to be trusted. Some best friend. Sylvia sure had Bambi fooled.

Gotta warn Bambi when I get out of this place.

He tried to sit up, but he couldn't lift his head off the mattress. His brain was a fog, but his recollection of those tense moments outside the club was clear enough. "Shut your mouth and keep your eyes forward," the man had told him. Unlike the first time around, however, he detected no Jamaican accent, and they didn't take Jeffrey's car. The man walked Jeffrey to another vehicle, shoved him in the trunk, and off they went. From then on, the second kidnapping was nothing like the first. This time, there was no disabling blow to the back of his head. No waking up in a dark garage on a concrete floor. No shackles or abuse. He was blindfolded for the walk from the trunk of the car to the house or apartment, he wasn't sure which. His room was windowless but air-conditioned, furnished with a comfortable bed, a chair, and a lamp atop the nightstand. It was like a small master suite. The closet was padlocked, but he was free to use the bathroom. There was a cooler filled with snacks and bottled water. And, biggest relief of all, Jeffrey still had all of his new gold caps.

Those first kidnappers had beaten and tortured him from the start, kicking him in the face with steel-toed boots, yanking out his nails and gold caps with pliers, laughing at his misery. They'd demanded to know how much money he had and where it was hidden. This new guy was very different, and not just because it was *one guy*. Jeffrey wasn't sure how long he'd been held captive, but it had been hours, and his kidnapper had yet to mention money. It was as if he knew that Jeffrey had blown through his cash, that he'd spent his last dollars on those bottles of Cristal for Sylvia—that the ransom would come from someone other than Jeffrey.

He heard footsteps on the other side of the door, then the rattle of keys. The deadbolt turned, and Jeffrey stepped back as the door opened.

"On the bed, face toward the wall," the man said from the dark hallway.

Jeffrey had the sinking feeling that the furlough was about to end. He lay on his side, his back to the door as the man entered the room.

"How'd you sleep, big guy?"

Jeffrey hesitated, puzzled by the cordial tone. "Fine," he said.

The man pulled up the chair. "You can look at me. Sit up."

Jeffrey rolled away from the wall, let his feet drop over the edge of the mattress, and sat facing his kidnapper. The man was wearing blue jeans, an "I ♥ New York" sweatshirt, and a rubber Halloween hood. Jeffrey was talking to Barack Obama.

"I like you, Jeffrey."

Jeffrey wasn't sure how to respond. "I like you, too."

"Michelle and I sincerely hope that we can get through this without having to fuck you up too badly."

"Michelle?"

"That was a joke."

The mask. "Ah. I get it."

"Do you?"

Jeffrey noted the change in tone, a bitter edge to it. "Do I what?"

"Do you *get it*?"

Again the tone confused him; the right answer wasn't at all clear. "I think I do."

The man leaned forward, resting his forearms on his thighs. "You *think* you do. That concerns me, Jeffrey. When someone gets kidnapped outside a strip club, and then he goes right back to the same strip club, it makes me wonder: Does he *ever* really get it? Or is he just a hopeless fuckup?"

"I'm not hopeless."

The man reached into his pocket and pulled out a pearl-handled knife with the blade still encased. He flicked it open, which made Jeffrey start. It wasn't technically a knife. He was holding a straight razor.

A lump came to Jeffrey's throat. "Please don't hurt me."

"Whoa, whoa," the man said, almost chuckling. "Hurt you? You're getting way ahead of the game."

"What're you gonna do with that?"

The man moved his chair closer and pushed the lamp to the edge of the nightstand, making room on the glass top. He pulled a palm-size packet of cocaine from his other pocket, neatly slit off the corner, and poured the contents onto the glass. "This is really good shit," he said as he cut the white pile into five lines with the razor's sharp edge. "Taste it."

Jeffrey collected a trace of powder on his fingertip and placed it on his tongue. The cool, numbing sensation almost sang to him. "That *is* good."

"You got a bill we can roll?" the man asked. "No, wait. I forgot. You pissed away all your dough, right?"

It was his kidnapper's first mention of money. Jeffrey didn't answer.

The man took a crisp hundred-dollar bill from his wallet, rolled it tightly, and handed it to Jeffrey. "Have at it, sport."

Jeffrey hesitated, still wondering what the man might do with that razor. His kidnapper seemed to sense the concern and put the blade away. Jeffrey leaned over the table and went at the coke like a vacuum cleaner, one line at a time, a series of glorious blasts to the pleasure center of his brain. Even the burn in his nostrils was oddly pleasant, and he savored the familiar bitter aftertaste in the back of his throat. He tilted back his head to catch the drip, then laid the rolled-up hundred-dollar bill aside and smiled at the buzz. "Wow," was all he could say.

"I told you it was good," the man said.

"You got any more?"

"You want more?"

"Once I get started, it's hard for me to stop."

The man opened the nightstand drawer, removed a much larger bag of cocaine, and rested it on the glass. It was as big as his fist.

"That's a lot of coke," said Jeffrey.

"Yes, it is. It's all for you."

Jeffrey glanced at the bulging bag, then back at the Obama mask. "I guess I'm going to be here a long time. Is that what you're saying?"

"No. You're going to do all of it . . . *now*."

Jeffrey chuckled nervously, but he detected no sense of humor behind the mask.

"Every last line," the man said, "till there is no more."

"But . . . that's enough coke to kill an elephant."

"You got that right, Dumbo." He poured the coke from the bag, spilling a white mountain onto the tabletop.

"Come on," said Jeffrey. "Seriously?"

"What's wrong?"

"That's too much."

"Too much of a good thing? A little late in the day to start humming that tune, don't you think?"

Jeffrey wiped his nose nervously, sniffing back the cocaine residue. "Please, man. Really. I don't want to die."

The man flipped open the straight razor and cut the first line. "We're all gonna die, Jeffrey. Let's get this party started."

46

•

Andie found her man in Key West Transit House, box number 47.

Valentín Cruz had given her a "general idea" of where to find the records relating to Octavio Alvarez, and his definition of "general" was among the broadest Andie had ever encountered. She'd sifted through scores of cardboard boxes, thousands of handwritten pages, and the flickering fluorescent light in the garage was a strain on her eyes. Having lived around migrant workers in Washington's Yakima Valley, Andie spoke Spanish well enough, but reading it was a chore in the best of circumstances, and the hastily written notes of overworked Transit House volunteers presented a special challenge. Hours into the task, she had her reward. The yellowed documents on the concrete floor before her were original intake sheets for Octavio Alvarez and the man she'd been looking for: Karl Betancourt. Each had identified the other as a raft mate, along with a woman and her fifteen-year-old daughter. Both men had reported the name of their vessel:

"*Se Vende*," said Andie, reading aloud.

Notes on Octavio's intake sheet explained that the Havana man who'd cobbled the raft together deemed the journey too dangerous, so he put it up for sale. The buyers kept the "For Sale" sign and dubbed their raft the *Se Vende*. Not exactly the *Niña*, *Pinta*, or *Santa Maria*, but heartwarming in its own way.

Andie sealed the intake sheets in an evidence bag and drove from the would-be museum to the FBI field office. Background checks were next, followed by more digging and brainstorming. At day's end, she walked into her unit chief's office to make her pitch.

"I think I've identified the second perp at the MIA warehouse," she said.

A mound of paperwork stretched from one end of Littleford's desk to the other. He peered over the top of his reading glasses and simply asked, "Who?"

"Karl Betancourt. He goes by Ruban. He manages a restaurant in Sunny Isles called Café Ruban."

"I've heard of it. Kind of a Russian-Cuban menu, right?"

Andie seated herself in the armchair facing his desk. "Exactly. Hence the name Ruban, a play on 'Russian-Cuban.'"

"Are you saying there's a Russian connection to this heist?"

"I don't know yet. But definitely a Ruban connection."

"Let's hear it."

She told him how Edith Baird had linked Alvarez to a boyhood friend in Cuba, and how she'd pieced things together through the Transit House records.

As usual—Andie was getting accustomed to his style—Littleford's initial reaction was skepticism.

"Edith Baird sounds like a money grubber. Why should we believe her?"

"First, because it makes sense. Alvarez and Betancourt grew up together, they risked their lives to come to this country together, they got rich together. Second, Edith Baird knows him well. Betancourt lived with Edith's daughter, and he pleaded guilty to domestic violence. No jail time, but he's a convicted felon."

"I'd be more impressed if the conviction was for armed robbery."

"There's more," said Andie. "Betancourt is married now. Get this: his wife is the niece of Craig Perez."

It took a second for Littleford to make a mental run through the limbs of the family tree. "Betancourt is related to Pinky?"

"By marriage."

"Remind me again: What's the status on Pinky?"

"You authorized surveillance, but we can't find him. I'm working an undercover angle with Priscilla from Night Moves, trying to set up a meeting. But Betancourt is a safer route that potentially ropes in the entire gang."

"I like it. The problem is that if you bring in Betancourt for questioning, Pinky will probably leave the country, if he hasn't already."

"I agree. I say we cancel the surveillance tail you approved for Pinky and shift it to Betancourt. Zero added expense. And we get a wiretap on Betancourt: two landlines—home and business—and his cell. I've already checked with his carrier. Four-hundred-dollar activation fee, plus ten dollars per day for access to his text, voice mail, and e-mail. Overall minimal impact on our budget."

The average person had no idea that the feds actually had to pay the carrier to surveil phone activity, and Littleford seemed appreciative of Andie's sensitivity to the administrative headaches that most agents at her level left to their supervisors. But he didn't look totally convinced. "If you add in the actual manpower expense of monitoring the surveillance, do you know what the average cost of a federal wiretap is, Andie?"

"I'm sure it's up there."

"Fifty-seven thousand dollars. That's why this office has done a grand total of twelve this year. This ain't TV, where we do one on every weekly episode."

"Are you saying no?"

"I'd be more inclined to say yes if we had a stronger application. I'm sure our friends at the U.S. attorney's office would feel more confident if we had recent contact between Alvarez and his old friend Betancourt. The rafting connection is a long time ago."

Andie, playing her ace, laid a thin file on his desk. "Cell-phone records," she said.

"Whose?"

"Betancourt's."

"How'd you get this?"

"I've never had good success getting historical information out of cell-phone carriers without a warrant. Betancourt's had no problem showing me what numbers he's been dialing for the past six months.

I highlighted every call to or from Alvarez's phone number."

Littleford thumbed through the records. "Nothing after the Fourth of July."

"Curious, don't you think? Talk, talk, talk. Then nothing. It's as if they reached an agreement not to make any more calls to each other before the heist."

Littleford handed back the file. "Follow up with the U.S. attorney's office."

"You'll sign off on the wiretap?"

"Let's nail it down ASAP," he said, returning to his paperwork.

Andie jumped from her chair and started for the door.

"Henning," he said, stopping her in the doorway.

"Yeah?"

"You do realize that you just talked yourself out of that undercover assignment with this Priscilla from Night Moves, right?"

"I know. Betancourt is clearly the better way to go."

Littleford looked at her with some combination of pride and curiosity, as if to acknowledge that not every aspiring undercover agent would have exercised the same judgment. "Good work," he said, returning to his paperwork.

Andie smiled to herself and hurried down the hall.

47

.

Jeffrey could not stop walking. Around the bed, to the door, to the lamp, back to the opposite wall. He paced with intensity, as if determined to burn a path into the carpet. His heart pounded, not only in his chest but in his temples and left tricep as well. His breathing was shallow and rapid. The room seemed to be getting inexplicably smaller. Hotter, too.

Don't get paranoid.

Two more jaunts around the room, faster and faster. He paused just long enough to check the thermostat on the wall. Eighty-one degrees. No, he wasn't paranoid; it was getting hotter by the minute. The march continued. His fastest leg yet. He stopped again at the thermostat and switched the fan from AUTOMATIC to the continuous ON position. Nothing. Obama had killed the air conditioning.

Son of a bitch!

He continued his walk, counting his steps from start to finish, then starting all over again: *eighteen, nineteen, one, two, three* . . . Sweat was soak-

ing through his shirt. The carpet was like hot
coals beneath his feet. His face and neck tingled
with fever. Cocaine fever. Skin on fire all over his
body—back, chest, arms, legs. He pulled off his
shirt, stripping down to his waist, but it made no
difference. He checked the thermostat one more
time: eighty-three degrees.

"Shit!" he said, banging his fist against the wall.

Coke had never done this to him before, but that
big bag on the nightstand couldn't have been more
than one-quarter cocaine. Anything purer would
have killed him in that quantity, for sure. Those first
five lines on the glass had been ass kickers, but the
bag had been diluted with something. The taste of
corn starch or some other sugar was unmistakable, a
common trick of dealers. But there must have been
a more volatile agent in that white mountain—a
chemical that was bubbling from within, boiling his
blood, scorching his skin.

Jeffrey ran to the bathroom. An icy cold shower
would do the trick. He didn't even bother removing his pants before turning the "C" valve. Not a
drop. He tried the "H" valve, turning, turning, and
turning as far and as hard as he could, using all his
strength. It snapped off in his hand. Still no water.
He pulled back the shower curtain, ripping it from
the rod, and threw himself at the sink. Nothing
but a strange vibrating noise in the pipes from the
"cold" faucet. Nothing at all from the "hot." Obama
had turned off the water.

Motherfucker!

Jeffrey dropped to his knees and raised the toilet
lid. *Water!* He scooped it with his bare hands and

splashed his face until the bowl was empty. He flushed for more, eagerly dunking his head and hair in the cool running water, the thought never occurring that he could have simply removed the lid from the tank and avoided the dirty bowl.

A noise from the hallway stopped him cold. He heard the deadbolt turn and the door open. Jeffrey climbed to his feet and stepped out of the bathroom. Mr. Obama was back.

"Sit on the bed," he said.

Toilet water dripped from Jeffrey's hair and face. "I can't. Gotta keep moving."

"Sit!"

The harsh tone frightened him, and Jeffrey quickly took a seat on the edge of the mattress. Both legs kept moving, bouncing up and down uncontrollably.

"You want more coke?" the man in the rubber mask asked.

"Yeah, yeah. I mean, no. I mean—shit!" he shouted, burying his wet face in his hands. "You got me all fucked up, bro!"

His kidnapper pulled up the chair, sat back, and crossed his legs, totally relaxed. "You're a mess," he said calmly.

Jeffrey kept vibrating. "I can't help it!"

"Yes, you can. I'm going to give you a chance, Jeffrey. Just one chance to help yourself."

The fever was gone; the toilet water had done the trick. Jeffrey was feeling cold. He folded his arms across his bare chest and started rocking back and forth. "Thank you, thank you, bro. I'll do whatever it takes."

The man pulled a photograph from his pocket and held it in front of Jeffrey's face. "Stop rocking and tell me who this is."

Jeffrey forced himself to sit still. "That's Marco," he said, and then resumed his rocking.

"I'm glad you didn't lie to me, Jeffrey. I know what you did at the airport. I know Marco Aroyo was part of the team. It's very important that you tell me the truth."

Jeffrey was rocking so fast he was short of breath. "I'm not gonna lie to you."

"Good. Do you know what happens if you lie to me?"

Jeffrey didn't answer. He didn't even want to think about it.

The man pulled another photograph from his pocket and held it so that Jeffrey could see. Jeffrey froze—no rocking, no leg motion, barely a breath of air. It was the "after" photograph of Marco Aroyo.

"Shit, man!" he said as he looked away, cringing. "I won't lie. I promise. Don't do that to me. Please, don't!"

He laid the photograph aside. "Now, about that chance to help yourself: here's how it works. We're going to make one phone call to your brother-in-law. It's a team effort. The two of us are going to remind him how much he loves you. You good with that?"

"Yeah, okay. Whatever you say."

The president took a cigarette lighter from his pocket, reached for the "after" photograph, and lit the corner. It burned slowly at first, and then burst into flames. Jeffrey watched nervously, until the man tossed it onto the floor, right at Jeffrey's feet. It singed his big toe, and Jeffrey cried out, in fear more than pain.

"Don't hurt me! Please, don't!"

The fire burned itself out, the remnants of the photograph only slightly more charred than the actual man who was in it.

"Nothing to worry about," he told Jeffrey, "as long as your brother-in-law shows us the love."

48
.

Ruban spent Friday's happy hour at the BMW car dealership.

He'd picked up his old Malibu from the paint and body shop around noon. The thinking was that a color change would make it safe to drive again, just in case someone had seen him with Octavio before the hit-and-run. It looked awesome in metallic blue, and Ruban decided it was at peak trade-in value, irresistible to any self-respecting gangbanger who had the cash to dress it up with chrome rims and low-rider suspension. The time had come to dump it.

"We have very attractive financing available," the salesman said.

It was just the two of them in the tiny sales office. A glass wall separated them from the cavernous showroom. Behind them, beneath the LED lights, an assortment of new German vehicles glistened.

"I'll pay cash," said Ruban. "Less five grand for my trade-in."

"Which vehicle are you interested in?"

"The Six Series. Convertible. In black."

"Let's see what I have on the lot," the salesman said, checking his computer.

Ruban watched from the other side of the desk as the salesman scrolled down the list. The sticker value on many of these cars approached six figures, but that was still a fraction of what he'd taken in the heist.

Hiding the money had been the smart plan, but not if Ruban was the only one doing it. He was fed up with Jeffrey and Pinky. He knew Edith Baird was a con artist who would scam him in a minute. Octavio's girlfriend had all the markings of a greedy bitch. Ruban wasn't sure how he was going to convince Savannah that he hadn't used "Jeffrey's money" to buy an eighty-thousand-dollar car, but he'd worry about that later. It was time he spent some damn money—before everyone else burned through it.

"We have two in black," said the salesman. "One's the sport package."

"That's the one I want."

"Excellent choice. Our mechanic will need your car keys to evaluate the trade-in. Meanwhile, let me check with my manager and see if I can get the very best price for you."

Ruban handed over the keys and tried not to burst out laughing as the salesman left the office. *The very best price for you.* The airport heist paled in comparison to the car-dealer dance of duplicity. *Talk about lying thieves.*

His cell rang and Jeffrey's number popped up. Ruban let it go to voice mail, but another ring followed immediately, the same number. This time Ruban answered. It wasn't Jeffrey.

"I have your brother-in-law, the fat one," the caller said.

No Jamaican accent; it wasn't Ramsey. "Who is this?"

"Your wake-up call. I know what you guys did, and I don't want to get involved with the feds or anything like that. That's not my problem. The only thing I want is my money."

"*Your* money?"

"Yeah. It's mine now. Half a million should do it."

Ruban checked his anger, then reached behind and closed the office door. "Listen to me, asshole. I don't know who you are, and I don't care. I'm not paying a dime to you or anyone else."

"You need a better attitude, or your brother-in-law is going to feel a lot of pain."

Ruban wasn't buying it. He'd put Ramsey in his place earlier, and this call smelled no less like a scam. He wasn't sure who this new voice was, the guy playing the role of "kidnapper," but Ruban couldn't resist calling his bluff. "Pain is temporary," said Ruban.

"What?"

"You heard me. Pain, schmain. Jeffrey will get over it."

"This is your brother-in-law we're talking about."

"I understand. But I have nothing to do with what Jeffrey's done with his life. Do what you gotta do, pal."

There was silence on the line, as if the caller couldn't quite comprehend. "Hold on. I want you to tell that to Jeffrey."

Ruban was tempted to hang up, but he wanted his brother-in-law to know that he was onto his game.

Jeffrey came on the line, his voice racing. "Bro, you got to fix this!"

"What do you want me to do?"

"Pay him! Where's your money?"

"I spent it all."

"No!"

"Strippers, cocaine, diamonds on my timepiece, tigers on a gold leash. It's all gone."

"Don't do this! Does the money mean more to you than me, than my life?"

"Hey, you looked for it, bro. Now you deal with it. I told you to get the fuck out of Miami, but you wanted to party. Now deal with it."

"I can't believe you're saying this!"

Ruban glanced over his shoulder, through the glass wall. No sign of the salesman in the showroom, but he was sure to return soon. It was time to put this nonsense to bed. "Jeffrey, I'm done playing these games. You're on your own."

"Please, please, don't say that. This guy is a killer, bro. He showed me Marco's picture."

Ruban hesitated. The mention of Marco made it seem less like a game, but Ruban stuck to his guns. "I don't believe you. You sound all coked up to me."

"Yes, I am! He made me do a mountain of coke!"

"Made you," Ruban said, scoffing. "Yeah, kidnappers are generous that way, always sharing their coke. What kind of idiot do you think I am, Jeffrey?"

"This is real, bro! If you don't pay, he's going to light me up like a Roman candle, just like he did with Marco."

"Stop it, Jeffrey!" he said bitterly. "I'm done playing this game. Ramsey called me this morning and fed me the same bullshit."

"Huh?"

"It was pathetic," said Ruban, turning on his Jamaican accent, mimicking Ramsey: "'Jeffrey rang me on my cell, mon. He's crying. He's scared. His voice is shaking. He says he's been kidnapped again and needs his Guardian Angel to help him.'"

"I never called Ramsey!"

"Don't lie to me. What'd you do, cook this up at the Gold Rush over a gram of coke and a thousand-dollar bottle of champagne? 'Hey, here's a *plahn*, mon,'" he said, turning on the accent again, "'let's call Ruban and tell him his *bruddah*-in-law be kidnapped, get a half million out of him.'"

"No, no! I never called Ramsey about being kidnapped. This is not a con, bro!"

"Who'd you get to play the kidnapper? One of Ramsey's buddies?"

"I don't know who he is, but he burned Marco to a crisp! This is *not* a joke! He is going to torch me!"

"Well, that's too fucking bad, Jeffrey. You can burn now. You can burn in hell. I don't care anymore. Don't call me again."

Ruban hung up, so full of anger that he was out of breath. He realized that to an outsider his words would have sounded cold as ice, but it was the only way to deal with a desperate drug addict who was out of money. This kidnapping wasn't real. Jeffrey was working with Ramsey. No one was going to burn Jeffrey. No way.

Unless it's not a scam.

There was that possibility. Ruban reached for his cell, ready to dial Ramsey's number, then stopped. If he was going to cut through the smoke, a phone call wouldn't do it. Better to have a face-to-face with Ramsey and catch him unawares—an ambush.

The door opened. "Good news," the salesman said as he breezed into the office. "I can let you drive away in a beautiful black Six Series convertible with the sport package for eighty-three thousand."

"That's three grand over sticker."

"I know, isn't that great? My manager has never done this on a back-ordered vehicle. A small premium puts you ahead of everyone on the waiting list."

Ruban rose. "Give me my car keys."

"Whoa, where you going, my friend?"

"Outta here."

"I see you drive a hard bargain. Maybe I can get my manager to see his way to eighty-two-five."

"I want my keys."

"Let's sit down and discuss—"

"My keys. *Now.*"

The salesman patted down his pants pockets, as if searching. "Damn. I must have left them with the mechanic. Unfortunately, he just went on break and won't be back till—"

Ruban grabbed him by the collar and got right in his face. "Give me my fucking car keys or I will snap your skinny neck."

Slowly, the salesman pulled the keys from his coat pocket. Ruban snatched them away and gave the salesman a little shove on his way out of the office, then hurried across the glitzy showroom and into the parking lot. That tired old game—*Keys, keys, who's got the car keys?*—had pissed him off, but nothing good would come from taking it out on a two-bit salesman.

Save it for Ramsey.

He climbed into his metallic-blue Malibu and drove toward the Gold Rush. The bullshit was about to end.

49

·

Around eight o'clock, Andie heard from the assistant U.S. attorney by phone. Friday evening wasn't the worst time for the AUSA to put an emergency request for a wiretap before a federal judge, but it was far from the best. Nonetheless, the news was good: "Application granted." Andie followed up with a tech agent about the landlines, and with the Wireless Intercept and Tracking Team for the cell. Agent Gustafson was her WITT contact.

"How soon do you need it?" asked Gustafson.

"Twelve hours ago," said Andie.

"You should have come to me then. No techie worth his salt needs a carrier's cooperation to monitor mobile devices."

"No crook worth his salt uses his cell anymore if he can avoid it. We needed landlines, too."

"There are ways to listen to cell-phone conversations before getting a warrant that covers the whole enchilada. That's all I'm saying."

Wireless intercepts were in the legal gray zone, but in Andie's thinking there was a time and place to test the limits of the Fourth Amendment. "I'll keep that in mind the next time I'm trying to stop a terrorist from blowing up a building. Right now I'm after a robbery conviction, not a constitutional debate over the admissibility of evidence at trial."

"Got it."

By nine p.m. the FBI had its target covered three ways: Ruban Betancourt's cell, and the landlines at Café Ruban and the Betancourt residence. Andie briefed the monitoring team and left the real-time surveillance to the experts. She was driving home from the field office when her cell rang. It was on the line she'd established for her undercover assignment at Night Moves. The call was from Priscilla.

"Hey, girlfriend, where are you?" asked Priscilla.

Andie's undercover role as Celia Sellers was technically over. She took Priscilla's call just to see if the seed she'd planted about Pinky had borne fruit.

"Staying home tonight," said Andie. "I think I'm coming down with a cold."

"Aww, too bad. I'm at the club now. I was hoping you could come."

Andie changed lanes, moving into slower traffic on I-95 as she spoke. "Did you follow up on what we talked about?"

"You mean Pinky?"

"Yeah. Did you talk to him about me?"

"I tried, but his cell has been disconnected, and I haven't seen him at the club. The guy just seems to have vanished."

Tell me about it. Andie stayed in role. "There must be someone at the club who's seen him."

"No one I talked to."

"Hmm. That's a bummer."

"There are lots of other men here at the club, Celia."

"I'm sure. But I was kind of looking forward to . . . well, you know."

"His big personality?" Priscilla asked with a chuckle.

"Right, *personality*. What every girl wants. Any idea how we can make this work?"

"Just one. I could ask his best friend, Pedro. But that's a really bad idea."

Andie wanted a last name, but it didn't seem like a question that Celia Sellers could ask. "Why would that be bad?"

"Pedro is one sick bastard."

A "sick bastard" by Priscilla's standards had to be quite a piece of work. "In what way?" asked Andie.

"If I tell Pedro that you're interested in hooking up with Pinky, you can bet he'll want in on the action. I've been down that road, and I don't recommend it. The craziness is only beginning when he whips out the fire tower."

"The what?"

"You've never heard of a fire tower?"

"No."

"Me neither," said Priscilla, "until I met Pedro. It's like that old trick where you cover your finger with grain alcohol, light it on fire, and dip it in water before it burns your skin. Except with Pedro it isn't his finger, and he doesn't dip it in water. It's also called a 'Greek fire,' which might give you a better idea of which end is used to put out the flame."

Andie maintained her law enforcement focus.

She was suddenly thinking of Marco Aroyo and the burn marks in the box truck. "So Pinky's friend likes fire?"

"He's a freakin' pyromaniac. 'Pyro Pedro,' we call him. I think he's a welder or something."

Death by blowtorch. "Pedro sounds kinky."

"He's beyond kinky. A night with Pedro is like having sex in the flames of hell. Literally."

Andie considered it. Strictly speaking, finding Marco Aroyo's killer was the job of Detective Watts and the homicide unit at MDPD, but it could also be the road to cracking the heist—which was Andie's job. "I'm not one to rule out anything too quickly. I may want to meet this Pedro."

"*What?* Are you serious?"

"Yeah, I am," said Andie. She forced a cough, still playing sick. "But not tonight. Let me sleep on it."

"Good idea," said Priscilla. "Think hard. You know, I have to say, when I first met you, I never would have guessed you would want any part of a guy like Pedro. You're just a box of surprises. Has anybody ever told you that?"

"All the time," said Andie.

"Feel better, girlfriend."

"Feeling better already," said Andie, and then she said good night.

50

·

Jeffrey could feel himself crashing.

The mountain of cocaine hadn't killed him, but he was starting to wish it had. He was alone in the windowless room, seated on the edge of the bed, staring at the wall. His gaze was fixed on a crack that ran from the top right corner of the door frame. It continued in a straight line for about another three feet before dropping straight down the wall all the way to the baseboard. He'd studied it from start to finish countless times, his gaze following the same path over and over again for almost an hour.

Seven?

It looked a little like a big number on the wall, but the angles were too upright. It reminded him more of the hangman game that he and Savannah used to play as kids. The paneled door was the dead stickman dangling from the gallows. If he stared at the door long enough, the "body" seemed to move, as if swaying at the end of a rope. The movement was starting to bother him, but he couldn't look away.

He cocked his head left, then right, trying to stop the motion, but that dead stickman kept moving.

Stop!

The door opened, and Jeffrey caught his breath. Obama was back.

"How we doing, fat boy?"

Jeffrey wiped away the sweat from his upper lip. His kidnapper still hadn't bothered to bind his hands. The cocaine crash was enough to immobilize him.

"I been better," said Jeffrey.

Obama had a cardboard bankers box with him. The rattling told Jeffrey that it contained something made of glass. His kidnapper pulled up the chair, set the box on the floor, and removed the lid. Glass vials, a beaker, and several bottles were inside. It was like a chemistry set.

"Have you ever freebased?" he asked.

Jeffrey shuddered. The last thing he needed was more cocaine; the thing his body craved was more cocaine. "A few times," he said.

"Those lines you did earlier had lots of junk in them. Not even close to pure."

Jeffrey wrung his hands. "Good thing. Or I'd be dead."

"True. But now it's time to get serious. We need to dissolve the shit away and get down to the good stuff."

He removed a small vial from the box. Jeffrey had seen it done before and knew it was just water inside. He watched as his captor spooned about a gram of cocaine into the vial. It dissolved before his eyes.

The man removed another vial from the box. "You know what this is?"

"Ammonia?"

"Very good. You *have* done this before."

Jeffrey watched the drops fall from an eyedropper, and the solution in the vial turned milky white. Then the man removed another vial from the box, which he handled with greater care than the ammonia. "You know what this is, don't you?"

Jeffrey didn't answer.

"Ethyl ether," the man said. "Very important final step in separating out the freebase, but also very dangerous. If you don't handle it just right it can spontaneously combust. *Poof.* Blows up right in your face."

"That's why I don't use it," said Jeffrey.

"Then you've never done it right."

The man started to open the bottle of ether, then stopped. "You ever hear of a comedian named Richard Pryor?"

"No."

"He was freebasing before you were born. Burned to a crisp. One of the first celebs to give the public a heads-up on how dangerous it is. Interesting thing is, when it first happened, there were a couple of rumors on how it went down exactly. Rumor one: freebasing. Ether blew up on him. But then there was rumor two."

Jeffrey watched with trepidation as the man put the ether bottle back inside the box and removed a much bigger bottle of liquor. He screwed off the cap, rose, and stood over Jeffrey. Jeffrey stared straight ahead, not moving a muscle.

"Rumor two has always intrigued me," the man said. "The story goes that in a drunken stupor, Pryor soaked himself in 151-proof rum and lit himself on fire. Cocaine psychosis, not freebasing."

Jeffrey felt the cold 151 pouring all over his body. The smell of rum soaked his skin, hair, shirt, and pants until the bottle was completely empty. The man tossed it aside, onto the mattress.

"These were just rumors, of course. But still, I wonder which would be the more painful way to go. I've seen ethyl ether burn a guy right up. Not pretty. That's what happened to your friend Marco. Dumb son of a bitch just wouldn't tell me where his money was."

He reached for his cell, brought up the image, and held it before Jeffrey's eyes. It was the same one Jeffrey had seen earlier in the glossy print, but it was no easier to look at the second time.

"Very painful," the man said. "At least I assume it was painful. Truthfully, I didn't get much feedback from Marco, unless you count all the screaming."

Jeffrey swallowed the lump in his throat. "Don't burn me, bro. Don't do that to me."

"I really don't want to," the man said. "I'm just having trouble believing that you don't have any money left."

"It's gone! I blew right through it."

"There's still a part of me that thinks you're lying."

"I'm not lying! I got nothing left!"

The man returned to his seat, staring at Jeffrey coldly through the eyeholes in that ridiculous-looking rubber mask. "Nothing, you say?"

"*Nada.* Not a cent!"

He reached inside his pocket and removed a pack of matches.

"No, man," said Jeffrey, his voice shaking. "Don't do this."

He opened the pack.

"My brother-in-law has money," said Jeffrey. "Lots of it. He'll pay you."

"He already said he won't."

"My sister will make him!"

"Your sister, huh?"

"Yeah, Savannah won't let you hurt me. She would never let that happen. Just put the matches away, please!"

"So, what you're saying is that I should keep you alive because your brother-in-law will pay?"

"Yes, exactly!"

"Makes sense, I guess. But I still don't believe you're out of money."

"I am, I swear! I'm an idiot, a total idiot. You can ask anybody. Even my own mother will tell you: she gave birth to a complete and total fucking idiot! I spent it all on strippers and watches and all kinds of stupid shit!"

"If there was ten cents of your money left, you'd tell me where it was, right?"

"Yes! Absolutely! But I have nothing left! I swear!"

He struck the match and held the yellow-orange glow by its cardboard stem.

"Please, please, don't!"

"Let's see if that's your story when we're done here," the man said. "Then I'll believe you."

51

The line was long outside the Gold Rush. Friday was always the busiest night of the week, and by nine o'clock the club had reached its fire-code maximum occupancy. Ruban stood outside the main entrance with a dozen other men who would rather wait than grease the bouncer's palm for immediate entry. The man behind him was alone, and everything from the bad haircut to the misspelled tattoo—*Villian*—screamed "loser." Ruban assumed he was a regular.

"How long does this usually take?" asked Ruban.

"Twenty minutes, tops. It's worth the wait."

A group of women arrived, drunk from happy hour, talking loudly and laughing way too much. Two young men at the back of the line started hitting on them, but the regular beside Ruban didn't look happy.

"I hate it when chicks crash our club," he said, grumbling.

Ruban didn't say anything, but Villian wouldn't let it go.

"You know what I'm saying, pal? They're everywhere. The golf course, the Dolphins games. Can't we at least have the fucking strip clubs to ourselves?"

Ruban dug his hands into his pockets and shrugged, not sure how to respond. "I guess it does make it harder to get in touch with your inner pervert."

"Exactly!" he said in a voice loud enough for the women to overhear. "How's a guy supposed to get in touch with his inner pervert with a bunch of giggly chicks at the next table?"

Ruban moved away, only to land beside a tourist wearing a Buffalo Bills jersey who was so awash in cheap cologne, so pungent, that he probably could have crossed the Florida Everglades without a single mosquito bite. Ruban sneezed, machine-gun fashion, five in a row.

"Shit, dude. Thanks for the shower."

Ruban didn't apologize. "Villian" the inner pervert and Buffalo Bill's synthetic musk were more than he could take. He slipped the bouncer a fifty and hurried inside.

It was Ruban's first visit to the Gold Rush, but it was what he'd expected, only bigger. The dancers seemed able to sniff out the big spenders who bribed their way past the bouncer. A tall brunette who was made even taller by a pair of spiked heels approached Ruban immediately. Her red leather pants and vest were full of strategically placed holes, leaving plenty for a roving eye to enjoy. Ruban's gaze was drawn to the Rolex on her wrist.

"Nice watch," he said over the music.

"Thanks." She was moving seductively to Lady

Gaga as she spoke, unable to stand still. "It was a gift."

"I know it was."

He walked past her, and she locked on to the next target as Ruban continued toward the bar. The music got even louder as he went deeper into the club. Every stool at the bar was taken, a mix of strippers and patrons, and people right beside each other were shouting to be heard. Ruban squeezed behind a blond stripper on a bar stool, accidentally brushing up against her trapezoids. She was hard like a bodybuilder.

"Don't touch," she said with attitude. "Unless I say it's okay."

"Sorry."

"Are you?" she said. More attitude.

"Yeah. I said I was sorry."

She turned to face him, flexing her overdeveloped pecs. "Say it like you mean it."

"What?"

"Say it like you mean it and I might let you drink my bathwater."

The kick-ass Nordic abuser was obviously her shtick, and there was probably no shortage of Gold Rush patrons who were into that sort of thing.

"Back off, Ingrid," said the bartender. His accent was Jamaican. It was Ramsey.

Ingrid shot Ramsey a playful look, then tossed her hair and stepped away, taking her dominatrix act to the other end of the bar.

"You here to see me?" asked Ramsey.

"I didn't come to give away Rolexes."

He wasn't sure Ramsey could hear him over the music, but apparently the message got across. Ramsey signaled to the other bartender to let him know he was going on break. Ruban followed him to the other side of the bar, around several tables, and toward the back exit. Ramsey stopped before they reached the door.

"Let's go outside," said Ruban.

"This is far enough."

They were halfway down the hallway, still in sight of the other bartender and at least one bouncer. It was quiet enough to have a conversation, and clearly Ramsey didn't feel safe stepping out into the parking lot with Ruban.

"All right," said Ruban. "Tell me what's going on."

"I told you, mon. I was telling the truth about Jeffrey."

Ruban stepped closer. "Let me explain something to you, Ramsey. The only reason I don't have both hands around your throat right now is that we're on your turf. But you can't hang out in this club forever. Sooner or later you gotta walk out that door. When you do, I'll be waiting for you. Unless you tell me the fucking truth here and now."

"What you threaten me for?"

"I don't believe Jeffrey called you this morning."

"Why would I lie about that?"

"Because this kidnapping is a scam. And you're part of it."

"No, mon. You got it all wrong."

"Look, I don't have time for games. One of the disadvantages of your having worked for me is that I know your immigration status. I know you came to

Miami on a ninety-day K-1 visa. I know you never married your cute little American fiancée and that your work permit expired a very long time ago. You're probably not the only illegal working here at the Gold Rush, but you're the only one I know about, and it's my duty as a responsible citizen to report you and your employer to Immigration."

"You suck."

"You lied about Jeffrey. Didn't you?"

"Okay, mon. Here's the truth. He didn't call me. But that was no lie about him gettin' kidnapped again."

"How do you know that?"

"He was here at the club last night. Sylvia was working him."

"Sylvia?"

"One of the dancers. She's friends with Bambi, so I'm sure she knows how Bambi played him for a pretty penny. I went over to Jeffrey's table and warned him, but he don't listen to nobody. Around two in the morning, Sylvia walks out to the parking lot with him, so I watch."

"What happened?"

"What I told you, mon. It's déjà vu all over again. Kidnapped."

"Same guys?"

"No. These be Sylvia's friends, not Bambi's."

"Where can I find Sylvia?"

"Who knows? These girls come and go."

Ruban's eyes narrowed. He stepped closer, his voice threatening. "You know where Sylvia is."

Ramsey didn't answer, but Ruban's tone had him swallowing the lump in his throat.

"First Bambi. Now Sylvia. Both times Jeffrey ends up kidnapped, and both times the money flows through you."

"I didn't say nothin' about ransom money."

"But that's where this was headed. That's why you called me this morning and said Jeffrey called you, like we're all in this together. Next step is for you to deliver the ransom. How much is your cut, Ramsey? Twenty percent? Twenty-five? How much of that goes to this Sylvia?"

"No, mon. That's not it at all."

He thumped Ramsey on the chest. "Your little scheme's not going to work."

"This is not a scheme. These are some bad dudes, mon. They be capable of some really gruesome things. I'm tryin' to help you."

"Help me?" Ruban said, scoffing. "Here's how you can help. Pass this message along to Jeffrey. Whatever 'gruesome things' these 'bad dudes' do to my brother-in-law—no, check that. Even the things they only *threaten* to do to Jeffrey, that's what I'm gonna do to you. Understood?"

Their eyes locked. Ramsey answered in a soft voice. "Yah, mon. It's understood."

Ruban glared at him another moment, long enough to make sure his message and his look were burned into Ramsey's memory. Then he headed toward the exit, counting the Rolexes he saw hanging on the wrists of strippers.

52

.

Pinky heard his nephew crying in the next room as he entered the building.

They were holding Jeffrey in low-rent warehouse space that Pinky had renovated for business purposes. Super Bowl XLIV was coming to Miami in February, along with plenty of men who were willing to pay for sex. Pinky had lined up half a dozen Guatemalan illegals for a full week. The young women didn't know it yet, but they would be staying well beyond the Super Bowl. Until then, the build-out was the perfect place to hold Jeffrey. There were two simple but comfortable bedrooms in front, each like a mini-suite. The building had no windows, so Jeffrey couldn't possibly figure out where he was; and it was in an isolated commercial area, so no passersby would hear the screams.

"Stop, please!"

Jeffrey's desperate pleas came right through the bedroom door. Pinky walked past the kitchenette and down the short hallway. He grabbed a rubber mask from the hook on the wall—he was George W. Bush—and went inside.

The bed and nightstand were pushed up against the wall. Jeffrey lay in the center of the room, staring up at his captor. He was hogtied, his wrists and ankles cuffed and chained behind him. It wasn't the first time Pinky had seen a man in that predicament, but Jeffrey was the first to bear such a bizarre resemblance to an actual hog.

"Welcome, Mr. President," said Pedro.

Pinky struggled not to laugh, and it wasn't just the absurdity of Pedro's Barack Obama mask. Jeffrey's arms, legs, and torso were wrapped tightly with silver-gray tape. He resembled an overweight mummy, only darker, the living precursor to *Fifty Shades of Grey.*

"Ahhhhhhhrgh!"

Forty-nine.

Pedro tossed the hairy strip of duct tape aside. The mummy had lost a foot-long swatch from his manly chest.

"You sure you're not lying to me, Jeffrey?" asked Pedro.

"I swear on my mother's grave. I got no money left!"

Pinky said nothing, knowing that Jeffrey would recognize his voice. He gave Pedro the "cut" sign and an unmistakable gesture to follow him out of the room.

"Not now, bro," said Pedro. "Fat boy is just two minutes away from begging me to set him on fire."

Pinky remained at the door, standing in the shadows. Even with the rubber mask over his head, he feared that Jeffrey might recognize him. He signaled again, more forcefully, demanding that Pedro come with him.

Pedro cursed under his breath and kicked Jeffrey in the kidneys, which made his victim groan. "I'm not done with you, fatty," he said.

He left Jeffrey on the floor and stepped out of the room with Pinky. He closed the door, and both men removed their rubber masks. Pedro's face was slick with sweat; torture was hard work.

"What the hell are you doing in there?" asked Pinky.

"Making sure he has no money left."

"I told you he doesn't have any."

"Marco told me the same thing," said Pedro.

It was Pedro who had chopped Marco's pickup, seen the TV reports about "a black Ford F-150" used in the heist, and then turned his blowtorch on Marco. Marco gave up Pinky's name, and so the Pedro/Pinky alliance was formed. Pinky promised him half of Marco's share, and so much more, if they teamed up, turned against the others, and reached the magic number: the five-million-dollar asking price for Night Moves.

"Marco wasn't lying. You tortured him for nothing."

"Not for nothing. For my peace of mind, bro. When I was done with Marco, I knew he was telling the truth."

"Just like I'm telling you the truth now! Jeffrey blew through his money!"

"No offense, bro. But I like to hear it straight from the horse's mouth before I decide if you're telling me the truth."

"Shut your mouth."

"Hey, Marco tells me you have his share of the money. How do I know that? You tell me Jeffrey's money is gone. How do I know that?"

"Don't you call me a fucking liar," said Pinky.

Pedro shook his Obama mask in Pinky's face. "Nobody calling nobody a liar. Simple White House policy: trust but verify. People soaked in 151 rum don't lie to a man holding a pack of matches. I'm just saying."

Pinky pushed the mask away. "You *can't* burn Jeffrey."

"Why not?"

"Because he's my *nephew*."

"He's a piece-of-shit worthless human being."

"Yeah, he is. But his mother is my little sister. We are *not* going to burn her son alive."

"Then what are we going to do with him?"

Pinky drew a breath as he looked away, thinking. "Keep him alive till Ruban pays," he said finally. "Then put a quick bullet in Jeffrey's head. Ruban you can burn."

Pedro returned to Jeffrey in the "guest room." Pinky went to the vault.

The vault was a wall safe in the closet. Only Pinky knew the combination. It was barely big enough to hold all the cash. Even after expenses, Pinky's original take from the heist, plus Octavio's and Marco's shares, had put him over the four-million-dollar mark, but a million of that was now Pedro's. He still had work to do if he was going to buy Night Moves from Jorge Calderón. It was his dream: own the annex and the club. What more could a man want?

He dialed the combination and opened the safe. Wedged between the stacks of bills were a 9-millimeter pistol and several ammunition clips. He removed the gun, loaded it. He had to push the metal door firmly against the bills to close the safe. Space was tight. He'd probably need to find another place to keep the gun once the ransom was paid in the form of another stack of vacuum-sealed bills. If it was paid.

Ruban will pay.

Ruban deserved to pay. He was the one who'd dropped the sixth bag, two million dollars, and left it on the warehouse floor.

Pinky tucked the pistol into his belt, grabbed his George W. Bush mask, and started down the hallway to the guest room. He stopped outside the closed bedroom door. He could hear Jeffrey crying and sobbing, and Pedro telling him over and over again to shut up.

"I'm not even hurting you, you fat fucking crybaby!"

Pinky hesitated again before entering. Pedro was right. Jeffrey was a loser, a drug addict, and a pathetic excuse for a human being. Pinky couldn't stand him. Never could. Not even when Jeffrey was a kid, especially not when he was a kid. The little shit was always in the way, always in places he shouldn't be. Probably foraging for food. One day he'd wandered into his sister's bedroom and found something he never should have found. Uncle Pinky had thought the door was locked, but in walked Jeffrey. Pinky had eight-year-old Savannah on the bed. Her shorts and panties were down around her ankles. Jeffrey had frozen in his tracks, his eyes like saucers. Then he'd turned and run. Pinky had sweated it out for days. Thankfully, not a word from anyone. Then, somehow, for the first and only time in his life, ten-year-old Jeffrey had found his spine: "Don't you even touch my sister again, or I will tell. I swear, I'll tell everyone."

It was the last time Pinky ever set foot in his sister's house. The secret remained a secret. Savannah seemed to have obliterated it from her memory. Every now and then, however, Pinky caught a piercing glance from Jeffrey that told him his nephew would never forget.

Payback's a bitch.

Pinky pulled on his mask, opened the door, and entered the room. He dimmed the light with the wall switch to make it even more difficult for Jeffrey to determine who was behind the rubber mask. Then he went to Jeffrey and put the gun to his head. Pedro knew the drill and did all the talking.

"My Republican friend here doesn't have very good aim," he told Jeffrey. "He might shoot you in the knee the first time. Hit you in the balls the second time. But eventually he'll get a bullet in your head. Unless you do exactly as I say. You understand?"

Jeffrey nodded. The gun remained pressed to his skull, moving slowly and in sync with his nod.

"Good. Here's the drill, fatso. I'm going to call your sister at her house. I'm not going to say anything. I'll put you on the line. You are going to tell her that you've been kidnapped and that your brother-in-law refuses to pay. You with me so far?"

"Yeah," said Jeffrey, his voice trembling.

"Then you're going to tell Savannah that she needs to fix it. Ruban has to pay. Your life depends on it."

"Uh-huh. I got it."

"Perfect," said Pedro. "Last and most important: right before you hang up, you are going to scream like you are in terrible pain."

Jeffrey shuddered before their eyes. "Okay, I can do that. I can scream. But we can pretend. You don't have to hurt me for real."

Pedro smiled through the hole in his mask. "Come on now, Jeffrey. Where's the fun in that?"

53

Ruban got home from the restaurant after midnight. The house was dark, and Savannah was in bed. Friday was her "sleep like a rock night," the evening shift at the dry cleaners followed by more drudgery on Saturday morning. He left the bedroom light off, tiptoed past her, and went straight to the shower. He needed one in the worst way, having absorbed an assortment of food odors from Café Ruban and God only knew what else from his visit to the Gold Rush. He swore he could still smell the musk from Buffalo Bill.

Inner pervert.

A cloud of steam filled the room. It was like a Turkish bath when he pulled back the curtain and stepped into the tub. The warmth felt good all over, but he focused on the crown of his head, a glorious scalp massage that sent hot water cascading down his neck, across his shoulders, and down his spine. It was hypnotizing, and he forced his eyes open every few minutes so as not to drift away. When he'd first met Savannah, he was the master of the two-minute rinse, saving all the hot water for her. The collapse of their financial world had changed all that. The shower became his escape, a place of solace for twenty minutes, thirty minutes, sometimes as long as an hour, while Savannah pleaded on the telephone with the customer service representatives in India, guys named "John Smith" or "Bob Jones" who tried to squeeze one last nickel out of them before the bank took the house.

A sudden noise startled him, and even before he fully realized that it was the sound of the bathroom door opening, the shower curtain peeled back like a scene out of *Psycho*.

"Ruban!"

"*Shit!*" he shouted back, clutching his chest. "Damn it, Savannah! You scared the hell out of me."

"Get out of the shower!" She was wearing a nightgown and clutching her cell phone.

He hopped out and grabbed a towel, the water still running. "*What?*"

"They just called," she said, her voice quaking.

"They—who?"

"Jeffrey! And his kidnapper!"

Ruban wrapped the towel around his waist and turned off the shower. "They called you on your cell?"

"No. Our home phone. I grabbed my cell and recorded it." She fumbled with the app. The on-screen image was a useless video of the earpiece on their landline, but the point was obviously the accompanying audio recording. "Listen," she said as she hit PLAY.

"*Savannah?*"

It was Jeffrey—a weak and frightened whimper. Savannah's recorded voice followed.

"Jeffrey? Is that you?"

"Uh-huh."

"Are you okay?"

"Nuh-uh."

"Jeffrey, where are you?"

The recording continued, but there was only silence. Ruban shrugged, as if to ask whether that was all of it.

"There's more," she told him.

Ruban moved closer, as if that might help. The next voice in the recording wasn't Jeffrey's. It was the same voice Ruban had heard in the call at the car dealer.

"He's alive," the man said. *"For now."*

"Don't hurt my brother. Please don't hurt him."

"It's in your hands."

"What do you want?"

"Money. Half a mil."

"I don't have that kind of money."

"Your husband does, but he told Jeffrey he won't pay."

"What?"

"You heard me. The money means more to Ruban than your brother's life."

"You're lying."

"Ask Ruban. Then tell him to get his priorities straight. I'll call him again this weekend. Your hubby better be singing a different tune."

"Don't hang up! I want to talk to Jeffrey."

"Sure. He wants to talk to you, too. Jeffrey, say something to your sister."

More silence followed, and it was hard to know if Jeffrey was refusing, afraid, or simply unable to talk. Ruban could see Savannah's cell shaking in her hand—a little at first, then almost uncontrollably, until her grip tightened and her eyes closed in anticipation of what they were about to hear.

It was a scream unlike any Ruban had ever heard before, a cry of pain so shrill that Ruban couldn't fathom what had caused it. Savannah gasped, and tears rolled down her cheeks. The scream lasted only a few seconds, but it seemed much longer.

The recorded voice of the kidnapper returned.

If you still think we're playing, you'll see we're not. A piece of your brother is on its way to you, special delivery. Pay the ransom, or that's the way he's coming home: bit by bit.

The recording ended. Savannah turned off the phone and let her arm fall to her side, emotionally drained.

"Did Jeffrey call you tonight, like the man said?"

Ruban hesitated, but he chose not to lie. "Yeah."

"Did you tell him we wouldn't pay?"

"I—" he started to say, then stopped, choosing his words carefully. "It wasn't like the call you got. I swear, Savannah. I thought Jeffrey was hard up for cash and scamming us."

Her glare tightened. "Did you tell him we wouldn't pay?"

"Listen to me, Savannah. I thought Jeffrey and one of the bartenders at the Gold Rush were playing me. I didn't think the kidnapping was real."

"Didn't think it was *real*?" She shoved him with the phone in her hand. "How does that not sound *real* to you?"

"I told you: it wasn't like that. Jeffrey sounded all coked up when he called me, the way he gets when he's been partying for days. It came across like a plan to get his hands on more money from the heist. We can't touch that money, remember? I told him no."

Savannah considered it, and some of the anger seemed to subside. But she appeared no less stressed. "I think it's time to call the police."

"We can't do that. Savannah, I have millions of dollars hidden away. You think the cops are going to believe I wasn't part of the heist? I'll go to prison for life."

The pain in her expression intensified. "Then we're going to have to pay the ransom."

Ruban didn't respond.

"We have to pay what they ask," she said. "Right? What choice do we have?"

He took her hand and tried to lead her to the bedroom. "Let's talk about this."

She shook free and stood firm, the showdown playing out in front of the bathroom mirror. "Talk about *what*, Ruban?"

"Let's just ask ourselves the question: What if we pay?"

"That's not the right question. What if we *don't* pay? They're going to chop my brother into pieces. You heard him: *bit by bit.*"

"Do you think they're going to turn Jeffrey loose if we come up with half a million?"

"We have to try."

Ruban drew a breath, hoping not to come across as heartless. "Savannah, like I said, I didn't believe Jeffrey before. Now I do. You should know this: he told me that his kidnapper is the same guy who killed Marco Aroyo."

She froze, speechless. Ruban spelled it out for her. "This guy is not going to let him go, no matter how much we pay."

"It's Jeffrey's only chance."

"We're throwing away money."

"Who cares about the money?"

"I do."

"What?"

"Savannah, don't you see? This money can change our lives."

"It's not our money!"

He paused, still not ready to tell her that he was the brains behind the heist. But he was almost there. "It could be ours," he said.

"Are you out of your mind? Do you hear yourself talking? This is stolen money. The only way it can change our lives is if we get caught hiding it and we both go to jail."

"We're not going to get caught."

"How can you say that?"

He laid his hands on her shoulders, looking her straight in the eye, making sure she understood. "There were four guys involved," he said, leaving himself out of it. "Marco Aroyo is dead. Octavio Alvarez is dead. Your uncle is missing and too smart to get caught if he's still alive. Jeffrey is . . ."

"As good as dead? Is that what you're saying?"

Ruban didn't answer.

Savannah looked at him, incredulous. "You want Jeffrey to die, don't you?"

"That's not true."

"I can see it in your eyes. You want Jeffrey out of the way. You want to keep that money."

"Savannah, I'm just saying—"

"Get away from me!" she said as she turned and hurried out the door.

Ruban followed her into the bedroom. "Savannah, listen to me."

She grabbed a suitcase from the closet, threw it on the bed, and started emptying dresser drawers.

"What are you doing?" asked Ruban.

She stuffed a sweater and whatever else she could grab into the suitcase. "What does it look like I'm doing?"

"We can't just run away from this."

"*We* aren't going anywhere."

"What, then?" he asked, scoffing. "You're leaving me?"

"Do you expect me to sleep in the same bed with a man who would rather see my brother dead than alive?"

"That's not what I said."

"It's what you *meant*!"

"Savannah, please—"

"Don't touch me!" she said, backing away.

Ruban watched in disbelief as she pulled off her nightgown and dressed in record time.

"This won't solve anything," he said.

"I can't stay here." She grabbed the suitcase and hurried out of the bedroom.

Ruban followed her down the hallway to the foyer. "Savannah, don't do this."

She continued toward the front door. Ruban rushed ahead and grabbed the knob before she could leave.

"Look at me," he said, stopping her. He was between her and the door, but she wouldn't make eye contact. "I'm asking you not to do this."

She didn't answer, still wouldn't look at him.

"We have to stick together," he said, and he could see the anger rise in her immediately.

"Like what?" she asked in a harsh tone. "Like a family? Do you even know what a family is, Ruban?"

"Yes, I do. I want us to have—"

"Don't even say it! You don't know anything about family. That was my *brother* I just heard screaming on the phone! My own brother!"

"Savannah, I'm sorry, okay?"

"No, it's not 'okay.' You've lied to me, you've deceived me, and now you've shown me a side of you that I can't . . . I can't . . ."

She stopped, and Ruban braced himself for what she might say: *Can't live with anymore?*

"I just can't understand," she said, stopping short of the bomb.

They stood in silence for a moment, Ruban looking at Savannah, her gaze fixed on the front door.

"You need to get out of the way, Ruban."

"Where are you going?"

"My mother's house."

He searched for something to say, anything that might change her mind.

"Ruban, please, get out of my way."

He stepped aside slowly. Savannah unlocked the deadbolt and pulled the door open. Ruban didn't stop her. He watched from the doorway as his wife walked down the steps, into the night, and, maybe, out of their marriage.

54

·

Andie met her unit chief at the FBI field office early Saturday morning. Littleford stood beside her in the A/V center as a tech agent replayed the phone conversation that FBI surveillance equipment had intercepted and recorded from the Betancourts' landline.

"If you still think we're playing, you'll see we're not. A piece of your brother is on its way to you, special delivery. Pay the ransom, or that's the way he's coming home: bit by bit."

The recording ended. Andie and her supervisor exchanged glances, but she let him speak first.

"Pretty chilling stuff," he said.

Andie checked the clock on the wall—7:09 a.m. "It's been over six hours. You think he's still alive?"

"I do."

"Looks like we secured that wiretap none too soon," said Andie.

Littleford settled into the office chair at the head of the rectangular conference table. "Connect the dots for me, Henning. Where does this Jeffrey fit in?"

Andie quickly recapped what the FBI knew, the direct line from Octavio Alvarez to Ruban Betancourt as raft mates; from Ruban to his brother-in-law, Jeffrey Beauchamp; and from Jeffrey to his uncle, Craig "Pinky" Perez.

"I think it's time we bring in Betancourt for questioning," said Andie.

Littleford pondered it, then spoke. "Why?"

"*Why*? How would Betancourt have the ability to pay a half-million-dollar ransom if he wasn't part of the MIA heist? It's pretty obvious that his old friend Octavio Alvarez brought him in."

"Fair point. But that's not enough for an arrest."

"I didn't say arrest him. I said bring him in."

Littleford flashed a quizzical expression. "I can't imagine you would want to do that at this point."

"A man has been kidnapped, and we just heard his kidnapper threaten to chop him to pieces."

"There was a threat, yes."

"A pretty convincing threat. He screamed like a wounded banshee."

"Maybe it was a wounded banshee."

"That scream was real," said Andie.

"Maybe."

"No maybe about it. Don't forget what happened to Marco Aroyo."

"We don't know that these are the same people who got Aroyo."

It was Andie's turn to wear the puzzled expression. "I'm feeling pushback here, and I don't fully understand it. We just heard a credible threat of serious and imminent bodily injury to the victim of a kidnapping. You can be sure that Betancourt isn't going to call the cops if, as I believe, he was part of the heist and is sitting on millions of dollars in stolen money. His brother-in-law might be a crook, too, but right now he's a kidnapping victim. We need to move in."

Littleford nodded slowly, but it was far from total agreement. "That's one side of it."

"If there's another side, I'm dying to hear it."

Littleford rose, walked over to the whiteboard on the wall, and grabbed a marker from the tray. "Here's what we don't know," he said, writing in red as he spoke. "One: Where's the money? Two: Where's Pinky? Three: Was anyone besides Aroyo, Alvarez, Betancourt, Beauchamp, and Pinky involved?

"Here's what we *do* know," he said as he put down the marker, facing Andie squarely. "If you haul Betancourt in for interrogation now, we will never get answers to any of those questions."

"I see it differently. Betancourt must be getting pressure from his wife to save her brother. We can use that angle to our advantage. We can save his brother-in-law and offer both of them a deal on the robbery if Betancourt tells us where Pinky is and where they hid the money."

"What if he doesn't know where Pinky is?"

Andie didn't have an answer.

"What if he tells us where *half* the money is and then digs up the rest when he gets out of prison in five years?"

Again she didn't answer.

"That's what I thought you'd say," said Littleford. "Your plan won't work."

"Again, I respectfully disagree," said Andie.

"You're respectfully overruled. Let the wiretap play out."

"That's a dangerous strategy. Jeffrey Beauchamp could end up dead."

"I'm not saying we let it play out that far."

"That's the problem. How do we know how far is too far? The kidnapper told Savannah that he would call her husband again this weekend. Jeffrey Beauchamp could end up like Marco Aroyo, and I don't want his mutilated body on my head."

"It's not on your head," said Littleford. "It's on mine."

She wasn't persuaded, but she respected his stand-up approach. Littleford was the opposite of what she'd experienced in Seattle, where shit flowed from top to bottom.

"The wiretap might not tell us everything we need to know," she said. "I'd feel better if we put a tail on Betancourt. And his wife."

"You got it."

"Okay," said Andie, sighing more loudly than intended. "So that's the plan."

"Yeah," Littleford said. "That is the plan."

55

Savannah rode the Metrorail green line toward Jackson Memorial Hospital and got off at the Civic Center station. She walked past the Miller School of Medicine campus and the University of Miami Hospital and then followed the cracked sidewalk beneath an interstate overpass to a place where life was less about hope and healing. The Miami-Dade County Women's Detention Center, a drab multistory building that butted up against the noisy Dolphin Expressway, looked exactly as it did in the website photo that Savannah had found. She knew from her quick online research that it housed 375 female inmates. Some were awaiting trial at the nearby criminal courthouse. Others were serving time.

One was about to receive an unexpected visitor.

"I'm here to see Mindy Baird," Savannah told the guard at the visitors' entrance. A pane of bulletproof glass stood between them. Savannah passed her identification through the slot, and the guard buzzed her through the metal door to the clearance center. Her phone, purse, belt, earrings, and everything in her pockets went into a metal storage locker. A female guard checked her with a handheld metal detector, gave her a quick physical pat-down, and then led her to the waiting area, which was filled with other visitors.

"Your first time here?" asked the guard.

Savannah wondered how she knew, but if she looked anywhere near as nervous as she felt, it was no wonder. "It is."

The guard handed her a printed copy of the visitation rules. "Be sure to read these, and wait here until your name is called."

Savannah promised that she would and found an open seat beside an elderly woman.

Betty the social worker from DCF had delivered on her promise to dig up the name of the accuser in Ruban's domestic violence conviction. Mindy Baird's incarceration complicated matters, but Savannah was determined to meet her. Nerves, however, were taking a toll. Savannah had barely slept at her mother's house, but she'd managed to head out early, no questions asked, her destination a secret. She was too on edge to converse with any of the other visitors in the waiting room, and she was glad the old woman beside her was busy praying aloud in Spanish, rosary beads in hand, no interest in small talk. It was exactly what Savannah's mother would have been doing if she were visiting her daughter in prison, and Savannah quickly shook off the disturbing thought that her own family could indeed find itself in that position—that in the eyes of the law Savannah was even more involved in the MIA mess than she realized.

"Savannah Betancourt?" the guard said.

Savannah stepped forward. The guard inspected her visitor's badge and led her down the hall to the visitation center. Savannah had stressed all night over being in the same room with Mindy Baird, but the rule sheet specified that contact visits were allowed only if scheduled in advance. The guard took her to a booth, and Savannah sat before a pane of glass that separated visitors from inmates. Savannah waited, noting the smudges on the glass, each fingerprint on her side matched by one on the other, the "contact" between loved ones.

The door opened on the cellblock side. A young woman dressed in orange prison garb entered the visitation room. Savannah tried not to stare as she approached the glass. She checked for a name on the coveralls to confirm her identity, but there was none: Mindy Baird was a number. She took a seat facing Savannah. Neither one reached for the phone on the wall. The first minute on opposite sides of the glass was their time to size each other up.

Mindy was prettier than expected, her face surprisingly fresh for a woman serving time on charges of drug use and prostitution. Her eyes were her most attractive feature, big and brown, with naturally long lashes. Her hair was shoulder length. Savannah surmised that the damaged ends had been cut off, like the other parts of her life that said "drug addict."

Mindy made the first move, and Savannah reciprocated by picking up the phone on her side of the glass.

"So you're Ruban's wife," Mindy said. She sounded unimpressed.

"How did you know?"

"Betancourt. Ruban doesn't have a sister. I didn't think the name was a coincidence. How long you been married?"

Savannah paused. She hadn't come to share information about herself. "A few years."

"Does he hit you?"

Savannah shifted in her chair. "Actually, no. Never."

"Well, aren't you the lucky girl? Did he tell you what he did to me?"

"Yes. That's why I'm here."

"What did he tell you?"

Savannah repeated her husband's words: Mindy strung out on drugs, begging Ruban not to leave and ripping off her blouse as he packed his suitcase; Ruban tackling her when she pulled a pistol; the police bursting into the apartment to find Mindy on the floor and Ruban in control, gun in hand.

Mindy laughed into the phone.

"Why is that funny?" asked Savannah.

"That's exactly what my mother told me to say."

"You mean when it happened?"

"No. Yesterday. It was the first time she's come to visit me since I been here. She wanted me to sign a sworn statement that says exactly what you just said."

"So it is the truth?"

"Hell no, it's not the truth. Why would anyone

pay me twenty-five thousand dollars to sign my name to a sworn statement if it was the truth?"

"What—twenty-five thousand? From Ruban?"

"*Yes*, from Ruban. Are you trying to tell me you don't know anything about this?"

"No, and I can't say that I believe you, either."

"I wouldn't want to believe something like that about my husband, either. Not that it matters. I'm not gonna sign anything for no twenty-five thousand dollars. Not when my mother gets five times that much."

Savannah blinked, startled by the number. "Ruban is paying you and your mother . . . how much?"

"One-fifty. That's how much he put on the table to clear his name. My mom says my cut is twenty-five. Can you believe that? She tells me that's the price I pay for getting knocked up at seventeen and making her raise my kid."

Apparently Grandma Baird hadn't said a word to Mindy about the adoption, but that wasn't the only thing that had Savannah's head spinning. "Wait a minute. You were *seventeen*?"

"Almost eighteen when she was born."

"But Ruban was—"

"Twenty-six."

Gross. Utterly and completely gross. It was Savannah's turn to speak, but her thoughts consumed her, and the words didn't come.

"Are you okay?" asked Mindy.

"Not really."

"Can I ask you one simple question?"

"Sure," said Savannah.

"It's been five years. Why is it suddenly so important for Ruban to clear his criminal record?"

Clearly her mother had said nothing about the adoption. Savannah wasn't sure if she should go there, but she eased into it, intentionally vague.

"We're thinking about adopting a child."

"Adoption, huh? I know a little something about that. My mother adopted my—"

Mindy stopped cold. Savannah could almost see the lightbulb above her head.

"Oh, my God," said Mindy. "Now I see what's going on. It seemed like a lot of money, a hundred fifty thousand dollars just for me to sign an affidavit and clear Ruban's name. But now I get it. That money isn't just for my signature. You and Ruban are buying my baby."

Savannah didn't answer.

"You bitch! You're *buying my baby*!"

The accusation crushed Savannah, but she didn't deny it. She wasn't sure where this one ranked in Ruban's string of lies—lies that brought everything into question, from his criminal past to his very denial of any involvement in the heist.

Mindy rose and leaned toward the glass. "You can't have my daughter," she said, hissing. Then she slammed the phone into its cradle.

Savannah watched as she turned and went to the door. The guard opened it, and before she disappeared into the cell block, Mindy looked back and shot Savannah the finger. Savannah hung up the phone, but she remained in the visitor's chair for a moment longer, unable to move.

"Miss, you have to go now," the guard told her.

Savannah didn't react.

"It's time to leave," the guard said.

Time to leave. Her thought exactly. "Yes," Savannah said, rising. "You got that right."

56

·

Pinky brought sandwiches back to the warehouse for dinner. He put on his Bush mask and walked down the hall to Jeffrey's room. He opened the door but said nothing, still mindful that even a single word might be enough for Jeffrey to recognize his uncle. He handed him an Italian salami sub with double meat.

"*No shanks*," said Jeffrey, his speech slurred.

They'd yanked out his gold caps with a pair of pliers to elicit that horrific scream in the phone call to Savannah. It was probably overkill to take his teeth and roots along with the caps, but Jeffrey deserved it, if he was stupid enough to buy replacement gold after the first kidnapping.

"*Jis shummin uh dree.*"

Pinky heard that as "Just something to drink." He gave him a bottle of water, then closed the door and locked it, pulling off his mask as he walked back to the kitchenette. Pedro was seated at the table. The foot-long roast beef on a hoagie roll was still on the counter, untouched. A small mirror lay on the tabletop, and the neat lines of white powder were the focus of Pedro's attention.

"Go easy on the coke," said Pinky.

Pedro snorted the first of five lines through a tightly rolled hundred-dollar bill. As soon as it was gone, another line magically appeared. Pinky did a double take, and then he realized that it wasn't a mirror and that the replacement line wasn't real. Pedro was snorting from his iPad screen. The real lines had been inhaled; their replacements on the "mirror" were virtual.

Pedro smiled. "It's my never-ending-coke app. The rolled-up bill acts like a stylus, so as you vacuum up the real coke, the app generates a virtual line to replace it. I'm investing my share of the ransom money in it. Brilliant, huh?"

"Brilliant, all right. What cokehead on the verge of drug-induced psychosis wouldn't want to be tricked into thinking there's more coke when it's really all gone?"

Pedro paused, seeming to take Pinky's point. A tap on the iPad screen erased the five electronic lines, leaving just the virtual mirror. Then he laid out five more lines of the real thing. He inhaled two of them, and the app did its job: still five lines on the screen, albeit two of them were mere computer graphics.

"Did you send the gold caps to Savannah?" asked Pedro.

"I decided not to."

"But we told her that a piece of her brother was on its way. 'Bit by bit'—remember?"

"I know what we told her." Pinky grabbed a beer

from the fridge, unwrapped half of the roast beef sub, and joined Pedro at the table. "I had them all packed up and ready to go, and then it hit me: if we start sending her body parts, she might call the cops."

Pedro was about to do another real line but stopped, incredulous. "Shit, bro. If you thought there's any chance she might go to the police, you should never have brought her into this."

"The only way Savannah might run to the cops is if her brother's gold caps or fingers or whatever land in her mailbox. Until that happens, Ruban won't let her go to the cops."

The third real line disappeared, and a virtual line took its place. Pedro pinched his nostrils as he spoke, savoring the real stuff. "Big mistake," he said, shaking his head. "Rule number one of kidnapping: Don't tell the family to look in the mailbox for proof that you mean business and then not send the proof."

Pinky drank more beer. "Just be patient."

Pedro rubbed his gums with the residue of a real line. "Here's where I come out on this, bro. On a gig like this, you're either all in, or you get out. Let's cut our losses and run. Just call Ruban and lower the ransom to something he'll pay."

"That's worse than not sending the gold caps. That shows weakness."

"It shows intelligence. Take what we can get before the cops get involved."

"You're panicking."

"Maybe with good reason. How do we know the cops aren't right on our heels, ten minutes away from arresting us for the murder of Marco Aroyo or Octavio Alvarez? I say we grab whatever money Ruban puts on the table and get the hell out of Miami."

"That's the problem. Right now there's nothing on the table."

"The only way to fix that is to get serious."

"This *is* serious."

Pedro rose, crossed the kitchenette, and opened one of the drawers. He found the knife he was looking for, walked back, and buried the tip of the ten-inch blade into the wooden tabletop. "I mean deadly serious."

The knife stood upright between them, still wobbling from the impact. Pinky looked past it and stared at Pedro. "What am I supposed to do with that?"

"This is how we lower the ransom and save face."

"I don't follow you."

"Let's keep Savannah out of this if you think she might go to the cops. We cut off Jeffrey's finger, send Ruban a picture, and tell him the ransom is slashed from five hundred to four-fifty. If he doesn't pay, we cut off Jeffrey's ear, send Ruban another picture, and lower it to four hundred. Every hour we whack off another piece and lower the ransom."

"That's insane!"

"No, it's hardball."

"Pedro, this is a fucking kidnapping, not a scratch-and-dent sale."

Pedro was down to his last two lines of real coke on the virtual mirror. They were gone in two quick sniffs and "replaced" just as quickly. "You're right. That is stupid," he said as he pressed his finger to the side of his nose, working it. "We need to speed this up, not drag it out."

"That's the real cocaine talking. It's making you paranoid."

"No, no. I'm seeing things very clearly. Okay, let's forget slashing the price a little bit at a time. Here's what we do: we call Ruban and tell him the ransom is cut in half—a quarter mil. No more negotiation. If we don't get the money in two hours, it's game over: we cut Jeffrey in half."

"That's even stupider than your first idea."

Pedro considered it. "You're right. Jeffrey's too fat to cut in half."

"Enough talk," said Pinky, groaning. "Just shut up and let me eat."

Pedro drummed his fingers on the table, thinking. "Bit by bit," he said. "That's what we told Savannah. We have to send something."

"Fine. Send the gold caps if you want to."

"Caps can be replaced. We need a more powerful message. I know it's overused, but I like the idea of a finger."

"We're not cutting off Jeffrey's finger," said Pinky.

"I know we aren't." Pedro pulled the knife from the tabletop and held it by the tip. "*You* are," he said as he offered the handle to Pinky.

"Forget it."

"It's only fair. I did Marco. You do Jeffrey."

"I ran over Octavio. We're even."

"You keeping score now?"

"No, you are! Look, you already pushed him to the edge of cocaine overdose, threatened to burn him alive, taped him up like a mummy, and yanked out his teeth. That's enough for one day. Jeffrey will drop dead of a heart attack if he sees George Bush and Barack Obama coming at him with a carving knife. Then we'll have nothing."

"That's lame, bro. Sounds to me like Uncle Pinky is stepping up to protect his nephew."

"I don't care what happens to that lazy son of a bitch."

"I know that's not true. You wouldn't let me burn him."

"Only out of consideration for his mother. I seriously don't give a shit about *him*."

"Prove it."

"I got nothing to prove to you."

Pedro was still holding the knife by its tip. With a quick flip of the wrist, he suddenly had it by the handle. The blade was pointed at Pinky, and Pinky's gaze locked onto it.

"You gonna cut me, Pedro?"

"Probably not. I think you get the message."

"What message is that?"

"The same one I have for Ruban, Savannah, and your whole damn family. I'm a reasonable man. I'm willing to negotiate on the ransom. But I want my money tonight. If I don't get it, things are going to get really unpleasant—and not just for Jeffrey."

Pinky's gaze shifted quickly up and down, from the blade to Pedro's face, then back to the blade.

Pedro shifted the knife, to get a better grip. "You on board, Pinky? Or you want to wrestle me for the knife?"

Pinky detected a hint of a smile, but he wasn't convinced that Pedro was kidding.

"And not just for Jeffrey."

He could have meant Ruban, Savannah, even Savannah's mother. Or he could have meant Pinky. It wasn't clear, but Pinky knew better than to press the point with a sadistic killer who had burned Marco Aroyo alive and who, at that moment, had a knife in his hand and a brain full of cocaine.

"Let's call Ruban," said Pinky. "See if we can wrap this up tonight."

57

A ndie spent Saturday at the Miami field office. Her preference was to monitor the Betancourt wiretap in real time, but holing up in the A/V room all day was impractical. She had a ton of paperwork to do, after all, and there was a conference room right across the hall from the surveillance center. The tech agent in charge of the Betancourt surveillance was on alert to rush over and grab her whenever the wiretap went active. Andie was reviewing a Form 302, the official record of FBI witness interviews, when Agent Gustafson hurried into the conference room.

"*Come now*," he said. "Betancourt is on with the kidnapper."

Andie dropped the 302, raced across the hall, and pulled on a pair of headphones. She recognized the kidnapper's voice from the previous call to Savannah.

"No, no, no! Don't hang up!"

It was definitely the same caller as last time, but the response was a voice she didn't recognize.

"I told you before," said Ruban, "I'm not paying a half million dollars. I swear I'll hang up if you say it one more time."

Betancourt, the tech agent scribbled onto a note-pad for Andie's benefit.

"Done. I won't say it again. The number is totally negotiable, bro."

"Don't call me bro. I'm not your fucking brother."

"No problem. I can tell you're a man who doesn't like to dick around, so I'm going right to the bottom line: two-fifty."

"Shoot him."

"What?"

"You want a quarter mil? I say shoot the dumb son of a bitch."

"But—"

"No 'but.' He's a pain in the ass and nothing but trouble. Shoot him right in the head."

"Dude, come on. This is your brother-in-law. How about two hundred?"

"No."

"I know you got the money. You did your thing. You're still coming out ahead. Shit, let me be on top, too."

" 'No' means *no*. You got it?"

"All right, all right. One-seventy-five. But that's my final offer."

"Shoot him. I'll pay for the bullet."

"Come on, man. Why are you making this so hard? I'm like the Salvation Army here, ringing the bell, and no one wants to pay for the fat boy."

"You should pay *me* to take him back."

"Fuck! This was supposed to be the easy part."

Ruban chuckled, but Andie didn't read it as enjoyment. "I tell you what," he said. "If you promise to stop calling me, I'll give you a hundred grand."

The kidnapper took a moment to consider it. "How about one-fifty?"

"How about seventy-five?"

"Okay, a hundred."

"Now you're at fifty."

"Shit! Okay, okay. I'll take fifty thou."

"Deal," said Ruban.

There was an audible commotion on the line, but the words were indecipherable. Andie surmised that the kidnapper was catching hell from his partner for going too cheap.

"All right, we're good on this end," said the kidnapper. "Fifty thousand, but it has to be tonight."

"Fine. Tonight."

"Do what you normally do on a Saturday night. We'll call you when it's time for the exchange."

The call ended. Andie removed her headset, walked around the worktable in the middle of the room, and went to the tech agent's computer station.

"Did you get it?" asked Andie.

"Triangulating now."

The display was a split screen: a map of Miami-Dade County on the left, which Andie recognized; a stream of numbers and letters on the right, which Andie could only assume were mathematical calculations. It was the key to "triangulation," the process of collecting and interpreting the electronic pulse that a cell phone in power-on mode transmitted to surrounding cell towers.

"Got it," he said.

The split screen vanished, leaving only the map. The target area was shaded.

"That's the best you can do?" asked Andie.

"Six million square feet. That's actually pretty good."

"Not if it's densely populated."

"That part of Hialeah is mostly commercial."

"Show me," said Andie.

The screen switched from map mode to satellite image. "Warehouses," said Andie.

"That's a good thing. There can't be a lot of cell phone signals coming from a cluster of warehouses on a Saturday night. You want to send in the Stingray?"

The Stingray was a mobilized tracking system that could roam through target areas and trick a cell phone into thinking it was connecting to a cell tower when, in reality, the user was revealing a more precise location than the FBI could obtain through triangulation based on actual cell towers.

"Is that our only option?"

"It's our best option."

Andie wasn't so sure. "The last time I sent in a Stingray, the perps spotted the van and were long gone before we could pinpoint anything."

"The Amberjack antenna is very low profile. We can mount it on any vehicle. Doesn't have to be a communications van."

"It wasn't the antenna or type of vehicle that was the problem. It was that methodic crisscrossing of the neighborhood that's needed to find the signal. Any crook with a lookout can see what's going on."

"That's a definite risk."

"I'm not sure it's a risk I want to take with a hostage involved."

"It's your decision. But you'd better make it fast. There's no guarantee our perps are stationary. That cell-phone call could have been made from a parked car anywhere in the target area, and that car could be mobile as we speak."

Andie glanced again at the satellite image on the screen. The Palmetto Expressway and dozens of side streets cut right through the targeted area, and the Florida turnpike was nearby. There weren't enough law enforcement officers on duty to cover six million square feet of a warehouse district.

"All right," Andie said. "Send in the Stingray."

Ruban poured himself another shot of tequila and belted it back. It was his fourth in the last hour. Maybe his fifth. He wasn't counting.

No way was he about to ransom Jeffrey—not for fifty thousand dollars, not for fifty cents. Once upon a time, his split from the heist had sounded like more money than he and Savannah could ever spend. How quickly things can change. Savannah was gone. If he wasn't careful, the money would be gone, too.

Ruban picked up the phone, started to dial Savannah's number, and then hung up. Calling her wasn't the answer. He wasn't going to beg. She'd be back. She would come to her senses, tell him it was all a mistake, and say she was sorry. All Ruban needed to do was play it cool. He was sure of it. Hell, she'd be the one begging, and he wasn't even sure he'd take her back.

Damn it, Savannah. Why haven't you called?

He put down the phone and poured himself another shot. Then he thought better of it. It was critical to remain sharp. He left the tequila on the table and went down the hall to his gun cabinet. *Do what you normally do*, the kidnapper had told him.

That voice had left him stumped. No recognition whatsoever. It could have been anyone. A friend of Ramsey's. A gangbanger. A random opportunist who saw Jeffrey giving Rolex watches to strippers. Maybe one of Pinky's buddies. There was no end to the possibilities, and if Ruban didn't make a statement, there would be no end to the kidnappings. Just saying no to ransom didn't seem to get the point across.

Ruban was about to unlock the gun cabinet, then stopped. There was plenty of firepower in his pistol collection for just about any situation. But this wasn't "any situation." He tucked the key away and continued down the hallway, past the kitchen, to the entrance to the attic. Using a stepladder from the pantry, Ruban climbed up and pushed through the trapdoor in the ceiling. The difference in temperature was at least fifteen degrees, and Ruban broke a sweat just climbing up into the dark, stuffy air. A hundred-watt bulb dangled from a wire; a tug on the chain gave him all the light he needed. His gaze drifted toward a wooden crate that was stashed behind the air-conditioning ductwork. He couldn't stand up all the way, but he was able to maneuver well enough in a crouched position. He dialed the combination, removed the lock, then opened the lid.

Most of Ruban's friends had seen the pistol collection he kept downstairs. No one, however, knew what he kept in the attic: his prized possession, an authentic Thompson 1928 West Hurley submachine gun, in mint condition.

Ruban reached into the box and removed the gun with care, almost lovingly. It had been a gift from Octavio. Braxton didn't just deliver cash; firearms were among the many valuables that shipped through the MIA warehouse. And on occasion items disappeared. This rare collectible never reached the licensed firearms dealer who'd paid twenty-seven thousand dollars for it in an online auction. When the Thompson submachine gun shipped through the warehouse, it practically spoke to Octavio. An authentic tommy gun was sure to convince Ruban that so much more—millions more—was theirs for the taking. He gave it to Ruban, and the partnership was born.

Ruban couldn't say for sure that Jeffrey's kidnapper had anything to do with Octavio's death. It didn't matter. At this point, the anger over losing his oldest friend had converged with the anger over Savannah walking out on him, over Grandma Baird working him for six figures, over cleaning up the messes made by a moron named Jeffrey. With a rate of fire in the mid–seven hundreds, the gun from Octavio could avenge all of it.

Could. But this was no time to get cute and play John Dillinger with a tommy gun. He laid the Thompson back in the box and picked up the semi-automatic UC-9 Centurion Uzi-style assault rifle instead. Fully legal, easier to hold on target, with a thirty-two-round 9-millimeter magazine—and best of all, with a folding stock, it collapsed to twenty-four inches in length, reasonably concealable in a backpack.

"We'll call you when it's time for the exchange."

Yup, there would be an exchange, all right. Ruban was ready to mow down anyone stupid enough to be on the wrong side of it.

58

Pinky checked on Jeffrey and found him snoring like a black bear down for the winter. It was hard to fathom how anyone could sleep so soundly after a cocaine binge, even if all but the first few lines had been cut with enough inert substances to make the most inefficient dealer profitable. The last time Pinky had seen anyone do that much coke, she'd set the club record at Night Moves for most double penetrations before midnight, and then danced around naked till dawn. Jeffrey's drug tolerance was off the charts. Then again, he did outweigh the average nymphomaniac by about two hundred pounds.

Pinky stepped quietly out of the room and returned to the kitchenette. Pedro was seated at the table, cutting a few actual lines of the purer stuff on his virtual mirror.

"You're ruining your iPad screen," said Pinky.

Pedro snorted another line, then smiled wistfully at the instant virtual replacement, as if wishing it were as real as the one that had just disappeared up his nose. "I'll be sure to mention that to the customer-service folks for the never-ending coke app."

Pinky dismissed it with a roll of his eyes. "Let me see your cell."

"What for?"

"Just give it to me."

Pedro handed it over. Pinky pivoted and threw it at the wall with the force of a major-league fastball, shattering it to pieces.

"What the hell did you do that for?"

Pinky gripped his own phone, went into another big-league windup, and nailed the wall again in almost the same spot. More pieces fell to the floor.

Pedro looked at him with disbelief. "And you're telling *me* to lay off the drugs?"

Pinky crossed the room and stomped the remains into tinier bits. "Haven't you ever watched any kid-napping movies? It's time for us to get new phones."

"These are *burn* phones," said Pedro. "Nobody can trace them back to us."

"That kind of thinking will land you in Florida State Prison."

"What are you, a tech expert now?"

"I checked it out on the Web. Prepaids still have an air card, and they still interact with cell towers. Just because the number can't be traced back to an account holder doesn't mean that a Kingfish, a Stingray, or some other gizmo can't follow the signal back to the guy who's physically holding the phone."

Pedro laid his iPad aside. The real coke was gone, and the virtual mirror went black. "What makes you think someone's trying to track our cell phones?"

"I wouldn't put it past Ruban. These gadgets are super expensive, but Ruban's got plenty of cash on hand."

"I don't think it's Ruban you're worried about," said Pedro, rising. "You're worried about your niece, aren't you?"

"I'm pretty sure Savannah doesn't have a Stingray."

"Don't get cute with me," said Pedro, stepping closer. "You're afraid Savannah went to the cops. That's why you did a Nolan Ryan on our cell phones."

"I'm just being careful."

Pedro's eyes narrowed, and Pinky gave it right back to him, the two men locked in a stare-down. "If the girl feels safe enough to call the cops, we need to change that," said Pedro.

"No. No one lays a hand on Savannah."

"I don't see a choice."

"I said *no*."

"Look, I don't care what kind of warm and fuzzy favorite-uncle feelings you have for—"

Pinky grabbed him by the collar, his voice hissing. "Don't even say it, Pedro."

"Say what?"

"That I got a thing for my niece."

Pedro winced at the suggestion. "Relax, bro. I wasn't talkin' sexual. I was just saying she's your niece, and obviously you got different feelings toward her than toward Jeffrey. That's all."

Pinky slowly released his grasp. Maybe he'd misread Pedro's meaning. Regardless, Pinky's over-reaction had exposed something, and the fact that it was out there made both men uncomfortable. The stare-down continued a moment longer, and then Pinky blinked. "Let's get new burn phones."

"Sure," said Pedro. "Jeffrey coming?"

"Wake his ass up and put him in the trunk."

Pinky grabbed the keys and pulled the car around to the back of the warehouse. Pedro brought Jeffrey out blindfolded so that he couldn't get a look at the driver. They taped his mouth shut, bound his wrists and ankles with nylon rope, and stuffed him into the trunk. Pinky pulled away slowly. Pedro rode shotgun, busy with another line of real coke on his virtual mirror.

"No blowing coke in the car," said Pinky.

"But it's the never-ending coke app."

Pinky reached over and bumped the iPad from the underside, knocking the powder onto Pedro's shirt. "Now it's a never-ending shame, bro."

The Mall of the Americas was less than two miles from the warehouse, just on the other side of the expressway, and the electronics store was, conveniently, open late. Pinky parked outside the main entrance and went inside. Pedro stayed in the car to make sure Jeffrey kept quiet in the trunk. Five minutes later Pinky returned with three no-contract cell phones, each with its own untraceable phone number and fully activated.

"Why three?" asked Pedro.

"One for you, one for me, and one for Ruban."

"Ruban?"

"Think about it: if the cops are tracking our phones on a Stingray, they're probably tracking

Ruban's, too. Doesn't do much good for us to be talking on new burn phones if he's still talking on his old phone, does it?"

"I guess not. But if we're gonna call and tell him where to pick up his new phone, we might as well call and tell him where to deliver the money, right?"

"Dumb shit. We don't call him on his old phone to tell him anything. We have the new phone delivered to him, and *then* we call him."

"Sounds good in theory. But who's the delivery man?"

"Someone Ruban will listen to," he said, and then he turned on a bad Jamaican accent. "Someone I can count on, mon."

59

It was Saturday night, and Café Ruban was hopping.

Ruban's instructions from Jeffrey's kidnapper were to follow his normal routine all the way up until the exchange. Ruban did so, bopping back and forth from the noisy kitchen to the crowded bar, checking on the night's reservations, and gracing his customers at their tables with his personal attention to make sure all were being cared for properly. Nothing about that night felt "normal," however—especially when Octavio's pretty fiancée showed up with a pissed-off expression on her face.

"You and I need to talk," Jasmine said. "In private."

The last time they'd spoken was on a jogging course, where Jasmine had threatened to pass along Ruban's name to the FBI if he didn't come up with Octavio's missing share of the heist. He'd explained how Octavio's backpack was stolen in the hit-and-run, and in a desperate case of wishful thinking he'd clung to the notion that she might cut him some slack, at least for a time. It appeared that his "time" was up.

"Let's take this in my office," he said.

She followed him from the bar, past the restrooms, to the office behind the kitchen. Ruban closed the door, which cut the decibel level of the crowded restaurant by half, at best. Jasmine didn't give him a chance to ask what this was about.

"You lied to me," she said.

"Can't say I know what you're talking about. But I do know that I've been nothing but truthful with you."

"Spare me, please. You kept Octavio's money."

"I told you: the backpack was stolen."

"I happen to know that the backpack was empty when you gave it to him."

"That's ridiculous. Who told you that?"

"Pinky."

Ruban froze. The Pinky connection had always troubled him about Jasmine. Apart from the actual heist, the three principal coconspirators—Ruban, Pinky, and Octavio—had been in the same place at the same time on only one occasion: a prep session the summer before at Night Moves, where Pinky had introduced Jasmine to Octavio.

"There was a million dollars in vacuum-sealed plastic inside that backpack," said Ruban. "That's why Pinky ran him down and stole it."

"Oh, so *now* you tell me it was Pinky who ran him over? Funny you never mentioned that the last time we talked."

"I wasn't sure it was him before. Now I am. How would Pinky even be able to tell you the backpack was empty unless he was the one who ran Octavio down and stole it? Have you thought of that?"

Jasmine didn't react one way or the other, and Ruban couldn't tell whether she'd thought through Pinky's role or not. Maybe it didn't matter to her.

"What about Marco Aroyo?" she asked.

Marco was a name he hadn't even bothered to share with Octavio, his role was so limited. "How do you even know about Marco?"

"Pinky told me that you made him disappear and kept his money."

"I gave Marco's share to Pinky! Pinky still has it!"

"That's not what Pinky says."

"Why would you believe a scumbag like Pinky over me?"

"Because *you're* the scumbag who hired Ramsey to kidnap your own brother-in-law."

"Did Pinky tell you that, too?"

"No," she said, her glare tightening. "Ramsey did."

Ruban suddenly felt cornered. The first kidnapping was a truth that tipped the credibility scales against him, and he had to explain it. "Okay, that part is true. But I was just trying to scare Jeffrey into cleaning up his act. It was never the plan to get any money out of him. I didn't screw over Octavio and give him an empty backpack, and I sure as hell didn't kill Marco."

"I don't believe you, but that's beside the point. I'm still going to give you this chance to make things right. Be at the Sunset Motel on Flagler at two a.m."

"For what?"

She laid a phone on Ruban's desk. "This is a pre-paid cell. Never been used, no call history, no trace.

Bring it with you. All the instructions you'll need to make the exchange will come over this phone. It'll be by text only. No more discussions."

"Whoa, wait a minute. You said I was a scumbag for hiring Ramsey to scare Jeffrey, but now you're the one running the exchange?"

"Just be at the Sunset Motel at two."

"Who will I see when I get there? The moron who called me at home and negotiated against himself? Or the real half-brain behind this operation?"

"You'll find out."

Ruban shook his head, still amazed that she could overlook Pinky's sins. "Pinky killed Marco. He killed Octavio. He's probably going to kill Jeffrey. And now you're working for him?"

"Wrong. I'm working *for me*."

"You're taking an unbelievable risk for a cut of a fifty-thousand-dollar ransom."

"Dream on, fifty thousand. Here's the new deal: bring Octavio's million dollars *and* Marco's. Then you get Jeffrey back."

"You've missed a few weekly episodes here, sweetheart. I honestly don't care if I get Jeffrey back."

"No. But your wife does."

"Leave Savannah out of this."

"Too late. She's in. All in."

"What does that mean?"

"You should ask Pinky that question when you see him. And then do what you gotta do, Ruban. For Octavio."

Ruban suddenly understood. "So that's your angle? You climb in bed with Pinky long enough to get your hands on Marco's share on top of Octavio's, and then you stand aside as I give Pinky what he deserves for taking down Octavio like roadkill?"

"It sounds so manipulative when you say it."

Ruban swallowed his anger, thinking about the assault rifle in his car, along with four magazines of thirty-two rounds apiece. "You're a clever one," he said, wondering if he had enough ammunition.

"Yes, I am. Don't be late."

She opened the door, and he watched her leave.

Too clever for your own good.

Andie watched on the video screen as Jasmine emerged from Café Ruban. An FBI surveillance van was parked across the street from the restaurant, and the two agents inside were streaming the images back to Andie in her car, which was parked a little farther down the street. Littleford was seated in the passenger seat, also watching the screen.

"That's definitely her," Andie said. "That's Octavio Alvarez's fiancée."

The surveillance agent's response came by radio. "You want us to tail her?"

"Not in the van," said Andie. "I'd rather call for another team."

"No time. She's heading for her car. We're going to lose her."

Jasmine's arrival at the restaurant had taken Andie by surprise. They weren't equipped to tail both her and Betancourt.

"Take the van and follow her until we can get another vehicle," Littleford told the surveillance agents. "We'll rendezvous later."

"Roger."

Littleford disconnected.

"What if Betancourt leaves the restaurant before we rendezvous with the communications van?" asked Andie.

"Then it's you and me in our bucar," said Littleford using the dated term for an FBI vehicle. "No Kingfish, no Stingray. We'll tail him the old-fashioned way."

Andie didn't see much choice. "All right," she said. "Old-fashioned is good."

Jasmine climbed into the car and closed the driver's-side door. Ramsey looked over from the passenger seat. The dome light blinked off, and the two of them were alone in the darkness.

"How did it go?" he asked.

"Perfect. I made it absolutely clear to him that Pinky is involved."

Inserting Pinky's name into the kidnapping had been directly contrary to Pinky's instructions to Ramsey, but Jasmine and Ramsey had their own agenda.

"Did he take the cell phone?"

"Yup. And I told him text only, no more phone conversations."

Ramsey opened the glove box and reached for the burn phone, the one Pinky had given him for delivery to Ruban. Two grand just to deliver a cell phone to Ruban had seemed like a good deal to Ramsey, but Jasmine had bigger ideas. It had been her brainstorm to drive by an electronics store, purchase another prepaid cell phone for Ruban, and keep the one from Pinky. Pinky had no way of knowing that the instructions he would text to Ruban would actually go to Ramsey, and that Ramsey would be texting a different set of instructions to Ruban—instructions that would make the "exchange" go down in a way that served his and Jasmine's purposes.

"Sistren, tell me. You think Ruban will be showin' up with two million dollars?" he asked.

"I really do. If for no other reason, he'll want to show Pinky what he's *not* getting before he kills him."

Ramsey drew a deep breath, reeling in his anticipation. "Whadda you goin' to do with your mil?"

"I don't know yet. What are you going to do with yours?"

Ramsey leaned across the console and gave her a quick kiss on the lips. "You a clever one, Bambi."

She smiled. "Funny. That's what Ruban told me."

60

Ruban left the restaurant around one and stopped by the house. It wasn't exactly on his way to the Sunset Motel, but he had plenty of time to get there by two, and he was hoping that Savannah would be home. He had no reason to think she would be, and of course she wasn't. Still at her mother's, he presumed. He used his real phone, not the prepaid, to type out a text message—*sorry . . . i love u . . . please come home*—but he didn't send it. No one down to his last out in the World Series of love had ever fired off a game-winning text message at 1:30 a.m.

Don't be pathetic.

He hit "cancel," opened the sliding glass door in the kitchen, and stepped outside. It was a clear, crisp night, and he walked to the far edge of the patio, beyond the fluorescent glow from the kitchen. A brick paver wobbled beneath his foot, and he stopped. There was money below him; there was money weighing on his shoulders.

Two million dollars, the equivalent of Octavio's

and Marco's share. Handing over that much to Jasmine would all but wipe him out. Ruban's entire take had been just two and a half, and he'd been chipping away at that on everything from Edith Baird's first fifty grand to the nonrefundable deposit on the house that Savannah didn't want. Pinky was angling to be the big winner—his share plus Marco's and Octavio's. Pinky and Jasmine, his new cohort. *Co-whore.*

It was time to change that.

He went back inside to his gun cabinet and selected two pistols, one for his belt and one for backup, in case the other jammed. The Uzi-style assault rifle made a more powerful statement, but he could conceal it only with the stock folded, so he couldn't count on using it in a pinch. He grabbed two extra ammunition clips, locked up the cabinet, and went to the bedroom closet. The balance of the money he'd set aside for Edith Baird was still in the backpack. He removed all but two vacuum-sealed packs of twenty-five thousand dollars each. It wasn't his intention to pay a ransom, but he needed to be able to bluff his way through the "exchange." The final touch was a windbreaker to hide the handgun on his belt. He locked up the house, went to his car, and retrieved the Uzi-style rifle from the trunk. With the stock folded, it fit just fine in the backpack. He laid it on the floor on the passenger side, started the engine, and drove.

Flagler is one of Miami's oldest and busiest streets, and the Sunset Motel was at its western end, midway between Miami's Little Havana and the Florida Everglades. Most of the old motels in this once-vibrant area were in decline and slated for demolition, and Ruban surmised that the last tourists to pull up and spend the night at the Sunset were probably on their way to Miami Beach in a 1966 Ford station wagon. The two-story building was typical of that bygone era. Rooms faced the parking lot and opened directly to the outdoors. Noisy climate-control units protruded from below the front windows. The neon letters on the roadside marquee were partially burned out, leaving the "Vacancy" sign to proclaim "Vaca," which Ruban read in his native tongue: *Cow*. Add that to the pigs that flocked to this place in search of prostitutes, and the Sunset Motel was a veritable barnyard.

Ruban found a parking space near the marquee and left the motor running. He was a few minutes early. The burn phone from Jasmine was on the console. One approach would have been to wait for the text message and play their game. Ruban had another strategy. He grabbed the burn phone and the backpack, got out of the car, and walked across the parking lot to the manager's office. The glass door was locked, a reasonable precaution in this neighborhood, but Ruban could see the manager seated behind the reception counter. She laid her cigarette in the ashtray, and with the press of a button her gravelly voice crackled over the speaker.

"Can I help you?"

"I need a room," said Ruban.

"I'll buzz you in. Leave the backpack outside.

And fair warning, mister: I have a gun, I've used it before, and I don't miss."

Well, then, we have something in common. "Understood."

The buzzer sounded and Ruban entered the small reception area. The elderly woman behind the desk watched him carefully as he approached the counter. She didn't say anything, but the name tag that was pinned to her blouse told him plenty: *Hello, My Name is A. Bitch.*"

Ruban laid a hundred-dollar bill on the counter. "That's for the room," he said, and he laid two more bills beside it. "This is for your help."

She took a drag from her cigarette, her eyes narrowing on the inhale, which brought out a whole new pattern of smoke-hardened wrinkles. "What kind of help?"

"I'm looking for a room with three men in it."

"Last guy to come in here and tell me that was a U.S. congressman."

Ruban smiled, gladder for the rapport than the humor. "Can you help me out?"

"I'd love to take your money, but I don't keep track."

That sounded true. Ruban tried another angle. "I'm guessing most of the rooms here go by the hour, am I right?"

"Most."

He laid another bill on the counter. "How about you tell me which rooms aren't your usual hourly clientele. And let's limit it to guests who arrived in the last eight hours."

She looked him over carefully, as if trying to discern why he might want that information. But she didn't ask and, apparently, didn't care. She checked the registry and jotted down a few room numbers on a Post-it. "You don't really want the room, do you?"

"No, ma'am." He took the Post-it, then pushed the hundred "for the room" toward her. "But you can keep all of it." Ruban turned and headed for the door, but she didn't buzz it open right away.

"I'm good with just about anything here," she said, "so long as no one gets hurt. You hear me?"

"Loud and clear."

The buzzer sounded, and Ruban stepped outside. He picked up his backpack and started down the walkway to the guest rooms. The burn phone in his pocket vibrated, and he stopped to check it. There was a text message at 1:59 a.m.

"Walk to the west stairwell. Wait."

Ruban glanced down the walkway. The motel had two external stairwells, one at each end. Like the first- and second-story walkways that ran the length of the building, the stairs were outdoors, but the stairwell was partially enclosed by three walls of painted cinder blocks. It would prevent anyone from taking a shot at him from the street or the parking lot, but it was impossible to know what was waiting for him behind those walls. Ruban wasn't foolish enough to walk into an ambush. He would stage his own ambush at one of the four rooms on the Post-it from "A. Bitch." But he played along and texted a reply.

On my way.

* * *

Pinky was getting antsy, pacing from one end of the motel room to the other. Pedro was seated on the double bed nearest the window. Jeffrey was locked in the bathroom, bound and blindfolded, but still alive.

"Check the cell again," said Pinky.

Pedro did so. "Nothing."

"Are you sure your text went through?"

"I sent it almost an hour ago. Told him to park in space number twenty-two at 1:30. He texted right back and said he'd be here."

Pinky stopped pacing. "Are you sure you told him the right motel?"

"Yeah. The Vagabond on Calle Ocho."

"Text him again."

"I already sent three follow-ups. No reply."

Pinky took the phone from him and checked it. The thread of messages confirmed it. "He's almost forty-five minutes late. He's not coming."

"Let's give him a few more minutes."

Pinky went to the window and pulled back the curtain just enough for a quick view of the parking lot. Each space was numbered on the asphalt, and number twenty-two was right beside a tall ficus hedge. It was empty.

"Ruban is messing with us," said Pinky.

"Maybe these burn phones are fucked up."

"Call him on his real cell."

"You sure?"

Pinky started to pace again. The burn phones had been a precaution, but he had no actual knowledge that law enforcement or anyone else was tracking Ruban's cell.

"Yeah," said Pinky. "He's fucked with me for the last time. Call him."

Ruban's cell rang. Not the burn phone, but his regular line. He didn't recognize the incoming number, but he took the call anyway.

"Who is this?"

"Where the hell are you?"

He recognized the kidnapper's voice from the previous calls. "On my way."

"You were supposed to be here at one-thirty."

"Your text said two."

"I said one-thirty."

"No, you didn't. You said—whatever. I'm here now."

"The hell you are! The parking space is empty."

"What parking space?"

"Number twenty-two!"

Ruban gripped the phone more tightly, confused. "I don't know what you're talking about."

"You lying sack of shit! I couldn't have laid it out any clearer. One-thirty. Space number twenty-two. Vagabond Motel on Calle Ocho."

"Dude, I'm at the Sunset on Flagler, like I was told."

"I never told you that!"

"Yes, two o'clock at—"

"Fuck you, Ruban! I've had it. Keep your fifty thousand dollars. Your brother-in-law dies."

The call ended before Ruban could respond. Jasmine had clearly told him the Sunset at two when she'd delivered the phone to the restaurant. It was confounding on many levels, right down to the last few words: *Keep your fifty thousand.* Jasmine had said two million. He was tempted to call back, but his burn phone vibrated with another text message:

"Stairwell. Where r u?"

Ruban stared at the screen. He didn't have the whole picture yet, but he could suddenly see right through Jasmine's double cross. He texted right back:

"On my way."

61

.

The FBI communications van was abuzz. Andie and Agent Littleford were in the middle of it.

The surveillance team had followed Jasmine to the Sunset Motel; Andie's "old-fashioned" tail on Betancourt had led to the same place. She and Littleford rendezvoused with the van just before two a.m. in the parking lot behind Snuffy's Tavern, a local dive across the street from the motel. The Stingray had locked onto the signal from the burn phone used by the kidnappers to call Betancourt. The wiretap on Betancourt's cell had picked up the entire conversation. The kidnapper's parting words—"your brother-in-law dies"—left Andie few options. She keyed the microphone and radioed the SWAT van, which was parked down the street.

"We have a direct threat against the hostage. New location: Vagabond Motel, corner of Calle Ocho and Red Road."

"Roger that. Room number?"

"Unknown. We are transmitting wire-card iden-tification now to your Kingfish." The Kingfish operated like a Stingray, but it was handheld and could literally pinpoint a cell phone to a specific room.

"Roger. Mobilizing now."

Andie keyed off the radio, and Littleford gave the next order.

"Let's pick up Betancourt."

"I think we should let the 'exchange' play out on this end."

"There is no exchange."

"That's my point," said Andie. "Based on that last phone call, it sounds to me like there's another player involved, some kind of double cross among thieves. It could be Jasmine, or maybe somebody else. If we pick up Betancourt now, we get only Betancourt. I say we watch, see who shows up, and move in against all of them. Clean sweep."

Littleford seemed to like the idea, but with reservations. "We need to wait for backup."

"Tell them to hurry."

"And put on your body armor."

"Yes, sir."

Ruban walked around to the back of the Sunset Motel, found a relatively private space behind the Dumpster, and opened his backpack. It was time to gun up.

He removed the Uzi-style rifle and unfolded the stock, which extended the weapon to its full thirty-one-inch length. The magazine clipped into place without effort, thirty-two rounds of 9-mil ammo. He doubted that any additional clips would be necessary, but he stuffed the extras into the pockets of his windbreaker anyway.

Jasmine had definitely tried to scam him. The kidnapper's reference to "fifty thousand dollars" had confirmed it: he was completely unaware of the two-million-dollar renegotiation. Ruban couldn't deny Jasmine's street smarts, but a move like this one had Pinky written all over it. Ruban's read was simple: Pinky had duped his partner into holding down the fort at the Vagabond with Jeffrey, waiting on the fifty-grand ransom, a sitting duck for the police if something went wrong. Pinky and his co-whore were at the Sunset, double-crossing Pinky's partner, thinking they could double-cross Ruban.

Way too clever for your own good.

Ruban ran one last weapons check. Pistol on his belt. Backup strapped to his ankle. The rifle was semiautomatic with closed-bolt action, which meant that it would discharge only as fast as his finger could squeeze the trigger, which was fast enough. All was in order. He stepped out from behind the Dumpster and started toward the west stairwell.

The Sunset Motel had four wings, each forming one side of a square that surrounded an open-air courtyard. Ruban stepped carefully across the courtyard. Weeds had sprouted between the stone tiles, some knee-high. The moonlight shone on a broken old fountain in the center of the courtyard. *Pitch a Penny for Luck*, the weather-faded sign read, but the fountain was dry, and Ruban had nothing smaller than a hundred-dollar bill anyway. He continued past the fountain and kept toward the edge of the courtyard, invisible in the shadows. He stopped a few feet away from the stairwell and pressed his back to the wall.

With his finger on the trigger, he waited. He listened. The night was eerily silent, but not for long. A noise in the distance changed everything. Sirens. No question about it: police sirens. It was time to move, and not slowly.

Run!

62

.

Pinky drove like a demon down Calle Ocho, tires screeching as he pulled a hard turn at the traffic light.

He'd left the car and Pedro back at the Vagabond Motel. He was in a four-door pickup with double-cab seating, just like the truck used in the heist, only this time Pinky was behind the wheel. Jeffrey was in the backseat, half sitting and half lying on his side, his hands bound and his mouth taped. He kept quiet until a string of potholes turned the ride into a virtual off-road excursion. Jeffrey's head slammed against the bench seat in front of him, and he groaned loud enough to be heard through the tape.

"Zip it, fatty!"

Jeffrey fell silent. Pinky kept driving.

Pinky didn't disagree with anything Pedro had told Ruban on the phone, but that brief call to Ruban's cell hadn't come close to expressing the depth of Pinky's anger. From the day Ruban and Savannah first started dating, he'd disliked Ruban. After she'd married that asshole, *hated* was a better word. He'd dug into Ruban's background himself, had even uncovered rumors about a seventeen-year-old girl. He'd held his tongue, however, never saying a word to anyone. Pinky had his own dirty laundry. He didn't stand a chance in that battle of accusations.

The truck stopped at a red light. Pinky leaned over the bench seat and grabbed Jeffrey by the collar, forcing eye contact.

"Listen to me, Jeffrey. We're going to call your brother-in-law. When I hand you the phone, you're going to say exactly what I tell you to say. You got that?"

Jeffrey nodded.

Before the start of the night, it had been Pinky's plan to turn Jeffrey loose if Ruban paid the ransom. No more. Ruban and Jeffrey would both get what they deserved. Ruban would tell Pinky where the rest of the money was hidden, and then Ruban would watch Jeffrey die. Ruban would follow him to the grave.

Pinky spotted an Italian restaurant ahead. It was closed for the night, the windows were dark, and the single row of parking spaces in front was empty. The engine rumbled as Pinky steered down the side alley to the larger lot in the back. Bumpy asphalt gave way to the crunch of gravel. He drove all the way across the lot and parked by the battered chain-link fence, away from the lone security light that shone above the restaurant's rear entrance. He killed the engine, then leaned over the seat, pressed his pistol to Jeffrey's forehead, and told him what to say. The burn phone didn't have Ruban's cell on speed dial, but Jeffrey's did. It made more sense to dial from a number that Ruban would recognize, anyway. He was more likely to answer.

Pinky dialed on Jeffrey's phone and let it ring.

Ruban was driving toward the expressway when he heard the ringtone—his cell, not the burn phone. He checked his pocket, but the phone wasn't there. He wasn't sure where he'd shoved it in his hurry to get away.

The backpack?

He'd left unfinished business at the Sunset Motel, but everything was secondary to staying out of jail. He wasn't sure whom he might have encountered in the stairwell if those sirens hadn't wailed in the distance, but he was confident that he would have been the better armed.

The ringtone continued. Ruban steered with his left hand while fishing through the backpack on the passenger seat. His cell was all the way at the bottom, wedged below the folded stock of the assault rifle. He pulled it free and checked the display. It pulsed with the personalized caller ID generated by his contact list: *Cokehead*. It was Jeffrey. He answered. The voice on the other end of the line wasn't the one he'd expected, but it didn't shock him.

"Guess who," said Pinky.

Ruban scoffed. "I knew you were behind this."

"Unfortunately for you, this is one of those situations where knowledge *isn't* power."

"Kiss my ass, Pinky."

"Your brother-in-law is in a black pickup truck parked behind the Blue Grotto Italian restaurant on

Red Road. I don't have time for this shit anymore. Keep your fifty thousand. Just take him."

"I don't want him."

"Stop being such an arrogant prick. My business partner is ready to put a bullet in his head. This is your last chance to see Jeffrey alive."

"How do I know he isn't dead already?"

Ruban could hear the tape ripping from Jeffrey's mouth, followed by the cry of pain that had become all too familiar. Then Jeffrey recited his lines through broken teeth.

"Bro, ah-yin thuh pickuh thuck. Cumma gemme!"

The line went silent; the call was over. Ruban tucked his cell away. He knew it was a setup, but he didn't care. If Pinky wanted a showdown, Ruban was cool with it. Ruban had the Uzi.

At the corner, he pulled into a gas station and turned the car around.

63

•

Andie kept her distance, careful not to tip off Betancourt to the bucar that was tailing him. Littleford was in the passenger seat.

"He's turning around in that gas station," said Littleford. "Don't go in there. Drive past the station and then pull a U-ey."

Andie would have figured that one out on her own, but Littleford had seemed compelled to give her a lesson in good old-fashioned surveillance since leaving the Sunset Motel.

Andie had been moments away from moving in to make an arrest. Betancourt had clearly come prepared. His assault rifle had been clearly visible through Andie's night-vision binoculars. For Andie, that was the end of the line: it was too dangerous to let him roam motel grounds so heavily armed. Something had spooked him, however. He had suddenly collapsed the rifle, stowed it in his backpack, and run to his car. Andie still wanted to make the arrest, but she was overruled: "Let him run a little longer," Littleford had told her. "See if he leads us to the kidnappers."

Andie drove past the gas station to a fast-food restaurant, where she turned around.

"He's picking up speed," said Littleford.

"I see him."

The radio crackled as Andie swung the car around and resumed their pursuit. It was the surveillance team from the communications van. The wiretap on Betancourt's cell phone had intercepted an incoming call.

"Play it," said Littleford.

Andie listened as she followed the orange taillights down Red Road. It took less than a minute, ending with Jeffrey's slurred words: *"Cumma gemme."*

Littleford immediately called for backup at the Blue Grotto restaurant. Andie radioed the SWAT leader at the Vagabond Motel.

"Hostage is no longer at the Vagabond," she said into the microphone. "Repeat, hostage is no longer at the Vagabond."

"Kingfish is still getting a cell-phone signal from room 207."

"Subject two is unaccounted for. He could still be there."

"Motel manager has confirmed that the only second-story room occupied on that wing is 207. Subjects specifically requested an isolated room when they checked in. MDPD has evacuated the first floor. Are you green-lighting a breach?"

Breach was the SWAT term for a tactical team's

forced entry. Not a good idea when a hostage's whereabouts were unknown, but that was no longer the case.

Andie glanced over at Littleford, who nodded.

"Green light," said Andie.

Pedro went to the window of room 207 and peeled back the corner of the curtain for another look at the parking lot. Nothing had changed. Same empty spaces. Same parked cars.

He checked the clock on the nightstand. It read 2:37 a.m.

It had been almost fifteen minutes since Pinky left with Jeffrey in tow. "I'll take care of him," Pinky had told him. "You wait here." Minutes later, police sirens wailed, louder by the second, as if approaching the motel. Pedro had expected to see blue flashing lights in the parking lot at any moment. Then there was silence. No swirling police beacons. Nothing. Nothing but waiting. Possibly the police had blown right past the Vagabond on their way to some other crime in progress. Maybe they'd stopped Pinky's truck. Maybe Pinky was already dead, killed in a shootout. Or in custody, ratting out his partner.

They could be out there, watching.

Pedro turned on the TV. "Breaking news" updates on police activity were a criminal's best friend. Nothing useful was airing. Channel after channel of the usual wee-hours programming—mostly infomercials for mattresses, sleep aids, and anything else that might spur insomniacs to open their wallets.

Pedro reached for his burn phone. Pinky had told

him to avoid cell usage—*"Burn phones still have an air card"*—but he needed information. It was time to make a move. Sitting in a motel room was no strategy at all.

Suddenly, a blast of white light shone through the crack in the draperies, slicing across the room like a laser, brighter than the morning sun. Pedro dropped the burn phone, grabbed his pistol, and turned off the lamp and the television. The slice of light pierced the darkness, searing a white line down the middle of the room. As quickly as he could move, Pedro flipped over the double bed, shoved the mattress and box spring against the window, and barricaded the door with the dresser. The line of light was gone.

The room's landline rang in the darkness. Once. Twice. Pedro yanked the wire from the phone jack. Silence. Seconds later, his burn phone rang, as if to tell him how the police had found him. Technology had given him up; the cops had literally plucked his phone number from the air. Pedro took the call and answered with two words.

"Blow me."

"It's over. You're surrounded. Give yourself up and save your own life."

"I said blow me."

He ended the call, tossed the phone aside, and checked his pistol. Fifteen rounds of 9-millimeter ammunition in the magazine. Two spare clips in his pocket. Maybe not enough to get out alive, but enough to go down fighting.

The window shattered on the other side of the barricade, and purely as a reflex, Pedro fired into his own protective barrier, squeezing off five quick shots into two feet of foam and springs. Smoke poured from inside and behind the mattress, the launched grenade having burrowed through the fabric. A cloud of chemical irritants burst forth and "Pyro Pedro" was savvy enough to realize that heat from an embedded smoke grenade could quickly set a foam mattress afire.

They're trying to burn me alive.

Something between panic and an acute sense of urgency washed over him, and in the back of his mind were the screams of Marco Aroyo, the hiss of Pedro's own blowtorch, and the smell of burning flesh. His memories vanished as the tinny voice of authority sounded over a loudspeaker from somewhere in the parking lot.

"Leave your weapon. Come out with your hands over your head."

The cloud of smoke thickened and crept across the room. Pedro's eyes began to water. He grabbed a pillowcase and covered his mouth and nose. It didn't help. He could barely breathe. Visibility was almost zero, nothing but smoke and darkness. Then he saw the flame, a burst of orange from the sheets and blanket on his mattress-barricade. Smoke grenades were nonlethal, but heat was heat, and this one was turning deadly.

"Thirty seconds," the man with the loudspeaker announced, "or we're coming in."

Pedro didn't wait. He pulled the dresser-barricade away from the door and flung it open. A blinding spotlight only exacerbated his temporary loss of vision from the smoke grenade, but he kept running, guided by instinct alone, exploding out of the room at full speed, squeezing off shots from his semiautomatic pistol even faster than his feet were moving.

The pop of return gunfire cut through the night, multiple shots from a host of strategic positions. Pedro felt a crushing blow to his chest, another to his shoulder, and an explosion in his belly. The repeated crack of his discharging weapon melded with the barrage from law enforcement. It was a single ballistic cacophony as he felt his hips slam into a railing, felt his feet whirling over his head, and felt himself floating in slow motion. For a brief but bizarre instant, he could see himself falling from the second-floor catwalk. He watched the pistol drop from his hand. He could even see the assortment of gold caps that spilled from his coat pocket and caught the flash of police searchlights in midair.

He saw the glint of gold all around him as his body slammed into the pavement.

64

.

Ruban parked in the alley behind a hardware store about a half block away from the Blue Grotto restaurant. Not another vehicle was in sight. It took only a few seconds to retrieve the folded assault rifle from his backpack, make sure the clip of full-metal-jacket ammo was secure, and run through the usual prefiring safety checks. All was in order. At the ready, finger on the trigger guard, he started walking.

Ruban was operating on the assumption that this was all a setup, that Pinky was waiting inside the truck for him, and that Jeffrey wasn't even there. His plan was not elaborate. Spray the driver's side with bullets. Change magazines. Walk to other side. Pump in another thirty-two rounds. Approach carefully. Make sure Pinky is dead. Run. Simple and effective. Even a steel door is no match for FMJ ammo fired straight-on at close range from an assault rifle.

But what if Jeffrey is in there?

The thought shredded his conscience like a weed

whacker. It was one thing to refuse to pay a ransom and allow Jeffrey to *be killed* thanks to his own stupidity. It was another thing to pull the trigger—to be his killer.

He stopped at the end of the alley. A gravel parking lot stretched before him, about half the size of a basketball court, with only one working streetlamp. The pickup truck was at the opposite end, parked against the chain-link fence. Ruban took a deep breath. It was justifiable on some levels. He'd warned Jeffrey. Stupidity has consequences. Jeffrey did this to himself.

"He's my brother, Ruban!"

Ruban started toward the truck, pushing Savannah's pleas from his mind as he raised the stock to his shoulder and took aim at the driver's door—when the voice of another woman stopped him.

"FBI! Freeze!"

Ruban stayed calm. "You're making a mistake. My brother-in-law has been kidnapped. He's in that truck over there."

"Drop your weapon and put your hands on your head."

"My car is parked in the alley. Look in my backpack. There's fifty thousand dollars in ransom money."

"I know there is. It's from flight 462, Frankfurt to Miami. Now drop your gun."

Busted. Ruban couldn't see behind him, but this seemed odd. *One agent? By herself?*

"You can't be FBI," he said. "Who *are* you?"

The engine cranked, tires spun, and the pickup was suddenly barreling toward them in reverse, bed first. Ruban and the agent hit the ground and rolled in opposite directions as the pickup passed between them. It skidded to a stop and then leapt forward, no longer in reverse. Gravel flew and a cloud of dust rose as the truck headed straight toward the agent on the ground. Ruban sprang to his feet and jumped into the open bed. Through the rear window he saw Pinky behind the wheel. A minute earlier, he would have put a bullet in the back of Pinky's head, but everything had changed. The truck roared past the agent, just missing her as she rolled out of the way. Ruban stayed low but raised his rifle above the tailgate and squeezed the trigger, again and again, unleashing a hailstorm of bullets that sailed across the parking lot as the truck crashed through the chain-link fence and peeled away into the night.

Andie climbed to her feet and ran down the alley. Littleford was in the car, racing toward her, and met her halfway. Andie jumped in the passenger seat, and Littleford chewed her out while speeding in reverse, back toward the street.

"Henning! What do you think you're doing? I told you to wait for backup!"

"Betancourt was about to empty an Uzi into that pickup truck," she said, breathless. "I had to move."

"Not by yourself, damn it!" The tirade continued as the car sped away from the alley. "You're lucky to be alive."

"Our hostage wouldn't be alive if I hadn't done something."

Sirens blared and lights flashed behind them. A

string of speeding squad cars joined their pursuit. They were suddenly part of a police armada.

"So *now* we have backup," said Andie. "Where were they two minutes ago?"

"They diverted to the Vagabond Motel. SWAT launched a smoke grenade to flush the perp out of room 207, and it ended up in the mattress. Huge fire. Half the building is burning."

"Anyone hurt?"

"Just subject one. Dead."

The radio crackled. MDPD had the pickup truck in sight: "Subject entering Palmetto Expressway, southbound from Flagler Street on-ramp."

Andie keyed the microphone. There was a good reason she'd held her fire in the parking lot, and she wanted to make sure MDPD did the same.

"Possible hostage inside the truck. Proceed accordingly."

"Roger."

Littleford hit the gas.

Andie glanced behind her. The string of squad cars was still with them. "All together now."

65

Ruban crouched low in the bed of the pickup, his windbreaker flapping as they sped onto the Palmetto. Pinky was at the wheel. The back of his head was an easy, stationary target through the cab's rear window. One bullet was all it would have taken, but Ruban had lost the spare clips in his roll across the parking lot and was out of ammunition. He laid his rifle aside, pulled the pistol from his belt, clicked off the safety, and then stopped.

The truck was moving like a rocket. At three a.m. the expressway was as wide open as a five-lane test track. The bed vibrated beneath him, and the wheel wells roared with the power of eight screaming cylinders. At this speed, a dead driver would mean a dead passenger.

Jeffrey's face suddenly appeared on the other side of the rear window. Their eyes met, a toothless mouth fell open, and Jeffrey shouted something that was impossible for Ruban to hear. He understood, nonetheless.

"Bro!"

The window cracked in spiderweb fashion as a bullet pierced the safety glass and punctured the tailgate just inches from Ruban's shoulder. Pinky was shooting at him! Ruban was about to return fire, but Jeffrey's face was in the way. Jeffrey was beating his fists against the cracked window, unable to shatter the safety glass, and shouting at the top of his voice.

"Ruban!"

The wind continued to howl. They were doing at least eighty, maybe ninety miles per hour. Ruban couldn't jump without killing himself. He couldn't shoot the driver. Through the cracks, beyond Jeffrey, he saw Pinky turn his head and raise his weapon. He was driving with one hand while taking aim with his pistol. Ruban was going to have to shoot first.

"Rooo-ban!"

He was unable to get off a clean shot, but his brother-in-law wasn't just getting in the way in his usual fuck-up fashion. Like a breaching Orca, Jeffrey somehow launched himself from the back of the cab. Hands duct-taped behind his back, he sailed nose first over the front seat and belly-flopped on Pinky's shoulders. The truck veered left, then right, then back again. Ruban thrashed from side to side. The tires screeched, the brakes screamed, and the smell of burned rubber rose from the asphalt. The truck fishtailed to a stop, and Ruban smashed into the side panel.

The pistol left his hand, sailing high over the side panel as if launched by catapult.

66

The FBI was second on the scene, right behind an MDPD squad car and the black pickup. Andie and Littleford jumped out. The truck's bed was empty. A uniformed officer was tending to an unconscious man in the front seat, driver's side. From the size of him, Andie knew it was Jeffrey Beauchamp, though she wasn't sure why his arms and legs were taped like a gray mummy.

"Two men fled on foot," the officer said. "My partner went after one of them. The other went that way." He was pointing toward a cluster of buildings in the darkness, just beyond the guard rail.

"Let's go!" said Littleford.

They drew their weapons, hopped the rail, and ran down the embankment to a two-lane access road that ran parallel to the expressway. Warehouses along the access road were built to zero lot lines, each building separated from the next by a narrow alleyway. Their suspect could have fled down any one of them.

A shot rang out. The agents instinctively went

down. It had come from one of the alleys, but a single gunshot in the night was hard to pinpoint.

"Wait for backup," said Littleford, his tone adding the words *this time*.

"That first-responder back at the truck said his partner pursued on foot. He could be down."

Two more MDPD officers arrived on foot, then another pair. They shared Andie's concern. A plan was hatched in seconds. They split into teams, one led by Andie, the other by Littleford. They sprinted to opposite corners of the warehouse, each team with its own alley to flush out before regrouping at the loading dock behind the warehouse.

With her back pressed to the brick face of the building, Andie poked her head around the corner, peering cautiously down the black alley. The warehouses were much deeper than wide, nearly the length of a football field from front to back. The alley had no streetlamp, or at least not a working one. The moonlight did little more than create confusing shadows in what seemed like an endless black tunnel. If there was an officer down, Andie couldn't tell; and if his shooter was in hiding, Andie couldn't tell that, either.

Andie hand-signaled to Littleford. He signaled back, and their coordinated sweep was under way.

Andie entered the alley, keeping close to the wall, her gun at the ready. The MDPD officer worked the other wall, directly across from her. They were ten feet into the darkness when Andie signaled a stop. They listened, and Andie reassessed. Roll-down steel shutters covered the windows and doors that faced the alley, blocking off escape routes. Corrugated boxes, flattened and stacked for disposal, one on top of the other, rose in cardboard towers along the wall near the Dumpster. She took another step forward, then stopped. There was a noise. Something—or someone—was behind the Dumpster. She and her partner took cover behind a thick stack of flattened boxes and waited. Her heart pounded. The chorus of sirens in the distance grew louder. More backup was on the way. It gave her comfort.

For another, it was cause for concern.

Two quick shots rang out. Andie heard the pops in the stacked cardboard. She hit the deck and saw a man running away from her.

"FBI! Freeze!" Andie shouted.

He turned and fired again in her direction, still running. Andie started to give chase but stopped quickly, her fears realized: an MDPD officer was on the other side of the Dumpster, motionless.

"Officer down!"

Andie checked his pulse. Still beating. The wound was to his upper thigh. He'd had the initial presence of mind to rip a ropelike fastener from the stacked boxes and make a tourniquet, but the blood loss had pushed him near unconsciousness. Andie checked the tourniquet. The other officer radioed for help. A third gunshot pierced the darkness, the bullet whizzing overhead as Andie dropped for cover between the shooter and the fallen officer. She braced for more gunfire, but heard only the echo of footfalls on asphalt. He was making a run for it.

The officer applied pressure to the first-responder's leg wound. "I was a paramedic. I got this," he told Andie.

She jumped out from behind her position of cover. The shooter was well ahead, rounding the corner and exiting the alley. Andie sprinted to the corner and stopped. Bursting carelessly into the open would have made her an easy target. She peered around the corner. The loading area was shut down and deserted, save for a single eighteen-wheeler that had backed up to the dock. The rig was parked with its external cab lights aglow. Andie could see the driver inside, behind the wheel, but he wasn't moving.

Asleep?

He'd probably driven all night and was sleeping in the cab until the warehouse opened, completely unaware that an armed killer was bearing down on him and his rig.

"Freeze!"

Her command was ignored. Andie took aim, well aware that a shot in the back was a dicey situation.

"I said freeze!"

He continued toward the rig. A string of dangerous possibilities flashed through Andie's mind. The driver might be taken hostage. He might be pistol-whipped, yanked from the rig, and viciously thrown to the ground. Or he might be shot in the head at point-blank range—a senseless murder—the way those New York thugs had shot Littleford's father in the armored truck.

Andie fired a warning shot into the sky. It woke the driver but didn't stop the gunman, who jumped up onto the running board and flung open the door. There was another shot—from inside the cab. The gunman's head snapped back. His gun flew as he tumbled backward and landed on the pavement.

Andie shouted to the driver—"FBI!"—and he raised his hands. He wasn't armed. Andie ran toward the rig, and as she approached she could see that the passenger door was also wide open.

Littleford was standing on the running board, gun in hand. In the sweep, he'd come around on the other side of the warehouse through the alley.

Andie checked the body and recognized the face. Pinky Perez was dead.

She climbed onto the running board and displayed her FBI shield to the terrified truck driver. His eyes were like silver dollars. "Are you all right, sir?"

"I guess so. What the hell is this about?"

Andie looked across the cab, straight at Littleford. He was still on the running board, but his mind seemed to be elsewhere. Somewhere in the past.

"It's about a lot of things," he said as he stepped down from the truck.

67

.

Ruban woke at 6:45 a.m. to the sound of an annoying buzzer on the nightstand. He sat up in the darkness, confused, momentarily forgetting that he was in a motel. The buzzer continued. He hadn't set the alarm clock, but apparently the room's previous guest had been an early riser. He silenced the damn thing with a slap of the button and settled back into the pillow.

Running from the cops was exhausting work. With such a huge head start, he'd easily won the footrace with the MDPD officers who'd given chase from the Palmetto Expressway. He needed rest, but the night had cost him much more than sleep.

His car: gone. The assault rifle and backup pistol: gone. The backpack was gone, too, along with the ransom money for Jeffrey. Another fifty thousand squandered. Ruban was down to three hundred dollars and change in his wallet, but it was more than enough to pay cash for the room. Plenty of guests paid cash at the Princess Lodge, a pink stucco motel with kitschy themed suites such as the Jungle Room and the Disco Room. Each unit had its own garage, a convenient cover for the businessman who might be worried that a divorce lawyer was hiding in the bushes, ready to snap a photograph of the new girl in HR stepping out of her boss's Porsche 911. Ruban found the garage particularly useful, having arrived in a stolen car. He'd lost one backup firearm, but he still had his ankle pistol, which had done the trick at the all-night gas station. The poor kid pumping gas into his car had wisely handed over the keys when staring down the barrel of a gun.

Gotta get some rest.

It was futile. He couldn't sleep, but it hurt to roll out of bed. The wild ride in the bed of the pickup had left him bruised and battered. He was actually worried about Jeffrey. His stunt had been amazingly courageous. Stupid, but courageous. Pinky must have been shocked. It was hard enough to drive and shoot at the same time, but virtually impossible with three hundred pounds of blubber pressing down on your neck and shoulders.

Ruban walked to the bathroom, splashed cold water on his face, and returned to the room. He wanted to call Savannah, but he couldn't possibly reach out to her. Surely the police were all over his wife and mother-in-law. If his cell hadn't been tapped earlier, it sure was at this stage of the game, and likewise for Savannah's. Going to his mother-in-law's house, or anywhere near Savannah, was out of the question.

The digital alarm clock sounded again. He'd hit "snooze" on the first try. He silenced it for good and noticed the time: 5:00 a.m. Everything that had happened after 11:00 p.m. would be on the morning news, sunrise edition. He turned on the TV, sat on the edge of the bed, and scrolled through the local channels until he found a news anchorwoman who couldn't have looked happier to have been awake since 3:00 a.m.

The lead story bore the tagline *"CA$H LANDING."*

"The driver has been identified as Craig 'Pinky' Perez, who was pronounced dead after a shootout with police that left one MDPD officer wounded. Sergeant Frank Sanchez was taken to Jackson Memorial Hospital and is reportedly in satisfactory condition. Perez's nephew, Jeffrey Beauchamp, reportedly found covered in gray duct tape, was also taken to Jackson and is in good condition."

Ruban smiled to himself, glad his brother-in-law had made it. The warmth quickly faded.

"Law enforcement is still searching for Karl 'Ruban' Betancourt, the suspected mastermind behind the multimillion-dollar heist at Miami International Airport just three weeks ago. Police are also searching for a second man who has disappeared with Betancourt's twenty-nine-year-old wife, Savannah."

Ruban felt chills as a photograph of Savannah appeared on the screen.

"According to police, Savannah Betancourt was staying with her mother when a man forcibly entered the house and took Savannah with him. That man is described as a black male, possibly Jamaican. He left in a white Japanese-model sedan. Anyone having information relating to Ruban Betancourt's whereabouts or to Savannah Betancourt's disappearance is asked to call Crime Stoppers at the number on your screen. In other news—"

Ruban tuned out. That was all he needed to hear.

Ramsey, you son of a bitch.

He reached for the landline but thought better of it. Caller ID on Ramsey's end would reveal Ruban's location. His cell was useless, but it occurred to him that he still had the burn phone that Jasmine had given him. He started dialing Ramsey's cell, but again he stopped. Did he dare dial Ramsey's number? The news report had said they were looking for a black man, possibly Jamaican. Had they figured out yet that it was Ramsey?

Ruban debated it. The bastard had Savannah. This was no time to be timid. But he also had to be smart.

Think, Ruban, think.

Then it came to him. The news report had made no mention of Jasmine, but Ruban had seen her true colors. He dialed her cell. It came as no surprise when it was Ramsey who answered.

"Been waitin' on dis call for two hours, mon. Where you been?"

"What did you do to Savannah?"

"Nothing. Got her right here. This one is going to cost you everything, mon. Keep the burn phone on. I call you later."

Ramsey hung up before Ruban could reply. He gripped the phone so tightly that he nearly cracked the LCD. "You do that, Ramsey," he said aloud. "You call me." He put the phone away and reached for the gun on the nightstand.

I can't wait to blow you away. Mon.

68

.

Room service brought him pancakes, bacon, and coffee. Housekeeping brought up six disposable razors and a pair of scissors. Ruban ate breakfast in his room and then shaved his head. He barely recognized himself in the mirror, which was exactly the point. It was safe to go outside, but he didn't take any unnecessary chances. He walked down the street to Target, bought clean clothes, a hat, sunglasses, and enough food and toiletries for three days. Then it was back to the motel. He kept the burn phone on.

No call came.

By late afternoon, he couldn't sit idle any longer. He started pacing. He checked to see if the phone had died. Over 30 percent battery left. He made doubly sure the ringer was on. Yup, Westminster chimes. For no reason at all, he checked his gun, a small Smith & Wesson revolver. Still loaded. He noticed that the naked babies patterned into the wallpaper were actually Cupids shooting their arrows of love, more proof that any man who would bring a woman to this joint didn't appreciate the value of hard-earned cash.

Cash. He had no way to pay Savannah's ransom. *Shit!*

Ramsey hadn't mentioned a number, but clearly he was thinking big: *"This one is going to cost you everything, mon."*

Refusing to ransom Savannah wasn't an option. This wasn't Jeffrey the cokehead. He had around two million left, by his count, but all of it was stashed at the house. He couldn't go home. He needed fast cash, lots of it; and he needed to get it from somewhere the police wouldn't be looking for him.

He knew just the place.

He put on his hat, which was actually one of those tight-fitting do-rags that football players wore under their helmets. Camouflage fabric. He liked the new look, especially with the sunglasses and the black shirt. The jeans were wide-leg, carpenter-fit style to accommodate the ankle holster. The new Ruban was ready to go. He called for a taxi and ten minutes later met it outside the lobby.

"South Miami," he told the driver.

The old Haitian gentleman cued the meter. The sun was setting as they pulled away from the motel, and the driver seemed to be having difficulty with the oncoming headlights. His ears weren't so good either. The radio was blasting, tuned to a crackly AM station and live coverage of the Miami Dolphins football game. Ruban's mind drifted back to another Sunday afternoon, when he was with Jeffrey and Pinky in Marco's pickup truck, the three men listening to the Dolphins game on the radio while waiting for the call from Octavio at the warehouse. A mere three weeks, and so much had changed. Ruban was the only one who wasn't dead or under arrest. And the Dolphins were out of contention for the playoffs. *Fucking Fins.*

"Stop here."

They were a half block from Whip 'n Dip, the ice cream shop where Jeffrey had bought a banana split for breakfast. From there, Ruban could walk. He paid the driver, crossed the tree-lined street to the hardware store, and purchased two lengths of nylon rope and a roll of duct tape. He used the store's rear exit, which faced the residential part of town, and followed the curved walkway into the quiet High Pines neighborhood.

Savannah kidnapped. It was his fault—again—just as it was his fault that she'd fallen off the back of his motorcycle. It was hard to find any silver lining in the motorcycle accident, but maybe the kidnapping was a godsend. This was his chance to step up and prove to Savannah how much he loved her, how he would do anything to get her back, how she meant more to him than money.

Sully's money, at least.

Ruban didn't know the address, and the ranch-style houses could look a lot alike after dark, but Ruban remembered the huge royal poinciana tree in the front yard. He walked around to the back. A thick, ten-foot ficus hedge ran along the property line. Sully liked his privacy. Good thing.

Ruban took the pistol from his ankle holster and went to the sliding glass doors in back. The house was the typical twenty-first-century renovation of

1960s construction, with all but the interior load-bearing walls removed to create that open "Florida" floor plan. Ruban listened. The television was playing loudly enough to be heard through the glass door. Sully was a Dolphins fan. Or maybe not. Ruban could see him sleeping on the couch.

He tried the door. It slid right open, unlocked. Ruban crossed the kitchen to the family room. Sully didn't move from the couch. He was on his back, snoring loudly. Much more than a five o'clock shadow covered his face, as if he hadn't shaved all weekend. He'd probably been out all night at the Gold Rush, selling Rolex watches. Ruban was betting on it.

He went to the couch and pressed the muzzle of his handgun to Sully's forehead.

Sully stirred, and then his eyes blinked open.

"Don't move," said Ruban, "or I will blow your brains out."

Ruban was back in his hotel room by eight. Sully, he presumed, was still locked in the closet, bound with nylon rope and his mouth taped shut. Ruban's take had been worth the trip: almost a hundred thousand dollars. He took six Rolex watches, too. Ruban knew they weren't worth Sully's asking price of twenty-five grand apiece, but maybe Ramsey would be as gullible as Jeffrey.

The phone rang. Westminster chimes. The burner phone. Ruban grabbed it. The incoming number was Jasmine's, the same number Ramsey had called from that morning.

"I'm listening," said Ruban.

"Ruban!"

He nearly dropped the phone. It was Savannah. She was whispering, her voice filled with urgency.

"Thank God you answered! I've been kidnapped!"

"Are you okay?"

"Yes! No! I mean—"

"Calm down, okay? Is Ramsey in the room with you right now?"

"No! He just walked out. I saw him use this phone to call you this morning. He doesn't know I have it. He left it in his bathrobe, so I grabbed it and hit redial."

"His bathrobe? Where are you?"

"It's a club. Ramsey brought me in the back door last night and locked me up in some kind of private sex room. This place is so gross. And Ramsey is creeping me out even more with all his talk about married people having sex with other married people."

"You're at Night Moves," said Ruban, his words simultaneous with the realization.

"Yes! That's it. You know it?"

"Your uncle practically lived there. Savannah, listen to me. You have to try to get out while Ramsey is away. Look around the room. Is there any escape?"

"No, I checked! There's no window. The door is locked from the outside. The first time Ramsey left me alone, I banged on the wall for help. He came back and slapped me so hard I thought my jaw was broken."

"I'm going to shoot that son of a bitch."

"Ruban, no! That's not the answer. If you know this place, just come. All we have is each other. Jeffrey's under arrest. If I call the police on this phone, we'll go to jail, too. The cops will never believe that we had nothing to do with the heist. Who knows what Jeffrey is telling them? We have to run as far as we can for as long as we can. Just bring whatever's left of Jeffrey's money, and you and I will run away to another country if we have to and never look back. Start over."

He swallowed hard. She was still referring to the money as "Jeffrey's." There was hope. "Are you serious about all this?"

"Yes. People like Ramsey will keep kidnapping us as long as they think we have the damn money, so we might as well have it."

Ruban's heart swelled. "I promise you, Savannah—everything is going to be okay. I love you so much."

"Ramsey is unlocking the door. I have to go! Hurry!"

"I will," he said, as the call ended. "I'm on my way."

69

·

Ruban didn't wait for a taxi. For two bills, a valet attendant at the motel was willing to "borrow" a Porsche from one of the overnight guests and drive him to Night Moves. They got there in fifteen minutes. The Porsche squealed out of the dark parking lot and headed back to the motel as Ruban hurried inside.

Sunday was not the busiest night of the week, but the club was never empty in late November, the official start of south Florida's "season." The dance room was straight ahead, beyond a set of double doors, but Ruban didn't get past reception. The attendant stopped him, a leggy blonde whose lips looked bee-stung.

"Can I help you, sir?"

He hesitated. The slightest hint at a kidnapping or criminal activity of any sort would prompt her to call 911, which would land Ruban in jail. "I'm here to meet up with my wife."

"So is everyone else," she said, and then she smiled. "A little Night Moves humor."

Ruban didn't find it funny. "I'm in a bit of a hurry. If you could let me inside to look around, I would really appreciate it."

"If you're not a member, you have to buy a day pass."

Ruban handed her a hundred. "Does this cover it?"

"Amply. Now if you could just fill out some information for me."

"No paperwork," he said as he handed her another hundred.

She took it, and he started past her.

"One more thing," she said, stopping him. "We have a strict no-drugs, no-weapons policy here."

The pistol was strapped to his ankle beneath his pant leg. "No problem."

"Good. Have fun."

Ruban continued to the double doors and entered the dance room. The loud music and flashing lights in a rainbow of colors were like any other club. The pornographic videos playing on flat-screen televisions around the room were distinctly Night Moves. About a dozen couples were on the dance floor, but it was more like group dancing, which made it hard to tell who was coupled with whom. No one was completely naked—it was still early— but several women would have caught Ruban's attention if he hadn't been on a mission. He took a good look around the entire room, keeping an eye out for Ramsey. The bar was to the right. To the left were couches and built-in lounge seating. Low-slung tables were outfitted with brass poles for wannabe strippers. Ruban saw no sign of Ramsey, but he spotted the table where he and Octavio had met with

Pinky to plan the heist. It had been several months, but he remembered Pinky saying something about private rooms in the back—the "baths," he'd called them. The entrance was behind the DJ.

Savannah had to be back there.

Ruban started across the dance floor. The music transitioned from a song Ruban didn't recognize to a remix of Rihanna's latest hit, which drew out even more dancers. Ruban zigzagged his way through a sea of wandering eyes. The dance floor was the epicenter in a land of opportunity, the place where hookups began. A woman started to dance toward him, a hot brunette wearing a sequined top that rode up above her navel when she raised her arms to the music. He avoided making eye contact, but she wasn't about to let him pass, playfully getting in his way.

"Wanna dance?"

"No, thanks."

She smiled and moved in toward him, close enough to be heard over the music, close enough to let him smell her perfume. "Aw, come on, handsome."

"No, I mean it."

She signaled to her girlfriend, who joined them. Blondes weren't typically his type, but this one was an incredible dancer. Great body. Ruban was suddenly at the top of a blonde-and-brunette triangle, the stuff of male fantasy. But he wasn't biting. He tried to move past them, but the blonde with the hot body stepped in his way, still dancing.

"You're cute," she said.

"I have to go."

"Shy, too. I like that. Would you blush if I took my top off?"

Ruban was starting to sweat. It must have been the lights.

"Let's get some champagne," said the brunette.

"And some baby oil," her friend said.

More sweating. It wasn't the lights. He was starting to feel like the guy who finally gets propositioned by Eva Longoria and Charlize Theron—on his honeymoon. They moved closer, one for each arm.

"Really, ladies. I don't—"

The next few moments were a blur. Before Ruban could even begin to appreciate what was happening, the brunette had his right arm, the blonde had his left, his hands went behind his back, and a pair of handcuffs closed over his wrists. It was one seamless motion, and it ended with Ruban down on the dance floor, flat on this belly. The brunette pushed his face toward the lacquered hardwood, and the muzzle of a gun was suddenly at the base of his skull.

"FBI. You're under arrest."

The music stopped. A barrage of white lights switched on. As the crowd dispersed there were a few screams, but things settled down quickly. The dancers on the floor were mostly law enforcement officers—FBI agents and MDPD officers from the joint Tom Cat unit headed by Agent Littleford—performing their very first undercover roles.

Andie flashed her FBI shield before Betancourt's eyes. The blonde removed her wig and read him his Miranda rights. "You have the right . . ."

"This is a terrible mistake! My wife is in danger!

She's been kidnapped. She's being held in one of those back rooms."

"Your wife was never kidnapped," said Andie.

"Yes, the kidnapper is a Jamaican guy named Ramsey. He called me this morning."

"A Jamaican FBI agent called you."

"What?"

"Ramsey was arrested at the Sunset Motel last night, along with his sidekick Jasmine."

"But—I heard it on the news. Savannah was kidnapped. She called me from here!"

"She called you from the FBI field office."

"Huh?"

"Your wife got herself a lawyer, told us everything, and agreed to do whatever was necessary to bring you into custody and to recover as much of the money as possible, Mr. Betancourt."

"No! Savannah would never do that!"

"She would, and she did. Deal with it, hotshot. And welcome to the FBI."

70

At nine o'clock Monday morning, Andie had a meeting at the U.S. attorney's office in downtown Miami. Littleford was with her at the table in a windowless conference room. They were silent observers, along with two other prosecutors from the criminal division. The chief prosecutor for the major crimes section sat in the middle, the FBI agents to his left, and the prosecutorial team to his right. The chief did the talking for the government. Savannah Betancourt wasn't there, but her lawyer was on the other side of the table. He did more talking than anyone.

"The deal was no jail time," he said.

The FBI appreciated Savannah's cooperation. After Ruban had told her that he was essentially trying to buy his child, Savannah was emotionally done with him. After meeting Mindy Baird and learning that Ruban had bedded a teenager, she was utterly disgusted. Savannah left him, went to her mother's, and contacted the FBI. Things got more complicated when she hired a lawyer. It was Savannah's attorney who had conceived the plan to stage her kidnapping. At first, the FBI had balked at the idea; they didn't need Savannah's help to capture Ruban. But they didn't know if he had more money stashed outside the house. If so, the best shot at recovering it was to lead Ruban to believe that Savannah was ready to run off to Antigua with him and whatever money he could get his hands on.

Her lawyer struck Andie as a pretty smart guy. His name was Jack Swyteck.

"A deal is a deal," said Swyteck.

The chief measured his response. "No jail time on the front end of the heist is fine. But I have a problem giving her a pass on accessory after the fact. It's clear that she took an active role in hiding the money."

"Savannah didn't hide any of the money."

"She admits she did."

"My client admits no such thing."

"She wore a Rolex watch to her birthday party that was purchased with stolen money. It's the judgment of our prosecutorial team that she has not been forthcoming about what happened to that watch. For all we know, she has it stashed away somewhere."

Andie showed no reaction, but the statement took her by surprise: that wasn't *her* judgment.

"She made her husband take the watch back to the dirtbag who sold it to him," said Swyteck.

The chief checked his paperwork. "That's not what Ms. Betancourt told us."

"Told you when?"

"The first interview with the FBI," he said, glancing toward Andie.

"That was before she hired me as her lawyer."

"I realize that. Nonetheless, here's the 302," he said, handing a copy to the lawyer. "It's all right there in black and white."

Andie watched from across the room as Swyteck read. As per standard FBI procedure, Andie had conducted the initial interview while another agent took notes. A "302" was an FBI agent's written record of what a witness said, created by the agent from the agent's notes; it was not a verbatim transcript or statement signed by the witness.

Swyteck looked up from the document when he finished. "Nowhere in this 302 does it say my client kept the Rolex."

"It doesn't say she made her husband take it back, either," the chief said.

"Maybe she was never asked that question."

"It's the kind of thing she would have mentioned even if not asked."

"Maybe she did say it, but the interrogating agent simply failed to write it down."

"I don't think so," the chief said.

Swyteck looked over at Andie, one-half of the FBI's presence in the room. She said nothing, but she wasn't entirely comfortable with the way the prosecutor was presenting the 302.

Swyteck accepted her silence and addressed the group as a whole. "If the FBI would join the twenty-first century and record interviews, we wouldn't be having this disagreement."

Littleford spoke up. "It's not the Bureau's policy to electronically record witness interviews."

"And the FBI is also the only law enforcement agency in the modern world that adheres to that policy."

"We do things differently."

"Yes, you do," said Jack. "And we all know that the reason the Bureau doesn't record interviews is Title 18 of the United States Code, section 1001, which makes it a felony for anyone to make a false statement to the FBI. If there's no verbatim record of what the witness actually said, whatever words the agent deigns to write in the 302 become, in effect, the witness's words. Whatever words the agent deigns to omit from the 302 become the witness's omissions. The witness can never contradict anything that the agent writes or chooses not to write in the 302 without facing the threat of felony charges under section 1001. Pretty nifty system you've got going there. Very J. Edgar."

"That is a complete distortion," the chief said.

"Is it? Well—excuse me one second." Swyteck grabbed his iPhone and dictated a message, staring straight at the section chief as he spoke: "Reminder to self: Write op-ed for the *Miami Herald* regarding abuse of 302s by the U.S. Attorney's Office for the Southern District of Florida." He put the phone away. "Sorry about that. Anyway, where was I?"

The chief assistant glanced toward the prosecutorial team to his right, then toward the FBI agents to his left, but his eye contact with Littleford lasted longest. Without words, recorded or otherwise, the two agencies seemed to come to an understanding that Savannah Betancourt wasn't worth the fight.

"I think we were all about to agree on no jail time," said the prosecutor.

The meeting ended around ten. Andie and her boss headed across the street to the Cuban coffee shop on the corner. The sun was shining warmly, the streets were utterly flat, and it felt nothing like the chilly walks that Andie and her old boss used to take down the steep hill from the Seattle field office to the Starbucks on Spring Street. But Miami was her new home, and Andie was getting used to it. They ordered two espressos at the counter and then found a table by the open window.

The FBI had recovered the money at the Betancourts' house and at Pinky's warehouse, as well as the hundred thousand that Ruban had taken from Sully. They'd actually believed Jeffrey Beauchamp when he swore on his mother's soul that he couldn't remember how much he'd given to his godfather for safekeeping, which was all he had left. In all, close to three million was unaccounted for.

Andie stirred a little spoonful of raw sugar into her demitasse. "Do you think we'll find any more of the money?"

"Nope," said Littleford.

"You think Savannah knows where any of it is?"

He thought about it. "I really don't believe she does."

Andie tasted her coffee. "How is she paying Swyteck?"

"Good question."

"He must be expensive."

"They're all expensive."

"But he strikes me as better than most. That can't come cheap."

"I suppose."

"Is he strictly criminal defense?"

"You're awfully inquisitive about this guy."

"No, I'm not."

"I'm picking up a certain vibe that you're hoping he might specialize in something other than criminal defense."

"I'm just talking."

"This case will be closed soon enough. If you'd like to meet him, I'm sure—"

Andie coughed on her espresso. "No. *No.* Not at all. I'm just saying he's a good lawyer."

Littleford smiled. "The lady doth protest too much."

"Now you're being ridiculous."

"His father was the governor of Florida. That was long before you moved here. The old man was a good guy, always supportive of law enforcement. Jack, on the other hand, made a name for himself defending death row inmates."

"Great. One from the dark side."

Andie glanced across the coffee shop and did a double take. Swyteck took a seat at the counter. He didn't seem to notice Andie or her boss by the window, even though they were close enough to hear him order a *café con leche* in Spanish. Really *bad* Spanish. Littleford caught Andie looking.

"You know, I'm good here sitting by myself," said Littleford. "There's an empty seat at the counter. Why don't you go over there and say hello to him?"

"You can't be serious."

"Hey, he can't be any worse than my wife's cousin."

Andie smiled, then shook her head. "It's pointless. FBI agent, criminal defense lawyer? How could that turn out to be anything but disaster?"

"You're probably right. Never work."

"Exactly," said Andie, glancing over once more. "That would *never* work."

Acknowledgments

•

All stories, I suppose, are to some extent inspired by actual events. For me, it's usually a collection of personal experiences and observations that twist and turn in my mind for months or even years before they can finally be woven into a seamless work of fiction. Every now and then, however, real-life events hit me like the proverbial lightning bolt, and from that spark of inspiration springs a complete work of fiction that seems almost to write itself. I'm grateful to the Honorable Paul Huck, U.S. District Court Judge for the Southern District of Florida, for cluing me in to the "actual events" that inspired *Cash Landing*.

As always, I'm also grateful to my editor, Carolyn Marino, and my agent, Richard Pine, both longtime friends who have guided my writing career from the very beginning. My beta readers, Janis Koch and Gloria Villa, have left their mark on more than a decade of my work. I still make plenty of mistakes, but they make me a better writer.

Finally, my deepest gratitude is to my wife, Tiffany. Thank you for encouraging me to follow my dreams, and for encouraging our children to follow theirs.